If she was pregnant, it was her own darn fault.

It would have taken all of one second to check the expiration date on the box of condoms that night, but she didn't. And she knew why she didn't. Ethan O'Connor's mind-numbing, toe-curling kisses had sucked the common sense right out of her head.

Physically, Ethan O'Connor was her dream man. Her every erotic fantasy come to life. He sent her hormones and pheromones into overdrive. And when he opened his mouth, he sent her temper there, too. The man stood for everything she stood against. There was not a single thing they agreed upon. If she said the grass was green, he'd say it was brown in that smooth, lawyerly voice of his.

And she might be having his baby.

Praise for Debbie Mason and
It Happened at Christmas

"Take another trip to Christmas, Colorado, and you'll be guaranteed a wonderful time."

—*RT Book Reviews*

"Christmas, Colorado, will get you in the spirit for love all year long."

—Jill Shalvis, *New York Times* bestselling author

"Come celebrate a Christmas you won't forget."

—Roxanne St. Claire,
New York Times bestselling author

"A passionate, liberal environmental activist and a straight-arrow conservative lawyer looking to the senate set the sparks flying in this nonstop, beautifully crafted adventure that skillfully unwraps a multilayered plot, adds an abundance of colorful characters and a familiar setting, and proves in no uncertain terms that opposites do attract."

—*Library Journal*

"*It Happened at Christmas* is the perfect story to begin the holiday season and would make the perfect gift for anyone—including treating yourself! Debbie Mason gives the best gift of all in this funny, heartwarming novel that touches the very core of Christmas. I know it has become part of my permanent Christmas book collection."

—FreshFiction.com

"This was a fascinating story to read. I found that these characters seemed to come alive on each page as you read through the story. There were several areas in this read that caused me to laugh out loud. The situations were so funny. I don't want to give any of it away other than to say you must pick up *It Happened at Christmas*. See for yourself how well this author gives us such a wonderful love story."

—NightOwlReviews.com

"Very sweet story. I laughed, I cringed. I sighed. This story is fantastic and filled with so much emotion."

—AfterTheFinalChapters.com

It Happened
at Christmas

ALSO BY DEBBIE MASON

The Harmony Harbor series

Mistletoe Cottage
"Christmas with an Angel" (short story)
Starlight Bridge
Primrose Lane
Sugarplum Way
Driftwood Cove
Sandpiper Shore
The Corner of Holly and Ivy

The Christmas, Colorado series

The Trouble with Christmas
Christmas in July
It Happened at Christmas
Wedding Bells in Christmas
Snowbound at Christmas
Kiss Me in Christmas
Happy Ever After in Christmas
"Marry Me at Christmas" (short story)
"Miracle at Christmas" (short story)

It Happened *at* Christmas

Debbie Mason

FOREVER

NEW YORK   BOSTON

Copyright © 2014 by Debbie Mazzuca

"Miracle at Christmas" is copyright © 2017 by Debbie Mazzuca

Preview from *The Corner of Holly and Ivy* copyright © 2018 by Debbie Mazzuca

Cover illustration and design by Elizabeth Turner Stokes. Cover copyright © 2018 by Hachette Book Group, Inc.

Forever

Hachette Book Group

1290 Avenue of the Americas, New York, NY 10104

forever-romance.com

twitter.com/foreverromance

Originally published in mass market by Grand Central Publishing in September 2014

Reissued: September 2018

Forever is an imprint of Grand Central Publishing. The Forever name and logo are trademarks of Hachette Book Group, Inc.

The publisher is not responsible for websites (or their content) that are not owned by the publisher.

The Hachette Speakers Bureau provides a wide range of authors for speaking events. To find out more, go to www.hachettespeakersbureau.com or call (866) 376-6591.

ISBNs: 978-1-5387-2933-5 (mass market reissue); 978-1-4555-2772-4 (ebook)

Printed in the United States of America

OPM

10 9 8 7 6 5 4 3 2 1

Acknowledgments

Thanks once again to the incredible team at Grand Central Publishing / Forever for all their efforts on behalf of my books, especially my fabulous editor, Alex Logan. I couldn't ask for a more dedicated, hardworking, supportive bunch. Thanks also to my wonderful agent, Pamela Harty, for all her support.

Many thanks to my brother and sister and best friends, Scott and Sharon LeClair, for the laughs and love. A big thank-you to the members of the Mazzuca and LeClair families. I'm so lucky to have you all in my life. To my beautiful children, grandbaby, and amazing husband, you know how much I love you. You guys are my world.

And to the readers, bloggers, and reviewers who take time out of their busy lives to spend a few hours with me in Christmas, Colorado, you have my heartfelt gratitude. Thanks for the lovely e-mails, tweets, and Facebook posts. You guys are the best.

Chapter One

Skylar Davis stood in the middle of Main Street wearing a sparkly purple dress with a wand in her hand and a cupcake tiara on her head, wondering where the magic had gone. For the last ten years, she'd flitted through life like a butterfly wearing rose-colored glasses.

Seven months ago, she'd had those glasses ripped right off her face, and her life had become stomach-churningly horrible. Six weeks ago, it went from horrible to downright scary. Which was why she was hiding out in the small town of Christmas, Colorado. Well, that and she only had a couple hundred pennies to her name.

Another reason for choosing Christmas, she had free room and board courtesy of her best friend Madison McBride—although she had a feeling that wasn't going to last much longer. The fact her best friend was married to a big, hot sheriff didn't hurt, either. At least Skye had protection if Scary Guy discovered where she was. But right now, the person she needed to avoid was her best friend.

Skye cast a nervous glance behind her, releasing a relieved breath when she didn't spot a familiar face among the crowd. In the middle of a wave of people heading down Main Street, she bent her knees and bowed her head in an effort to make herself less visible. Granted, it was a little hard to be inconspicuous wearing a Sugar Plum Cake Fairy costume. And somehow she'd wound up in the middle of a group of tourists from Japan. Up ahead, she spotted a couple of men taller than she was and started toward them.

One of the tourists snagged her arm. "Picture." He smiled, holding up his camera.

Two more men held up their cameras. "You. Picture."

"At the park. Okay?" Skye smiled, pointing to where the Fourth of July festivities were being held. They'd draw less attention there, and if she spotted Maddie, Skye could duck behind a tree. She went to walk away and caught a glimpse of a tall, broad-shouldered man in a light gray suit, the sun glinting off his tawny blond hair as he held court on the sidewalk with a statuesque brunette at his side.

Skye's smile froze on her face, a drawn-out *no* echoing in her head. She'd overheard someone say that Republican senatorial candidate Ethan O'Connor had another speaking engagement and was heading out of town. If she'd known he was sticking around, she would've hidden out at the bakery. She'd been humiliated enough for one day, thank you very much.

Her gaze shot to the pastel-painted shops across the street to her left. *Seriously?* she thought, at the sight of the beautiful blonde wearing a floral sundress standing beneath the purple-and-white-striped awning of the Sugar Plum Bakery. It was her best friend, Maddie McBride.

And one more example of how dramatically Skye's luck had changed.

Since bemoaning the situation wasn't going to save her further humiliation and neither was standing there, Skye did the only thing she could think of and dropped to her knees. Forcing a smile for the worried faces looking down at her, she said, "I lost my wand," surreptitiously tucking the aforementioned item beneath her dress.

"Excuse me. Pardon me. Lost wand," she explained, duckwalking through the crowd as fast as the position allowed.

"I'll help you find it, Sugar Plum Cake Fairy," offered a little girl, her dark curly hair caught up in red, white, and blue ribbons.

"Me too," volunteered a little boy, a miniature American flag clutched in his small hand.

Before long, Skye had a line of children waddling after her. She was like a mother duck with her ducklings following behind. They looked so darn cute that she would've had an *aw* moment if she didn't feel like throwing up. She'd been feeling that way a lot lately.

Her day so far wasn't helping matters. Because she hadn't contributed to the Jack-and-Grace fund, Maddie no doubt suspected that Skye, who'd once had more money than God, was now as poor as Jesus. And then there was Ethan O'Connor, the man she'd had a one-night stand with—and Skylar Davis did not do one-night stands— who was in town looking even more breath-stealingly gorgeous than she remembered. And if that wasn't bad enough, the first time she saw Claudia Stevens, the bane of her teenage existence, she was in Christmas on Ethan's arm instead of in Texas where she belonged.

Skye's father, William Davis, referenced Claudia—an old family friend—in every one of his it's-time-to-grow-up lectures. "Why can't you be more like Claudia?" was his constant refrain as he compared the other woman's many accomplishments to Skye's nonexistent ones.

With the reminder of just how crappy her day had been, Skye was more determined than ever to avoid all three of them and crouched lower. As she made her way to the front of the crowd, beads of perspiration rolled into her eyes, blurring her vision. She went to rub the drops away with the hand that held the wand. *Oops.* "Look at that," she said, turning to the children. "It's my magic wand. Silly me, I should've wished for it sooner."

She winced at the crestfallen expressions on their cute little faces because she'd found her wand without their help. In an effort to counter their disappointment, Skye raised it, nodding at the sparkly sugar plum on the end. "You know what, my wand just told me it didn't find me because of *my* wishes, it was because of all of yours. Yay, you guys." She clapped her hands, relieved when they joined in.

"That makes us your fairy helpers, doesn't it?" said the first of her volunteers.

"Yes, it does." Skye smiled, looking through a sea of legs to get her bearings. A few more yards and she'd be on the path to the park. She felt like clapping her hands again. "I have to go now. Thanks for all your help."

"Can we have tiaras like yours?" asked a little girl, her blue eyes hopeful behind her pink-framed glasses.

Skye fingered the jeweled crown with the tiny cupcakes glued to each point. She'd love to give the tiara away. When

Grace, her friend and boss, had first broached the idea of Skye being the Sugar Plum Cake Fairy, she'd jumped at the chance. But that was when she thought it was a paid position. When she found out it wasn't, she kind of thought it was cool that she'd be the face of the Sugar Plum Cake Fairy in the book. It wasn't until they fitted her with the costume, and she realized they meant for her to wear it in public, that she wanted to say, *No way, no how.* But she couldn't. Even though Grace didn't have the money in her budget to hire Skye, she'd given her a job at the bakery. So Skye had no choice but to accept the role as the bakery's mascot to repay Grace for her kindness.

Today was Skye's debut as the Sugar Plum Cake Fairy. And as her newfound bad luck would have it, she'd been in costume when she saw Ethan for the first time in three months and Claudia for the first time in ten years. Ethan had restrained his laughter. Claudia, not so much. And the woman was bound and determined to get a picture of Skye looking like an idiot to post on social media.

"I wish I could, sweetie, but there's only one tiara like this in the whole, wide world." At the little girl's disappointed look, Skye did a quick head count. She got paid next week, so she should be good. "But because you're my special helpers, you all get a free cupcake from the bakery this week. You just tell them the Sugar Plum Cake Fairy sent you."

"Yay." The little girl bounced up and down, and her friends joined in.

Oh, gosh, they're getting kind of loud. Afraid they were going to draw unwanted attention, Skye put a finger to her lips. "Shush, we don't want anyone else to know. It's our secret. Okay?"

They nodded, and Skye went to stand up. Several of the children threw their arms around her. "We love you, Sugar Plum Cake Fairy."

"Aw, I love you guys, too." Maybe this job wasn't so bad after all. She'd always enjoyed spending time with kids. Some people told her it was because she still thought she was one. She didn't know what the big deal was. In her opinion, the world would be a better place if more adults kept their inner child alive, holding on to that natural curiosity, the ability to appreciate the simple things in life and have fun. She supposed that was easy for her to say. She'd never had to work for a living or worry about paying bills or putting a roof over her head or clothes on her back.

She sighed. Not until now she hadn't.

Skye waved good-bye and speed-walked to the path.

Maddie's stepdaughter, Lily, ran toward Skye, her chestnut-colored ponytail bouncing, and caught her by the hand. "Auntie Skye, I've been looking all over for you. Mommy wants to talk to you."

Skye couldn't help but smile. She loved that Maddie's stepdaughters called her Auntie. In a way, it was true. Since she was an only child, Skye thought of her best friends, Maddie and Vivi, as her sisters. But she wasn't quite ready to face her *sister* just yet. Skye needed time to put a positive spin on her situation.

Her gaze darted to the park, and she spotted the bright blue port-a-potty in the distance. "Tell Mommy I'll catch up with her in a bit. I have to go." She nodded in the direction of the portable outdoor toilet.

Lily frowned. "Mommy's at the bakery. It's closer."

Too bad Lily was as smart as she was adorable. Skye shot a look at the crowd working its way up the street and caught sight of the tourists. "Right, but I promised some people I'd take a picture with them. I won't be long."

Skye waved and headed down the path. To her left, a man shouted out for Ethan. *Please, let it be another Ethan.* She glanced in the direction he'd called from. Sure enough, there was the man himself entering the park with Claudia on his arm. Skye took off at a run. By the time she reached the port-a-potty, she was out of breath.

This hiding-out crap is exhausting.

A big, burly man with a full beard stepped out of the port-a-potty and gave her an apologetic shrug.

How bad could it be? Skye thought, stepping inside. She slapped a hand to her mouth and nose. It smelled like someone had died in there. Several someones, and a long time ago. She whipped around, about to get out, when she heard, "Is that Kendall?"

Skye ducked inside, slammed the door, and locked it. There was only one person who called her by her legal name, and that was Claudia. Skye had started using her middle name when she left Texas. The one her mother had chosen. It was Skye's way of thumbing her nose at her father's attempt to change her into the daughter he wanted her to be. Someone William Davis, the former governor of Texas and right-wing Republican, could be proud of.

Someone like Claudia.

Breathe, Skye told herself in hopes of calming her jackrabbiting pulse. *For goodness' sake, you idiot, don't breathe!* She lifted the hem of her dress and pressed it to her face, gagging into the silky fabric. The claustrophobic space was closing in around her, and the temperature felt twenty degrees hotter than outside. Holding her breath, she fanned herself with her dress. When the lack of oxygen began to make her dizzy, she once again buried her nose in the purple fabric and released it.

Okay, relax. Think of walking through the forest in winter, the snow crunching underfoot, your breath a crystallized cloud. Yes, she almost cheered; it was working. The room felt cooler, the space less confining. But the smell... she retched, automatically leaning toward the black hole. She jerked back when she realized what she was doing. *Hurry up, think of... think of something that smells amazing, something you want to... Do not think of that!*

She couldn't help it. Once the images started, she couldn't make them stop. The memory of that night with Ethan played out in her mind. *Oh, but he had smelled amazing, and all that lean, sculpted muscle, his large... arms, his arms!* Voices coming in her direction snapped her back to the here and now.

Good, that was good.

"Claudia said she saw her going in there, Madison."

Bad. Very bad.

That was Ethan's voice. Ethan's incredible, swoonworthy voice. She scowled as the thought popped into her head. The sewage must be poisoning her brain, she decided, pinching her nose and breathing through her mouth. The man was a right-wing, judgmental conservative who was as critical of Skye's lifestyle as her father was.

Oh no, now she could taste it. She made small, retching sounds as the cupcakes she'd eaten earlier curdled in her stomach.

"Skye, are you in there?" Maddie asked, tapping on the door. "Skye?" She tapped again.

If Skye stayed quiet, maybe they'd leave. She moved away from the door, which put her closer... She started gagging, and stumbled backward, bouncing off the wall.

"Skye, Lily said she saw you running over here. Are you okay? Do you need help?"

"I'm fine. I'll be out in a minute. You can go..." She gagged again before she got *back to the bakery* out.

"You don't sound *fine*, and we're not going anywhere until we know you're all right," Ethan said, his voice whiskey smooth and deep.

"I am. It's the door." She rattled it for effect. "It's stuck, and I can't get out. So if you could go and get someone... if *all* of you could go and get someone, that'd be great. Thanks." And when they did, she'd escape to the woods. The sweat trickling down her chest and back had turned the sparkly purple fabric to shrink-wrap, while the humidity had turned her long, wavy hair into a frizz ball. There was no way she was going to face Mr. and Ms. Perfect looking like something the dog had dragged in and shaken a couple of times before he did.

"Okay, I'll try and get it to open," she heard Ethan say.

"No, that's not a good idea." The door handle moved, and a metallic scraping sound came from the other side. "What are you doing?"

"Picking the lock."

"You can't pick locks," she blurted in desperation, swiping her arm across her damp forehead. "You're a lawyer, and you're running for political office."

"Appreciate the concern for my reputation, cupcake. But it's a port-a-potty, and I'm rescuing a damsel in distress." She heard the amusement in his voice.

"I don't need rescuing. Go away." She stupidly took a

deep breath to calm herself and started retching again. She sounded like she was horking up a hairball. Covering her mouth and nose with both hands, she turned away, hoping to muffle the noise.

"Hang in there, sweetheart. Just a little bit…There, got it."

Her eyes widened, and she whipped her head around, reaching for the handle just as it turned. She dug her heels in the damp floorboard, holding on to the handle with both hands.

"Huh, the lock released, how come…" He pulled on the door, a sliver of light entering the space.

They played a silent game of tug-of-war; she leaned back, he inched her forward, she leaned back, he inched her forward. Then, with one last yank from his side, she went flying out the door. Landing hard on her hands and knees at his feet, her tiara askew, Skye threw up on Ethan's Italian leather shoes.

*　　　*　　　*

The last thing Ethan expected was for Skylar Davis to come flying out of the port-a-potty and land on her hands and knees at his feet. Considering how any interaction he'd ever had with her ended in some kind of drama, he shouldn't have been surprised.

Moving his shoes out of the line of fire, he crouched beside her and gathered the thick mass of sweat-dampened butterscotch curls in his hand, holding them back from her face. It reminded him of that night a few months ago when he'd had those long locks wrapped around his fist. Unlike now, she'd been making soft, sexy sounds in her throat, her incredible body moving in a sensual rhythm beneath his.

Caught up in the memories, it took Ethan a minute to realize Skye was looking at him from under her ridiculously long lashes. "Sorry, I—" She nudged her chin at his shoes before being overcome by a dry heave.

He grimaced. "Don't worry about it." At a loss as how to help her, he went to rub her back, but the lilac wings attached to the sparkly purple fabric got in the way, and rubbing any lower would only get him in trouble. Eight hours after she'd rocked his world that night in April, she'd made it clear she didn't want him to touch her again. Oh yeah, he had enough experience with a ticked-off Skylar Davis to know better and dropped his hand to his side.

Behind him, Claudia Stevens, his campaign manager, choked out, "Oh, my God, I've never smelled anything that bad. I think I'm going to throw up."

Skye's cheeks went from pasty white to hot pink. "It wasn't me. There was a man..." She sighed, pushing herself upright. "It's a port-a-potty. What do you expect?"

Given the squinty-eyed look Skye aimed at Claudia, Ethan figured he could do both women a favor. He'd seen Skye's face when Claudia had recognized her at the ceremony earlier today. Added to his campaign manager's comments, it was obvious the two women had a history. In Skye's case, it didn't appear to be a happy one. Then again, she hadn't been happy to see him, either. Too bad—he didn't plan on going anywhere until he knew she was all right.

He turned to Claudia, who stood a few feet away in a conservative red dress with a handkerchief pressed to her nose. "Why don't you head to the booth? I'll be there shortly."

Her glossy red lips pursed as she looked from Skye to

the port-a-potty. "All right, but you're scheduled to take part in the hamburger-eating contest in fifteen minutes."

As a weak groan escaped from Skye, Ethan stood up and offered her a hand. "Might help to settle your stomach if we move away from here."

"There's your mother." Claudia waved. "Over here, Liz."

Skye groaned louder this time, her gaze shooting to the trees. "Don't even think about it," Ethan said, helping her to her feet. "You're too weak to make a run for it."

"I wasn't going to make a run for it," she scoffed, tugging her hand from his, but he didn't miss the way her eyes darted from his mother back to the woodland path.

Raising a skeptical brow as he grabbed his bottle of water from the trampled grass, he moved her upwind of the port-a-potty. She rolled her eyes at him, but he wasn't buying it. His mother, Liz O'Connor, and Skye weren't exactly on speaking terms. Three months ago, Liz had threatened to have her arrested.

Ethan offered Skye his bottled water. She gave him an as-if look. "I'll take some gum if you have any."

He should've known better. In their brief time together, Skye, an environmental activist, had lectured him about the damage bottled water did to the environment and the amount of chemicals contained in the plastic. Handing her a stick of gum, he said to Claudia, "Do me a favor and cut my mother off at the pass. I need to speak to Skye for a sec...in private."

"Skye? Oh right, I keep forgetting that you changed your name, Kendall. Don't be long, Ethan. We don't want to keep people waiting. Kendall, come find me later. We have lots to catch up on, and I have to get a picture of you in your adorable costume."

He heard Skye mutter "Not if I can help it" under her breath before she forced a smile and said, "Sure."

Claudia bent down to tug her red-spiked heel from the grass, then gingerly made her way down the incline to meet his mother.

"So," Ethan said, returning his attention to Skye, "how do you know Claudia?"

Head bowed, she yanked on the low-cut bodice. He imagined the effort was intended to keep her full breasts from practically falling out of her dress. Other than distracting him, it wasn't working. With one last frustrated tug, she blew out a breath and looked up at him. "Our fathers are friends. Richard helped get my dad elected. How did you end up with Claudia as your campaign manager?"

"Richard and my dad were both aides in the Ford White House. They stayed in touch. He advised my parents on their breeding stock, sold them a couple of horses. When my mother told him I was running for the state senate, he suggested I hire Claudia."

"Small world."

"Yeah, it is." He shoved his hands in his pants pockets and asked her the question that had been bugging him since he'd discovered who she was. "How come you never told me your dad was William Davis or that your real name is Kendall?"

She gave him a bewildered look. "Why would I?"

"Oh, I don't know, Skye. Maybe because we spent the night together."

"I…" she began, then frowned. "You're serious." She shrugged. "We slept together, Ethan. It's not like we had a relationship."

She was right, of course. But that didn't stop the slow burn building in his gut. Because the thing was, she had rocked his world that night. He moved closer, leaning into her. "Yeah, well, when I'm deep inside a woman and shouting her name, I'd like to know it's the right one."

"Quid pro quo, Ethan. It would've been nice to know before we made love that you thought I was some flighty, spoiled rich girl who needed to grow up, and that the causes I supported were nothing more than a joke to you. For that matter, everything I believe in, everything I feel strongly about, you—"

It was kind of hard to take her seriously when she was standing in front of him wearing wings, her cupcake crown sliding onto her forehead. He reached out to straighten it while fighting back a grin. "That's not what I said. You didn't give me a chance to explain before—"

Her eyes widened, and she pushed his hand away, shoving the crown back on her head. "You're doing it again. You think I'm a—"

At the sound of someone approaching, Ethan looked up to see his mother marching toward him with Claudia in tow. "Uh, Skye," he went to interrupt her, but she was off on a tangent and didn't stop to take a breath.

"You know what? I don't care. What happened between us was a mistake, and one I have no intention of repeating. I will never sleep with you again, Ethan O'Connor."

Because Skye's voice got increasingly louder the more agitated she became, his mother heard her and shot him an accusatory stare. Claudia shot him a disbelieving one. And Skye, who'd just then realized she had an audience, looked like she wanted to turn him into a toad.

"Mom, you remember Skye, Madison's best friend?"

He gave Liz a warning look, one he hoped she wouldn't ignore.

"Ms. Davis." His mother directed a tight nod at Skye and looped her arm through his. "Darling, they're waiting for you to start the hamburger-eating contest."

"Hi, Mrs. O'Connor," Skye said politely. "I have to get going, too. Cake Fairy duties, you know. Have fun eating all those cows...I mean burgers." She started to walk away, then turned and took the bottle of water from his hand. "We can't have the senator-to-be looking less than his best, now can we?" Before he realized what she was up to, Skye unscrewed the cap and doused his shoes with water.

Ethan raised his eyes from his now-clean but soaked shoes. With a withering smile, Skye handed him the empty bottle. "When you get tired of killing poor, defenseless animals to adorn your feet, let me know. Target has a great deal on pleather ones."

Her mouth hanging open, his mother stared after Skye. "I can't believe she just did that. What is wrong with that girl?" She pinched his arm. "And what is wrong with you? I can't believe you slept—"

"I'm thirty-six years old, Mom, who I...spend time with is none of your business." He watched Skye, wings flapping, flounce toward Madison, who was jogging up the path with a man in a blue uniform shirt.

"It most certainly is my business. You're running for state senate. Being involved with a woman like Skylar Davis would destroy your chances."

"We're not involved. But I think you're being overly dramatic." And he'd had about all the drama he could take for one day.

Claudia looped her arm through his. "I'm happy to hear that, Ethan, because Liz is right. She's a campaign manager's worst nightmare. Well, the manager of a Republican candidate's worst nightmare, at least," Claudia said with a laugh, then tilted her head to study him. "I'm surprised you were involved with her. You two have nothing in common."

Ethan was only half-listening to Claudia. He was too busy watching a group of kids swarm Skye. They wrapped their arms around her legs and waist, tugging on her hands. She laughed, playfully spinning in a circle as they hung off her.

"Ethan O'Connor, get that smile off your face and stop looking at that girl," his mother snapped. "You're like a dog in heat."

"Nice, Mom, real nice," he said, as they headed in the direction of the sign-up booth. Both women clung to his arms as if they didn't trust him not to go chasing after Skye with his tongue hanging out and his tail wagging.

A distinct possibility.

Because from the first time he'd laid eyes on Skylar Davis, he'd wanted her with an intensity that nearly knocked him on his ass. And once he got her in his bed, he didn't want to let her go. But he was smart enough to realize that both Claudia and his mother were right. Any involvement with Skylar Davis would kill his chances in the election.

She was a bleeding-heart liberal who believed in same-sex marriage and gun control and could turn a simple difference of opinion into a reason for all-out war. And there was nothing Ethan wanted more than to win a seat in the state senate. He'd made a promise to his father, and he planned to keep it.

Chapter Two

Her cheeks heating with embarrassment, Skye stomped away. The least Ethan could've done was warn her his mother was within earshot. Liz O'Connor had looked at her like she was the lowest of the low, a sleazy ho. Admittedly the costume Skye wore pushed her B-cup boobs into the C-cup vicinity, but she was so not a ho.

Skye didn't know why she let Liz O'Connor's opinion of her bother her, anyway. A few months ago, she'd threatened to have Skye arrested after Skye had accidentally dumped champagne on Ethan's head. Okay, so maybe she'd done it on purpose—but really, talk about an overprotective mama bear. Skye never would've taken Ethan for a mama's boy, but obviously he was.

Too bad he was also one of the most drool-worthy men she'd ever met. And not only was he off-the-charts gorgeous, he knew how to put his strong, athletic body and talented hands to good use. He'd given Skye one of the most incredible, unforgettable nights of her life. And despite being in the middle of throwing up, when his hand brushed her neck as he caught up her hair, she felt a heated tremor course through her body at the memory of what those clever fingers could do, of how gentle, considerate, and kind he could be.

If she hadn't been tossing her cupcakes, she might have thrown herself into his arms and let him kiss away all her worries and fears. And that would've been just one more mistake to add to the mile-high pile she'd made in the last several months. She didn't need another straitlaced, uptight conservative telling her how to live her life. She got enough of that from her father, thank you very much.

Maybe it was a good thing Liz O'Connor hated her after all. She'd do everything in her power to keep Ethan away from Skye. Granted, Skye had probably achieved the same results all on her own when she'd drowned his Italian leather shoes.

She groaned at the sight of her best friend coming up the path with the port-a-potty man. Skye didn't need this right now. When several of her fairy helpers darted with excited squeals past Maddie to converge on Skye, she sent her thanks to the universe. A little boy clung to her leg, two girls to her waist, while two other boys grabbed her by each hand.

"Hi, guys," Skye laughed, her earlier embarrassment and temper dissipating.

For Maddie's benefit, she forced herself to laugh louder, twirling in circles with the kids hanging off her in a bid to get further away from her best friend.

It didn't work. "Hey, kids, I have to steal the Sugar Plum Cake Fairy from you," Maddie said, stopping Skye mid-twirl.

From the determined look on her best friend's face, Skye realized the jig was well and truly up. It was probably for the best. Maybe her stress levels would diminish once she confessed to Maddie. Keeping her financial predicament from her best friend had bothered Skye. Especially since she'd already told Grace. But her other secret, the Scary Guy secret, she couldn't bring herself to share. Because while losing her trust fund wasn't entirely her fault, what happened with Scary Guy pretty much was.

Maddie took her by the arm, leading her unto the path. "You're green and"—she picked up a lock of Skye's hair—"what's this?"

"You don't want to know," Skye said. Lately, Maddie's stomach had been as queasy as Skye's. Only her friend's queasiness had nothing to do with stress and port-a-potties and one obnoxiously gorgeous man. Maddie was pregnant.

Her best friend grimaced, dropped Skye's hair, and put a hand to her mouth. "Did you...?" She nodded in the direction of the port-a-potty.

"Mmm-hmm, right there in front of Ethan and Claudia. Actually, right on Ethan's shoes." Skye forced a laugh, her cheeks warming at the memory. She perked herself up with the thought that her day could only get better. It sure as heck couldn't get worse.

"That's what I love about you. You always see the humor in life. You never let anything get you down."

This was true, or at least it had been. The old Skye, the one who walked around wearing rose-colored glasses, never got down. The new Skye forced her lips to curve. "That's me, little Miss Sunshine."

Maddie gave her a searching look as they reached Main Street. "You sure you're okay?"

"Sure I'm sure. Why do you ask?"

"Because you've been avoiding me. And I know it's none of my business—you can spend your money any way you'd like—but I was wondering why you didn't contribute to Jack and Grace's house?"

Everyone but Skye had pitched in to buy the house on Sugar Plum Lane for Jack and Grace Flaherty. Jack had been a POW in Afghanistan for seventeen months, and he and Grace deserved all the happiness in the world. Last year, Skye would've gifted them the house on her own. It'd been hard not to be able to contribute.

"Skye?"

She took a fortifying breath before saying, "I'm broke."

Maddie stood stock-still on the sidewalk outside the bakery, her mouth hanging open in disbelief. "I, ah, I think I heard you wrong. You didn't just say you're broke, did you?" her best friend asked with a thick Southern drawl. When Maddie was nervous, she spoke Southern.

"You didn't hear me wrong. I'm broke." It felt kind of liberating to finally admit the truth to her best friend.

"Skye, this isn't funny. You can't be broke. You have more money than—"

"*Je suis fauché. Que significa. Non ho un Euro.* Diggin' for dinero. In pursuit of pesos."

"I think I need to sit down," Maddie said.

Not surprising. Her best friend was the most fiscally responsible woman Skye had ever met. Actually, she was cheap. She was also brilliant when it came to investing and making money. Skye wouldn't be surprised if in the near future, Maddie had more money than God.

"It's not a big deal, really. I'll be fine," Skye said, taking the key for the bakery from her best friend's limp hand. "It's not like I have a family to support. And I have a job."

"You have a job...like in a real job?"

"Yes." Skye opened the door and nudged Maddie inside. "And I'd appreciate it if you didn't act like the concept was foreign to me. Volunteering is work, you know."

"Sorry, that's not what I meant. I guess I'm still in shock."

Makes two of us, Skye thought. She locked the front door and followed Maddie through the swinging half doors to the kitchen. As Maddie pulled out a stool by the stainless steel prep table, Skye went to the sink and turned on the tap.

"So how did it happen—the money, I mean? How did you lose your fortune?"

"It seems Big Al made a slight miscalculation on a few years of tax returns. 'Slight' as in 'millions.' I had to divest several properties in order to cover the back taxes, and with the market the way it is..." She shrugged. "I should've kept a closer eye on him. Some of his investments were on the shady side." She should've known an accountant-slash-money manager with a name like Big Al didn't bode well. She finished rinsing off her hair and got a glass of water before turning off the tap. Taking a tea towel from the drawer, she dried her curls.

"But that still doesn't explain how you're broke. You had more money than—"

"Please don't say it. I haven't had that much money in years."

Maddie made a frustrated sound in her throat. "Because you couldn't say no to anyone, not a cause or a person with a sob story. Skye, I can't believe you—"

"FYI, feeling bad enough, thanks." Skye turned back to the sink, rinsing her mouth with water before saying, "Look, I know I messed up, but what's done is done. It's time to move on, and I have."

"You're right. I'm sorry. At least you have your condo and your communications degree. Who are you working for?"

She's going to lose that hopeful expression on her face pretty darn fast. Skye considered running for cover before answering, "I had to sell my condo. But it was too big for one person anyway. And I'm tired of New York."

Maddie gave her a since-when look with a side order of Lord-help-me thrown in for good measure, then she offered Skye an overly bright smile. "So you decided to take the fund-raising position with that environmental company in Belize you invested in." Maddie nodded. "That's great. It's perfect for you."

It would have been if the company still existed. Two days after Skye invested, Emmanuel closed up shop and fled the country.

"Skye?"

"I'm working for Grace. I think I've found my calling."

"Here. You're working here? Since when, and why did I not know this?"

"Two weeks. And I didn't tell you because I knew how you'd react." She crossed her arms and gave her best friend a pointed look.

"All right. Okay. But come on, Skye, you have not found your calling. I saw the cake you made today, remember? And you're a vegan. You don't eat cake and cupcakes. At least not the kind Grace makes."

Up until a couple of weeks ago, that would've been true. But lately, Skye couldn't seem to help herself. It was like she had a tapeworm or something. And since she'd unsuccessfully been trying to convert Maddie and her family to a vegan lifestyle, her new cupcake obsession wasn't something she could share. And now that she thought about how many cupcakes she'd eaten in the last ten days, Skye realized why she'd been nauseated. "Hey, it didn't turn out too bad for my first attempt at making a sugar plum cake."

"Two words, Skye. 'Minimum wage.' You can't support yourself on that. How are you going to live on . . . Oh."

Skye had sensed she'd overstayed her welcome, but that didn't stop the small pinch of hurt at the oh-crap look in her best friend's eyes. "Don't worry, I should have enough to buy a tent next paycheck, and I found a perfect spot at the campgrounds. I'll be out of your hair in a few days."

"Don't be ridiculous. You're staying with us or we'll find you an apartment. I'll help out with your rent until you get on your feet. Have you thought about calling your dad? I'm sure—"

"I'm not calling my dad to ask for a handout. And while I appreciate the offer, I'm not taking one from you, either. I'm twenty-eight years old and fully capable of taking care of myself. Despite what some people seem to think."

"I never said . . ." Maddie trailed off when Skye arched a brow at her. "No, I didn't. I may have said you're a little gullible and overly generous, but I never said you had to grow up."

"I said take care of myself, not grow up. It's good to

know how you really feel," Skye said, and began tidying up the mess she'd made earlier, picking up the mixing bowls from the prep table to put them in the sink.

Maddie reached for her hand. "I love you. I'm worried about you."

Skye sighed, setting the bowls on the table. "I love you, too. But I'm going to be fine."

"Sit down." Maddie pushed a stool toward Skye with her foot. "We need a plan. I have contacts in New York."

"No. Christmas is perfect for me. Cost of living isn't high, it's beautiful and mostly pollution-free. Plus, you're here, and I can help out when the baby comes." All true, and one of the biggest selling features: Scary Guy didn't live there. Ethan did, though. But for the next several months he'd be on the road campaigning. And since the man was *GQ* handsome, smooth, and debonair—not to mention smart—she had no doubt he'd win the election and spend most of his time commuting between Denver and Washington.

"I like having you here, too. But even in Christmas, seven dollars and sixty-eight cents an hour isn't enough for you to live on."

"Eight. Grace is paying me eight dollars an hour, and I told her I can work more than forty if she needs me to." Skye barely managed to stifle a groan when Maddie took a pen and pad of paper from her purse and began jotting down numbers.

"How many hours a week are you averaging?"

"Twenty," Skye mumbled, making it sound more like thirty. Maddie scribbled something on the paper. Given that even thirty hours probably wouldn't impress Maddie, Skye added, "Business has really picked up. I'm sure Grace will increase my hours any day now."

"She's using all her extra funds to hire another baker. Jack doesn't want her putting in as many hours as she has been."

Well, there goes that, Skye thought, but she didn't blame Jack. Grace worked harder than anyone she knew. Taking note of the twitch in her best friend's left eye, Skye realized she had to put a positive spin on the situation or she'd be subjected to a twenty-minute fiscal-responsibility lecture. And since that lecture would undoubtedly depress Skye further, she blurted, "My blog. I'll start charging people to advertise."

"Mmm-hmm," Maddie said, but kept on writing, a frown furrowing her brow.

Skye glanced at the budget, and her still-queasy stomach got queasier. She'd done a budget of her own, and it hadn't looked half as bad as Maddie's. "Are you sure you didn't miscalculate..." She trailed off when Maddie gave her the *look*. "Right, but I don't need health insurance. I'm young and healthy. And I'm serious about camping out. So if you get rid of those expenses, I'm back in the black." When her best friend opened her mouth, no doubt to refute Skye's perfectly valid points, she added, "And you're totally ignoring the income I can generate from my blog. I had close to fifty thousand followers last time I checked. You probably don't know this, but there are bloggers who are making six figures a month. All I have—"

"Are *you* making money from your blog? Any money at all?"

"Well, no, but I haven't—"

And she was off. Skye propped her face in her hands, half-listening to Maddie while mentally going over a

list of influential bloggers she could get in touch with.
Because no matter Maddie's success-to-failure ratios,
Skye latched on to that tiny nugget of hope like an envi-
ronmentalist hugging a tree.

Twenty minutes later, Maddie stopped lecturing long
enough to say hello to Grace, who'd come through the
swinging doors, jarring Skye out of her transcendental
state. Skye was good at tuning people out. It was how she
survived living under her father's dictatorial thumb for all
those years.

Grace, a classic blonde beauty who wore a white feminine sundress, couldn't hide her dismay at the state of
her kitchen. Skye loved her boss, but the woman was a
cleanaholic and a perfectionist. Over the last couple of
weeks, Skye had been working with Grace on her issues.

Grace took a calming breath and smiled. Progress,
Skye thought with a sense of satisfaction. "Don't worry,
Grace. I'll have the kitchen spic-and-span in no time."
After all, Skye had been the one to make the mess icing
the sugar plum cake.

"No, you relax and let me do it." Grace gave Skye's
shoulder a comforting squeeze. "I heard you were sick.
Are you feeling any better?"

She should've known how fast word of the embarrassing episode would spread in the small town. "Better now.
Thanks."

Grace cast her a worried look. "That's the third time
you've been sick this week, Skye. Maybe you should
make an appointment with Dr. McBride."

At least it wasn't as often as the week before. "I—"

"And why is this the first I've heard about it?" Maddie
asked, a hurt expression on her face.

"Because it's not a big deal. It's probably just the flu." More like cupcake overload.

"You have been awfully tired. She fell asleep decorating the cupcakes yesterday," Grace confided to Maddie.

"I did not. I—"

Maddie laughed. "You sound like..." Her laughter faltered, and her eyes widened. "You're not pregnant, are you?"

"No." Skye snorted. "Unless it's an immaculate conception. I haven't had sex in over a..." She trailed off. She'd been about to say a year, but it wasn't a year. It was three months ago. With Ethan.

Not surprisingly, she'd been trying to put that night out of her head. But there was no way she could be pregnant. They'd used protection each and every time. She had had the condoms for a while... Surely she hadn't had them *that* long.

She didn't like the calculating look in Maddie's eyes or the speculative one in Grace's. Skye needed to think of something fast. "I had my period last week," she blurted, at the same time trying to recall how long it had actually been. She fought to keep her expression neutral when she realized her last period had been two weeks before Maddie's wedding.

Her breath came in short, shallow puffs. Stress, it was just the stress. She filled her lungs to prevent hyperventilating. Yes, that was it exactly. The stress. Her breathing evened out. Lots of people missed periods due to stress. And no way would the universe pull a cosmic joke of this proportion on her. As if she could be pregnant by the Republican Party's poster boy. The Fates wouldn't be that cruel. Thinking back to the last few months, she realized, yes, they darn well could. She jumped off the stool. She had get to Maddie's and check the expiration date on the condom box.

"You know, I probably should go home and change," she said, and headed for the swinging doors.

Grace's voice stopped her cold. "You can't. You're scheduled to read the Sugar Plum Cake Fairy story in the park."

Skye counted to ten before slowly turning around. "I thought we'd canceled the reading. The book wasn't supposed to be here in time."

"We got them to do a rush order. Isn't that great?" Grace smiled and reached for a box under the prep table.

Maddie leaned over to help Grace and held up a book. "Aw, look how cute you are."

Skye's anxiety took a backseat to her excitement over finally getting to see the finished product. She walked over and took the book from Maddie. "I am, aren't I?" She grinned.

They'd been working on the book for a while now. Grace had done the illustrations, and Skye had been responsible for editing the story her best friend, Vivian Westfield, had written. Since Vivi had been going through a man-hating phase while writing the story, Skye'd had her work cut out for her. She wanted the Sugar Plum Cake Fairy to have a happy ending after all. And Vivi kept killing off the prince.

Skye flipped through the pages, captivated by the pastel watercolor images. "Grace, your illustrations are amazing."

"Skye's right, Grace. You outdid yourself. I was pretty sure we'd make a fortune off merchandizing the Cake Fairy, but now I'm positive."

Too bad Skye wasn't going to share in their good fortune. But she was happy for Maddie and Grace. Until she flipped to the page that introduced the Sugar Plum Cake Fairy's prince. It took a moment for her to regain her power of speech. "Grace, I told you I wanted my Prince Charming to have dark hair and dark eyes. Not this. I did not want him to look like this." She stabbed her finger into the tawny-haired prince's obnoxiously gorgeous face. "Ethan O'Connor is not my Prince Charming."

Chapter Three

"Nice look," Gage McBride said, eyeing the crown on Ethan's head with a grin. "Lucky for you, Harlan had the stomach flu."

Ethan wasn't feeling so lucky. He'd won the hamburger-eating contest. If he would've known the prize was a crown, he wouldn't have tried so hard. But Gage had been chowing down beside him, egging him on. He raised his hand to remove the crown.

"Not yet. We don't want to offend anyone." Claudia angled her chin at the crowd gathered around the stage. "I'll be right back." She smiled, then headed in his mother's direction.

"Shut up," Ethan said under his breath to his laughing best friend. "I should've let you win." He lowered his hand, feeling some sympathy for Skye.

Then again, she probably loved wearing a crown. She was twenty-eight going on twelve. She was one of the most uninhibited, fun-loving women he'd ever met. She inhaled life: sailing through it with all the ease of a trust-fund baby. Which was probably why she drove him nuts. And not in a I-can't-keep-my-hands-off-her kind of way. Claudia was right. They had nothing in common. He needed to remember that the next time Skye was within ten feet of him.

"Yeah, right, you hate to lose," Gage said.

"Says the guy who tripped me so he could win the hundred-yard dash in sixth grade." Ethan wasn't a sore loser. He just didn't believe in doing anything half-assed. Whether it was winning a hamburger-eating contest, going after a conviction in his previous job as assistant district attorney, or going after the seat in the state senate. When he set his sights on something, he gave it his all.

"Yeah, and you're the one—" Gage broke off at the sight of his nine-year-old daughter, Lily, bounding up the stage steps with a candy apple in her hand. Her older sister, Annie, followed behind.

Gage smiled at his daughters. "You girls having fun?"

"Yeah," Lily said, bouncing up and down.

Annie rolled her eyes. "She's had too much sugar again, Dad."

Ethan grinned. "Hey, I've been out of town for a few weeks and you two forget about me? Where's my hug?" He loved his best friend's kids. Annie and Lily were great. And Gage was one hell of a father. He'd pretty much raised the girls on his own. It hadn't always been easy, and Ethan was glad Gage now had Madison in his life. He envied him. At thirty-six, Ethan wanted what his best friend had: a wife and family.

Annie gave him a one-armed hug. "Like the crown,

Uncle Eth. Is that what all the candidates are wearing these days, or just the Republicans?"

He blinked at what sounded like sarcasm in her thirteen-year-old voice. Taking in her innocent expression, he figured he'd heard her wrong.

"Annie," Gage said in a warning tone.

Not so innocent after all. And Ethan had a good idea who was behind the attitude.

"I like your crown, too, Uncle Ethan. You look like a prince. Can Daddy have one?" Lily asked, wrapping her arms around Ethan's waist.

"Sure," he said, tweaking her ponytail. "He can have mine."

Gage gave him an in-your-dreams look. "Uncle Ethan won the hamburger-eating contest fair and square. The crown's his."

Annie crossed her arms, narrowing her eyes at Ethan while Lily drew back to give him a disappointed look. "You shouldn't eat burgers. They make them out of someone's mommy and daddy."

Skylar Davis strikes again. The damn woman was going to turn Lily and Annie against him. He tried to think of something to say. Thankfully, Gage intervened, "Have you guys seen your mother?"

"She's at the bakery," Lily said, lifting Ethan's arm to look at his watch. "Annie, we gotta go. Auntie Skye's reading the Sugar Plum Cake Fairy story at four. I wanna get a good seat."

Ethan thought about going with her. He had a bone to pick with the Sugar Plum Cake Fairy.

"Aw, Dad, do I have to?" Annie said.

Before Gage could respond, Ethan's mother came

over to say hello to the girls. Liz O'Connor was Lily and Annie's honorary grandmother. She'd been Gage's mother's best friend. Anna McBride had died of breast cancer nine years ago. Five years later, Ethan's father suffered a fatal heart attack. Neither Gage nor Ethan liked the idea of their parents spending the rest of their lives alone and had been trying, unsuccessfully, to get them together. It was obvious they liked one another, but neither one would act on their feelings.

"I swear you two have grown a couple of inches since I saw you last," his mother said, giving the girls a hug. "It won't be long before you have a new baby brother or sister. Are you getting excited?"

Annie shrugged as if she couldn't have cared less, but the hint of a smile gave her away.

Lily nodded enthusiastically. "We want a baby sister, right, Annie?"

"Hey, I'm outnumbered as it is," Gage protested.

Ethan's mother patted Gage's arm. "You don't fool me. You love having a house full of girls to wait on you."

Gage snorted. "You *have* met my wife, haven't you?" Looking down at Lily, who was dancing in front of him, he said, "Okay, I'll meet you over there."

Liz smiled as Lily dragged a protesting Annie off the stage, then returned her attention to Gage. "You're a lucky man, and you know it. If I could find someone half as wonderful as Madison for my son, I'd be a happy woman. I need some grandbabies of my own to spoil. But from the looks of it, that's not going to happen anytime soon."

Ethan didn't miss the assessing glance his mother sent in Claudia's direction. She'd been touting his campaign manager's wifely attributes at an annoying frequency. Ethan couldn't deny that Claudia was a beautiful woman and would be an asset to a man holding political office, but he wasn't attracted to her. Considering the woman he *was* attracted to, maybe he needed to rethink that.

"You have two daughters. Get on Chloe's and Cat's cases," Ethan told his mother, whose long-suffering expression made it clear she thought he was her only hope. It was possible she had a point.

Chloe was an actress who lived in LA, and the only man she was interested in was a golden statue named Oscar. Last year, it'd looked like Cat, a police officer with the Denver PD, might be the one to make his mother's dream come true. Until his sister found out that her fiancé was running a Ponzi scheme right under her nose. Cat lost not only the man of her dreams but her job. She now worked in LA as her twin sister's bodyguard. And while Ethan loved Cat and Chloe, he wasn't exactly disappointed they lived a thousand miles away. He'd had enough of their drama growing up, especially Chloe's. But there were times, like now, when he wouldn't have minded having them around to take the heat off him.

"You're the oldest. It's up to you to set an example." His mother straightened his crown and sighed. "Look how handsome you are. I don't understand why someone hasn't snapped you up yet."

"What I look like, Mom, is an idiot." He scowled at his best friend, who he knew was silently laughing his ass off. Once again, Ethan went to remove the crown.

Claudia, who chose that moment to rejoin them, stopped him. "Ten more minutes." Her smile turned into a frown as she moved his arm and leaned back. "That little girl ruined your jacket. She got candy apple all over you."

Gage winced. "Sorry about that, Eth."

"It's not a big deal," he said, and wasn't happy Claudia was making one out of it. She had to know Lily was Gage's daughter. Then again, it was possible she didn't. Unless someone was of voting age, they didn't appear on her radar. Ethan was more than happy to get rid of his jacket. He hadn't wanted to wear a suit, but Claudia insisted. He took the jacket off, rolled up the sleeves of his white dress shirt, and decided to lose the tie as well.

"No. Leave it on." Claudia stilled his hand with hers, then took the jacket. "I'll get the stain out."

"I'll help," his mother offered.

"Your mom and Claudia get along well," Gage said as the two women left the stage.

"Too well, if you ask me."

"Liz has her pegged for the front-runner in her campaign to find Mrs. O'Connor, does she?"

"Was it that obvious?"

"Not to anyone who doesn't know Liz." Gage cocked his head. "Are you interested? She's beautiful. And with her connections and political savvy, she'd make a great politician's wife."

"You sound like my mother." And like his old boss, Jordan Reinhart, who'd been the one to put Ethan's name into the race. Only Jordan had touted his daughter Sam's good-wife attributes. Ethan had dated Sam five years ago, but their relationship ended when he'd left his job as assistant district attorney and moved back home. "Come on, let's get out of here. I need a break."

"Interesting," Gage said, following him off the stage.

"You didn't answer my question. So should I assume that's a yes?"

"Yes, she would, but no, I'm not interested." It's too bad he wasn't. A recent poll indicated that while Ethan's single status increased his popularity with the younger, more liberal voters, it hurt him with the older, conservative ones. Ethan smiled, shaking hands with several people in the crowd.

"Thanks, appreciate it," he said at their promises of support, then walked away with Gage by his side. "Okay, I think I've worn this thing long enough."

"Maybe you should leave it on. Here comes your fairy princess." Gage's laughter turned to a groan. "Oh hell, she looks pissed. What did you do now?"

"Nothing," Ethan said, lowering his arm as Skye marched toward him with Grace and Madison in tow. He'd been approached by at least ten beautiful, very sweet, reasonable women today, so why was it that the only woman who set his pulse racing was the ticked-off fairy shooting daggers at him?

"You"—Skye jabbed him in the chest with a book—"are *not* my Prince Charming."

"Yeah, you've made that pretty clear, cupcake." He straightened her crown, looking into her flashing caramel-colored eyes. "What did I do now?"

She made a frustrated sound in her throat and went up on her toes. Her sweet, sexy body brushed against him, sending a familiar zing of heated awareness to every nerve ending. He fought the urge to dip his head and kiss her rosebud lips when she reached up, whipped the crown off his head, and waved it in his face. "How do you explain this?"

"I won..." He trailed off. Telling her that he'd won the hamburger-eating contest wouldn't go over well, and they were already drawing attention.

Her gorgeous eyes narrowed, and she thumped the crown against his chest. "You won the hamburger-eating contest, didn't you? Oh, you..." She made a growly noise in her throat, turned on her slippered feet, and flounced off with her wings flapping.

"Sorry, Ethan," Grace said over her shoulder as she hurried after Skye.

"What was that all about?" Gage asked his wife.

"She, ah..." Madison glanced at Ethan and continued in a thick Southern drawl, "She's a little stressed, is all."

Gage put his hands on his wife's shoulders and ducked his head to meet her eyes. "Not buying it, honey. What aren't you telling me?"

"Nothing." She cast a nervous glance in the direction Skye had fled. "I'd better go and calm her down before she starts reading the story. She's liable to kill off the prince. Don't take it personally, Ethan. She's not feeling like herself these days." Madison patted his arm, kissed her husband's cheek, and took off.

"Do me a favor," Gage said, rubbing the back of his neck. "Give Skye a wide berth for the rest of the day."

"Plan to," Ethan said, unable to keep from searching the crowd for a flash of purple.

"Yeah, right, I saw the way you looked at her. Trust me, you don't want to go there, buddy. I like Skye, but she's not for you."

Ethan had heard the same thing from his mother and Claudia. He'd even said it himself. So why did his best friend warning him away from Skye leave Ethan with a hollowed-out feeling in his chest? "Any idea what she's stressed about?"

"Who knows? Tired, maybe. She's been helping Grace out at the bakery. I doubt she's ever worked before."

His best friend was probably right, but it didn't stop Ethan from feeling defensive on her behalf. "You're being a little unfair, don't you think? Just because she's rich doesn't mean she hasn't put in an honest day's work before."

Gage released a low whistle. "You've got it bad, buddy."

"No, I . . . okay, yeah, I do," he admitted at Gage's knowing look. "But it's nothing more than a physical attraction. I'm not a fool." Though he was beginning to feel like one when it came to Skye. "I know better than to get involved with her, especially now. I just have to keep my distance."

"Good luck with that. You've been searching the park for her ever since she left."

"You may not have noticed, but she doesn't want anything to do with me. Besides, I'll be on the road, and she'll be leaving town."

"It's probably a good thing you'll be hitting the campaign trail, because it doesn't look like she's leaving anytime soon." And Gage didn't appear overly thrilled about it.

Before he could question Gage further, several older women surrounded Ethan.

Ten minutes later, as the blue-haired ladies walked off, his best friend grinned. "You always did have a way with older women. From what I've seen and heard today, you're a shoo-in." He clapped Ethan on the shoulder. "You'll make a great senator. I'm proud of you."

"Thanks, but we still have a long way to go. Bennett is running a solid campaign. We'll—" He broke off when his mother rejoined them, his jacket draped over her arm. "Where's Claudia?" With another Fourth of July BBQ to attend in the next county, they had to hit the road.

His mother handed him his jacket. "She wanted to get a picture of some Kendall person. Ethan, where are you going?" she called out, as he took off in the direction Skye had gone.

"What's up?" Gage asked, jogging up to him.

"Skye's Kendall." And he'd seen her reaction when Claudia mentioned taking a picture of her in costume. "I have to get to Claudia before she finds her."

Several yards away, adults ringed a group of children who sat on the grass under a weeping willow. Ethan made his way through the crowd toward Grace and Madison. Out of the corner of his eye, he caught a flash of red and zeroed in on the tall brunette. "Claudia," he called out. She didn't hear him and raised her iPhone.

Skye, who sat on a rock surrounded by at least thirty little kids, glanced in his direction at the same time Claudia said, "Smile, Kendall."

Skye glared at Ethan as she continued reading the story and, in graphic, gory detail, killed the prince.

"I can't believe she just did that," Madison said, covering her face with her hand.

Neither, it appeared, could Skye. With a horrified expression on her pink-cheeked face, her gaze went from the book to the little kids gathered around her.

"Oh no, Madison, look, they're crying," Grace said.

"I can't."

Aw, hell, Ethan thought, when Skye looked like she

might do the same. He started through the crowd with the idea of rescuing her. Gage stopped him with a hand on his arm. "Keeping your distance, remember?" he reminded Ethan. "From the way she reacted to you earlier, you'll only make it worse."

"No, don't cry," Skye pleaded. "The prince isn't dead. He's in a coma."

Ethan bowed his head when two little girls in the front row cried louder. He raised it in time to see their mothers rush into the circle, scooping them into their arms. Whatever the two women said to Skye deepened the color on her already flushed cheeks. "Grace, Madison, come on. Do something," he said. If they didn't, he would.

Lily jumped up, pointing to the trees behind Skye. "Sugar Plum Cake Fairy, look. It's the Evil Queen!"

"What? Where?" Skye asked, whipping her head around.

Thank God for Lily, Ethan thought.

Gage chuckled. "That's my girl."

Lily ran to Skye, grabbed her wand, and brandished it at the invisible Queen. Waving the wand, she murmured what sounded like a chant, then said, "She's gone Sugar Plum Cake Fairy, and I made her take the spell off the sugar plum you ate. It was poisoned."

"Lily's getting a raise on her allowance," Madison murmured.

"Maybe we can make her the Sugar Plum Cake Fairy," Grace whispered.

"Thank you, Lily. I wondered what that awful taste was." Skye hugged the little girl while making a comical face that had the kids laughing. "So, did I do anything bad when I was under her wicked spell?"

Hands shot up in the air. Several boys didn't wait for her to call on them and shouted what she'd done.

As shock and horror contorted Skye's beautiful face, Ethan decided she should win an Oscar for her performance. She flipped through the pages, holding the book open for her audience. "See, my prince didn't die. He rescued me from the Evil Queen, and we lived happily ever after."

Chapter Four

The next morning, Skye sat on the edge of the bed numbly staring at the expiration date on the condom box in her hand. *If* she was pregnant, it was her own darn fault. Flopping onto the fuchsia satin comforter in the guest bedroom at Maddie's, she stared at the pink chandelier overhead. It would have taken all of one second to check the box that night, but she didn't. And she knew why she didn't. Ethan O'Connor's mind-numbing, toe-curling kisses had sucked the common sense right out of her head.

She supposed the three glasses of champagne she'd had at Maddie and Gage's rehearsal party might have had something to do with it, too. As soon as Skye had seen Ethan standing by the bar in an expensive black suit that fit him to perfection, she'd been drawn to him like a bee to a daisy . . . or maybe a rose. Ethan was too sophisticated to be a daisy.

And the morning after, he'd looked even better. Which

proved that champagne goggles weren't to blame. Lying in bed with a muscular arm tucked behind his head, he had a lazy, satisfied grin on his sinfully gorgeous face. The tangled sheets rode low on his waist and bared an impressive six-pack and a sculpted chest. She'd barely resisted the urge to crawl back into the king-sized bed and run her fingers through his sleep-tousled hair. She released a resentful sigh at the memory.

Physically, Ethan O'Connor was her dream man. Her every erotic fantasy come to life. He sent her hormones and pheromones into overdrive. And when he opened his mouth, he sent her temper there, too. The man stood for everything she stood against. There was not a single thing they agreed upon. If she said the grass was green, he'd say it was brown in that smooth, lawyerly voice of his.

And she might be having his baby.

Hot and cold shivers raced up and down her spine, her stomach rolling on a nauseous wave. *You're not pregnant*, she told herself firmly and sat up. Sliding a hand under the waistband of her black yoga pants, she brushed her fingers over her stomach. Firm and concave. No changes there. She brought both hands to her black, pink-trimmed sports bra and cupped her boobs. Definitely a change there. It hadn't been the Cake Fairy costume after all. And not only were her boobs bigger, they were more sensitive, too. Cupcakes—it had to be all the sugar-laden cupcakes she'd eaten. Sugar was poison, and she'd been poisoning herself on a daily basis.

Dear universe, please let it be the sugar, Skye thought as she picked up her iPhone. The one extravagance from her old life that she couldn't afford to let go. Even if she kind of couldn't afford to keep it. Because no matter what

Maddie said, Skye's financial future rested on her blog. But before she checked for responses from the bloggers she'd e-mailed last night, she Googled pregnancy symptoms.

Missed period. She mentally checked off the box. *Morning sickness.* She gave it a half-check. Hers was an all-day sickness, or at least it had been up until a few days ago. *Tender breasts.* Another check.

She gave a guilty start as the bedroom door opened. Quickly closing the site, Skye tossed her iPhone and pulled up her legs to sit cross-legged on the bed, wrapping her right elbow over her left in a seated eagle pose.

Maddie stuck her head in. "Hi ... What are you doing?"

"Yoga."

"Oh, okay. How are you feeling this morning?" she asked, a touch of Southern in her voice.

Pregnant. "Fabulous."

"You look better than you did yesterday. Your face is all glowy."

Darn it. Skye mentally checked another box.

"Did you sleep well last night?"

"Like a log." *Dammit.* Her stomach did a panicked dance as she checked off that last box. At any other time, with any other man, she would've blurted her fears to her best friend. But she couldn't. *If* Skye was pregnant, as soon as she started showing, she'd leave Christmas. She wouldn't tell Ethan.

There's no way she'd subject her child to the same harsh censure she'd endured growing up. And she knew only too well that as conservative as Ethan was, he'd insist she marry him. She didn't believe in marriage. Especially to a man who didn't like her, let alone love her. What kind of environment would that be for a child to grow up in?

She knew exactly what kind, since it was the one she'd grown up in.

"That's good, because I just got off the phone with Grace," Maddie said as she walked into the room. "She needs you to help out today."

Skye had been mortified yesterday. Devastated that she'd made the little girls cry. She didn't know what had come over her. Okay, so she did. Ethan had driven her to it. Ethan and her worries over their maybe baby. Seeing Claudia take a picture of her, a picture that made Skye look like a fool, only made it worse. Ethan already thought she was a joke. One more reason for her not to tell him if she was pregnant.

"I can't work today. I have plans." She was picking up a pregnancy test. And she'd have to drive halfway across the state to ensure no one saw her do so. "Grace told me yesterday that she didn't need me." She hadn't said so in so many words, but after Skye had killed Ethan...the prince...she figured Grace didn't trust her to help out at the fund-raising event Liz O'Connor was hosting for her son. The Sugar Plum Bakery was catering the Strawberry Social at the O'Connors' ranch today.

"You have to. Desiree called in sick."

"Liz O'Connor hates me. She won't want me there." And that was one more reason to add to the why-not-to-tell-Ethan list. "And I don't want to see Claudia again." Especially since Skye would be working the type of event she'd usually attend as a guest.

"Since when do you care what people think? You've always marched to the beat of your own drum, so keep marching. Grace needs you, and you need the money."

Skye's stomach dropped to somewhere in the vicinity

of her toes at the reminder. She hadn't moved past the initial shock and horror of thinking she *might* be pregnant to think about all that entailed. Supporting herself on minimum wage was one thing, but supporting a baby, too...? She'd need health insurance. She'd need... Tears prickled at the backs of her eyes as the weight of her worries came crashing down upon her.

Maddie frowned and sat beside her on the bed, taking her hand. "What's wrong?"

Skye wanted to tell her, but she couldn't ask Maddie to keep a secret from her husband. Gage and Ethan were best friends. And she wouldn't put her best friend in the middle of the mess. Resting her head on Maddie's shoulder, Skye swiped at the tear burning a trail down her cheek. "I feel like a failure. I'm twenty-eight, and I have no money, no home, no career. I don't have anything."

"You have me, and you have Vivi. And you're not a failure. Come on." Maddie squeezed her hand. "What happened to the woman who always told me, 'When one door closes another one opens'? Or what about 'It always looks darkest before the dawn'?"

Skye snorted and rubbed her nose. "She had her rose-colored glasses ripped off her face."

"Maybe that's not a bad thing. I bet one day you'll look back on this and say it's the best thing that ever happened to you. Everything for a reason, remember?"

"Are you going to quote every platitude I ever spouted?"

"Yeah, it's kind of fun. How about this one: 'Breathe and find your happy place'?"

Skye half-laughed, half-cried, and put her arms around Maddie. "I really do love you, you know."

"I know you do, and I love you, too." Maddie rubbed

Skye's back. "We're going to figure this out. I checked out your blog last night. You weren't kidding. It really is popular. I made up a list of potential advertisers that would fit your target audience."

Wiping her cheeks with the back of her hands, Skye eased out of Maddie's arms. "Really?"

"Yeah, really. We'll talk about it tonight. You'll be back on your feet in no time."

With Maddie putting her stamp of approval on the plan, Skye felt more hopeful and positive. It made it easier for her to push her fears away. "You're right. I will."

"That's more like it. But until you are, you're staying with us," Maddie said as she came to her feet.

Skye shook her head. "You know how much I love camping. I'll be fine. Besides, I don't want to wear out my welcome."

"Don't be silly. Lily and Annie love having you around. Their auntie Skye is way cool in their eyes."

"I am pretty cool, aren't I? But you and Gage are newlyweds. You don't need a third wheel."

"We have two kids and another one on the way. What's one more?"

Skye narrowed her eyes at her best friend.

Maddie laughed. "Come on. Grace wants you to wear black pants and a white blouse. I've seen your closet, so we'll have to raid mine. Let's see what I have that'll fit you." She gave Skye a quick once-over and frowned. "Have your boobs gotten bigger?"

*   *   *

The colorful glass beads holding up Skye's messy topknot clinked as the delivery van bounced along the one-tract dirt road. "Geez, I thought the O'Connors were rich. You think they could pave the road." She sounded a tad cranky, and Skye was rarely cranky. Her mood was probably due to the motion causing a return of her nausea. Either that or her inability to convince Grace that her working the event was a bad idea.

"You're not feeling well, are you?" Grace said, shooting her a concerned glance.

"No, I'm good. Just a little carsick," Skye lied. She wished it was the truth. Because she really didn't want to think about the other explanation. After she'd changed into Maddie's short-sleeved white blouse and black Capri pants, Skye had locked the bathroom door and filled one of the expired condoms with water. She repeated the experiment three times. They were all fine... no leakage. So she'd convinced herself she had nothing to worry about.

"I really wish I didn't have to ask you to do this, Skye. But it's my first big catering event, and I need your help. There's a lot of influential people attending, and it'll be great publicity for the bakery. I don't want to mess it up."

One more reason she shouldn't be there, Skye thought. Half the people attending the social were on her hit list. But after hearing how important today was for Grace, she decided she had to get over herself and suck it up. She'd do whatever she had to to make the event a success. "You won't. Once they taste your strawberry shortcake and strawberry tart, you'll be booked through to next year." And thinking of the theme for the social, her voice grew more enthusiastic. At least the Sugar Plum Cake Fairy wouldn't be expected to make an appearance.

"I'm so glad you moved to Christmas. You're good for

my confidence. I hope you don't plan on leaving anytime soon." Grace's smile faded when Skye inadvertently grimaced. "You're not leaving, are you?"

"You know me, footloose and fancy-free," Skye said, forcing a lighthearted tone to her voice. "Never know when the mood will strike me. But don't worry, I'll give you plenty of notice."

New York had been Skye's home base for the last ten years, but she spent so much time travelling to remote corners of the world with her environmental causes that she was rarely there. Over the last year, even before she'd lost her money, her bohemian lifestyle had started to lose its appeal. She'd been thinking of settling down and starting a foundation of her own. But her financial problems had effectively ended that idea.

"Oh, I thought you were happy here." Grace wrinkled her nose. "Is it Madison? Did you guys have a fight when you told her you lost your trust fund? You seemed to be getting along okay."

"No, we're good. I, uh, I don't want to overstay my welcome." Skye stared out the passenger-side window at the aspens nestled against the rocky cliffs that encircled the private valley. As the landscape blurred into a verdant blob, she blinked back tears. She didn't know why the idea of leaving the small town—Maddie and her girls, the friends she'd made—left her feeling so darn emotional. She cleared her throat. "I'll probably camp out for a while, see how it goes."

"You're not living in a tent, Skye," Grace said firmly, tapping her finger on the steering wheel. "Promise me you won't do anything for now. I have an idea, but I have to talk it over with Jack first."

"I don't plan..." Skye began, then groaned as they drove through the open wrought-iron gates and up the long, paved circular drive. And it wasn't because the last time she'd driven through those gates she had been with Ethan. No, it was because she recognized the man standing on the cobblestone walkway in front of the O'Connors' stunning home talking to Liz O'Connor. Ethan's mother looked youthfully pretty with a black headband holding back her toffee-colored, shoulder-length hair. She made even a white denim skirt and black-and-white T-shirt look coolly elegant.

"What's wrong? Are you going to be sick?"

Skye sunk down in her seat. "The man in the black Stetson is Richard Stevens, Claudia's father. You have to do me a big favor, Grace. No one can find out I'm broke. If anyone asks, tell them I'm just helping you out," she said desperately. All she'd need was for her father to hear she'd lost her trust fund. He'd never let her live it down, and neither would Claudia.

"Of course. Madison is the only one who knows you're on the payroll." Grace made a face. "And Jack."

"You don't think he'd tell Gage or Ethan, do you?" Skye asked, bending down to dig her cell phone from her purse.

"I don't think so, but I'll call him just to make sure."

"Thanks. I'd better call Maddie." Skye already had her phone to her ear. When the call went to voice mail, she left a message. They were heading to Lily's baseball game, so hopefully Maddie would get it before coming to the social.

Liz and Richard turned when Grace pulled the white van in front of the house. Catching sight of Skye, Ethan's mother's lips set in a disapproving line. *Let the fun begin*, Skye thought. She forced a smile for Richard, who offered her a surprised one in return. He opened her door. "Kendall Davis," he said in a booming voice as he hauled her into his arms. Richard was a loud, gregarious man in his midsixties who looked like Robert Redford. "Claudia told me you were here. I was going to look you up before I left. You haven't changed a bit. Still pretty as a picture. How long has it been?"

"It's been a while." Skye smiled. She'd always liked Claudia's dad. "You look great, Richard. You're doing well?"

"Can't complain, darlin'. Now, tell me what you're doing here. Last I heard from your father you'd been arrested for chaining yourself to a tree in Brazil."

Her cheeks heated. "Um, that was about six years ago."

"Oh, right, it was a forklift up in Montana."

"No, that was—"

He snapped his fingers. "Gotcha. Canadian embassy in Washington to protest the tar sands." Grinning, he hooked an arm around her neck. "This little gal's a pistol, Lizzie. Never knew what she'd get up to next. When she was ten, she snuck out of the house one night and set the neighbor's horses free." He chuckled. "Surprised your father still has a hair left on his head. Have you—"

"Richard, we probably should let Ms. Davis get to work," Liz interrupted him in an unamused voice. "The guests will be arriving shortly."

He frowned, looking from Skye to Grace, who'd started to unload the van. "You're working at a bakery?"

"Just lending my friend a hand." She patted his arm. "It was great to see you, Richard."

"You too, darlin'. We'll talk later."

"Grace, the boys are in the back setting up the tables. Get them to give you a hand. You can go through the house to the backyard," Liz said. She looped her arm through Richard's. "Come and see that horse I was telling you about."

"You should let Skye have a look at him. She's a regular horse whisperer." He chuckled and winked at Skye. "On second thought, you better not. She's liable to set him free."

Ethan's mother, whose lips were once again pressed in a disapproving line, gave a disdainful "Hmm."

Grace, standing with two containers in her arms, stared after Liz and Richard. "Okay," she said. "I thought you were exaggerating, but you're not. Mrs. O'Connor is definitely not a fan of yours."

"Yeah. And hopefully Richard cans the reminiscing or you'll be on your own. If he tells her about my run-in with the NRA last year, she'll have me tossed from the premises."

Pulling a tray from the back of the van, Grace cast Skye a nervous glance. "I think there's a man from the NRA on the guest list. You won't—"

"Don't worry, Grace. I won't do anything to embarrass you or the bakery. I promise." She grabbed two trays from the van and turned to head up the stairs.

Ethan stood on the porch in a white dress shirt with the sleeves rolled up to bare his tanned forearms. A pair of navy dress pants showed off his narrow waist and long, muscular legs. "Glad to hear that, cupcake," he said, taking the trays from her.

She sighed. "Can you please give the 'cupcake' thing a rest?"

His hazel eyes warmed and his lips tipped up at the corners. "You prefer Cake Fairy?"

"Maybe you didn't notice, but I'm not wearing my costume. I'm not the Sugar Plum Cake Fairy today." *Thank the universe.*

"Oh, I noticed," he said as his eyes took a lazy head-to-toe tour of her body. "And you still look good enough to eat."

Chapter Five

Ethan never lost his temper. His colleagues at the district attorney's office used to call him Mr. Unflappable. But at this precise moment, Mr. Unflappable was having a difficult time keeping his cool. He didn't know which woman to lay the blame on: his mother or Skye. Probably Skye.

Every time she walked by him in her frilly purple-and-white-striped apron, she'd snort or say something derogatory under her breath. As far as he could tell, she hadn't been saying the same to his supporters or soliciting votes for his opponent. Yet. And of course Ethan knew this because he couldn't take his eyes off her. Something his hawk-eyed mother didn't miss and which had already earned him two sharp-toned lectures.

Even now, he watched as Skye approached a white-linen-draped table with a glass pitcher of strawberry punch. He tensed when he recognized Frank Riley, the local NRA representative sitting with five other members at the table.

His mother nudged him. "Ethan said the exact same thing the other day, isn't that right, dear?" Liz said, addressing him through a tight smile.

She was annoying, but right. Ethan had to start paying attention to the conversation at hand. Mrs. Rich, a long-time Democrat with considerable influence, was talking about throwing her support behind him. "Yes, I—" He broke off when Skye bent down to pour the punch in Riley's glass, and the older man patted her butt at the same time he loudly denounced the anti-gun lobbyists to his friends. *Aw hell.* Ethan recognized the look that came over her face. "Excuse me for a moment," he said to Mrs. Rich and headed for the table.

"Skye," he called out, trying to gain her attention. She glanced up at the same time as she tipped the pitcher, pouring pink liquid onto the man, a strawberry coming to rest in the lap of his gray pants. At Riley's bellowed obscenity, Ethan heard his mother gasp from behind him and saw Grace's frantic expression as she hurried over.

"Oh, I'm so sorry. I'm such a klutz," Skye said, looking anything but apologetic until she caught sight of Grace. Then she winced and reached for the strawberry, apparently thought twice about it, and grabbed some napkins off the table instead.

Riley glared at her, snatching the napkins from her hand as she prepared to pat him down. "I'll be sending you the cleaning bill, young lady. And I suggest you start looking for another job."

Ethan rested his hand on Riley's shoulder. "It was an

accident, Frank, and Ms. Davis apologized. I'll take care of your—"

Claudia, wearing a nautical blue-and-white dress, swooped in to save the day. "Come with me, Mr. Riley. I'll have you fixed up as good as new in no time." She poured on the charm as she led the man toward the house, drawing a laugh from him. Given the look Riley shot in Skye's direction, Ethan figured the joke had been at her expense.

Skye's cheeks flushed as she mopped up the folding chair. Ethan went to offer his help, but the men at the table diverted his attention with a question about his stance on armed security guards in local schools. Skye lifted her head and opened her mouth. Thankfully, his mother and Grace arrived at the same time and cut off her response.

"I'm really sorry, Grace," Skye said as she picked up the container. "I—"

His mother took the crystal pitcher from Skye. "I realize you're understaffed, Grace, but I think it would be best for Ms. Davis to leave. I'll take care of the punch."

Once again, Ethan excused himself and herded the three women out of earshot. He took the pitcher from his mother and handed it back to Skye. "She's not going anywhere, Mom," he said, even though he thought it might be a good idea if she did. But seeing the vulnerable expression on her face, he couldn't help but defend her. "Grace needs her, and it was—"

"—an accident," Skye said, glancing at him from under her long lashes. "I spilled the punch because he startled me when he patted my bottom, Mrs. O'Connor. I could legitimately charge him with sexual harassment, you know. But I won't. Now, if you'll excuse me, it's about a hundred degrees in the shade, and your guests are thirsty."

Grace cast a nervous glance from his mother to Skye and retrieved the pitcher. "I'll take care of the punch, Skye. You can serve the cupcakes, okay?"

Before Skye had a chance to respond, his mother said, "I have another pitcher. I'll give you a hand, Grace. Ms. Davis, if there's one more incident—"

"I'll handle it, Mom," Ethan said, placing a hand on Skye's shoulder.

"I don't need to be *handled*, Ethan." She wriggled out from under his hand as Grace led his mother away. "It was his fault I spilled the punch."

"Tell that to someone you haven't poured champagne on. I saw your face, cupcake. You spilled the punch on him because of what he said, not what he did."

"Only a sexist nincompoop would say something like that." He struggled to keep a straight face at her word choice, and her caramel eyes narrowed at him. "Did you actually expect me to stand there and smile while some aging lothario groped my bottom?"

"No. I don't like anyone groping you but me." Her jaw dropped, and he continued, "If you'd given me a chance, I would have taken care of him, Skye."

"You are such a…" She made a frustrated sound in her throat. "I don't need you to protect me, Ethan. I've been looking after myself for a long time."

At her raised voice, heads turned in their direction. Exactly the kind of attention Ethan wanted to avoid. Once again, he was reminded why he needed to keep his distance from Skylar Davis. "I realize that, but are you forgetting your promise to Grace?"

"You're right," she said, looking suitably chastened. "I don't want her to lose business because of me." She nibbled on her fingernail. "Maybe you could tell him I have a medical condition?"

And this was why he had a difficult time keeping his distance. She was cute as hell. "Any particular condition you had in mind, cupcake?"

She pressed her lips together. "Forget it. I'll apologize and pay his dry cleaning bill."

"Don't worry about it. I'm sure Claudia smoothed things over. And I'll take care of his dry cleaning bill."

"I'm sure she did. No one does sucking up better than Claudia," she said with a curl of her upper lip. Something caught her attention, and she frowned at him. "You invited Fred and Ted?"

"Of course I did. Why wouldn't I?" he said, glancing over his shoulder to see the two older men, who looked like the actors from *Grumpy Old Men*, taking their seats at one of the tables. Then he realized why she'd ask. "If you would've let me get a word in edgewise at Gage and Madison's wedding instead of ripping into me after misconstruing what I'd said, you wouldn't have to ask." His response came out clipped at the reminder of how, after the amazing night they'd shared, she'd turned his best friend's wedding into a shit show over a simple misunderstanding and a difference of opinion and refused to speak to him.

"No? So if I offered to marry them, right here, right now, you wouldn't object?"

"Okay, for the last time, Fred and Ted are not gay."

"As if they're going to come out to *you*, Mr. Poster Boy for the Republican Party."

There was no reasoning with her, and he didn't know why he bothered to try. Sure he did, but he was slowly coming to the realization that everyone was right. It was about time he got his head in the game and that meant keeping away from Skye. "I'm not getting into this with you now. And for Grace's sake, if you can't put your own agenda aside, then it's best if you leave. I'm sure Claudia, my mother, and Nell won't mind pitching in to help Grace."

"Ethan." His mother waved him over to Mrs. Rich's table. He walked away, leaving Skye staring after him.

Ethan spent the next hour working the tables. He managed to keep his distance from Skye. Ignoring her? That was easier said than done. Every time she laughed—and that was just one more thing he liked about Skye; she laughed a lot—he'd find himself seeking her out. In his defense, she had an amazing laugh. He returned his attention to the CEO from Albright Energy, who'd been railing against the stranglehold that newly proposed legislation would put on his company.

Since he'd heard it before, Ethan easily picked up the thread of the conversation. "I agree with you. You're heavily regulated by the state as it is, and the additional rules are unnecessary. We need to empower local self-government and put an end to the one-size-fits-all government that Bennett endorses," he said, referring to his opponent.

After another ten minutes of discussing a recently released report by the Energy Department that determined fracking didn't contaminate drinking water, the three men assured Ethan he had their endorsement. Slapping him on the back in turn, they headed to a table. Claudia stopped to have a word with them before joining Ethan, his mother, and Richard. "That went well," Claudia said with a pleased smile as she reached his side.

"Were you able to smooth things over with Mr. Riley?" his mother asked Claudia.

"Yes, Ethan has his full support, and he's quite taken with your housekeeper. Rosa found him a pair of pants and got the stain out of his. She's pressing them as we speak."

"Well, that's good to hear at least. I still can't believe the nerve of that girl. I told Grace in no uncertain terms that if I host another event, I don't want her here."

"Mom, relax, it was an accident."

Claudia's father laughed. "I highly doubt it, son. That little gal came out of the womb with a protest sign clutched in her tiny fist. She stands up for what she believes in, and Lord help you if you get in her way. Her father had his hands full, let me tell you. She's got gumption, that one. Might not agree with her politics, but always did admire her passion for the issues. And don't let her fool you, she's smart as a whip. Made the mistake of debating the merits of a vegetarian lifestyle with her when she was twelve. She won."

"That's not what you said when you had to bail her out of jail at sixteen for throwing red paint on Mrs. Harmon's fur coat, Daddy," Claudia said with a petulant look on her face. "For Ethan's sake, let's hope she keeps her leftist politics to herself for the rest of the day."

"Claudia's right, Richard. You should save your admiration for someone who deserves it. Your daughter is amazing." His mother looped her arm through Claudia's and patted her hand. "I don't know what we'd do without her. She's a marvel, isn't she, Ethan?"

"Yes, she is," he agreed, then wanted to take it back at the familiar gleam in his mother's eyes.

"I've had several people ask if you two were an item, you know," she said. "Don't you think they'd make the perfect couple, Richard?"

Claudia smiled and gave Ethan what he prayed was a here-we-go-again look and not a hopeful one.

*   *   *

With a forced smile on her face and a tight grip on the tray of cupcakes, Skye walked toward the table where the idiots from Albright Energy were seated. *Nice men from Albright Energy*, she corrected herself. After the strawberry punch incident, she couldn't afford another slip-up. Grace, being Grace, of course, hadn't said anything about it. But Skye knew she was upset with her. And so was Ethan, even though he'd defended her to his mother. She didn't want to admit it, but he'd hurt her feelings when he suggested she leave. Or maybe it was the way he'd said it in his cool, emotionless voice that bothered her most.

He didn't look cool and emotionless right now, she thought, sneaking a furtive glance to where he stood talking to several older men. With the sun glinting off his thick, tawny hair and the flash of his warm smile, he looked dangerously hot and sexy. She dragged her gaze away as the CEO of Albright Energy waved her over. Liz O'Connor sat with a group of her friends at a table beside theirs, making it difficult for Skye to ignore her overly loud conversation with the two women at her table. "You're right, Claudia's a darling." Ethan's mother looked directly at Skye as she continued, "She'd make a wonderful daughter-in-law. The two of them are perfect together."

Skye rolled her eyes. Did Liz actually think it bothered her that she wanted Ethan to marry Claudia? At the sinking feeling in her stomach, Skye realized that maybe it did bother her, just a bit. But it was only because Ethan didn't know Claudia like Skye did. The woman was an uptight conservative who didn't care who she stepped on to get to the top. Cold and ambitious, Claudia Stevens cared more about polls than people.

Maybe they were a perfect match after all, Skye thought, as Claudia walked to Ethan's side. He laughed at something the tall, elegant brunette said and put his arm around her shoulders, introducing her to the men. Skye might not be a fan of Claudia, but she had to admit with her high cheekbones, long, wavy dark hair, and dark eyes, Claudia was a beautiful woman.

At the sight of Liz beaming at the glamorous couple, Skye turned and started doling out cupcakes to the Albright Energy table with a forced smile.

"Well, hello, sweetheart." The CEO grinned, the sun glinting off his wedding band. "Why don't you join us?" he asked, holding out a chair for her.

"I…" Skye was about to politely refuse the man's invitation when she overhead Liz say, "Who knows, by this time next year, I might have a grandbaby like the both of you. They'd make beautiful babies, don't you think?"

Skye didn't know why—maybe it was the thought of Claudia having Ethan's baby, or that the married CEO flirting with her probably had children of his own—but a spurt of anger fired up inside her. "Seriously? You want *me* to sit with *you*, a man whose company is single-handedly destroying Colorado's pristine wilderness, and poisoning the water table, all to make a dishonest buck? Yeah, that's not going to happen."

The man gave her a tight smile. "You might want to stick to baking, sweetheart. Don't worry your pretty little head about things you know nothing about."

Skye slammed the platter of cupcakes on the table, causing the glasses of punch to shake. "You'd be surprised how much information my pretty little head can hold." The Albright CEO's face pinked as she listed instances of documented well water contamination and health problems directly linked to fracking.

"Ms. Davis, I'd like a word with you," Ethan said, his strong fingers encircling her arm. Skye's gaze flitted from his hand to everyone staring at her openmouthed.

At the sight of Grace coming toward them with a panicked expression on her face, Skye felt like crying again. And her out-of-control emotions were ticking her off. "Sorry," she mumbled and jerked her arm from Ethan's hold. Her only thought to get away before she started to cry, she brushed past him and ran for the wooden bridge, heading for the privacy of the red barn.

Once inside, she sat on the bales of sweet-smelling hay and tried to figure out how she could make this up to Grace. She looked up to see Ethan standing in front of her. His concerned gaze roamed her face. "What's going on?"

She focused on her hands and smoothed the apron. "I don't know what you're talking about."

Nudging her chin with his knuckle, he forced her gaze to his. "I know how you feel about fracking, but there's more to what just went on out there. You promised Grace you wouldn't embarrass her or the bakery, but you did. Twice. And yesterday you made the kids cry when you killed off the prince. You told me you were a pacifist, so even if it's in a book, that's not something you'd normally do."

Up until her run-in with Scary Guy, Skye thought she was a pacifist, too. She supposed it didn't count if you were acting in self-defense, but some people might think putting a man in the hospital constituted violent tendencies. "It's my diet," she said, because she wasn't about to tell him what was really going on.

"What are you dieting for? You have an incredible body."

"Thanks," she murmured, ignoring the tiny spurt of pleasure his compliment engendered, "but I'm a vegan, and I've been eating too many cupcakes." When he looked confused, she said, "Sugar's poison. You may not be aware of this, but there's a correlation between violent behavior and sugar."

His mouth tipped up at the corner. "Is that right?"

"Yes. And I haven't been exercising, so my serotonin levels are probably low." No wonder she'd been feeling so crappy and emotional. It was such a relief to finally figure out what had been going on with her that she gave Ethan a bright smile. "Thanks, I feel much better now. I'll just go..." She went to stand, and he slid his strong hands up her knees to her thighs, holding her in place.

"There's more to it than that, and I want to know what it is. You're not leaving here until you tell me."

"You can't keep me here against my will. Besides, you're wrong. I'm totally fine." But the way his thumbs caressed her inner thighs lulled her into submission, and she didn't move. She wasn't even sure she could speak without moaning. She'd forgotten the power of his sensual touch, how amazing his warm hands felt on her skin.

"Skye?"

"Hmm."

"Cupcake, are you falling asleep on me?" he asked, a hint of amusement in his whiskey-smooth voice.

She blinked and sat up straighter, pushing her hair from her face. "No, of course not. I should be going. I really do appreciate your concern, Ethan, but I'm honestly fine."

"Madison said you're stressed."

"Really? When did she say that?" Obviously her best friend hadn't told him about her financial problems or, like her father, Ethan would be lecturing her on her irresponsibility.

"Yesterday when you whacked me with the crown and killed the prince."

"Oh right, sorry about that. It was stage fright. And I think Maddie's projecting. She's stressed about the baby, you know."

"I'm a criminal prosecutor. I can tell when someone's lying. Others might not be able to see through you, but I can. I just wanted to offer my help, but if you don't want it, that's fine."

"No, I'm not...Thank you," she said, clearing the emotion from her voice. He was being so kind and sweet that she was tempted to tell him about their maybe baby. It'd be so easy to unload her worries on his broad shoulders. He was a strong, responsible man and so gorgeous he sometimes made her lose her train of thought. Like now, for all of a few seconds, she forgot he was a Republican. "Thank you for worrying about me. That's very nice, considering I reamed out one of your biggest supporters. I hope none of your guests will hold it against you or Grace."

"I'll tell them you're suffering from mood swings due

to a medical condition." He stood and offered her a hand, helping her to her feet.

"I didn't think of that. Maybe I have hypoglycemia. It would explain…" Catching herself, she said, "That's a great idea."

"I have them every now and again. But I can't take credit for that one. It was yours, remember?" He smiled, holding her gaze as he tucked her hair behind her ear. "If you're in trouble or need anything, you have my number."

She nodded, wishing she really did have magic and could turn him into a Democrat. "Thanks," she said, having a hard time fighting back tears.

"Hey, are you going to cry?" he asked with a frown. Taking her chin in his hand, he stroked her cheek with his thumb. "You're starting to worry me, cupcake."

"I think I'm coming down with a cold," she said, faking a smile.

"Ethan." They turned as his mother entered the barn. "Some of the guests are leaving," she said, her narrowed gaze moving from Ethan to Skye. As though she sensed her son's hesitation, she added, "Mr. Riley is looking for you."

"Thanks. I'll be right there. You sure you're okay?" he asked Skye as he lowered his hand and took a step back.

"Positive. Go and say good-bye to your guests. I'll just hang out here for a bit, if you don't mind."

"No problem. Just remember what I said. If I can do anything, anything at all, let me know."

"Thanks, Ethan." She walked to one of the stalls as he headed from the stables with his mother. She heard them talking in low, aggravated tones and had a fairly good idea who was the topic of their conversation. A few seconds later, another voice joined in, and their voices faded.

Skye passed several empty stalls until she found one with an occupant. She put her foot on the rail. "Hey, pretty boy," she said to the horse. He was a beauty with his shiny black coat, white socks, and a spattering of white dots on his hindquarters. The horse snorted and tossed his head, pawing the hay-strewn floor.

"I suggest you back away, Ms. Davis. He's a rescue horse and very temperamental." Skye startled, turning to see Liz coming toward her. She drew her attention back to the horse and prepared for a confrontation with Ethan's mother.

"He's beautiful," Skye said, instead of telling the woman the horse should be left free to run wild. To the O'Connors' credit, they'd rescued the animal, and their stables were immaculate; the horse was obviously well groomed and cared for. Unlike Skye's neighbors' horses in Texas. In response to Liz's approach, the horse double-kicked the rear wall of his stall, releasing a high-pitched whinny, his ears flattening.

"Don't come any closer," Skye quietly advised, then made soft, chuffing sounds to gain the horse's attention. He settled enough that Skye slowly reached her hand in the stall. "Good, boy. That's a good boy," she said in a low voice. The horse approached and nudged her arm. Skye praised him as she raised her hand to gently rub the middle of his forehead. It wasn't long before he was completely calm and nuzzling her neck.

"Richard was right," Liz said in an amazed tone of voice. "We've had him for a month, and he hasn't let any of us near him."

Skye moved her forefinger and thumb in small circles along the horse's neck. "Walk up slowly behind me."

When she felt Liz at her back, Skye said, "Bring your fingers alongside mine."

Skye waited a couple of minutes before moving to the side and allowing Liz to take her place. But the horse had other ideas and followed her to the edge of the stall. Skye felt the weight of Liz's gaze upon her as she murmured good-bye into the horse's neck, then stepped away.

"I'm not sure what to make of you, Ms. Davis."

Neither had her father and teachers. "I get that a lot," Skye said, then cleared her throat. "I'm sorry about earlier. I hope you won't hold my actions against Grace."

"Of course I won't. But in the future, I'd prefer that you didn't help out at our events," Liz said, as they walked from the barn together. "My son has an excellent chance of winning the election, Ms. Davis. It's something he's wanted since he was a little boy. I won't let anyone or anything stand in the way of him realizing his dream." She stopped Skye with a hand on her arm. "It would be best if you stayed away from him. You're not the type of woman he needs in his life."

Even if for a moment Skye kind of wished she was, she knew Ethan's mother was right. But that didn't mean she appreciated Liz warning her off or disparaging her character. "Mrs. O'Connor, you don't know me well enough to make that call."

"Perhaps not, but I do know my son. He may be attracted to you at the moment, but it won't last. He needs a woman of strong moral character and values, a woman who believes in what he stands for and will help him realize his dreams. Acquainted as you are with the world of politics, you know as well as I do, Ms. Davis, that you are not that woman."

Chapter Six

Ethan made his way through the crowded fairgrounds with his mother and Claudia at his side. Laughter and high-pitched screams filled the mid-August night air, competing with the music from the bandstand and the whir of sirens as the rides picked up speed. When the smell of fried food wafted past his nostrils, he decided that last corn dog he'd eaten was responsible for the dull gnawing in his gut. He dug in his leather jacket for a roll of antacids. Except for a piece of tinfoil he withdrew from his pocket, he came up empty.

"I'm going to head home instead of going back to the hotel, Ethan," his mother said, as they reached the parking lot.

Maybe he wouldn't need the antacid after all. For the last ten days, his mother had been campaigning for him to put a ring on Claudia's finger almost as hard as she'd campaigned for him to win a seat in the state senate. He kissed her cheek. "Careful on the road. Text me when you get in. I'll probably make it home for the Labor Day weekend."

"You better. Madison's baby shower is on the Sunday. You can keep Gage occupied. Maybe get him out for a game of golf. You could use a little R & R. You look tired," she said, rubbing his arm. "At least I know I'm leaving you in good hands." She turned to hug Claudia. "Make sure he eats and doesn't stay up half the night working, dear."

"Don't worry, I'll take good care of him," Claudia said with a suggestive look in his direction.

So maybe he'd need that antacid after all. Over the last couple of days, he'd noticed a change in Claudia. She'd gone from friendly professional to friendly flirty. But she was too damn good at her job for him to consider firing her now. Not to mention the negative impact it would have on his campaign if he did. His mother would probably just rehire her anyway. He hoped it was a passing phase, but obviously he was going to have to deal with it before it went much further. And the first chance he got, he'd tell his mother to knock off the matchmaking.

"You're coming home with Ethan on the long weekend, aren't you?" she asked Claudia.

Duct tape, that was what he needed. "I'm sure Claudia wants to go home and spend some time with her dad, catch up with friends."

"Pish." His mother responded with a flick of her hand. "I'll invite Richard. We can all spend a nice, long weekend together. I could use his advice. When you were saying good-bye to the mayor, I got a text from Raul," she said, referring to the ranch foreman and Rosa's husband. "Bandit, the rescue horse, kicked down the gate to his stall." She sighed and got in her truck, glancing at Claudia before she closed the door. "Don't let me ruin your plans, dear. I understand if you'd rather go home."

Claudia cast Ethan a sidelong glance before saying to his mother, "No, I'd love to come, and I'm sure Dad would, too."

So much for a relaxing weekend. He wondered if his mother was using Richard as a means of getting Ethan and Claudia together or if she was interested in the man herself. Ethan didn't like either scenario.

"Perfect. I'll call your father tonight."

They said good-bye, walking to the Escalade as his mother's taillights faded from view. "You don't mind me coming home with you, do you?" Claudia asked.

He pressed the Unlock button on his car key fob. "Of course not, but you've been working twenty-four seven this last month. You deserve a break."

"So have you. But we really can't afford to take time off. I was thinking of it more as a working holiday. I'd like to spend some time mapping out the next couple of months leading into the election."

As dedicated as she was, Ethan knew he shouldn't be surprised. "You want the rest of the team to come along?" he asked, as she buckled her seat belt and he closed his door. Having everyone there would cut down on his one-on-one time with Claudia. And his second in command, Pete Travis, had a major thing for her.

She made a face. "I don't think that's necessary."

At her answer, the gnawing in his gut increased. He leaned across her to open the glove compartment. When his search failed to produce a roll of antacids, he said, "I've got to stop at a drugstore on the way to the hotel."

Ever the efficient campaign manager, she took out her BlackBerry. "Okay. There's a Walgreens off the highway." She punched the directions into his GPS. "I'll let Peter know we'll be a few minutes late."

"Thanks." They were expecting a volunteer update from the district managers within the next hour.

She was still on her BlackBerry when Ethan pulled into the brightly lit parking lot. "I'll be back in a minute," he said as he undid his seat belt.

"Okay, I'll wait for you here." She looked up from her phone and angled her head. "Is that Kendall?"

Ethan followed the direction of her gaze to the leggy, butterscotch blonde in a black motorcycle jacket, knee-high black boots, and Daisy Duke denim shorts entering the store. Oh yeah, he'd recognize that hair and body from a mile away. And if he wasn't mistaken, five parking spots over was Jack's black Harley. It gave him heart palpations just thinking of her on that bike. And not the I'm-so-hot-for-her kind. More like the panic-attack kind.

"Yeah, looks like her." He hadn't seen Skye since the Strawberry Social. He'd thought about her...a lot. But hadn't seen her. He'd been worried about her. Worried enough that he called Gage every few days and somehow found a way to work her into the conversation. Of course his best friend figured out what he was up to and busted his balls. But in the end, he'd relented and told Ethan what he needed to know. She was good and still helping Grace out. A couple of weeks ago, the Flahertys had moved into their new place, and Skye had moved into their apartment above the bakery. A piece of news Gage had been very happy to share.

"I wonder what she's doing this far from Christmas."

Claudia shot him an uneasy glance. "You don't think she's stalking you, do you? We're a good two hours from there."

He wished she was. "Since no one's been picketing our events, I'd say no. Looks like she took Jack's bike out for a ride," he said, lifting his chin to the Harley. And that was something he planned to talk to her about. Right. He'd have more luck talking to Jack.

Claudia unbuckled her seat belt. "I think I'll come in with you. I just remembered a couple of things I have to pick up."

"Tell me what you need. I'll get them for you," he said. He wanted to talk to Skye on his own.

"Um, they're sort of personal. Feminine products, you know."

"Gotcha. Come on." When they reached the entrance to the pharmacy, Ethan held the door open for her. "I'll meet you at the checkout."

He didn't spot Skye right away and searched several aisles before he saw two male clerks hanging around one of the rows. Great—she was in the feminine products aisle. Head bowed, studying the box in her hand, she didn't notice him. It gave him an opportunity to do a leisurely perusal of the woman who played a frequent role in his dreams. His gaze lingering on her shapely, tanned legs, he didn't realize Claudia had come up behind him until she scooted past him. "Kendall, what are you doing here?"

Skye's head jerked up, and she dropped the box. "Ah, I'm..." She scooped the box off the black-and-white-tiled floor and grabbed a couple more off the bottom shelf. Her arms now full, she straightened. "Sorry. You startled me. What are you guys doing here?" she asked with a strained smile, her face flushed. She walked backward, pulling more items off the shelf.

"Campaigning in the area, and I needed—" Ethan began, before she cut him off.

"That's great. Gotta go. Nice seeing you both." She whirled around, dropping one of her items as she took off in the opposite direction.

"Is it just me or was she acting more weird than usual?" Claudia asked as she walked over to pick up the box Skye had dropped. "Maybe she's just really anxious to get home and put these to good use." She laughed and held up a box of magnum condoms.

*   *   *

Seriously? She drove all this way to make sure she didn't run into anyone from Christmas, and she ran into the man she most wanted to avoid. If only she hadn't put off picking up the pregnancy test until now. In her defense, she'd been busy. Busy in a way that made her think her luck was turning around. She had a place of her own, and Grace had reduced the rent. In exchange, Skye opened and closed the bakery and took a cut in pay. And just last week, she'd signed on two advertisers for her blog.

The cashier stood snapping her gum as she talked on her cell phone. Skye dumped her purchases onto the conveyer belt. "I'm kind of in a hurry, so if you don't mind..." She smiled and nodded at the cash. The woman ignored her and kept talking.

"Okay, seeing as you're busy, I'll give you a hand." Skye ran the pregnancy test past the scanner, leaned over the counter, and grabbed a plastic bag. "Um, do you have paper?"

"What do you think you're doing? This isn't one of those self-serve counters, you know." The forty-something woman shoved her phone in her pocket, then grabbed the box and bag from Skye.

"Sorry, my mistake." Skye leaned back to look past a rack of magazines and saw Ethan headed her way. "I've really gotta go," she said, and started sliding her other purchases over the scanner.

"If you don't stop that, I'm calling my manager."

"I think you forgot something," a deep voice said from behind Skye.

She turned, and sprawled across the conveyor belt, leaning on her elbow in what she hoped was an I'm-cool-and-totally-relaxed pose to hide her purchases from Ethan's observant gaze. He handed her a box of condoms. "Thanks," she said, tossing it over her shoulder.

"Ow," the cashier yelped, then pushed Skye. "Get off of there right now and stop throwing things at me. Are you high?"

"Yes, I am. I'm high on life," Skye said in a voice that sounded slightly manic even to her. She straightened, tilted sideways, and stretched her arms, glancing over her shoulder to make sure the damning evidence was now concealed in the bag. "Beautiful night out there, isn't it?" she said to Ethan, who crossed his arms and raised a brow. It was a look that she imagined he used in the courtroom to intimidate witnesses. He was a little too good at it for her liking.

"What are you doing?" he asked, using his smooth, lawyerly voice. She didn't like that voice. At all.

"Kink in my shoulder. Just stretching it out." She smiled, added one more stretch for good measure, and snuck a quick peek behind her. Thankfully, everything was in the bag.

"Sixty-two fifty," the woman said, looking past Skye with a flirty smile. "You're Ethan O'Connor, aren't you?"

Skye rolled her eyes, then briefly closed them when she realized the amount. What the heck had she bought? She fished out her black AmEx from the back pocket of her shorts and handed it to the woman, who took the card without looking at her. She was too busy batting her eyelashes at Ethan. "I love your ads. Me and my friends are voting for you. We need someone like you representing us," she said as she ran the card through the machine.

"Could've called that one," Skye said under her breath.

"Did you say something?" Ethan asked, once he'd thanked the woman.

Skye smiled sweetly up at him. "No, I didn't say—"

"Your card was declined," the cashier said with a smirk in her voice.

Skye's smile faltered, and her face got hot. "There must be a mistake." She hadn't used that card in almost a year. "Can you try again, please?"

The woman released a loud, put-upon sigh. "I'll have to call it in."

Skye avoided looking at Ethan while listening to the cashier. Claudia appeared at his side. "Problem?" Claudia asked.

"No, there's something wrong with their—" Skye began, then stopped when the cashier hung up the phone, took a pair of scissors from the drawer, and cut her credit card in half.

"You can't do that," Skye said, trying to grab a piece of plastic as it fluttered to the floor.

The woman gave her a smug smile. "I can when the

credit company authorizes me to confiscate the card. Can you pay or should I put it all back?" she asked, even as she began taking the items out of the bag.

"No, I can pay. Stop that," Skye said, grabbing the bag and clutching it to her chest with one hand as she dug into her back pocket with the other.

"Are you kidding me, Kendall?" Claudia shook her head. "I don't know why I'm surprised. Your father always said you were ridiculously inept at managing your money. He tried to get her trust fund changed because he was sure she'd blow it before she hit thirty," Claudia confided to Ethan in a superior tone of voice. "I guess you're lucky you have so much money, Kendall. No one, not even you, could spend your fortune."

Wanna bet? Skye thought miserably.

"But you really should pay your bills if you don't want to destroy your credit rating," Claudia added.

If she only knew. Claudia had always been jealous of Skye's fortune. She had no idea that Skye had bailed out Richard when he'd run into financial trouble several years ago. He'd been too embarrassed to go to Skye's father, so he'd come to her instead. "FYI, Claudia, I forgot to send them my change of address. And really, what do I care about my credit rating? It's not like I'll ever need to borrow money," Skye said in a flippant tone of voice, ignoring the disappointed look on Ethan's face. She tossed a couple of crumpled twenties on the counter, reaching in the bag to remove a box of magnum condoms and a box of small ones. "Can you take these off the total and see what it comes—"

Ethan handed the cashier his credit card. "I'll take care of it."

"Thanks, but I'm not taking your money. I'll just—"

He held her gaze as he stuffed the condom boxes back in the bag, a little more forcefully than she thought was necessary. "It's worth the money to ensure you're protected."

"But I—" She was about to tell him it wasn't what he thought, but she'd never seen Ethan angry, so she hurriedly said, "Okay, thanks. I'll pay you back," just to get out of there.

The cashier snorted, handing Ethan his receipt. "If her pregnancy test comes back positive, she won't have to worry about protection. At least not for that."

Skye stared at the woman. She didn't just say that? Yeah, she did, Skye realized, taking in both Ethan and Claudia's shocked expressions.

She had to think of something fast. "Oh, come on, you can't seriously think that test is for me? It's for Grace. Why do you think I came all this way to buy it? She doesn't want Jack to know. She wants it to be a surprise if she is. So you guys better keep this on the down-low, got it?" She narrowed one eye and made a gun with her fingers.

Ethan visibly relaxed. "We won't say anything. I hope Grace gets the news she wants."

"Oh, God, me too," Skye said.

Ethan's gaze narrowed at her as he paid cash for a roll of Tums and a pack of gum.

"Antacids aren't good for you, you know. They'll give you leaky gut syndrome and pollute your colon and liver. Try cutting back on the greasy food and sugar," she said as a means of distracting him. Plus, it was true. "Ciao." She waved and hurried off, leaving Ethan and the two women staring after her.

As Skye roared out of the parking lot on the Harley, she thought how a session of primal therapy might be just what the doctor ordered to alleviate the stress from her run-in with Ethan and Claudia. She didn't, though, not with the possibility she had a baby on board.

Three hours later, it was no longer a possibility but an actuality. The stick had turned blue. And sitting on the cold floor in the bathroom of her apartment, Skye indulged in a fifteen-minute primal therapy session. And when she finished screaming, she cried really loud and really hard for a good twenty minutes straight. By the time she pulled herself to her feet and looked in the mirror over the sink, her eyes were practically swollen shut, her cheeks were blotchy, and her nose was red and two times its normal size. She stared back at the terrified, exhausted woman in the mirror and said, "Suck it up, buttercup."

Chapter Seven

Under trees lit up with miniature white lights, Ethan danced with Samantha Reinhart in the backyard of her father's Denver mansion.

"Claudia's giving me the evil eye and so are half the women here. You probably should have danced with someone else this time." Sam smiled up at him, her platinum-blonde hair brushing against his chin as they swayed to the cover band's rendition of Jeff Healey's "Angel Eyes."

"Too bad. You're the only one I want to dance with."

The amusement left her eyes, a vulnerable expression crossing her delicate heart-shaped face. "Don't say something you don't mean, Ethan. You broke my heart five years ago. It took me months to get over you. I've enjoyed spending time with you this week, but I didn't fool myself that we could be anything more than friends. But tonight it seems—"

"I never meant to hurt you, you know." He'd been

dating Sam for several months when he'd gotten the call that changed his life. No one knew about the conversation he'd had with his father only hours before Deacon O'Connor suffered a fatal heart attack. Not his mother. Not even his best friend. A month after his father's death, devastated and guilt-ridden, Ethan had left Sam, his job, and Denver to try and fill his father's shoes. He'd spent the last five years trying to make amends to a man he'd loved and admired more than anyone else. "It was a tough time."

"I know it was. I'm not blaming you. You never made me any promises." Her arms tightened around him. "Your dad would be so proud of you. Do you remember the night we went for dinner at Racine's?" She laughed. "All he talked about was you running for the state senate. He used up all the napkins on the table mapping out your campaign strategy."

"Yeah, I remember," he said quietly, struggling to keep the emotion from his voice.

A flash went off. Sam glanced to her right and sighed. "Look at him. I'll bet that picture ends up in the newspaper tomorrow morning."

"Your dad's not very subtle, is he?" Ethan said with a laugh, relieved to change the subject. "What is it with our parents playing matchmaker? My mother is as bad as your father."

"They want us to be happy. They've had great marriages. They want us to have the same. But you're lucky *my* mother hasn't jumped on the bandwagon. She'd have the church booked."

"Still hasn't forgiven me, has she?"

"No, but don't feel bad. She's hasn't forgiven the boy

who broke up with me in second grade, either. And she has her sights on someone else."

"Tall, dark, and broody, who's shooting me death glares?"

She laughed. "That would be him."

"Does he have a chance?"

"I don't know. Maybe. He's an investigator for the district attorney's office. You'll be meeting him shortly. He has some information for you on that blogger, and he had me do a profile. He's good at what he does, but we didn't exactly get off to a great start. We went out a couple of times a few months ago, and he went all alpha male on me. He came close to putting one of my clients in the hospital."

Sam was a psychiatrist and dealt with some unsavory characters. Ethan had prosecuted a couple of them. "He must have had good reason to, Sam."

"I suppose he did. Not that I'd tell him that. He's arrogant enough as it is."

Ethan saw something in Sam's eyes when she talked about the man. "You should give him a second chance. You deserve to be happy."

"So do you. You're not involved with Claudia, are you?"

"No, despite how hard my mother's working to make it appear that I am." It was as if Sam's dad and Ethan's mother were playing dueling matchmakers in the press. One day a photo of him with Sam would appear. The next day, one with him and Claudia. Ethan had had more coverage in the last ten days than he'd had from the start of his campaign. He couldn't complain, though. Up until a couple of days ago, he'd had a positive uptick in the polls. Then Envirochick's latest blog post went viral. He was anxious to hear what Jordan's investigator had to say.

"I'm glad you're not involved with Claudia. She's too much like you. You need someone who doesn't take life so seriously. Someone who will make you laugh and challenge you."

She could have been describing Skye. But the night he'd run into her at Walgreens, Ethan had finally realized that while he wanted more than a one-night stand, she didn't. Any woman who bought boxes of condoms in various sizes wasn't looking for a relationship. She was too wild, too outspoken, and too free-spirited for him. "Is that your professional opinion?"

"Yes, it most definitely is," she said at the same moment the lead singer crooned "Angel eyes" one last time.

And instead of the words invoking thoughts of the pretty blue eyes looking up at him, Ethan pictured caramel eyes lit up with laughter, and his response came out more terse than he intended. "Then I'm afraid I'd have to disagree, Dr. Reinhart."

She gave him a surprised look, but her father called them over before she could respond. They joined him beside the kidney-shaped pool that was lit up with red spotlights. Sam's would-be suitor pushed off the wall and ambled to her father's side. Tall with a military bearing, his dark eyes were trained on Sam. "Ethan, this is Adam Blackwell. He does investigative work for me," Jordan said.

"Nice to meet you." Ethan shook Blackwell's hand. "Sam was just talking about you."

"Is that right?" the other man said in a gravelly voice. The corner of his mouth quirked, indicating he got Ethan's message.

So did Sam, and she gave Ethan a you're-so-dead look.

He grinned in response. Her father didn't miss the byplay, and he gave Ethan a brief, disappointed look before saying, "I asked Adam to look into that blog for you."

When the blogger Envirochick took aim at Ethan's relationship with Albright Energy, his recent gains in the polls began a downward slide.

"Hang on, I'll get my iPad." Adam lifted his chin at Sam. "You can fill him in on your profile," he said, then headed for the French doors leading into the kitchen.

"Why don't we sit down?" Jordan Reinhart said. Ethan's former boss, a distinguished man with a thick head of silver hair, gestured to the white wrought-iron table as Claudia joined them.

Ethan held out a chair for her. "Sam's got some insights to share on the blogger."

"Thank you," Claudia said, smoothing her black dress as she took a seat. "I'm glad someone is taking her seriously. She has it out for Ethan. I think we should put her on a watch list and increase his security."

"I'm not increasing my security, Claudia," Ethan said, loosening his tie. They'd had the same discussion repeatedly over the past few days. "She may be having a negative impact on my numbers at the moment, but she's not a danger to me personally."

"Ethan's right, Claudia," Sam said. "Although I do agree the latest attacks have become somewhat more personal. What you're dealing with, I believe, is a twentysomething woman who is an independent thinker, bright, and with a strong sense of what is right and wrong. She champions the underdog and gives voice to those she identifies as marginalized in society. So I don't feel Ethan's personal safety is in any way at risk. As for his numbers, if her focus remains on Ethan, she does pose a significant problem for you. She has an engaging voice and is very accessible and relatable. I suspect her following and influence will continue to grow in the weeks leading up to the election."

Ethan heard the admiration in her voice. "You like her, don't you?"

"Well, yes I do. And in the interest of full disclosure, I probably should tell you I'm following her now. I'm still voting for you, though." She gave him an impish grin.

"Please tell me you're joking," Claudia said in a horrified tone of voice.

"I can assure you, she isn't," Jordan said. "But really, Sam, that was not well done of you. What if someone in the press discovers you're following this woman?"

"No one will know who I am. I have..." she began, then trailed off when Adam pulled up a chair beside her.

Adam leaned over and whispered in her ear.

"How did you know that?" she asked, her face flushed.

The man winked. "I'm real good at my job, Doc." He straightened and redirected his attention to the rest of them. "And in case you're wondering, I agree with Sam's risk assessment. The woman isn't dangerous, but it is possible that one or two of her followers are. I'll continue to monitor the situation from my end. Up until a couple of months ago, she didn't have any paid advertisers. Now that she does, her followers have almost doubled. Ten days ago, Tom Green, a man I'm sure you're all familiar with, signed on as an advertiser and is backing her not only financially, but he's also using his extensive connections to get the word out. He's the reason her latest post went viral."

This was not the news Ethan hoped to hear. Tom Green

was a multimillionaire whose attack ads in the last election were attributed to the incumbent Republican senator's failure to retain his seat. "Who the hell is she?"

"Here's where it gets interesting. It usually takes me an hour at most to uncover a blogger's identity. This one took me two days. She's either incredibly tech savvy or has someone working for her who is." He turned his screen. "Her—"

"Oh. My. God. It's Kendall," Claudia gasped at the same time Ethan said, "Skye."

"You know her?" Sam asked, leaning forward to get a look at the screen.

"Yeah, I know her." *And I'm going to kill her*, he thought, pinching the bridge of his nose.

Sam watched him, a smile spreading across her face. "Ethan, in my professional opinion, she's exactly what the doctor ordered. She's perfect."

"If you think that, you're as crazy as your patients," he muttered.

"You have to do something, Ethan. Maybe you can talk to her friend Madison. And while her father doesn't have any influence over her, mine does. I'll call him." Claudia pulled out her BlackBerry. "This couldn't be worse. Tom Green worried me, but Kendall has as much money as he does. Together—"

"I can alleviate your worries on one count," Adam said. "Skylar Davis is broke."

* * *

"Hey," Skye said to Vivi as she took the stairs to the apartment two at a time. "You better not be calling to cancel." Vivi had promised she would be there for Maddie's shower two days from now.

"No. And you're on FaceTime, so all I can see is the inner workings of your ear. Which I have to tell you is kind of scary."

"Ha-ha." Skye held the phone in front of her as she opened the door. "Better?"

"I'm not sure. Why are you all sweaty and flushed?"

"Just back from a run. We'll go for one when you're here. You have to see these trails; they're amazing. The trees are changing colors, and the scenery's gorgeous. Don't you just love this time of year?" These days, Skye was pretty much in love with life. Her life specifically. Tom Green's check had just gone through, and her bank account was in the black, like Texas-crude black, for the first time in months. And the night two weeks ago when she'd pulled her terrified self off the bathroom floor seemed a distant memory.

She'd done exactly what she'd told herself to do. She'd sucked it up. She'd started running again, doing her daily yoga routine, and sticking to a strict vegan diet. Instinctively her hand went to her still-flat stomach. And now that she felt better and had a steady income stream, she was feeling more confident about her ability to raise baby Apple on her own. And she was more determined than ever to keep the knowledge of her precious child's existence from the sperm donor who appeared to be sleeping his way through Denver.

Since his mother had stopped by the bakery the other day to talk to Grace about engagement cakes, it appeared Claudia didn't mind his hound-dog ways as long as she ended up with a ring on her finger. As if Skye would saddle an innocent child with a father and stepmother like that.

"Give me a gym over your pretty trails any day. I hope you're being careful. There's bears and wolves in that area, not to mention mountain lions. I know you think you're an animal whisperer, but you're not."

"You're such a city girl," Skye said as she opened the fridge and took out a protein shake. "So what time are you getting in tomorrow? We still have a few things to do for the shower."

"I'm actually boarding in twenty minutes," Vivi said, showing Skye the view from the airport. "I'll be in around eight tonight."

"Really? That's fantastic. I'm so excited to see you. I didn't think you could get away from work early."

"Um, can you do me a favor and sit down?"

Skye laughed. "Sorry, am I giving you motion sickness?"

"No, but when I tell you what I have to, you might just toss your cookies."

"Oh no, what's wrong? Are you sick? Did you lose your job? It's okay, sweetie. Whatever it is, we'll handle it. I can take care of you. You can come live with me in Christmas. And you don't have to worry about Hot Bod. I haven't seen him since I've been in town," she said, referring to Gage's older brother, Chance.

Last year, during a Skype conference call, the man had walked behind Vivi bare-chested with a cowboy hat covering his face, earning him the title of Hot Bod. Because he really did have an impressive physique. But at the time, that was all Skye and Maddie knew about him. Vivi hadn't known much more. It wasn't until they were in Christmas last December that they'd learned who he was and what he'd been doing in New York. His great-aunt Nell had sent him to investigate Maddie, and he'd ended up investigating Vivi instead, breaking her heart in the process.

"Oh my God, dial it back a notch. You're giving me a headache." Vivi rubbed her temples. "Skye, it's not me you need to worry about it. It's you."

She couldn't believe it. Somehow Vivi had found out that she was pregnant. She'd been so careful... "How did you know?" Skye asked as she flopped onto the couch. "I haven't told anyone. Not even Maddie. I didn't think I was showing. Is it my boobs? Did my—"

"Because it's all over social..." Vivi began, then her eyes narrowed. "Hold it. What did you just say?"

Skye closed her eyes and squinched up her nose. She didn't plan on telling anyone just yet but she'd obviously misunderstood her friend. "No, you go first. What were you going to say?" And hopefully she'd forget what Skye had inadvertently blurted out.

"Skylar Davis, are you pregnant?" Vivi asked in a fierce, raspy voice.

"Um, yeah. Maybe. Just a little."

"For God's sake, you can't be a little pregnant. How pregnant are you?"

"Eighteen weeks, I think."

"You think... you think. Have you not seen a doctor?"

"Well, no, I don't have insurance. And would you stop yelling at me? This hasn't exactly been an easy time for me, you know."

"Okay... okay. Just give me a minute to think." Vivi rubbed her forehead and took a couple deep breaths. "All right, who's the father?"

"I prefer to think of him as a sperm donor, so a name isn't necessary."

"And I prefer to know what we're dealing with, so spill."

She chewed on her fingernail and reluctantly admitted, "Ethan O'Connor."

"This just gets better and better." Vivi rubbed her face. "Okay, so from your sperm-donor comment, you've obviously made up your mind not to tell him. I'm not sure I agree with that, but for now I'll support your decision. We're going to have to go apartment hunting when you come home. My place is too small for the three of us." Of course, as soon as Maddie had found out Skye was broke, she'd called Vivi.

Skye blinked back tears. Her emotions were all over the place, but even if they weren't, her best friend's offer to move in with her would make her cry. "I love you. And Apple and I would love to move in with you, but we can't."

"Who the hell is Apple?"

"My baby. I thought I'd name her Apple, what do you think?"

"Yeah, sure. But why can't you move in with me?"

Skye took a deep breath, preparing herself for Vivi's reaction. She would not be happy about this piece of news. But if anyone knew how Skye should deal with Scary Guy, it would be Vivi. And Skye had to know she'd be safe if she planned to head to New York when she started showing. "Well, there's a small problem I haven't mentioned. Have you heard of Jimmy Moriarty?"

"Jimmy 'the Knife' Moriarty, sure. How do you know that lowlife?" Skye forgot they were on FaceTime and grimaced. "Oh no, you can't be. Do not tell me you're the woman he put a hit on?"

Skye jerked upright and spilled her protein shake in

her lap. "He put a hit on me? *He* attacked *me*. All I did was defend myself." She grabbed tissues to mop up the green mess in her lap.

"You ruptured his balls and dislocated his jaw."

"Really? Wow. But how do you know all this?"

"I'm a crime reporter. He's a criminal. I'm supposed to know these things."

"Right. I forgot." Vivi had left her old job with the online *Daily News* and a couple of months ago took a job as an investigative reporter for the *Daily Spectator*.

"There's a rumor going around that the woman was a paid escort. Please tell me you weren't that desperate. I still can't believe you kept your financial situation from Maddie and me."

"I've apologized . . . like a hundred times. I was embarrassed. But you know me better than to think I'd do something like become an escort. Geez, that's just . . . gross. You remember Gina Ricci, don't you?" The three of them had met Gina their last year of college.

"Yeah, she's connected, Skye."

"Connected?"

"To the mob. An uncle on her mother's side. Forget about it. Tell me the rest."

"Oh, I . . . Okay, well, Gina called me and said she had a friend who needed a date and would I please do her a huge favor and go out with him. She sounded desperate, so I agreed. The guy was nice enough. He didn't make a move on me or anything, but I kinda felt uncomfortable. So when she called a week later, I said I was busy, but she gave me a sob story about Jimmy being her cousin and how he'd recently divorced and was going through a hard time . . . yada yada yada. And I agreed." She looked into her best friend's violet eyes. "I didn't mean to hurt him, Vivi. But he really scared me."

"I know you didn't, but with the rumors circulating about the guy, it's probably a good thing you did." Vivi held her gaze. "Gina skipped town before Jimmy got out of the hospital. She was using you, Skye. She ran a high-end escort service. Does he know who you are?"

Skye bowed her head. Why . . . why did she have to be so gullible? She couldn't believe she hadn't realized what Gina was up to. Skye tried to see the best in people. She had to start being more like Vivi and see the worst. Vivi didn't trust anyone. "No, Gina told me his ex was stalking him and to use a fake name . . . Tawny Brown. But he took a picture of us at the restaurant."

"At least she tried to protect you, and I have a feeling she still is. But if I get my hands on her, I'm going to kick her ass. Let's just hope Jimmy doesn't find her first. There's a guy I've worked with on a couple of stories. I'm going to contact him. He's good. Like scary good. He got me out of a few tight spots."

Skye frowned. Her best friend's voice took on an amused softness when she talked about the guy, and her face had gotten kind of glowy. "Who is he? Where and when did you meet him?" After Vivi's breakup with Hot Bod, Skye was extra protective when it came to Vivi and men. She didn't want to see her hurt again.

"We haven't exactly met. He contacted me when I first started working at the *Spectator*. Gave me a lead. He's been working with me ever since."

"What's his name? Have you checked him out?" Skye asked.

"He calls himself Superman," Vivi said with a hint of a

smile on her face. "I tried to check him out once. He shut me down pretty fast. But it doesn't matter. All I care about is the information he gives me." She cocked her head. "I've gotta go. They're calling my flight. I'll see you in a few hours. Oh, and, Skye, don't look at your Facebook or Twitter accounts until I'm there."

"Why? What's going on? I'm going to look right now if you don't tell me."

Vivi sighed as she hefted a bag over her shoulder. "Everyone knows you're broke. I traced the leak to Claudia. And Skye, somehow they found out you're Envirochick. They're using the fact that you lost millions of dollars to counter your influence. They're making..." She made a face. "They're making you out to be a spoiled socialite who never had to work a day in her life and that your blog is just a scheme to make money."

"I can't believe Ethan would do that to me," she whispered, her heart hammering against her rib cage.

"Your blog did some damage, Skye. You had to know they'd go after you."

"But not like this, Vivi. I didn't attack him personally."

"Candidates don't always control the message their team puts out. Don't panic. Call Tom. He'll know what to do. And I'll start working on damage control."

Maybe Vivi was right. This had Claudia's fingerprints all over it. But Ethan could have stopped her if he wanted to. "Okay. I'll be at the airport at eight." And she'd make a stop at Bob Bennett's Denver campaign office and sign up as a volunteer. If Ethan thought she'd go down without a fight, he didn't know her very well.

Chapter Eight

Skye meditated while doing a headstand, her tension releasing as her body rested comfortably against her living room wall. Until a raspy voice startled her out of her transcendental state, yelling, "What do you think you're doing? Stop that right now. You're going to hurt the baby."

Skye sighed and opened her eyes to see her best friend's bare feet, her toenails painted black. Lifting her gaze, she met Vivi's aggravated one. Who would've thought "Kick-Ass" Vivi Westfield could be such an over-protective worrywart?

"I'm not going to hurt the baby by exercising," Skye said as she lowered one leg at a time. "Do you really think I'd do anything to put my baby at risk? Look at all the books I've read." Over the past few weeks, Skye had downloaded ten baby books to her iPhone. There were a couple she stopped reading because they freaked her out, but she'd made it to the end of five. "I know what I'm doing."

Vivi made a noncommittal sound in her throat.

Since discovering she was pregnant, Skye had taken a hard look at her life and made changes to ensure that she was the kind of mother her baby deserved. Which was probably why her best friend's reaction bothered her so much. "Whatever," Skye said as if it didn't, then thought to add, "You better keep your lips zipped at the shower today. No one can know about the baby."

"Yeah, well, when you finally break the news to Maddie, make sure I'm at least a thousand miles away. She's going to be furious with you, not to mention hurt."

"I know, and I really wish I could tell her," Skye said, chewing on her fingernail. "It totally sucks that I'm pregnant at the same time as one of my best friends, and I can't share any of the fun stuff. But I'm not putting Maddie in the middle of this."

Vivi gave her a one-armed hug. "You can share with me. When it's safe for you to come home, we'll go shopping for baby Apple."

"Oh, I forgot to tell you. I've changed her name to Willow," she said as she hugged a now-grinning Vivi in return. "Did you hear back from Superman yet?"

"No, and he usually responds quicker than this." Just then, Vivi's cell vibrated on the coffee table. "Maybe that's him."

"Don't slip if it's Maddie." Vivi's appearance at the shower was supposed to be a surprise. With her arriving two days earlier, they'd already had a couple of close calls.

"I won't...it's Superman."

Studying her best friend as she read the text with a smile spreading across her face, Skye realized she'd been right after all. "You have a crush on Superman."

"Please. I've never even met him or spoke to him. For all I know, he's an old guy with a beer gut."

"I don't think so. He's probably a hot undercover cop. And he can only correspond by text or e-mails, or he'd risk breaking his cover. Either that or he's married."

"You have an overactive imagination," Vivi murmured without looking up from the screen, but Skye's comment about him being married seemed to bother her. Which meant Skye was right. She did have a thing for the guy, and Vivi hadn't had a thing for anyone since Hot Bod dumped her. With her lush, dark hair, olive skin, and violet eyes, Vivi was a stunning woman. She should have had men lining up to date her, but she didn't. Probably because she was also a ballbuster. Skye hadn't seen that look in her best friend's eyes in a long time, and she decided to take a wait-and-see approach where Superman was concerned.

"So what did he say?"

"Hang on." Vivi tapped out her response, then said, "He wants you to lay low. No social media, no pictures in the paper, and if you can swing it, a name change. He also thinks you need to shut down your blog now that your identity is out there."

"I can't, Vivi. I can't shut down my blog. You know that. It's my only source of income. I mean, I work at the bakery, but it's not enough, not with the baby coming. This is all Ethan's fault. If they hadn't outed me . . ."

Vivi gave Skye's shoulder a comforting squeeze. "Okay. Give me some time to think about the blog. The media coverage is fairly localized. But your social media accounts link you to New York so—"

Skye picked up her cell phone from the couch. "I'm giving it another couple of hours, and then I'm shutting them all down. I just want to make sure my friends"—she made air quotes—"have a chance to read my post."

Vivi cast her a nervous glance. "What did you say?"

"Well, these are people who borrowed money from me over the years and then had the nerve to post smartass remarks or lecture me on my spending habits after I was outed. So I messaged every one of them. I told them what they owed me and that I'd accept a check or they could make payment arrangements."

"Did anyone respond?" Vivi asked, head bowed as she pressed the keys on her iPhone. Skye figured she was logging onto Facebook to check up on her.

"Only four people out of two hundred. They can't pay me back, but they apologized, so I took them off the list. And last night I posted every single one of the hundred and ninety-six names and what they owed me on my Facebook page and posted the link on Twitter."

"You gave Lydia Baker money for a boob job?" Vivi said, looking up from her phone.

"I wouldn't have said what I gave her the money for, but her comments were some of the nastiest. Hey… Where did my page go?" she said when it disappeared. "What did you do?"

"I didn't do anything." Vivi's cell pinged, and her lips started to curve. "But I think I know who did." She read the text. "He says you're a sweet woman, but you need a keeper. And he's got enough on his plate without you making more enemies. He's wiping your social media history now." Her eyebrows raised, and she nodded. "He suggested putting it out that *I'm* Envirochick. He said you could make some noise about suing Ethan's campaign for releasing private information about your finances and insinuating your blog is just a scam to make money. It should be enough to shut them down. If you're okay with it, he'll start putting things into place so that when they dig deeper, I'll show up. We can put out a blog post on Monday introducing me as Envirochick. What do you think?"

"If you're good with it, sure. I don't care as long as I can keep up the blog. And I don't think Tom and my other advertisers will, either. As long as the content doesn't change."

"Okay, I'll tell him to go ahead." Vivi sent the text and seconds later, Superman responded. Whatever he said made her best friend blush.

She motioned to Vivi. "Let me see."

"No"—she shoved her phone in her jean shorts pocket—"we've gotta get going."

"You so have a crush on him," Skye said as she walked from the living room. "I just have to get changed." Five minutes later, she found Vivi sitting at the kitchen table on her computer. Her best friend was a workaholic.

"What's this?" Vivi asked when Skye waved a purple strapless cover-up under her nose.

"I made them for the three of us. Maddie's is pink." Hers was yellow with a yellow-and-white-polka-dot bow beneath her boobs.

"Oh no, I am not wearing this. I don't want to catch what you two have. And it seems to be contagious. I still can't believe my two best friends are pregnant."

"And that Maddie's a stepmommy and wears pink." Skye laughed. "We better get going. I can't wait to see her face when she walks in. And it'll be so much fun to see all the baby stuff." Skye was looking forward to the shower. She couldn't be happier for Maddie. But for all of a second, she felt a little sorry for herself and her baby. There'd be no shower for them, no one to wake up in the middle of the night when she got scared or went into labor, or when the baby said its first word or took its first step.

She mentally gave herself a slap. She wasn't alone. She had Maddie and Vivi. And women all over the world did this all the time. "Don't forget your bathing suit. We're playing Toss the Baby." At Vivi's raised brows, Skye explained, "Not a real baby, water balloons. And you have to get in the pool for the rubber ducky race."

"Shower games, are you serious? And why do I have to bring a bathing suit and you don't?"

Skye lifted her cover-up to reveal her yellow polka-dot bikini.

"Wow. You look amazing. No one would guess you're eighteen weeks pregnant," Vivi said, then bit her lip as she eyed Skye's flat stomach. "I don't think that's right. Maybe something's wrong. You're making a doctor's appointment before I leave. No excuses," she added when Skye started to argue. "You have enough money, and there's a thing called doctor-patient confidentiality."

"I'm healthy and so is baby Willow. Stop being such a worrywart." At Vivi's don't-mess-with-me face, which was way scarier than Maddie's, Skye relented. "Okay. Fine. If it'll make you happy, I'll make an appointment. Now go put your bathing suit and cover-up on." Skye wouldn't admit it to Vivi, but every once in a while, she worried something might be wrong with the baby, too.

*   *   *

Skye nudged Vivi, who stood in front of the stone fire-place in Paul McBride's living room, staring at the family photos on the mantel. "What are you...Oh." She'd forgotten about Hot Bod. Gage's older brother, Chance, stood in all his dark blond, sun-bronzed glory with his brothers in a family photo. But as she looked more closely at Vivi, Skye realized it was the wedding photo beside it that held her attention: Chance McBride's wedding photo.

"She died two years after the wedding," Skye said quietly, looking at the beautiful, petite blonde in the photo. She'd heard all about the tragedy when Chance was a no-show at Gage and Maddie's wedding.

He hadn't been home since his wife died. Kate McBride had been Chance's childhood sweetheart. She'd gone off the road in a snowstorm, killing both her and her unborn child.

"I know." Of course she did. Maddie and Skye hadn't told her, but as soon as Vivi had discovered Hot Bod's true identity, she would've found out everything she needed to know on her own.

Skye needed to distract her. She nudged Vivi and whispered, "Can you take some of the presents from me? I probably shouldn't be carrying this much in my condition."

Vivi snorted. "I'm fine," she said and took two boxes decorated with baby's footprints from Skye.

"I know you are." But she didn't look fine, so Skye said, "Did I tell you how hot you look in that cover-up? If I was gay, I'd totally want to do you."

"You're nuts." Vivi laughed. "And I hope my niece is just as nutty as her mommy," she said, patting Skye's stomach.

Skye shot a panicked look around the room. "Vivi, shush."

Vivi winced. "Sorry. I won't forget again. Promise."

Behind them, Grace opened the front door and welcomed more guests inside. Skye glanced over her shoulder, then shot a frantic look at Vivi. "Ethan's mother brought Claudia. What am I going to do? I didn't think she'd be here."

"I'll tell you exactly what *we're* going to do," Vivi said, and took Skye by the hand, walking toward the two women. They looked like a pair of socialites heading to their country club in matching white Capri pants and lightweight indigo blue sweater sets. Their hair was perfectly coiffed, their makeup impeccable. As Skye and Vivi approached, Claudia shared a raised eyebrow with Liz.

"This is a bad idea," Skye whispered, dragging her feet.

Ignoring her, Vivi tightened her grip on Skye's hand. "Mrs. O'Connor, nice to see you again. I don't think we've met," Vivi said to Claudia, extending her hand first to Ethan's mother.

"Ms. Westfield," Liz O'Connor said with a nod before smiling warmly at the dark-haired beauty by her side. "This is Claudia Stevens. My son's campaign manager."

"Ms. Westfield," Claudia said with a condescending smile. Neither of the women acknowledged Skye.

"You both know my best friend Skye, of course."

"Actually, I know her as Kendall. And I need a word with you," Claudia said to Skye in a snippy tone of voice.

"I'll take these." Grace smiled nervously while gathering up the presents. "Are you going to be all right?" she said for Skye's ears alone as she brushed by her.

"I think so," Skye said under her breath, "but I doubt

Claudia will be once Vivi gets through with her. Think
Maddie on steroids."

"Oh." Grace's eyes widened, and she hurried off.

"Actually, I need a word with you, Ms. Stevens. Or,
I should say, my lawyer does." Vivi checked her watch.
"You'll be receiving a request to set up a conference call
any minute now."

"Your lawyer? In regards to what?" Claudia asked, her
earlier bravado fading.

"The lawsuit I plan to file against your candidate.
Maybe it would clarify matters if I reintroduce myself.
I'm Envirochick."

"No, you're not. Kendall is."

"Uh, no, you got that wrong. Hence the lawsuit for disparaging my best friend's character and releasing information about her personal finances. You want to start
slinging dirt, you sling it at me. And I'm not as nice as
Skye. You're going to get real dirty playing with me. So
dirty that you won't be able to wash the muck off your
candidate before election day."

"I don't believe you."

"Tell whoever you hired to dig deeper. He might be
good, but I'm better. And now that I think about it, I
should have my lawyer check into privacy laws. You must
have broken a few of those."

Nell McBride, who looked like a gingerbread granny
if you discounted the flaming red streak in her softly
curled white hair, was accompanied by the diminutive
Evelyn Tate and Stella Wright, who had a white streak
in her long, dyed-black hair, as they pushed through
the door. "Maddie's coming up the driveway. Hurry. Go
hide."

*   *   *

"This was the best surprise ever. I love you guys." Maddie stood up when she'd finished opening the last of her presents and threw her arms around Vivi and Skye. "I can't believe you kept it a secret from me." She sniffed, looking at everyone congregated in Paul McBride's backyard. A group of women sat in lawn chairs under the shade of the towering pines, the mountains a purple shadow in the distance, while Liz O'Connor led the others on a tour of Paul's extensive gardens.

"What is it with pregnant women? You're all so weepy."

Madison drew back and wiped at her eyes. "Who else do you know who's pregnant?"

Skye furtively elbowed Vivi, and her best friend covered her "oomph" with a cough. "Generalization," Vivi said, once she recovered. "Isn't it time for more games or something?"

"No, let's go check out the presents," Skye said, gesturing to the table overflowing with baby gifts.

"Auntie Skye, Auntie Skye!" Lily waved to her from where she stood in the shallow end of the pool. "Come and get me," she called, and started toward the deep end.

Skye grinned and shimmied out of her cover-up. "I'm coming."

"Oh, my God, look at you," Maddie said to Skye, then patted her own rounded stomach. "Enjoy it while it lasts. One day you'll get pregnant and look like you swallowed a beach ball like me."

"I doubt it," Vivi muttered, "more like a golf ball."

Skye gave Vivi a zip-it look and headed toward the pool. As soon as she got close, Annie did a cannonball, soaking both Lily and Skye. "Get her, Auntie Skye. Get her." Lily sputtered, holding on to the side and wiping her eyes.

"I'll get her, Lily. Don't you worry." Skye ran to the edge of the pool. She was in midair, arms wrapped around her knees, when she heard Vivi yell, "Skylar Davis, you're pregnant. You can't—"

The cool water closed over Skye's head, and she sunk to the bottom of the pool. She thought about staying there, but didn't think holding her breath for that long would be good for the baby. Blurred faces peered over the edge, staring down at her as she swam her way to the top. She changed direction and headed for the stairs. As soon as she stood up, Lily threw her arms around her. "Yay. We're going to have another baby."

For one heartwarming second, Skye allowed herself to forget about the consequences of being outed and reveled in Lily's excitement.

It didn't last long.

"You're pregnant, and you didn't tell me? You told Vivi, and you didn't tell me?" Madison gritted out as she hauled Skye from the pool.

"I can explain," Skye said, nervously glancing at the women who moved within earshot.

"You have a lot of explaining to do. How many months are you?"

Vivi grimaced, sending Skye an apologetic glance. "Maddie, why don't we—"

"No. I want to know how long she kept this a secret from me."

"She's almost eighteen weeks. Now can we—"

Skye knew Vivi was trying to help, but she was making

things worse. Maddie's brow furrowed, then her eyes widened. "You got pregnant in April. Who...Ethan." She covered her mouth with an oh-shit look in her eyes. Then quickly grabbed Skye by the arm. "Okay, ladies. I—"

Claudia pushed to the front of the crowd. "That night Ethan and I ran into you at Walgreens you were buying a pregnancy test for yourself, not Grace."

"Grace, you're pregnant, too?" Nell said. "Geez Louise, there must be something in the water. Evelyn, we're drinking bottled from now on."

"I'm not pregnant," Grace said, looking at Skye, who mouthed an apology.

"My son? You're pregnant with my son's baby?" Her eyes wide, face pale, Liz O'Connor pressed her fingers to her mouth.

This couldn't be happening. Skye grabbed Vivi's hand. "No, no, Vivi and me, we're partners. I had artificial insemination. We're so happy, aren't we, sweetie?"

Vivi sighed and bowed her head. Maddie covered her face with her hands.

Apparently Liz didn't hear Skye because she said, "*She's* having my son's child. My grandbaby. Oh, my God, I'm going to be a grandmother."

"Liz, are you all right? Liz, what's wrong? Someone help me," Claudia cried, as Ethan's mother collapsed in her arms.

Chapter Nine

I'm sure it's nothing, Eth," Gage said as they ran up the walkway of his father's gray stone bungalow. They were playing a round of golf and got the call about Liz on the seventh hole. Thankfully, Dr. McBride's girlfriend Karen, a nurse, had been invited to the shower. Ethan thought it was a good sign that she hadn't called an ambulance. Then again, she didn't like his mother very much.

"I shouldn't have let her campaign with me."

"Stop beating yourself up. Liz loves going out on the stump," Gage said, as they reached the front steps.

"Where is she?" Paul asked Karen, who met them at the door, his voice gruff and edgy.

Her brow furrowed. "On the couch in the living room. She's fine, Paul," she called after them.

The thirtysomething redhead wouldn't be happy about Paul rushing to Liz's side. She would've been less happy if she'd witnessed Paul's reaction when they got the call.

He'd been as worried about Liz as Ethan. Under different circumstances, his obvious concern for Liz would have had Ethan and Gage high-fiving each other.

At least forty women were crowded into the great room with its high-beamed wooden ceiling. They parted to let Paul, Ethan, Gage, and Richard by. Lily, in a flowered bathing suit, ran over to grab her father's hand. "Daddy, Auntie Skye's having a baby, and Nana Liz fainted."

Several groans met Lily's announcement. Ethan suspected one might have come from him. He felt like he'd been sucker-punched. Which was stupid. He knew she wasn't the woman for him. But the thought that Skye was pregnant with another man's baby ... No matter how hard he tried, he couldn't stop himself from searching the room for her. "Holy hell," he said under his breath when he caught sight of her standing in the corner in a yellow polka-dot bikini.

"Geezus," Gage said, and Ethan turned to give him an are-you-kidding me look. "What? I'm married, not dead."

Ethan ignored him and blocked the *Sports Illustrated* image of Skye from his mind as he reached the couch. He stood beside Paul, who crouched at Liz's side and took her wrist between his fingers. She had a white cloth folded on her forehead and looked a little wan, but nowhere near as bad as Ethan had feared. Claudia, who sat on the arm of the couch, looked worse than his mother. "Mom, what happened?"

Both women stared at him with betrayed expressions on their faces. *What the hell?* "I need to talk to my son," his mother said, attempting to swing her legs off the couch.

Ethan reached for her at the same time as Paul. "You're

not going anywhere until I say so. Your pulse is erratic," Paul said, letting go of her wrist to open the black doctor's bag he'd dropped at his feet.

"Your girlfriend said I'm fine."

"She's wrong. You're not fine. You have mitral valve prolapse." He held up a hand. "No, I'm tired of you dismissing it and carrying on like you're in your thirties. You need to start acting your age and—"

Aw hell, Ethan thought as he caught Gage's eye. His best friend gave him a here-we-go look.

"Evelyn, tell me my nephew didn't just say what I thought he did," Nell muttered from somewhere in the crowd.

"You have some nerve telling me to act my age, Paul McBride. You're the one getting it on with a woman who is young enough to be your daughter."

"Now, Lizzie, I'm sure the doc meant nothing by it." Richard rubbed Liz's arm. "You just relax, darlin'. I'll take you home as soon he's checked you out."

"Do you mind giving me some room here, Richard?" Paul said, his gaze narrowed on the other man.

"Sure thing, Doc."

Paul went to place the stethoscope beneath Liz's sweater.

His mother pushed him away. "You are not putting your hands under my top."

"For God's sake, Liz. It's not like I'm trying to cop a... Look, if you don't let me check you out, I'm taking you to the hospital."

Ethan tried to stay focused on his mother, but he kept getting distracted by thoughts of Skye. Given how much of her knockout body the yellow scraps of material revealed, she had to be in the very early stages of pregnancy. He wondered who she'd been sleeping with and when.

The gnawing in his gut that had started when he first heard the news increased with a vengeance. Unconsciously his gaze once again searched her out. She glanced his way, gave him a startled look, then quickly averted her eyes.

"Ladies, let's give them some privacy," Gage said, taking control of the situation. As he started to usher the women to the backyard, Nell walked by and leaned past Paul to pat Liz's leg. "She fainted when she thought Skye was having your baby," Nell informed Ethan.

"Nell," his mother grumbled, "I didn't faint. I had a weak spell, that's all. And I really need to talk to—"

"Hold it. What did you just say, Nell?" He must have misunderstood her. He scanned the crowd of women heading toward the patio doors for Skye and spotted Madison and Vivian Westfield hustling her out of the room.

"Skye." Ethan took off after her. From behind him he heard Nell say, "But she's gay and had the artificial thingamajig done."

Like hell she did. "Stop right there, Skye. You're not going anywhere until we talk," he said just as she reached the front door.

"Ethan, do not use that tone of voice with Skye. She's in a delicate condition and can't be upset," Madison said.

Gage must have followed him because he walked past Ethan to take his wife's hand. "Honey, he's not going to upset her. He's just wants to talk to her. Right, Eth?"

"Yeah, right," he muttered.

Vivian stepped in front of Skye and crossed her arms.

"I'm not going anywhere. He leaked personal and hurtful information about Skye, and then he trashed her reputation in the press. So if you think I'm going to leave her alone with him, think again."

He hadn't approved Claudia's press release, but by the time he'd heard what she'd done, it'd been too late to stop it. And that'd led to the first real argument he'd had with his campaign manager. He started to respond, but Claudia approached him, shooting an apprehensive glance at Skye and Vivian.

"Ethan, I need a word with you," she said, putting a hand on his arm.

"It'll have to wait, Claudia. I need to speak to Skye."

The woman in question looked from Claudia to someone coming up behind Ethan. He glanced over his shoulder to see that they had an audience, Annie and Lily among them.

Skye sighed and nudged her friend out of the way. "I'll talk to you, but not here."

"Use my dad's bedroom," Gage said.

"Back through the living room," Ethan said to Skye, waiting for her to go ahead of him.

She crossed her arms and arched a brow when Claudia started off, obviously intending to join them.

"Claudia, I need to speak to Skye privately. This doesn't concern you."

She turned. "You're wrong, Ethan. As your campaign manager, it very much *concerns* me."

"And it concerns me, too," his mother said, pushing aside Paul's restraining hand to sit up.

Skye threw up her arms. "I'm outta here. You can call me."

Ethan snagged her hand. "You're not going anywhere." As he pulled her through the living room, he pointed to his mother and Claudia. "Both of you, stay where you are."

He opened the door to the black-and-white master bedroom and nudged Skye inside. She flounced across the white shag area rug and sat on the black leather ottoman at the foot of the bed. Like it always did, his body reacted to the sight of her long, toned frame. And it was damn inconvenient that it was doing so now. Annoyed with himself for still wanting her as much as he did, he reminded himself of the damage she'd done to his campaign and closed the door harder than necessary. She jumped. Okay, so maybe he'd slammed it.

If he wanted to have a conversation without drooling, he decided he needed to cover all that smooth, sun-kissed skin. He found what he was looking for in the en suite bathroom and tossed her a white robe. He took a moment to rein in his temper, another thing that was damn annoying since he didn't usually have one.

"Thanks," she said, and shoved her arms in the sleeves. "They turned up the air for your mother. It was freezing in there."

Her comment drew his gaze to her breasts. She was cold. And now he was hot.

"Are you having my baby?" That cooled him off pretty quick.

"No, I had artificial…" He crossed his arms. She sighed. "Yes, I'm having your baby. Happy now?"

"No, I'm not. How long have you known you were pregnant?"

"I didn't know for sure, but around the Fourth."

"The Fourth of July? You knew since the Fourth of

July, and you didn't think this was something you should share with me?"

"Sharing with you now."

"And you're positive the baby's mine?"

"I'm eighteen weeks. Do the math."

"And you're telling me there's no possibility it's another man's? Because we used protection."

Her face flushed. "Yeah, we did, and it didn't work. Nice to know how high an opinion you have of me. I guess I shouldn't be surprised. But don't sweat it. You're the sperm donor, nothing more. I don't expect anything from you."

"I wasn't passing judgment, Skye. But it's not like you keep your lifestyle a secret. If the baby is mine, I will take responsibility for it." He pulled his cell from the pocket of his khaki shorts. "I'll set up a DNA test."

"Are you crazy? I'm not putting my baby at risk because you don't believe me." She stood up. "I've fulfilled my obligation to you. Whether you like it or not, whether you believe me or not, none of that matters to me. We're done here."

She was right. He shouldn't have questioned her. She had no reason to lie. It's wasn't as if she was trying to use the baby against him. Obviously, since she hadn't been in a hurry to tell him the news. In fact, he had a sneaking suspicion she never intended to tell him about the baby, and that infuriated him. "No, we're not, so sit the hell down. As the baby's father, I have rights, Skye."

"Oh, what, now you believe the baby's yours? I don't think so, Ethan. You—"

"Be quiet and listen to me. This baby is as much mine as yours." He shoved his fingers through his hair, his voice rising as it finally hit home that he was having a baby...with Skye. A woman who thought of him as nothing more than a sperm donor. *Who the hell does she think she is?* If she thought she could limit his involvement in his child's life, she'd better think again. "I'm a lawyer, Skye. And I can assure you that no judge in his right mind would grant you sole custody. You can't do this on your own. You don't have a steady income. You probably don't even have health insurance. Half the time you act like a kid yourself, and you really expect me to believe you can handle raising a baby on your own? I'm not trying to be mean, but you're irresponsible and flighty. Jesus, Skye, you had millions of dollars, and now you're broke."

She crossed to him, lifting her chin, her eyes glassy. "I made some mistakes. Not everyone is as perfect as you, you judgmental jerk. And I was turning things around until you trashed my name. Until you"—she poked his chest with her finger—"revealed my personal business and made me look like a fool in the press."

The press. He hadn't given any thought to what this would mean to his campaign. The hit he'd taken because of her blog was nothing compared to the hit he'd take if word got out she was pregnant with his baby. He'd lose the support of his conservative voters unless... "Calm down and lower your voice." He put his hands on her shoulders. "Look, you don't have to worry about any of that now. I'll take care of you and the baby. I'll put a rush on the marriage license. We should be good to go on Friday. We'll go to the courthouse and—"

She jerked back. "Married? Have you lost your mind? I'm not marrying you. I don't believe in marriage. And even if I did, I wouldn't marry you if you were the last man on God's green earth."

*   *   *

Later that evening, Ethan sat at a table in the local sports bar, the Penalty Box, with Gage and their mutual friend Jack Flaherty. Brandi, wearing her waitress uniform—a black-and-white-striped jersey and a short black skirt—approached with a tray of drinks. "Compliments of the house. Sawyer named the drink after you, Mr. Senator-to-be. It's a Prince Charming. Bourbon, cinnamon schnapps, Goldschläger, and root beer rimmed with coarse salt," she explained as she set the drinks on the table. "Sawyer suggested you have a couple of them before you speak to your baby mama again."

Gage and Jack laughed. "Har har," Ethan muttered, slanting a look to where the owner, Sawyer Anderson, stood behind the bar taking orders. The tall, broad-shouldered ex-captain of the Colorado Flurries, a professional hockey team, gave Ethan a two-fingered salute and grinned. "Your friend's a real comedian," Ethan said to Jack.

"Yeah, he likes to think so," Jack said, "but maybe this time he's right. From what Grace said, you could use all the help you can get."

"At least your wife's talking to you. Thanks to him"—Gage jerked a thumb at Ethan—"mine isn't."

"She was until I defended him. Now I'm in the same boat as you," Jack said, taking a long pull on his beer.

"Would someone like to explain how I'm the bad guy in this? She had no intention of telling me about the baby. As far as she's concerned, I'm a sperm donor and have no rights." And once his initial shock had passed, he started to get excited about the baby. He'd always hoped to be a father one day, and he was not about to let Skylar Davis take that away from him. "I asked her to marry me."

He didn't realize Brandi had hung around until she said, "No, you didn't ask her. You told her you were getting married. At the courthouse. On Friday."

"Yeah, and you also told her she was irresponsible and flighty and threw losing her trust fund in her face," Gage said.

Brandi gasped. "You didn't?"

"Come on, I didn't say anything that any of you haven't said or thought. Besides, I was pissed off. And I had good reason to be." He might've had good reason to be angry, but he shouldn't have let his temper get the best of him. The temper he didn't have until he met Skylar Davis. "I sent her flowers and an apology, okay?"

Gage grimaced.

"What? You don't think she'll like them? The florist told me any woman would love them. I sent her three dozen roses." Who knew flowers could be that expensive? But even Ethan realized he had to make some kind of gesture after what he'd said to Skye.

"Most women would, just not the one you sent them to," Gage said.

Gage's dad approached their table before Ethan could argue his case. Paul pulled out a chair and sat down. Now it was Ethan's turn to grimace. He didn't feel up to another lecture. After Skye had left the room, Gage's father had stopped Ethan from going after her. "Why aren't you home looking after your mother?" Paul asked him.

Because she was driving him nuts. So was Claudia.

They hadn't gotten a foot out of Paul's house before the two of them started in on Ethan. Claudia had already set up a focus group to see how it would play with his supporters if word got out about the baby. "Mom's resting." More like strategizing. "Richard and Claudia are with her." At Paul's disgruntled expression, he decided he shouldn't have mentioned Richard.

Gage caught Ethan's eye, angled his head at Paul, and grinned at his father's jealous display. At any other time, Ethan would be grinning, too.

"How can she rest with them around? Stevens is loud and never stops talking. And Claudia will get your mother all worked up about your campaign. She's worked up enough as it is. She's happy about the baby, but she's not exactly crazy about the baby's mother. I don't know why. Skye's a sweet girl."

Yeah, Ethan had heard exactly how unhappy Liz was about the mother of his child. About twenty times in twenty different ways. And then, looking like she'd sucked on a lemon, she told him she expected him to do the right thing and marry Skye. He would; of course he would. But that didn't mean he had to like it. He'd hoped to be in love with the woman he married. There was no doubt he lusted after Skye. But love? She drove him crazy, and Ethan didn't do well with crazy. He'd had enough drama growing up with Chloe and Cat. He liked his life drama-free and predictable. Something it would never be with Skye in it.

Fred and Ted sauntered over to the table. "Heard what went on at the shower today. We thought you could use our help," Fred said as he and Ted pulled out chairs to join them. "Me and Ted helped Jack here win back Gracie, didn't we, Jack?"

"Yeah. You guys were a big help," Jack agreed, fighting back a grin.

"I appreciate the . . ." Ethan's cell rang. Claudia's name popped up on the screen. "I've gotta take this," he said, and answered.

She began talking before he had a chance to say hello. "I just got off the phone with Peter. He's fielding calls from reporters asking if it's true you're going to be a father. They don't seem to have a lot of information, but we have to do something before the whole story gets out there, Ethan. This isn't going to play well with conservative voters. God, I can't believe I'm going to say this, but I think the only way to combat the negative publicity is for you to marry Kendall. Peter agrees."

A couple of days ago it looked like he had a shot at fulfilling his promise to his dad. And now everything was going to hell in a handbasket. "I don't know what you expect me to do, Claudia. I asked her and she said no." The four men at his table stopped talking and looked at him.

"Pay her off. She needs the money."

"No. I'm not going to do that. And she wouldn't accept even if I did," he said, angry at Claudia's insinuation that Skye was a gold digger.

"Okay, I'm sorry. But I'm desperate, Ethan. I don't know. Tell her the marriage will be in name only. After a year or so, you can quietly divorce."

"I'll take care of it, Claudia. For now, try and hold off the press." She agreed but didn't sound hopeful, and Ethan hung up.

"Word got out?" Gage asked.

"Yeah, and I—"

"We got work to do, boys," Fred interrupted him, rubbing his hands together. "Grace was easy. I don't think this Skylar gal is going to be. But don't you worry none, Ethan. We'll figure it out."

"I appreciate the offer, boys. But I think I can handle it." He'd apply his courtroom skills to the problem. He'd never lost a case yet. And he'd already laid the groundwork with his apology and flowers. All he had to do was…

Nell McBride, Evelyn Tate, and Stella Wright ambled over, dragging chairs to the table.

"What are you girls doing here?" Ted asked the older women.

"Same thing you are," Nell said. "We're going to help him win Skye over so he doesn't lose the election. And, Ethan, if he gives you advice, don't listen to him." She gestured at Paul. "As he proved today, my nephew doesn't know a thing about women."

"What are you talking about, Nell? I—"

Ethan interrupted Paul. "Thanks, ladies, but I think—"

Evelyn beamed at him. "Don't you worry, Ethan. We're the love experts. And, dear, those roses you sent me were beautiful." She fluttered her lashes.

"Yes, Ethan, that was very sweet of you to send them to us. But a little extravagant, don't you think? I hope you didn't send them to all your female supporters. Their husbands might not be as understanding as mine," Stella said.

Ethan rubbed the bridge of his nose between his thumb and forefinger, ignoring Gage's I-told-you-so look. "Did all three of you get a dozen roses?" he asked in hopes he misunderstood them and that Skye hadn't sent his peace offering to the three older women.

"Yep, me, Stella, and Evelyn. But you didn't have to bribe us. We'd vote for you anyhow. We want one of our own in the state senate, don't we, girls?" Nell said as she pulled out a pad and pen. "And just as an FYI, when you put from a secret admirer, you're not supposed to sign your name."

Chapter Ten

Skye looked at the clock on the bakery wall and released a heartfelt sigh of relief. Twenty minutes until closing time. After spending eight hours dealing with the well-meaning citizens of Christmas, she felt like doing a happy dance at the thought. Four days had passed since Vivi blurted Skye's news at Maddie's shower, and the marry-your-baby's-daddy campaign had started at nine a.m. sharp the very next morning. Oh, yeah, it had been fun times at the Sugar Plum Bakery.

Skye picked up the cloth she'd used on the glass display case and rounded the counter. As she went to wipe down the tables, the bell tinkled over the door. She looked up, stifling a groan at the sight of Nell, Evelyn, and Stella. Ted and Fred had dropped in two hours ago to plead Ethan's case. She should've known the three older women wouldn't be far behind. She wondered if Ethan had offered money to whichever team could change her mind. It would be just like him to have someone else do his dirty work.

Though, in fairness to the man, he texted her every day to see how she was feeling and plead his own case. She hadn't responded. She hadn't forgiven him for the hurtful words he'd said in that smooth, emotionless voice in Paul McBride's bedroom. Maybe if she told the older women what he'd said, they wouldn't be so determined to marry her off to the man. Then again, he hadn't said anything she hadn't heard before. And maybe that was why his words hurt so much. She was worried he might be right.

She shoved the thought from her mind. He wasn't right, and she was going to do everything in her power to prove him wrong. "How are you ladies doing today? I bet you came in to try Grace's caramel apple cupcakes, didn't you?" she said as she made her way around the counter.

If she had to put up with them touting Ethan's good-daddy attributes for the next twenty minutes, the least they could do was buy something. The women exchanged she's-on-to-us glances, then nodded and placed their orders. Skye grabbed a pastry box and began filling it with cupcakes.

"Evelyn, Stella, did you see Ethan on *Wake-Up Denver* today? I tell ya, if I was younger, I'd take a run at the man myself," Nell said.

Skye closed her eyes and counted to ten in order to calm the uptick in her pulse—an uptick that had nothing to do with the image of Ethan in his golf attire that popped into her head. So what if he was a perfect ten, maybe twenty, in the looks department, and she lusted after him every now and again? In the end, looks didn't matter. It was what was on the inside that made the man or, in Ethan's case, unmade him.

"Oh my, yes, Nell, I did. He gave me a hot flash, and I haven't had one of those in twenty years," Mrs. Tate said, fanning herself.

Skye taped the box and set it on the counter with a thump. If they didn't cut it out, her rising blood pressure was going to blow off the top of her head. Obviously Stella didn't take the hint because she said, "If he asked me to marry him, I wouldn't say no. And I bet there are hundreds of girls who would jump at the—"

"Okay, you three, I've had it," Skye said, placing her hands on the display case and leaning toward them. "You're stressing me out. All this pressure isn't good for me and my baby. I can't take it anymore. So I'm going to tell you once and for all, I...am...not...marrying Ethan O'Connor. Not now. Not ever."

"But why not, dear?" Evelyn said, looking distressed.

Skye sighed. She shouldn't take her frustration out on them. This was Ethan's fault. She gentled her voice. "Because, Evelyn, he doesn't love me. And besides that, I don't believe in marriage."

"But you're having the man's baby. You need someone to look after you. To support you."

"No, I don't, Stella. I can take care of myself, and I'm perfectly capable of taking care of my baby." Skye hoped they didn't start listing all the reasons that made her unfit to be a single parent. Late at night, when she lay alone in her bed, Ethan's words played over in her mind. Her own worries would get the better of her then, and her chest would tighten as she struggled to breathe.

Nell looked at her, and her expression softened.

"Skye's right," she said gruffly. "It's not like it was in our day, Stella. She doesn't need a man to look after her. She's a smart girl. She can support herself."

"Thanks, Nell." Skye gave the older woman a grateful smile and rung up their order. As they were about to leave, Nell leaned over the counter. "Just because you can take care of yourself doesn't mean you have to, you know. Ethan's a good man, not to mention damn fine looking. Don't cut off your nose to spite your face, girlie." Nell patted Skye's cheek, then followed her friends out the door.

Skye didn't let herself linger over Nell's parting remark. All she could think as she locked the cash in the safe was that she'd finally put a stop to the matchmakers from hell. *They weren't that bad*, she silently amended. It was kind of sweet how they stuck their noses in everyone's businesses. She snorted. Fine to say now that they were going to leave her alone. She hadn't been feeling so magnanimous earlier today. As Skye set the alarm and locked the bakery, she looked forward to a quiet night working on her next blog post. She tried the door to ensure it was locked, then turned to . . .

"Hello, Mrs. O'Connor," she said, doing her best to clear the frustration from her voice as Ethan's mother approached with an armload of what appeared to be photo albums and scrapbooks. "How are you feeling?"

"Better. Thank you." The fiftysomething woman's lips curved in what Skye supposed she meant to resemble a smile. She actually looked like she might throw up. "Do you mind if I come up? I'd like to talk to you," Ethan's mother said.

Skye nodded and reached for the books. "Here, let me help you with those."

Ethan's mother clutched them protectively to her chest. "No. That's all right."

Skye shrugged and led the way to her apartment. As she unlocked the door, she realized she should've sprinted up the stairs ahead of Ethan's mother. Skye wasn't exactly Suzy Homemaker. She moved quickly into the living room, shoving her pajamas, bra, and panties under the floral cushions of the couch. Liz O'Connor entered the room before Skye could get rid of the leftover protein shake and bowl of half-eaten cereal from the coffee table.

"Can I get you something to drink...a cup of tea?"

"A glass of water, if you don't mind," Liz said, brushing off the couch before sitting primly on the edge of the cushion. She wrinkled her nose as she delicately moved aside the glass and bowl to put down the albums and scrapbooks.

Heat suffused Skye's cheeks as she gathered up the dishes and headed into the kitchen. She opened the fridge, sticking her head inside to cool off before grabbing the container of purified water. She checked the glass for spots then poured Liz's drink. Skye walked into the living room and caught the look of distaste on Ethan's mother's face as she took in her surroundings. She cleared her expression when Skye handed her the glass.

"Thank you," she said, giving Skye a sidelong once-over.

Self-consciously, Skye brushed a speck of white icing from her black uniform pants. There wasn't much she could do about the spot of red food coloring on the sleeve of her white shirt. And her hair...

"I don't want to interrupt your dinner. You can eat while we talk."

"That's okay. I'll fix something later," Skye said, taking a seat at the far end of the couch.

"Have you seen a doctor yet?" She gestured to Skye's stomach. "You don't look pregnant. Are you sure you're eighteen weeks?"

Okay, she couldn't take it anymore. "Look, Mrs. O'Connor, I get that you don't like me. I get that you don't think I'm good enough for your son. I even get that you wish it was Claudia carrying his baby and not me. But if you want to be part of *my* child's life, you better get over it."

"All I asked was if you'd seen a doctor. I was worried—"

"No, I haven't had time, but I will. And the pregnancy test I took told me how many weeks I am. I'm not worried that I'm not showing. I'm healthy, and so is my baby. Now, if that's all..." She went to stand up.

"No." Liz reached for her. "I'm sorry. I'd like to start over. Will you give me another chance?"

For the sake of the baby, Skye gave a tight nod and sat down.

"I'm very protective of my son," she said, picking up a photo album. "Of all three of my children, really. You'll understand when your baby comes."

"I already do. But your son isn't a little boy anymore, Mrs. O'Connor. He doesn't need your protection."

"Please, call me Liz. And you're wrong, Skye. He will always be my little boy." She opened the album, smiling down at the page before returning her attention to Skye. "Ethan says you're not speaking to him. He's worried about you and the baby."

"You can tell him we're both fine. If that's all you—"

"I know he upset you the day he found out about the baby. The news took him by surprise. And then he thought you meant to keep the baby from him... You won't, will you? He'll be a wonderful father. He loves children."

She knew he did. She'd seen him with Annie and Lily. And while in the beginning, Skye had planned to hide the baby's existence from him, once her pregnancy was out in the open, she knew she wouldn't be able to keep him from seeing his child. "No, despite what you and your son think of me, I wouldn't do that. Mrs. . . . Liz, what are you doing here?"

The older woman hesitated, appearing to weigh out her options before admitting. "I'm worried once Ethan confirms the baby's existence that his conservative base will abandon him. He's managed the press so far, but it won't last. I thought if you knew how much the election meant to him, you might reconsider and accept his proposal." Before Skye could answer, she rushed on. "My husband used to bring Ethan with him when he went to political events." She pointed to the picture of an adorable young boy with a heartbreaking grin holding a tall, handsome man's hand.

"He was about five here." As she turned the pages, Liz told Skye where each of the photos had been taken and what Ethan had been like as a little boy. "Ethan adored his father. He wanted to be just like him. My husband worked in the Ford White House with Richard. Deacon lived and breathed politics. I think he regretted not making a run for the state senate himself. He never doubted Ethan would. About a year before he died, he'd started mapping out Ethan's political career. He and Richard would have weekly strategy meetings over the phone. Deacon would be so proud of Ethan right now." She sniffed and swiped at her eyes. "Sorry, I . . ."

"No, don't apologize. It must have been hard on all of you when you lost Mr. O'Connor."

"It was, but I think it was hardest of all on Ethan. That's why this election is so important to him, Skye. It's his way of honoring Deacon. Making both his and his father's dream come true." She leaned over and pulled a piece of lined paper from the scrapbook. "This is the speech he wrote in sixth grade for a public speaking competition. He went on to represent the state." She passed a well-worn paper to Skye with a look of pride in her eyes.

After she read the speech, Skye understood why. Even at his young age, Ethan showed signs of the man he would one day become. Smart, eloquent, passionate in his beliefs. But Skye wondered if she was the only one who noticed that when he talked about the justice system, giving a voice to the victims, he sounded more like a lawyer than a politician. Liz held up his medal and a picture of him receiving it. Skye smiled at the tall, lanky boy in a rumpled suit with a mop of unruly tawny-blond hair. "He was very handsome, and it's a great speech. You should have Claudia release it to the press."

"That's a good idea. I'll mention it to her," Liz said as she carefully tucked her treasures away. "Does that mean you'll reconsider Ethan's proposal?"

"Your son didn't propose to me. He told me when and where we were getting married. I understand your concerns, Liz, but we can't get married just to appease the voters. We don't—"

"Why not? It can be a marriage in name only. And the baby won't be born out of wedlock."

Skye couldn't help it. She laughed. "Liz, I don't think that matters anymore."

"I'm sure your father would disagree with you. I'm surprised he hasn't called Ethan demanding that he marry you."

"I, um, haven't told my father yet." She'd been putting it off. She hadn't told him she'd lost her trust fund, either. She supposed it was time to put on her big-girl panties and make the call.

"Seeing as how Claudia and Richard know, you may want to take care of that soon. It's not something a father wants to hear from someone else or read about in the paper," Liz said as she packed up the albums and books.

Especially hers, Skye thought. "I will." Her stomach gave a nervous jitter, and she frowned. It felt like butterflies taking flight inside her. "Oh," she gasped.

"Are you all right? Is something wrong?"

"I think the baby just moved," she said, her voice filled with awe.

Liz smiled, her eyes growing misty. "It's a wonderful feeling, isn't it?"

"It's incredible." Skye gently rubbed her stomach. "It all feels so real now. I have a little person growing inside me. Hi, baby," she said, feeling embarrassed when she remembered Liz was still there.

"It's a very special time for both you and Ethan. I wish you'd reconsider." Focused on her stomach, hoping to feel her baby again, Skye didn't respond. Liz gathered up her books and patted Skye's arm. "I know you don't have a mother to call for advice, so please, phone me anytime."

No, she didn't have a mother. She hadn't had one since the age of ten. Her father had sent her packing when she put his election at risk. She'd been too free-spirited for him to control and wouldn't toe the party line. It was something Skye needed to remember, because for a moment there, her resolve not to marry Ethan had weakened. Seeing him as a little boy who dreamed of making the world a better place had touched her. And feeling her baby kick for the first time filled her with both panic and wonder. She wanted to share that with some-one, with him.

"Thank you, I will," Skye said, and got up to walk Liz to the door.

"No, I'll see myself out." As she went to leave, Liz turned to Skye. "Do you mind if I tell Ethan that you felt the baby kick, or would you prefer to?"

"I...you can tell him." It was better if Skye didn't speak to him just yet. She was too vulnerable, and Ethan could be very persuasive. A dangerous combination.

They said good-bye, and Ethan's mother left. Skye wondered if the baby had sensed the tension caused by her one-on-one with Liz. Actually, it hadn't been as bad as Skye had feared. But she didn't like to think she'd stressed out her baby, and she decided to go through her yoga routine before getting to work on her blog.

She changed into black yoga pants and her sports bra. Grabbing her iPod off the dresser, she headed for the liv-ing room. She put in her earphones, and Deva Premal's melodious voice calmed her almost instantly. Skye felt even better by the time she completed her routine with a headstand, her body relaxed against the wall.

She closed her eyes and let the last of her tension seep through her legs, down her body, down...

"Kendall Skylar Davis, what the hell is going on?" Her

father's furious voice jerked her out of her peaceful state. Skye snapped her eyes open to see him staring down at her. She lost her balance and fell sideways. Her legs took out the table and lamp. She rolled in a ball to protect the baby, and down went her father.

Chapter Eleven

Ethan stabbed the elevator button several times. "Calm down," Claudia said, rubbing his arm. "I'm sure the baby is fine."

"I am calm," he muttered, waiting impatiently for the doors to open. He'd broken every posted speed limit to get here. He'd been in Denver when Gage called to let him know Skye was in the hospital.

It'd been bad enough getting the call about his mother four days ago; this had been worse. And when Gage told him Skye had fallen while doing a headstand—a headstand, God damn it—Ethan made his decision right there and then. No more Mr. Nice Guy. No more giving her time to see that marrying him was the best choice. She'd proven him right, and he'd taken matters into his own hands. Thanks to his connections, he had the marriage license in his jacket pocket and a preacher on the way.

Whether she liked it or not, she was signing the paper-work and they were getting married tonight.

"I understand why you're upset. But I'm not sure marrying Kendall is the best solution anymore. I think we overreacted when the news first leaked and forgot one important thing. She's a loose cannon and a rabid Democrat. That hasn't changed because she's carrying your baby. You've done a good job throwing off the press. All we have to do is get her to agree—"

"My decision to marry her has nothing to do with the campaign." At that moment, it didn't. His focus was on his baby's well-being, which meant looking after its mother and making sure she didn't pull crap like she did today.

"Oh, I didn't know you were in love with—"

"I'm not," he said as the doors opened. He headed for the nurse's station with Claudia following close behind.

"Ethan," his mother called from the waiting room before he reached the desk.

He backtracked, glancing down the empty hall. "Which room is she in?"

"Four fourteen, but the nurse is with her now. Paul said her blood pressure is a little high and they're going to keep her overnight for observation. But she and the baby are fine, honey. They did an ultrasound."

Some of the tension left Ethan at the news. "Why's her blood pressure high?"

Madison and Gage, Grace, and Nell piled out of the waiting room as he asked the question.

"It's my fault," Grace said, looking distraught. "She's been working a lot of hours this week. I'm so sorry, Ethan. If I had known, I wouldn't have taken time off."

"It's not your fault, Grace," Madison said. "Skye wanted the extra hours."

"I'm sure she's making enough money from attacking Ethan on her blog that she doesn't have to work," Claudia sniped.

"Claudia, that's enough," Ethan said, although he agreed with her. Not the "attacking" part—Skye had toned down the rhetoric some—but she now had several more advertisers on board. Despite retracting their previous comments linking Skye to Envirochick and issuing a public apology to her in the press, Ethan didn't believe for one minute that her friend Vivi Westfield was Envirochick.

"Yes, her—" Madison corrected herself "—*their* blog is doing very well despite *someone's* attempt to shut it down. But Skye's saving every penny she makes for the baby."

"So what is—" Ethan stopped, his gaze narrowing at his mother when she got a guilty look on her face. "Mom, what did you do?"

"Nothing. I stopped by to have a visit with her earlier. She seemed fine then." Tears filled her eyes. "She felt the baby move, honey. I was going to tell you when we talked tonight."

Another bit of good news at least. And it reinforced his decision to marry her. He didn't want to miss out on those moments. He wanted to share them with Skye, not his mother.

"And why exactly were you visiting, Mom?" He knew her too well to let her distract him.

She sighed. "Do you have to be so suspicious? I just wanted her to know that you'll be a wonderful father. And to make her understand how important the election was to you."

"Oh, well, that it explains it then," Nell said. "You were pressuring her just like the rest of us. When me and the girls dropped by this afternoon, she told us we were stressing her out and it wasn't good for her and the baby."

"What do you mean, you were pressuring her? And who's the rest of you?" Ethan had an uneasy feeling Nell had gone through with her plan. He'd shot down the idea when she'd mentioned it at the Penalty Box the other night. He should've known she wouldn't listen to him.

"Don't get your shorts in a twist. I activated the hotline. No one's going to be bothering her anymore. Won't work anyway. She said she isn't going to marry you."

"No wonder she's stressed," Madison said, shooting a perturbed look at Nell. "And I'm sure it didn't help that her father's in town."

"Her father's here?" Ethan asked.

"Yeah," Gage said, "And you would've known that if you didn't cut me off earlier. He's the reason Skye fell. He surprised her."

"He won't do that again. She broke his rib," Nell said.

"Oh my God, are you telling me she hit William? You see, Ethan, this is exactly the kind of behavior I'm worried—"

"What the Sam Hill are you talking about?" Nell interrupted Claudia. "She didn't do it on purpose. She was trying to protect the baby when she fell."

Ethan pinched the bridge of his nose. If they were giving him a headache, he didn't want to think what the last few days had been like for Skye. Maybe he'd jumped the gun. "Where's her dad now?"

"X-ray," Gage said.

A nurse with steel-gray hair and an attitude that matched marched toward them. "Are you the baby's father?" she addressed Ethan in a no-nonsense tone of voice.

"Yes, I—"

"You can go in now. And if you want a healthy baby, you get that girl to eat. All that hippie nonsense. I don't need a blood test to tell me she's anemic," she said as she strode to her desk.

"Settle down, honey," Gage said to Madison, who was scowling after the older woman. "I'm sure she didn't mean anything by it."

"Yes, she did, the old battle-ax. We call her Nurse Ratched," Nell said.

"We'll wait for you here," Liz said to Ethan, indicating the room behind her as he set off down the hall.

He found Skye's room and entered without knocking. She sat cross-legged on the bed in a green gown, her long, tumbled mass of butterscotch curls hiding her face as she pushed at the food on the hospital tray.

"Skye," he said as he approached the bed.

She looked up at him, tears rolling down her cheeks. His chest tightened as he moved the hospital tray and sat beside her. "Hey"—he stroked her hair—"what's wrong? The baby's okay."

"She...she said I was being foolish. And...and if I didn't start eating meat I'd put the baby at risk."

"Come here, cupcake," he said, taking her into his arms. "Don't listen to her. You're not hurting the baby."

He might not know much about a baby's nutritional needs, but Skye was in incredible shape, so her vegan diet obviously wasn't hurting her. But he was thinking seriously of hurting that damn nurse. He planned to have a word with her as soon as Skye calmed down. And he was going to call the preacher and cancel. She'd dealt with enough today. She didn't need him putting any more pressure on her.

He gently patted her back and her arms went around his waist, her face buried in his neck. "Stop crying. You're going to make yourself sick."

She relaxed against him, her shuddering breath warming his neck. She didn't pull away, and he was okay with that. He liked the feel of her soft, supple body in his arms. Even more, he liked that she let him hold her, let him comfort her. He leaned over to grab a couple of tissues off the table at the side of the bed.

She drew her arms from his waist and sat up. "Thanks," she sniffed, accepting the tissues and wiping her red-tipped nose. "Sorry for the meltdown. It's just that I've tried so hard to do everything right. I've read all these books and done exactly what they said, and then she... she..." Skye hiccuped a sob.

He took her in his arms again and kissed the top of her head. "Don't pay any attention to what Nurse Ratched said. I'm going to take care of her. I—"

She pulled back. "Nurse Ratched?"

"Yeah, that's what Nell calls her."

"She is kind of scary. She said she's going to make sure the doctor doesn't release me until I eat some meat." Skye cast a disheartened look at the hamburger in the plastic dish. "I can't do it, Ethan. I'll be sick."

"You don't have to." He lifted her hand to his mouth, kissing her palm before he got to his feet and picked up the tray. "I'll go talk to her now and get you something else to eat. I'll be back in a few minutes."

"Good luck. She's really mean."

"Cupcake, I prosecuted murderers and rapists. She's no match for me." She gave him a small smile. "Lie down and relax. I won't be long."

The nurse didn't look up when Ethan set the tray on her desk. She sighed and rolled her eyes. "What did she do... cry, throw a temper tantrum? The women today have you boys whipped."

"Did you tell her that she was putting our baby at risk if she didn't eat meat?" he asked, barely keeping his anger in check.

He heard a gasp from behind him and held up a hand before Madison and Grace, who'd been talking outside the waiting room, charged over. The nurse glanced in their direction before returning her gaze to his. She lifted her chin, but some of the defiance left her eyes. "I might have."

He planted his hands on the desk. "If I hear you've spoken to her, gone within ten feet of her, I'm going to file a complaint against you. Get her doctor up here."

"You can't—"

"Page her doctor. Now."

"Yes, sir. I'm paging her," she said, holding up the phone to indicate she was going to do as he asked.

He joined Madison and Grace. "I could strangle that woman. I can't believe she said that to her," Madison muttered.

"Don't worry, she won't be upsetting Skye again." He reached in his back pocket for his wallet. "Would one of you mind picking up something for her to eat? I'd go, but I want to talk to her doctor."

"I will," Grace offered, waving off his money. "Don't be silly. It's the least I can do."

As Grace headed for the elevators, Madison said, "Despite the nurse from hell, she's in good hands. They've hired a new ob-gyn. Dad says she's wonderful," she said, referring to Paul. "How's Skye doing?"

"Traumatized." He shoved his fingers through his hair. "She was crying when I got in there."

She searched his face. "You really do care about her, don't you?"

"Of course I do. She's having my baby." He ignored her knowing smile. "I better get back in there."

"You do that, Daddy."

He gave his head a bemused shake. "I don't think it really sunk in until now."

"Pretty amazing, isn't it?"

"Yeah, it is. Kind of scary, too."

"You'll be a great dad. And take it from me—my best friend, she's going to be an amazing mom."

"That's probably something I should tell her." He thought of how hard Skye was trying to be one, and remembered the comments he'd made the day he'd learned about the baby. He'd been an ass. No wonder she didn't want to marry him. Which reminded him—he had to call the preacher.

Madison looked over his shoulder. "There's the doctor. Let me know when I can see Skye."

"Sure." He headed toward the tall, attractive, dark-haired woman Nurse Ratched had cornered outside Skye's room. The older woman headed in the opposite direction as Ethan approached. The doctor extended her hand. "Hi, I'm Dr. Evans."

"Ethan O'Connor." He glanced in Skye's room. She was on her phone. He thought he heard her say something about Superman, but figured he must have misunderstood. She looked up. He smiled, held up a finger, and closed her door a few inches. "Sorry, I'd like to talk to you privately. I don't want to upset Skye."

"I don't want her upset, either. I'm concerned about her blood pressure."

"How concerned?"

"Enough to keep her overnight for observation." She touched his arm. "Sorry, I didn't mean to alarm you. Other than her blood pressure, Skye and the baby are fine."

"Are you worried about her diet?"

"Not at all. She's in great shape and very knowledge-able. She's adjusted her supplements to compensate for her pregnancy. I wish all my patients were as healthy as she is."

"You might want to tell that to her nurse." He repeated what the older woman had said to Skye and added, "I don't want her near Skye while she's here."

"I understand completely. I'm sorry. Skye didn't need that right now. I better recheck her pressure. Is there anything else?"

"No, that's it for now," he said, holding the door open for her. He followed her into the room and rounded the bed. "You okay?" he asked, noticing the way Skye nervously eyed her phone. "Who were you talking to?"

"Just Vivi. I'm good. I didn't expect to see you again tonight, Dr. Evans. Is something wrong?" *Ah, so that's why she's nervous.*

"Your husband...I mean, the baby's father, is worried about you. I'm sorry the nurse upset you. I thought it might be a good idea to recheck your blood pressure," Dr. Evans said as she slipped the cuff on Skye's arm. "As I told your..." She sighed. "Sorry. As I told Mr. O'Connor, I'm not concerned about your diet. You're doing everything right."

"Thanks." Skye kept her eyes focused on the expanding cuff. "Ethan and I are getting married tomorrow, so you can refer to him as my husband. I'll be Mrs. O'Connor tomorrow. Mrs. Kendall O'Connor," she said in an over-the-top excited tone of voice.

"We are? You will? But just the other day you said you wouldn't marry me."

"That was the other day. Now I think it's important that we're married when Willow is born. I don't want anyone to be mean to her because she's illegitimate."

Ethan felt like he had whiplash. "Cupcake, who's Willow?"

"Your daughter."

"We're having a girl?" he asked, looking at Dr. Evans for confirmation, but she'd turned away, her shoulders shaking.

"The baby's legs were crossed on the ultrasound, but I'm sure we are."

"Oh, okay. That's—" Ethan looked up when a white-haired man wearing a black suit and white collar peeked into the room.

"Mr. O'Connor, are you ready for the ceremony?"

Skye gaped at the preacher, then turned to Ethan. "How did you get him here so fast?"

The older man smiled. "Mr. O'Connor called me

a couple hours ago. I'm a big supporter, and I dropped everything to get here. I'm honored to officiate the wedding of our soon-to-be state senator."

"You called him a couple of hours ago?" Skye asked, looking less thrilled with the idea of marrying him than she had a few minutes ago.

Ethan didn't respond. He was watching as Dr. Evans released the pressure on the cuff. "How is it?" he asked.

"Still higher than I'd like. I'm not sure this is the best time for you to get married. Perhaps in the next day or so..."

"No problem. We can wait until Skye—"

"No, it's better to get it over with. You know, like a bandage. Rip it off fast so it doesn't hurt so much."

The three of them stared at her. "Ha-ha," she said. "It was a joke. But honestly, Dr. Evans, I'll feel better once we're married. Weddings are very stressful, you know. All the planning..."

"What planning? We weren't getting married until a few minutes ago."

"Well, obviously we were, Ethan. You called the preacher."

"Perhaps it's a good idea after all. Just keep it as short as possible. And no more than four other people in the room." Dr. Evans looked at Skye. "Six maximum."

"Thanks, Dr. Evans." Skye said.

"You're welcome. I'll check on you in a few hours. Congratulations, the next time I see you, you'll be Mrs. O'Connor."

"Mmm-hmm," Skye said with a weak smile.

Ethan frowned. He knew from Gage's experience with Madison that pregnant women's emotions were all over the place, but this seemed extreme. "Skye, are you sure..."

"Totally, let's do this. Oh, and make sure it's Kendall O'Connor on the marriage certificate. And when Claudia puts out the press release, list Texas as my home." She chewed on her fingernail. "Never mind, I'll take care of the press release."

A big man with a barrel chest strode into the room. "Daddy, you're just in time for the wedding. Meet your son-in-law, Ethan O'Connor. I'm sure you'll love him. You have a lot in common." From the look on Skye's face, that was not a compliment. And Ethan had finally figured out what, or whom, was behind her sudden desire to get married.

"Pleasure to meet you, son. I've heard a lot of good things about you from Richard. You'll make a fine senator," the man said, taking Ethan's hand in a powerful grip.

"I appreciate you saying so, sir."

"Now, what's this about you two getting married?"

"I'm pregnant, Daddy, remember?"

"A little hard to forget with how you carried on when you busted my rib. But you were never one to conform to society's rules. Don't know why you'd start now." The man rubbed his side. "You sure you know what you're getting into, son? She kicks like a mule and is as stubborn as one, too. You say the grass is green, and she'll say it's brown."

"Careful, Daddy, you'll scare him off, and you'll have to tell all your friends at the country club that your daughter not only lost her fortune, she's a single parent who had her baby out of wedlock."

And that set off a political war of words between

father and daughter. The gnawing in Ethan's gut returned, and he started to worry, not only about Skye's blood pressure, but that Claudia had been right after all. The preacher slowly lowered himself into a chair. He looked as if he were praying. Ethan hoped he was saying a few for him.

Chapter Twelve

Skye looked up when Ethan popped his head in the hospital room the next morning. "You almost ready to leave?"

"Yes, but can you come in here for a sec?" She motioned him into the room.

"You okay?" he asked, giving her a concerned look as he entered.

"I'm good. Just stand against the wall and smile." She raised her cell phone then lowered it. "Could you at least try to look happy?"

"You wanna tell me why you're taking my picture?"

No, but obviously she had to tell him something. "It's our first morning as husband and wife. I want to memorialize the occasion." She forced a bright smile.

He rubbed his hand over his mouth and nodded. "Okay. Whatever makes you happy," he said, and gave her a sexy, amused smile.

She scrutinized the picture. His black suit was rumpled, and he looked tired after spending the night in the chair by her bed. But there was no denying that Ethan O'Connor was one exceptional-looking man. It was too bad listening to him talk half the night away with her father reminded Skye why he wasn't the man for her. And she'd kind of needed reminding after he'd held her in his arms and protected her from Nurse Ratched.

"Are we good now?"

"I just need to make sure I didn't leave anything behind. Go ahead, I'll meet you out there."

"Okay, I'll pay the bill, and I have a call to make."

So did she. As soon as he left the room, Skye phoned Vivi. "It's me. I don't have long to talk."

"Well, if it isn't Mrs. O'Connor. How was the wedding night?"

"Ha-ha. Listen, I need a favor. I'm sending a picture of Ethan to you now. Remember that Halloween party I went to as a Texas Republican?" Skye had to make sure that no one recognized her in the press release announcing their marriage. It was why she'd decided to take matters into her own hands.

Vivi snorted. "How could I forget?"

"Do you have it?"

"Yeah, I think so. Why? Never mind, I know where you're going with this. You want me to superimpose you into the one I just got of Ethan for the press release?"

"I'm so lucky to have a friend as smart as you." Skye grinned. "What do you think? Scary Guy wouldn't recognize me if he saw it, would he?"

"No. Your own father wouldn't recognize you. And speaking of the governor, how did he and Ethan get along?"

"Love at first sight. My father always wanted me to marry a lawyer. He assumed I was going to need one so it'd save on legal fees. By the end of the night, they were finishing each other's sentences. Because of you and Superman, I've married my father, Vivi," Skye accused.

"Superman figured since you were having the man's baby, anyway, you might as well marry him and take advantage of the name change. I thought it was a great idea. You cover your tracks, and other than the press release, you won't be doing any publicity photos. And it's not like you're going to be out on the campaign trail."

"Not after the stories my father shared with him. If we hadn't already been married by then, I'm positive Ethan would've left me at the altar." It was a good thing her father was on his way back to Texas.

"You were married in your hospital room."

"You know what I mean." She sat on the edge of the bed. "Any more word on Jimmy and Gina? Are the police any closer to pressing charges?"

"The woman he put in the hospital recanted her statement. The cops figure Jimmy got to her. But there's new evidence on the woman who went missing last year. They think he killed her, Skye. If they can prove it, he'll never see the light of day."

"Oh, God, Vivi. He really is a scary guy. Would it help if I gave a statement? I don't want—"

"No. There's no evidence he attacked you, but he has proof you attacked him. Superman thinks Gina's the key. He's got people looking for her now."

"Okay, Vivi, I've been thinking. How does he do it? Superman, I mean. He's saved you from a couple of close calls. He always knows what you're doing and what story you're working on. It's kind of creepy. And he knows where I am and what I'm doing. I don't like it. How—"

Skye stood up as it hit her. She knew who Superman was. At least she thought she did. Chance McBride. He used to be special ops and now worked for a private security contractor. The man had contacts all over the world, and she knew exactly who was feeding him information on her.

Nell McBride. His great-aunt. Master manipulator and busybody extraordinaire. Nell, who'd indirectly put Vivi in Chance's cross-hairs. Since Skye didn't want to upset Vivi, and the man was protecting her, after all, she couldn't mention her suspicions to her best friend. "Uh, Vivi, can you give me Superman's e-mail? I have a question for him."

"I can't. Sorry. I gave it to one of my friends at the NYPD, and Superman didn't get in touch with me for a week. I can't risk losing contact with him right now."

Because she had a crush on the man. Skye wondered how Vivi'd feel if she found out Superman was Chance.

"Skye, what are you . . ."

At the sound of Ethan's voice, Skye went down on her hands and knees, pretending to search under the bed. "Gotta go," she whispered to Vivi, then said to Ethan, "I lost my phone."

He rubbed his jaw. "It's in your hand."

She stood up. "I know that. I just found it." She looked at the wheelchair he'd pushed into the room and shook her head. "No way. I am walking out of here. I'm not riding in a wheelchair like some decrepit old woman."

"Hospital rules. Get in. I'll take you for a ride."

She grabbed her knapsack off the bed and plunked

herself down in the wheelchair. "Yeah, and knowing you, it'll take us twenty minutes to get to the front doors."

She gave a startled yelp when he tipped the chair backward. "You haven't seen enough of my moves to judge, cupcake." He smiled down at her before lowering the front wheels.

He was right. And the moves she'd witnessed that night in April were pretty darn spectacular. She didn't think her heart would survive if he showed her more. Living under the same roof with the man might end up being her undoing if she didn't lay down some ground rules. She was about to lay down a few when she saw Nurse Ratched at the end of the hall speaking to another nurse.

"Don't worry. If she says anything, we'll run her over."

"Why, Ethan O'Connor, if I didn't know better, I'd say there was a bad boy inside you after all."

"Like I said, you don't know me very well."

Her body got warm and tingly in response to the promise in that whiskey-smooth voice of his. "I'm beginning to realize that," she murmured.

"Am I making you nervous?" he asked with a hint of laughter in his voice.

She almost said *No . . . hot,* but caught herself before she blurted out the words. They passed Nurse Ratched on the way to the elevator. The woman smirked and said something to her friend, whose eyes widened.

Skye grabbed Ethan's black silk tie and pulled him down. "Did you see that? She's up to something."

"Yeah, I did." He was so close she could see the dark blond stubble on his face and had an almost uncontrollable urge to lick his chiseled jaw. "You think you could let me go now, cupcake? You're strangling me." The corner of his mouth twitched as he tugged his tie from her fist.

She stared at her clenched hand and slowly lowered it to her lap.

"You all right?" he asked, his brow furrowed as he pushed the down button.

No. There was something wrong with her. Something seriously wrong with her. "I'm good. Just trying to figure out what Nurse Ratched is up to," she said, her voice as raspy as Vivi's. Self-consciously, she cleared her throat.

"She won't bother you again, so don't worry about it," he said. The elevator doors opened and he pushed her inside.

His cell rang. "Hey, Claudia."

Skye could hear the other woman, her voice raised and agitated. Ethan got that scary-calm look on his face. The only thing that gave his emotion away was the muscle ticking in his cheek. "I'll take care of it. No, Claudia, I said, I will." He looked at Skye and lifted his chin, indicating they'd reached their destination. She got out of the wheelchair and Ethan, still on the phone with Claudia, took her hand. Every so often, he'd respond to his campaign manager with a yes or no.

"What's wrong?" Skye asked when he disconnected and jammed the phone in his jacket pocket. He glanced at her as he took out his keys. "Our wedding was leaked to the press. They're playing up the fact that I didn't marry you until you were over four months pregnant and included a bunch of pictures that were in the society pages a couple of weeks ago. At least there's no mention of your blog. Looks like they believe that Vivi is Envirochick and not you."

She stiffened. And her reaction had nothing to do with him figuring out that they'd lied about Vivi being Enviro-chick. No, it was the reminder of those pictures. "I used my given name on the marriage license. They wouldn't make the connection. And you could always say we just found out we're pregnant. But I guess it'll be harder to explain why you were sleeping with half of Denver, and Claudia, when you're supposedly in love with me." She jerked the seat belt over her shoulder and snapped it into place.

Ethan rested a hand on the roof and the other on the open door. "If I didn't know better, I'd think you were jealous."

She snorted. "As if."

"Sam's an old friend, and—"

"Oh, is 'old friend' the euphuism they're using for 'lover' these days?"

"You are jealous." He stared at her and, ignoring her "I am not," added, "I dated Sam five years ago. We're friends. And I never dated Claudia."

"No, you were just going to *marry* her." Before he could deny it, Skye said, "Your mother was picking out your engagement cake last week."

"It doesn't matter. We're married, and those photos are easily explained. Claudia's more worried about you being a Democrat and a vegan. It's not like our marriage is front-page news, so it's possible they won't dig deep enough to make the connection. But if they do, we'll have to deal with a lot of crap about you boycotting the meat industry."

She noticed he didn't deny that he'd been going to marry Claudia. "Too bad you aren't a Democrat. None of this would matter. My being a vegan would win you votes." She felt a small pinch of regret that he'd lose votes because of her. It was those darn pictures of him as a handsome little boy looking adoringly up at his father. A man he wanted to honor and a lifelong dream he wanted to fulfill. She might not agree with Ethan's politics, but it was hard not to admire him.

He gave her a half smile, and closed the door. She dug her phone from her knapsack and texted Vivi. By the time Ethan had started the SUV, Skye had what she needed.

"What's Claudia's e-mail address?"

He shot her an apprehensive look. "Why?"

"I'm not going to go all jealous wife on her, if that's what you're worried about." She held up her phone. "I want to send her the press release. It should help to counter the negative publicity."

"I appreciate you trying to help. I really do. But I don't see how a picture of me with some big-hair blonde model is going to . . ." He glanced from the screen to his suit. "Is that the picture you took of me this morning?"

"Yes, and that's me. Do you really think I look like a model?"

He laughed. "That's not you."

"Yes, it is," she said, wondering why she was offended when she should be happy he couldn't tell, because that meant Scary Guy wouldn't recognize her, either. "I'm going to emphasize my father's accomplishments as governor of Texas, and list the local charities I was involved with. I'll also include the fact that my father owns a cattle ranch. We just won't mention that I haven't eaten meat since I was ten."

"You've been a vegan since you were ten?"

"Vegetarian. Vegan since I was sixteen. Now let me type this up and send it off to Claudia."

"Hey." He gently tugged on her hair. "Thanks for doing this," he said when she looked up at him. "We can take another picture of us when we get to the ranch."

"No, this one's good. I look like a Republican."

He shook his head. "You've got a warped perception of Republicans, cupcake. We're going to have to work on that."

"Don't waste your energy. My dad's been trying to convert me since I was ten."

"I've been told I can be pretty persuasive."

"Republican women are easy," she said, ignoring the effect his swoon-inducing voice had on her.

"Yeah? I seem to remember a certain Democrat who was pretty easy." He waggled his eyebrows at her.

Jerk. But who was she trying to kid? She had been easy. "What was her name?" She ignored his laughter. "Stop talking so I can get this done."

He grinned as he fiddled with the sound system. The Rolling Stones' "Midnight Rambler" came through the speakers. His fingers tapping on the steering wheel, Ethan moved to the beat. Her lips twitched, and she struggled to focus on typing up the release. When he started singing, she started laughing.

"Hey, I've been told I have a good voice."

"No, it's not that. I like the Stones, too. We finally found something we agree on."

"There's hope for us yet, cupcake."

The smile she gave him was forced. Once Jimmy was behind bars and Ethan won the election, their marriage would be over. A fluttery sensation in her stomach distracted her. It was stronger than before.

"What's wrong?"

"It's the baby. She's moving. Here." Skye took his hand and placed it on her stomach. When there wasn't any movement a few minutes later, she said, "Sorry, looks like she got her exercise for the day."

"Never know, he might do it again." Her husband's hand felt heavy and warm and far too good where it was. He glanced at her, his thumb moving in a slow up-and-down caress.

"Maybe," she agreed, her voice breathy, but then she realized what he said. "Peanut's a she."

"Peanut?" His lips twitched. "I thought it was Willow."

"It was, but I like Peanut better. And don't try to distract me. Our baby's a girl."

"A boy. But Peanut works." He returned his hand to the steering wheel. "I've got to stop for gas. You need anything?"

"You should buy a hybrid."

He gave her a look and turned up the radio, singing as he pulled into the station. Skye was about to roll her eyes when she felt the now-familiar movement. "She kicked again. I think you like your daddy's voice, don't you, Peanut?"

Pulling up beside the tanks, Ethan took off his seat belt. But instead of getting out, he placed a hand on her upper thigh and leaned over, bringing his mouth to her stomach. He started to sing one of Skye's favorite songs, "Wild Horses." She pressed her lips together to hold back a moan. She really needed to think before she spoke.

"Do you feel anything?" he asked, turning his head to look up at her. Skye swallowed and croaked, "No."

His eyes darkened, and he brushed his lips over her

stomach, the muscles clenching in response. "You sure?" he asked, his voice a seductive rasp.

"Mmm-hmm, very sure." She turned her head and saw a man on the other side of the pumps staring at her, his bushy silver brows meeting his hairline. "Um, Ethan, there's a man looking at us, and I think he's getting the wrong idea."

Ethan smiled into her stomach and sat up. Scrubbing his hands over his face, he waited a couple of seconds before he shifted in the seat and curved his hand around her neck. He drew her closer and gave her a sweet, tender kiss.

When he released her, she sat there stunned for a moment before she managed to say, "What was that for?"

"With everything going on yesterday, I never got a chance to say I'm sorry for being an ass when I found out you were pregnant. In case you haven't figured it out yet, I'm happy about the baby."

"Thanks. I should have told you sooner. I'm sorry I didn't."

"You're forgiven, cupcake. You sure you don't need anything?"

A cold shower. "No, I'm good. Thanks."

As soon as he closed the door, Skye called Maddie. "Hey..." she began.

"Would this be Skylar Davis, now Mrs. O'Connor, the woman who vowed never to marry?"

Maddie had stood up for her at the hospital-room wedding. She'd kept interrupting their vows with snorts of laughter, especially when they got to the "obey" part. Which Skye had made the preacher change. "Okay, it's getting old now. I need to ask you a question before Ethan gets back," Skye whispered into the phone, glancing at Ethan as he filled the SUV. He caught her watching him and winked. She sunk lower in the seat.

"If he's not with you, why are you whispering?"

"Because it's embarrassing. Okay, don't laugh, but does, um, being pregnant make you horny?" Skye sighed when Maddie burst out laughing. "If you dare tell Gage, you're no longer one of my best friends."

"Sorry . . . sorry. I know I shouldn't laugh. And I don't know if it's the same for all pregnant women, but I want to jump Gage all the time. I think I'm wearing him out. He slept on the couch last night."

"All right, that was more than I needed to know. So what am I going to do? I can't have sex with Ethan."

"Why not? You're married, and you're already pregnant."

"Because . . ." Skye couldn't tell her that if she had sex with Ethan again, she was afraid she'd fall in love with him. And she couldn't fall in love with him because they'd end up as unhappy as her parents and destroy each other. "We don't love each other."

"Well then, I suggest you invest in a really good vibrator. You're going to need it."

Chapter Thirteen

"We just pulled in. I'll be there shortly. I want to settle Skye in first." Holding the phone with one hand as he responded to Claudia, Ethan unloaded Skye's suitcase from the Escalade. Madison had gone to the apartment and packed up for Skye, and Gage had delivered the suitcase to the hospital this morning. Ethan had been surprised there'd only been the one and called Madison. An uneasy feeling had come over him when his wife's best friend said that since Skye never stayed in one place long enough to settle down, she didn't have much to pack. It made him wonder if one day she'd come to resent him and the baby for having to give up her wanderlust ways.

He pushed the concern from his mind when Claudia, in a perturbed tone of voice, said, "Peter isn't here yet."

Ethan doubted her attitude had anything to do with Pete being late. At least not this time. When she'd realized Ethan was actually going through with the marriage the previous night, she'd tried once again to change his mind. It wasn't her half a dozen reasons against the idea that had him second-guessing himself. He'd gotten cold feet after listening to William Davis's stories about the crap Skye had pulled as a teenager. Only by then it'd been too late to back out. They were already married.

On the drive to the ranch this morning, some of those fears had dissipated. Her father had been talking about a young girl, not the woman Ethan had married. And as her press release had proven, Skye was smart and politically savvy. She intuitively knew what message to send out to get his supporters on board. He appreciated that she did that for him.

The fact that his feelings for her hadn't changed, no matter how hard he tried, didn't hurt, either. She was gorgeous and incredibly sexy. He'd had a hard time keeping his hands off her on the drive to the ranch. From her flushed face and her breathy response to his kiss, she wasn't immune to him, either. They might not love each other, they might not exactly have a lot in common, they might not...

At least they had the physical attraction thing going for them. They'd build on that and everything else would fall into place over time. They both wanted the best for the baby. And Ethan believed that was happily married parents. He was going to do his damndest to give his child the same life he had growing up.

"Ethan?"

Right. "Don't worry about Pete. He'll get here when he gets here." Ethan set the suitcase on the gravel drive and locked the Escalade. He lived in the guest house, and they held their meetings at his mother's place when he was in town. She liked to feel part of the action. Since his father died, Ethan had been doing all he could to fill the void. After all, if it wasn't for him, Deacon O'Connor would still be alive. Ethan shoved the thought aside. It wasn't something he let himself dwell on. "Any feedback from the press release?"

"No, nothing yet. But I think you should've let us handle it. Skye—"

"—did a fantastic job," he finished for her. Claudia's constant need to bash his wife was getting old fast. Neither of the women liked each other, but he wasn't about to let their past history cause friction in his campaign or stress out his wife.

"If you're happy with it, I suppose—"

Skye stormed onto the wooden porch of the guest house, the screen door slamming behind her. "Claudia, I gotta go." He disconnected. Picking up the suitcase, he walked toward his irate wife. "What's wrong?"

Wearing pink leggings and a long-sleeved black T-shirt, she stomped down the steps. "I'm not staying here. Put my suitcase back." She wrapped an arm around her waist and pressed her fingers to her lips. "I think I'm going to be sick. There's dead animals everywhere, Ethan. Dead animals," she said, her voice rising on a hysterical note.

He put a hand on her shoulder. "Calm down. I'll take care of it." His dad had been an avid hunter, and the guest house had served as his man cave. Knowing Skye as he did, Ethan should have anticipated her reaction, but . . . "You didn't have a problem with them the last time you were here."

"It was dark, and we were in your bedroom, and I was . . ." Her face flushed. "I'd had too much to drink."

"You didn't have that much to drink." He didn't seduce drunk women. "We didn't make it to the bedroom until round three, cupcake." He'd been so hot for her that they were lucky they made it through the front door. And remembering that night, he was hot all over again. "First time was—"

"Don't remind me. We did it in every room in there, and *she*"—Skye patted her flat stomach—"is the result. But that doesn't change the fact that I am of sound mind and body right now, and I am not stepping foot in that place again."

"Getting yourself worked up isn't good for either you or the baby. I told you I'd take care of it, and I will. Why don't you go for a walk?"

She glanced toward the stables and nodded. "I'll visit Bandit. At least you people haven't killed every animal on God's green earth." She started off, then whirled around, jerking her hand at the house. "Did you kill any of them?"

He used to hunt with his dad all the time. But none of the stuffed heads on the wall belonged to him. It had disappointed him as a kid. Now he was thinking it was a good thing they didn't. She'd probably divorce him. "No, none of them."

Her eyes narrowed at him, then she set off toward the stables. He took out his cell and texted Claudia that he'd be delayed.

He was boxing up the head of a bighorn sheep when his mother walked in. She frowned. "What are you doing? Those are your father's prized possessions."

Oh, yeah, this was going to go over real well. "Mom, if you want us to live here, I've gotta clear them out. Skye is an animal-rights activist. I'll bring everything over to your place. We'll set them up in the den." He looked at the stack of heads on the hardwood floor. "And one of the spare bedrooms."

His mother pressed her lips together and crossed her arms. "Of course she'd be an animal-rights activist. Honestly, Ethan, whatever did you see in that girl? Next thing you know, you won't be allowed to eat meat, let alone have it in your home."

He hadn't thought about that. Hell, he hoped Skye wouldn't expect him to become a vegetarian, too. "Don't go there. And let's not forget who pushed for this marriage."

"You'd already let the horse out of the barn, so what else could I do? You have an election to think about, and we always taught you to take responsibility for your mistakes. I'm not about to have an illegitimate grandchild. I just wish the baby's mother was normal. I pity her father. She must've driven the poor man crazy."

"My baby is not a mistake, and if you don't have anything nice to say about its mother, I suggest you keep your opinions to yourself. I mean it, Mom. This has to stop. You have to figure out a way to get along with Skye. Now, I've gotta get this done. I'm already late for my staff meeting."

She sighed and picked up a box. "I'll finish up. What time do you expect Skye to arrive?"

"She's already here. She went to the stables... What's wrong?" he asked at her wide-eyed expression.

She dropped the box. "Doc's coming to put down Bandit."

"Why the hell are you putting the horse down?" Ethan asked as he ran out the front door after her. Given Skye's reaction to the heads on the wall, he figured his would be joining them once she heard the news.

"Because he attacked Rebel and Shiloh."

Okay. All Ethan had to do was get to Skye before she found out or Doc got there. As they ran down the gravel path toward the barn, he heard a man and woman yelling in Spanish. He couldn't understand what they were saying, but he recognized his wife's voice— especially because she'd used that spitting-mad tone on him before.

But that time she'd had a bowl of punch in her hands. This time she was wielding a pitchfork at Raul when Ethan entered the stables ahead of his mother. Skye's hair was wild, her eyes the same, as she stood in a protective stance in front of Bandit's stall. The horse tossed his head, kicking at the back wall.

"Skye, get away from there before you get hurt," Ethan ordered. He understood why she was upset. He didn't like the idea of the horse being put down, either. But Raul and his mother wouldn't have come to the decision lightly, and Ethan didn't want Skye anywhere near the animal.

"I'm not the one going to get hurt. He is if he comes near Bandit." Her hot-tempered gaze flicked from Raul to Ethan as he approached, her eyes bright and accusing. "How could you—"

"Loco, your wife, she is as loco as the horse," Raul said to Ethan.

"*I'm* loco? I'm not the one going to murder an animal because he's acting like...like an animal. What is wrong with you people? You rescue a horse only to turn around and abuse it in the worst way possible."

"Your blood pressure, remember? Settle down. Let's

talk about..." he began as he reached for her. The horse charged to the front of the stall and bared his teeth at Ethan, forcing him to take a step back. "Skye, he's dangerous. Come here."

"He's not going to hurt me, are you boy? Show them what a good boy you are," she spoke to the horse in a low, comforting tone—and damned if he didn't nuzzle her neck. She set the pitchfork down, bringing her hand up to stroke Bandit.

His mother led Shiloh out of her stall and pointed to the mare's bandaged right foreleg. "This is why we're putting him down, Skye. He's attacked two horses now. We don't know if Rebel"—she lifted her chin to the stall at the other end of the barn—"will even recover."

"He's just establishing his place in the pack. This isn't his fault. It's yours. If you didn't think he was ready, you shouldn't have had him with the other horses. You don't have to kill him. Let him go," she said.

Ethan saw her hand go to the latch on the gate. "Skye, don't. You're not letting him out."

"Why not?" Her delicate jaw was set in a determined line.

Ethan took a step toward her, and Bandit stamped his hoof with an aggressive snort.

Raul lifted his bandaged hand. "He attacked me. He is dangerous."

Skye rubbed her cheek against Bandit's nose. "Right, I can see how dangerous he is."

"Raul, take Shiloh to the ring," his mother said.

The older man must have sensed the resignation on his boss's face because he said, "Thirty-seven years working here, and you are going to listen to her over me?"

Grabbing the reins from his mother's hands, he said, "I will have nothing to do with that animal."

"You don't have to. I'll take care of him," Skye said, and turned to hug Bandit. "We'll show them, won't we, boy?"

As Raul stomped away, muttering in Spanish, Skye called after him. Ethan didn't know what she said, but the old man threw up his hand and said, "Loco."

His mother sighed and went to walk away. "I'll try and reach Doc. Save him a trip."

"Skye, come here. Now," he said when she ignored him. She turned and arched a brow.

"Please." When she reluctantly did as he asked, he put his hands on her shoulders, ducking his head to look her in the eyes. "I understand why you're upset. But you have to know my mother and Raul are as protective of these animals as you are." The horse strained to reach his wife, giving Ethan the evil eye. He took a couple of steps back, bringing Skye with him.

She glanced over her shoulder, then back at Ethan with a grin. "You're scared of him."

"No, I'm not. I am not," he said when she responded with a brow lift. "Skye, I grew up around horses. I'm not afraid of him. But I am worried about you. You and the baby. I want you to promise me that you'll be careful." His cell rang. He figured it was Claudia and said, "I have to get going. I've got a staff meeting. If you need me, I'll be at my mom's. No going in his stall, all right?"

"Ethan, I'm not stupid. I wouldn't do anything to put the baby at risk." She crossed her arms, a defensive yet vulnerable look on her face.

"It's not you I'm concerned about. It's Bandit. Just

because he's docile around you now doesn't mean he won't turn on you later."

"I've been around horses since I was in diapers, Ethan. I think I know what I'm doing." She stepped away from him. "Honestly, how do you expect an animal that's born to run free to behave when you take away its freedom and trap it in a five-by-five stall?"

Ethan couldn't help but think his free-spirited wife was talking more about herself than the horse. "He didn't know any different, Skye. His previous owner mistreated him and...look, don't judge Mom and Raul until you've spent some time around Bandit."

* * *

Skye winced as she lifted the lasagna out of the oven. She'd have to be careful to hide the reaction from Ethan. Bandit had swung his head, sending her flying, when Raul approached his stall earlier. Who was she kidding? The older man probably ran to Ethan as soon as she'd left the stable. She'd find out soon enough, she thought, hearing footsteps on the front porch.

"Hi," she said when Ethan came through to the kitchen. He'd changed into well-worn jeans and a white button-down shirt for his meeting. He filled both to perfection, and her female parts were apparently very happy to see him. Holding the pan with her oven-mittened hands, she cast a surreptitious glance at her chest to see if he'd be able to tell just how happy her female parts were, angling her body away from him when she realized he most definitely would. "How was your meeting?"

He leaned his hip against the counter and crossed his arms. "Fine. How was the rest of your day?"

Oh, yeah, he knew. He had his lawyer face on again. Granted, it was a very hot lawyer's face, all chiseled jaw, firm lips, and a touch of steel in his hazel eyes. "Good. I did an energy cleanse on the house, got settled in, went to the grocery store, and made your dinner." She set the pan on the wooden cutting board, giving him a bright smile and fluttering her lashes.

She'd have to remember to do that more often, she thought, as his expression softened and his eyes warmed. Then she realized he wasn't looking at her. He was looking at the pan of lasagna. With all his attention zeroed in on her, he mustn't have noticed until now. She didn't mind cooking for him so that was good. It was the least she could do since he refused her offer to split their living expenses and insisted on paying for her hospital stay. But there was a part of her that wished it was her smile that had taken him from annoyed to nice.

"You cooked for me?"

"Yeah, well for—" She broke off at the sound of his mother's voice.

"Hi," Liz said, coming into the kitchen with a foil-wrapped dish in her hands. "Rosa made you your favorite, honey. Chicken and dumplings." She glanced at him. "You look tired."

"Uh, Mom, Skye made dinner for me."

"Oh, I didn't think...Well that's fine. We can put one in the fridge for tomorrow. Which would you prefer tonight, honey, chicken or lasagna?"

Unable to help herself, Skye said, "Yes, *honey*, which would you prefer?"

With a glint of what looked to be amusement in his eyes, Ethan said, "No contest. Your lasagna, cupcake."

A warm, fuzzy feeling filled Skye at both his answer and the expression on his face. She frowned at her reaction. She didn't want him making her feel warm and fuzzy, making her feel like this was real. Ground rules, that was what they needed. And as soon as his mother left...

"That's fine," Liz said, walking over to put the dish in the fridge. "Do you want me to make a salad, Skye?"

"I already made one. Thanks," she said, tilting her head and raising her eyebrows at Ethan. He grimaced and gave her a what-can-I-say look.

"Okay, I see it here." Liz pulled her head out of the fridge. "Ethan, why don't you open a bottle of wine and we can toast the baby? A cabernet would go well with the lasagna, I think."

It would, but it wasn't like Skye could have a glass.

"Here's some apple juice for you, Skye," his mother said, plunking the container on the counter along with the salad. She then opened a drawer and handed Ethan three place mats. "Here, dear, set the table. And while you're at it, put on a fire."

Oh, yes, Ethan, do put on a fire. We'll have a lovely romantic dinner. You, me...and your mother. As soon as the snippy thought entered her mind, Skye realized having Liz around was probably for the best. Nothing like a mother-in-law to curb those warm-and-fuzzies.

"I thought you were a vegetarian," Liz said when Skye placed a slice of lasagna on her plate.

"Vegan," Skye replied as she sat across from her mother-in-law at the table.

"So you eat meat on occasion?"

"No, I don't eat meat or any animal by-products." Well,

she hadn't until she'd come to Christmas and developed a cupcake obsession. And now, because Nurse Ratched had terrified her, Skye had bought some free-range eggs at the grocery store today. She refocused on Liz and saw the way she eyed the lasagna. "It's polenta pesto with soy cheese."

His mother exchanged an I-told-you-so look with Ethan, which he pointedly ignored as he took a tentative bite.

"Don't worry, honey." His mother patted his hand. "You can come home for dinner anytime. He's just like his father," she confided to Skye, "a meat-and-potatoes man."

*   *   *

Three hours later, Liz left. Skye, sitting cross-legged on the couch, looked at Ethan, who sat on the other end. "Your mother needs to get a life or get la..." She trailed off, realizing that wasn't something she should say to an uptight conservative like her husband. Really, it wasn't the type of comment to make to any man about his mother, but dinner had gone from bad to worse with Liz marking her territory at every opportunity.

Ethan choked on a mouthful of coffee. He put the mug on the table and turned to her. "Did you just tell me that my mother needs to get...laid?" he asked, and started to laugh when she grimaced and nodded.

His reaction surprised her, and that worried her. She didn't want him to have a sense of humor, and she could do without that deep, sexy laugh, too.

"You're right, about the life part at least. Gage and I have been trying to set up our parents for a while now. As you can tell, it hasn't been working."

"Of course it hasn't. They have nothing in common."

"Now wait a minute. You're the one who said they'd be a perfect match." At her confused look, he said, "Last Christmas at the pageant? Matching auras?"

"I forgot all about that." She hadn't forgotten about seeing Ethan for the first time, though. He'd driven her and Vivi from the Denver airport to Christmas last December. She'd never felt that instant attraction, that crazy zing of chemistry, with anyone else. "I was going to suggest Richard, but you know your mother better than I do. And auras don't lie."

Sitting back, he rested his arm along the back of the couch and twirled her hair around his finger. "Sorry about how tonight turned out. I didn't plan on my mother joining us, but I couldn't say no. She's lonely since my dad died." He gently tweaked her hair. "I liked the lasagna, you know."

"I know." She smiled. "You told me about ten times. I don't think your mother did."

"Yeah. Sorry about that," he said, rubbing her arm. His eyes narrowed when she wasn't able to hide her wince of pain. "Raul said Bandit knocked you around. You seemed fine, but obviously you're not. Let me have a look."

"No." She moved her arm. "I am fine. He head-butted me. Oh no, don't give me that I-told-you-so look. It was Raul's fault. Bandit doesn't like him."

He wrapped his strong fingers around her wrist. "Show me."

She sighed and did as he asked, pushing up her sleeve. Tiny sparks danced under her skin as he gently probed the outer edges of the bruise. He shifted closer, enveloping her in his familiar, masculine scent. He smelled so good, clean, with a hint of spicy, expensive cologne, that she found herself leaning into him. At the feel of his warm, hard body against hers, she squirmed on the couch. He raised his gaze to hold hers. "You okay?" he asked, but the corner of his mouth quirked, and she realized he knew exactly how she was feeling.

"Ethan, I, uh, I think we need to lay down some ground rules."

Chapter Fourteen

Skye." Ethan tapped on her half-closed door, pushing it open when she didn't respond. Her suitcase sat in the middle of the bed, clothes spilling onto the quilt, a lacy pink bra and thong panties catching his eye. Considering the ground rules she'd laid down last night, Ethan figured that was about as close to seeing her bra and panties as he was going to get.

He'd agreed that making the house a politics-free zone was a good idea. Her moratorium on sex? Not so much. But he didn't have a chance to argue, because she went to bed as soon as she'd laid down the law. He'd been determined to talk to her about it today, but seeing as how she'd yet to unpack, and it didn't look like she intended to, he decided to bide his time so he wouldn't send her running for the door.

He knew she was as attracted to him as he was to her. He'd seen the way her breathing had quickened when he touched her soft skin last night, the way her caramel eyes had darkened with desire. Oh, yeah, she wanted him. And he planned to remind her of that today.

He called her name as he walked into the kitchen, glancing at the dishes in a sinkful of water. A piece of paper on the table caught his eye, and he picked it up. Scanning the long list of changes she wanted him to make to the guest house, he rubbed his jaw. He supposed he shouldn't be surprised that a woman who called herself Envirochick wanted to make the house eco-friendly. Some of the changes were easy and cheap enough—inserting solar panels on the roof, not so much.

He shoved the list in his jeans pocket and headed to the stables. "Hey, Raul, have you seen my wife?" he asked the older man, who was bent over cleaning a horse's hoof with a pick.

"She took the beast for a walk. I told her it's a horse, not a dog. She didn't listen." Raul cast him a sidelong glance. "You should have married Claudia. Your mama likes her. I like her, too. This one..."

So much for hoping the older man would warm up to Skye. Raul hadn't appreciated her challenging his authority. He ruled the ranch with an iron fist. Taciturn and stubborn, Raul had been like a surrogate grandfather to Ethan. He and Rosa had been with the family before Ethan was born. He was about to tell Raul that Rosa didn't like Claudia, but decided to ignore him and instead asked, "Any idea which direction Skye went?" They owned more than six hundred acres.

"West. Toward the entrance to the national park."

Great. The park was only a mile up the road, and there were about a million acres of trails running through it.

"Thanks." On his way out of the barn, Ethan stopped and turned to Raul. "Wait a sec. Are you telling me she got a bridle on Bandit?"

The older man muttered something in Spanish, then said, "Yeah."

Ethan fought the urge to rib him. It wouldn't endear Skye to the old ranch hand if he pointed out that she'd accomplished in one day what his mother and Raul had been trying to do for more than a month.

Twenty minutes later, Ethan caught sight of his wife in the meadow. She was lying on her back, propped on her elbows and chewing on a blade of grass, with her gaze fixed on the horse in the field. He took his time, enjoying the view. She had on a purple sweatshirt, a pair of Daisy Duke shorts, and tennis shoes. With the sunlight turning her long hair to a burnished gold, she looked like a woodland fairy, a sweet, natural beauty that had him cursing her damn rules. He cleared the frustration from his face as he approached.

"Hey," she said and sat up.

"Hey yourself," he said, joining her on the grass. "Is he going to attack me if I sit too close?"

"Possibly. But don't worry, I'll protect you."

"Good to know," he said, reaching over to brush the grass from her hair. He didn't miss her reaction to his touch, the slight hitch in her breath. He thought about continuing to play with her long, soft curls, but she wasn't the only one having a reaction, and he lowered his hand. "You were up early. You should've waited for me. I would've joined you."

She averted her eyes, picking a piece of clover. "I heard you on the phone and didn't want to bother you. It sounded like you had a full day ahead of you."

"I do, but you wouldn't have been bothering me. I want to spend some time with you, show you around the ranch before I head out."

"Don't worry about me. I like exploring on my own." She drew her gaze from Bandit and smiled. "This is the most amazing place. It's incredible. I passed a pond back there." She pointed beyond the gravel path lined with yellow-and-orange-leafed bushes. "You must have had a great time growing up here."

"I did. There's five ponds on the property. Two of them are stocked with rainbow trout. I'll take you fishing...uh, guess not, huh?"

She opened her mouth, then closed it and shook her head. He figured he was lucky she didn't tear a strip off him for his suggestion. Bandit trotted toward them, and Skye stood up, brushing off the back of her shorts.

"I'm impressed that you got him to wear the bridle. Bet Raul was surprised," Ethan said as he forced his gaze from her heart-shaped behind.

She shrugged, taking hold of the bridle. "He didn't say much, other than muttering a couple Spanish curse words. I don't think he likes me."

"Don't let him bother you. He's more bark than bite. He'll come around." Ethan walked along the narrow path beside Skye, with the horse trailing behind them. "When did you learn to speak Spanish?"

"When I was ten. One of my nannies was Latina."

"You had more than one?"

"I think I went through eight of them before my father finally gave up. Why do you look so surprised? He told you what I was like growing up, didn't he?"

"Well, yeah, I just didn't realize...That must have

been tough on you." He felt sorry for the little girl she'd once been, but he knew better than to say that out loud. He got the impression from Richard that Skye's parents had had a tumultuous marriage, and her mother hadn't been in the picture much when she was growing up. At least he knew where her negative view of marriage came from. He wondered if it was the reason she was afraid to give theirs a chance.

"Tougher on the nannies, I think. So, where are you off to today?" Ethan wanted to know more about her childhood. But she obviously didn't want to talk about it, and for now he'd let her get away with changing the subject.

"Luncheon with the Ladies Auxiliary and then I'm heading to Fort Carson."

"Will you be home in time for dinner?"

"No, don't worry about me. I'll probably be late."

He'd liked that she'd cooked for him last night. It had felt like she was settling into the marriage, maybe even putting down roots, making the house her own. A few hours later, she'd ended the fantasy. But they had the baby to think about, and he wasn't going to give up on them that easily. He glanced at Bandit docilely following Skye and had a flash of inspiration. He'd handle his wife like she handled the temperamental horse. He had to be patient and gain her trust. "Mom will be around if you need anything, and I'll call to check in on you. You going to take it easy for the rest of the day?"

"No, I've got things to do. I'm going to head into town…" She sighed. "Ethan, I'm fine."

"Yeah, well, I want you to stay that way. Do me a favor, just for the next couple of days, take it easy."

"Okay. Two days tops."

"Let's play it by ear."

"Let's not." She glanced at him. "You're not going to turn into an overprotective daddy-to-be, are you?"

"Looks like it." He smiled. "And speaking of baby, how's Peanut doing today?"

She patted her stomach. "Good. I was thinking of calling her Clover, what do you think?"

"It's... Are you serious?"

"You don't like it?"

No. "Yeah, but we're having a boy and a name like that would get him teased. How about Liam or John?"

"You're kidding, right? They're so... pedestrian. Okay, here's the deal. *If* we have a boy, you can name him. I get to name the girl."

"I got your number. The only reason you're giving in is because you think we're having a girl."

"I know we are." She grinned, then touched her stomach and looked at him. "She really does like your voice. She kicked again."

"Yeah? Let me see," he said, taking her arm to get her to stop walking. He crouched in front of her, placing his hands on her stomach, and talked to the baby. He felt the muscles in Skye's stomach tighten, saw the heat in her eyes, and realized he'd found the perfect excuse to touch his wife. "I'll have to do this every day."

"Um, that'll be a little hard to do when you're on the road." It sounded like she was more relieved than disappointed.

"Come with me," he said as he stood up, his hand on her arm. "I'd feel better if you did."

"I don't think it's a good idea, Ethan. You know how—"

With a toss of his head, Bandit trotted over and inserted himself between Ethan and Skye.

"Hey, get your own girl," Ethan said when the horse nuzzled Skye's neck. Bandit responded by head-butting Ethan, causing him to slide on the loose gravel down the embankment. Ethan lost his footing and ended up standing ankle deep in the muddy creek that ran alongside the path.

Skye looked around the horse, her lips pressed together, her eyes dancing with suppressed laughter. "Do you need a hand?"

"No, I think I can manage, thanks," he said, his running shoes making sucking sounds when he pulled them from the mud. He sloshed his way up the embankment.

And if that wasn't bad enough, much to his wife's amusement, Bandit kept pushing Ethan around all the way back to the barn. "I have time for a coffee before I leave," Ethan said in hopes his wife would join him.

Bandit shoved his nose in Ethan's chest and began eating the buttons off Ethan's chambray shirt. "Knock it off." He pushed at the horse.

Skye grinned and tugged on the reins. "I need to rub down Bandit. I'll see you tonight."

It looked like he'd have more luck getting his wife's attention if he was a horse. As Ethan walked away, Bandit whinnied. It sounded like a snicker.

* * *

It had been three weeks since Ethan had asked Skye to join him on the campaign trail. Ten days since he'd been home. If she'd known how long he'd be gone, she might have reconsidered her response that day. She missed having him around. Sure they talked on the phone, Skyped almost every night, but it wasn't the same. Maybe it was the early October weather. It'd been dreary, cold and gray, for the past week.

Skye kept herself busy during the day. Filling her time with Bandit and her blog, heading into town to visit with Maddie and Grace. It was the nights that were the hardest, a little scary, too. She had yet to adjust to the noises the house made, the branches scraping across the roof and windows, how dark and isolated it was.

Last night, the howling winds had knocked out the power, and she'd had a mini meltdown. Probably because before the lights went out, she'd been talking to Vivi about Jimmy the Knife. And despite her best friend telling her that everything was status quo, Skye spent the night with the covers around her ears, jumping out of her skin at every creak and groan, convinced Jimmy had found her.

Tucking her legs beneath her, she curled up on the couch, her eyes glued to the open computer on the coffee table as she waited impatiently for a connection. A shiver of anticipation raced up her spine when Ethan appeared on the screen. He sat on the edge of the bed in his hotel room, adjusting a cuff link in the sleeve of his white dress shirt.

"Hey, cupcake, how are you doing?" he asked, reaching for his black suit jacket.

"Good...I'm good." Ethan looked better than good. He looked delectable, lickable, kissable. She couldn't believe she'd just thought that. Right, who was she trying to kid? Lately, all she thought about was the night they'd spent together. Darn pregnancy hormones were sending her libido into overdrive. She cleared the husky quality from her voice and asked, "Are you going out?"

"Yeah, Jordan is hosting another fund-raiser for me."

He glanced at his watch. "Sorry, I won't be able to talk for long."

She covered her disappointment with a forced smile. "That's okay. I have to get some work done on my blog anyway. I guess Sam will be there tonight."

He raised a brow as he shrugged into his jacket. "We've had this conversation before, Skye. Sam and I are just friends. And speaking of your blog, I read it last night."

Given his cool, unemotional voice, he obviously wasn't happy with what she'd written. She'd done a piece on cheating politicians. In her defense, so had most of the major news outlets. A married New York senator had gotten caught with his pants down...literally. Admittedly, some of her own worries may have crept into her post.

Two days ago, pictures of Ethan surrounded by the Broncos cheerleaders had ended up on the front page of the Denver newspaper. Skye had never been jealous a day in her life, and it irked her to no end that she was. When the green-eyed monster reared its ugly head, she'd reminded herself that Ethan wasn't the type of man to cheat. He didn't have a sense of entitlement or an over-inflated ego like some politicians. He was honorable and loyal. But he was also a married man whose wife wasn't really his wife.

"Yeah, it was very popular," she said in a defensive tone of voice. "Resonated with a lot of women, I guess."

Now his face got that lawyerly look. "If you have something you want to say, say it. I don't have time for passive-aggressive bull—"

Skye blinked. Ethan never swore. It didn't matter that he'd stopped himself before he did. She ignored the pinch of hurt in her chest. "There was nothing passive-aggressive about my post, and I resent you insinuating that there was. Nothing I wrote reflected on you. And if you felt like it did, that's not my problem, it's yours. No one knows I'm Envirochick, and even if they did, I'm entitled to my opinions." And since they had gotten married, she'd been careful to temper her posts so that they didn't negatively impact Ethan.

He raked his fingers through his hair. "You're right. I probably shouldn't have called you tonight. It's been a long couple of days. I'm tired."

"Don't let me keep you. I'm sure you have more important things to do than waste your time talking to me."

His expression softened. Probably because he sensed how close to tears she was. She hated how emotional she was, but she'd been looking forward to his call all day. "Come on, cupcake. You know that's not true. Talking to you is the best part of my day. So tell me what you've been up to."

"It's okay. You don't have to humor me."

"I'm not. How's the baby?"

Because she had news she'd been anxious to share, she relented. "I think she's getting bigger. I popped."

"You popped?" he said in a confused tone of voice.

"I'll show you." She stood up, angled the screen, and lifted her long-sleeved, powder-blue T-shirt, giving him a side view of her baby bump. It wasn't that big, but at least she looked pregnant now. She rubbed her bare stomach, the waistband of her pajama bottoms riding low on her hips. "Can you see it?"

"Yeah, I, uh, I can see it," he said, his voice low and gruff.

The way he was looking at her made Skye feel warm all over, and her groundless worries disappeared. Ethan still found her attractive. He still wanted her. And as hard as Skye had been fighting it, she wanted him, too. All this pent-up desire couldn't be good for her or the baby, or for that matter, Ethan. He was probably as frustrated as Skye.

And right then, looking at the stunning example of male perfection staring at her with a hot, hungry expression on his face, Skye's desire won out over her fear that she'd fall in love with her husband. She hadn't fallen in love with him back in April, so why would this time be any different? Now she had to figure out a way to let him know she'd changed her mind about her no-sex rule without coming out and saying it. She'd rather he did the asking; begging would be better.

With that thought in mind, Skye said, "I don't think you're getting the full effect. Here, let me just…" She glanced at her powder-blue pajama bottoms with the cows on them. Not exactly the thing to put her husband into a lust-filled state, but there wasn't much she could do about it now. Taking a deep breath, she hooked a finger in the waistband of her pajamas and shimmied, lowering the bottoms several inches. "How's that? Can you see now?"

"No, I think you're gonna have to lower them a little more, cupcake," he said, a slow smile curving his lips.

"Really?" she croaked, trying to remember if she'd put on granny panties or a thong.

"Oh, yeah, sweetheart. Really."

Somewhat awkwardly, she lowered them some more. Relieved when black lace came into view, she snuck a peek at Ethan. The appreciative look in his eyes gave her the confidence to continue. She added a sexy little bump and grind, smiling when she heard his low laugh. Humming a stripper song, she gave another tug and wiggle. As her pajama bottoms puddled on the floor, she kicked them off in a move that would do the Rockettes proud.

"Ethan, can you help me with my zipper? It's..." Claudia, a hand pressed to the front of her black dress, her back completely bared, widened her eyes as she caught sight of Skye. "Kendall, what are...Oh."

"Skye," Ethan began.

She heard him swear as she slammed the computer closed.

Chapter Fifteen

Ethan pulled up to the guest house. He'd put in an hour at the fund-raiser, did the meet-and-greet, then headed for home. Claudia wasn't happy about his decision, and neither was his mother, but his head wasn't in the game. Skye wouldn't take his calls. And all he could think about was the devastated expression on her face before the screen went black. During her sexy little striptease, he'd been imagining what it would be like to finally have her in his bed again. Now he had to explain what Claudia was doing in his room.

After her latest blog post, he suspected his chances of convincing her that nothing was going on between him and Claudia were slim to none. But it was true. There was only one woman he wanted and that was his wife. It was probably why her post pissed him off. She'd basically said that all politicians of the male persuasion thought with one head, and it wasn't the one on their shoulders. He smiled as he turned off the engine. While he didn't appreciate or agree with her comments about a politician's propensity for adultery, Sam was right. Skye was funny as hell and had an engaging voice.

His smile faded as he locked the SUV. He'd taken a lot of heat because of her blog. She might have convinced everyone else that her friend Vivi was Envirochick, but his team knew it was his wife. Claudia, of course, had voiced her disapproval the loudest. If she had her way, Ethan would be divorced immediately after the election. And oddly enough, she might now get her wish. With that thought weighing on him, he bounded up the front steps. A pool of light illuminated the porch, the weather-beaten boards littered with autumn leaves. It was after midnight, and the house was dark and quiet. He locked the door behind him and headed for Skye's bedroom.

Moonlight filtered into the room through the window over her bed. He froze. She wasn't there. As he turned in hopes he'd find her in his room, a blow to the shoulders nearly took him to his knees. He stumbled, regained his balance, and whipped around to face his attacker. Adrenaline pumped through him at the thought someone had broken in, hurt Skye, hurt the baby. He needn't have worried.

He grabbed Skye's hands before she whacked him again with the rolling pin.

Her eyes went wide. "What are you doing here? I-I thought you were..."

Nudging her against the bedroom door, he pinned her hands over her head. His heart still racing, relief coursing through his veins, he lowered his mouth to hers and kissed her. It wasn't a soft and gentle kiss. It was demanding, full of need and a hot, searing desire.

She trembled in his arms, and he raised his head. "Sorry I scared you," he said, his voice a rough rasp. Releasing her wrists, he took the rolling pin from her and tossed it on the bed.

She wrapped her arms around his waist, burying her face in his chest. "I was so scared. I thought..." She shook her head, her voice muffled and shaky.

He stroked her hair. "Makes two of us." Lifting her into his arms, he ignored the dull ache across his back and headed for his room.

Her gaze jerked to his. "What do you think you're doing?"

"What I've wanted to do since the moment you walked back into my life."

"Oh no, not after what I saw tonight. Let your girl-friend take care of you," she said, her eyes flashing as she struggled to get out of his arms.

He tightened his hold. "Calm down, and I'll explain everything." He flipped on the light before he placed her on the middle of his bed. She went to scramble off.

He looped an arm around her waist. "We need to talk. Your room's freezing. Mine will be warmer once I get a fire going." And it was going to get a hell of a lot warmer before the night was over. He wasn't about to let her ruin the first opportunity he had to make this a real marriage because she'd jumped to the wrong conclusion.

She scooted to the edge of the mattress, crossed her arms, and glared at him. "Talk. You have two minutes."

"You'll give me as long as I need. Get in," he said, pulling back the covers. He reminded himself that he'd scared her, and reined in his irritation. "Do you want anything, something to drink?"

"I want you to stop being so bossy and let me go back to bed. I'm tired," she grumbled, even as she crawled under the blankets, pulling them to her chin.

"So am I." He took off his jacket and tie, glancing at her as he rolled up his sleeves. She averted her eyes. He got the fire going, turned off the light, and walked back to the bed. "You going to keep ignoring me?" he asked, sitting beside her.

Her gaze moved from the flickering flames to him. Along with her anger, he sensed she was hurt, and maybe a little embarrassed that Claudia had seen her in her panties. Ethan didn't think any woman who looked as good in her panties as his wife did had anything to be embarrassed about. And maybe that was why Claudia hadn't said a word, acting as though she hadn't caught them in the middle of some sexy tech time.

"You're making a big deal out of nothing. And if you would've taken my calls, you wouldn't have spent the night worrying about it."

"I wasn't."

"Yeah, you were." He took her hand in his, rubbing his thumb over her knuckles as he held her gaze. "There was a mix-up at the hotel, and we ended up in a suite. My mother shared one of the bedrooms with Claudia. She couldn't ask her to help with the zipper because Mom had already left for the Reinharts'." He let go of her hand and took his phone out of his pocket. "Call Claudia if you don't believe me."

She pushed his phone away. "I'm not calling her."

"You believe me, then?" She shrugged, and he bit back a frustrated sigh. "If I was in love with another woman, wanted to be with another woman, I wouldn't have married you, Skye."

"Oh, please, of course you would have. I'm having your baby, and you were worried how that would play out with your supporters. You were worried if you didn't marry me, you'd lose the election."

"I married you because of the baby, not the election." When she raised an eyebrow, he toed off his shoes. "Move over," he said, giving her a gentle nudge. She complied, and he stretched out beside her, propping himself up on his elbow. "Seems to me you're forgetting that you asked me to marry you."

"I did not."

"You were the one who insisted we get married that night. I was all set to back off. I didn't want to pressure you. I know the only reason you wanted to get married was because of your dad, but I don't care. I'm just glad that you did."

Her gaze roamed his face. "You are?"

"Yeah, I am. And I'm slipping if you didn't get that." He drew her into his arms. "I'm sorry I haven't been around. I told Claudia to fix my schedule so that I can come home at night."

"I'm glad." She plucked at the buttons on his shirt. "I've been nervous here by myself."

"You should've told me. Is that why you had the rolling pin?"

She nodded, then reached around to stroke his back. "I'm sorry I hit you. I heard footsteps and...Did I hurt you?"

"I don't think anything's broken. I'll probably be black-and-blue tomorrow, but that's okay." She grimaced, and he kissed her forehead. "I'm teasing, cupcake. I'm fine. And I'd be even better if we could pick up where we left off."

He waggled his brows and started humming the stripper song.

With a mischievous glint in her eyes, she gave him a light push. "Get up there, Mr. Senator-to-be. Show me what you've got."

"I don't know, cupcake. With the problem you've been having with your blood pressure, it might be dangerous for you to see what I've got."

"I'm willing to take the risk."

He could tell she didn't believe he'd take her up on her challenge. "All right, you sit back and prepare to be amazed." He saw the surprise in her eyes when he stood up and danced his way to the end of the bed. "I should warn you, my mother and Rosa forced me to watch *Magic Mike* with them. I picked up some moves." He did a slow swivel of his hips as he started to unbutton his shirt.

Propping the pillows behind her, she put two fingers between her lips and whistled. "Whoa, baby. Shake it."

He shook it, then turned and looked at her over his shoulder as he moved his hips and lowered his shirt in a slow back-and-forth motion.

Skye clapped and sang "It's Raining Men."

He did a spin, whipped his shirt off, and twirled it over his head before tossing it at his laughing wife.

Since she was too busy laughing to sing, he took up the song where she left off and drew his belt through the loops. Swiveling his hips, he dropped it on the floor, then danced his way to the side of the bed. He undid his pants, slowly inching the zipper down. He mimicked the sexy bump and grind she'd done earlier and dropped his pants, kicking them out of the way. She stopped laughing.

"You're looking a little flushed, cupcake. I better check

your pressure." He crawled into bed with her and gently eased her onto her back. She held his gaze, her breath hitched when he took her wrist between his fingers and kissed the soft skin there. "On second thought"—he released her hand and lifted her T-shirt, placing his palm on her breast—"this might be the best way to gauge how you're holding up. What do you think?"

"Good...really, really good idea."

"Now I don't usually let the women touch me, but for you, I'll make an exception."

She gave a strangled laugh and reached for him, her fingers digging into his shoulders when he lightly nibbled on her neck. He smiled against her sweet-smelling skin and kissed his way to her lips. He grazed her mouth with his, teasing her until she begged him to kiss her. He did, and when he raised his head a few moments later, she released a frustrated groan. "Hang on, cupcake. I'm gonna take care of you real soon."

Her stomach quivered as he trailed his tongue along the waistband of her pajama bottoms.

"I need...oh, yes, yes," she said when he lowered her pj's and headed south.

*   *   *

Skye woke up to a phone vibrating on the nightstand and a warm, hard body spooned against her back. Ethan's arm was wrapped around her waist, his big hand lying protectively on her stomach.

He groaned, lifted his hand, and reached across her to pat down the nightstand. He rolled onto his back with the phone in his hand. Skye grumbled a protest at the loss of his warmth and turned to face him, snuggling against him.

"Morning, cupcake," he said, wrapping an arm around her and bringing her closer. "Should've turned the damn thing off. Sorry it woke you up."

"It's okay," she yawned, lifting his arm to glance at his watch as he answered the phone. "I should get up anyway." Not that she wanted to, not after their incredible night together. She'd rather spend the day in bed with him. But from the conversation he was having with Claudia, that wasn't going to happen. Skye smoothed her hand over his broad chest and reluctantly pushed herself upright.

"I'll be there as soon as I can," he said to Claudia at the same time as he looped his arm around Skye's waist. "Oh no you don't. I'm not done with you yet." He disconnected and tossed his phone on the bed.

She glanced over her shoulder with a hopeful smile. "You don't have to head back to Denver?"

"I do," he said, pulling her down beside him. "But it doesn't mean I have to leave right away."

"Claudia won't be happy," she said, tracing around the edges of his firm lips.

"Too bad." He smiled and nipped her finger. "I'll have enough time to prepare for the debate."

She drew back. "The debate's tonight?"

"Yeah." He rubbed the bridge of her nose. "What's with the frown?"

"You never said anything about it to me."

"No politics, remember? You're the one who laid down the ground rules."

She pulled away from him and crossed her arms over her chest. "I also said no sex, but you didn't have a problem breaking that rule."

"You didn't seem unhappy about me breaking it last

night." He angled his head to study her. "You're upset I didn't invite you to the debate?"

"No . . . Well, yes. Your mom and Claudia will be there. I'm sure Sam will be, too. Won't people wonder why your wife isn't there to support you?"

"Not anyone who knows you," he murmured.

"That's not fair, Ethan. Just because we don't see eye to eye on the issues doesn't mean I don't support you. I know how much the election means to you." She moved to get out of bed.

He pulled her back, caging her in with his body. "I'm sorry. I didn't think you'd want to come."

She did. She wanted to be there for him. She didn't completely understand her change of heart. Though it was possible the night they'd shared had something to do with it.

"I do." She glanced up at him. "Can I come?"

"I don't think it's a good idea. Not with your blood pressure. You—"

"My blood pressure wasn't a problem last night."

"No, it wasn't. But that's because when we're making love, we're on the same page. We don't argue. You like everything I do to you, and I feel the same way." He nuzzled her neck, then brought his mouth to her ear and reminded her exactly how much she'd liked what he did to her.

He was right.

In fact, she would have gone so far as to say she'd loved every single minute she spent in his bed. She loved it so much she didn't want to ruin her chances of it happening again. But it didn't change the fact that she wanted to be there to support him tonight. She didn't like being treated like . . . like an embarrassment. Like someone he had to hide away because he was ashamed of her, because he thought she was a loose cannon, a flighty, irresponsible woman who had no idea how to conduct herself in the political arena.

He was wrong. He forgot who he was dealing with. She'd been spoon-fed Republican policy since she was a baby. "All right, if you need proof, I'm going to give it to you."

"You don't have to prove anything to me." Sliding his hand up her inner thigh, he held her gaze as he stroked her with his long, talented fingers. "I can feel exactly how much you love when I touch you."

"That's not . . . oh, that feels good." And he was very good at distracting her. "No, that's not what I meant." She shook her head when he raised a brow. "I mean it feels . . . oh, yes, yes." She strained against his hand, threading her fingers in his thick hair. It was only when he stopped stroking that she regained her ability to speak without moaning. "What I'm trying to say is that just because we disagree doesn't mean we can't talk about the issues like two reasonable adults."

His lips quirked, and he lowered his mouth to her breast. "It's not me who has a problem being reasonable." Given where his mouth was, his voice was muffled, and she wasn't entirely sure she'd heard him correctly. Plus it sounded like he was laughing.

"You're not funny." She tugged on his head. "Look at me."

"I'm kinda busy." And he got busy again, in a way that had her moaning her appreciation. Several orgasm-inducing moments later, he raised his head. "You sure you want me to stop?"

Her eyes fluttered open. "Huh?"

He laughed. "You're real easy to distract, you know."

She really was easy where he was concerned. She nudged him onto his back and crawled on top of him. "Or maybe you're just really good at distracting me. But I'm serious, Ethan. We can talk about politics without having a disagreement. I know we can. Let me prove it to you."

He patted her bare bottom, a lazy smile on his gorgeous, beard-stubbled face. "Okay, go ahead. Prove it to me."

Twenty minutes into their discussion, Ethan had her flat on her back with her arms pinned over her head. "That answer was a total cop-out, and you know it. When I ask your stance on gay marriage, Ethan, you can't say the state doesn't belong in people's bedrooms."

"Yes, I can. And a couple of seconds ago, you agreed with me."

"Moaning doesn't constitute an agreement."

He gave her a hard, fast kiss. "Sorry, cupcake, I've gotta go," he said, and got off the bed. "But you proved your point. As long as we're in bed and naked, we can talk politics."

She threw a pillow at his tight behind as he walked into the bathroom. His cell rang at the same time she heard the shower turn on. She glanced at the caller ID, and seeing it was Claudia, picked up.

"Ethan, where are—"

"Hey, Claudia. He's in the shower. Is there anything I can help you with?"

"What do you mean, he's in the shower? He should be on his way here."

"Relax. He'll be there shortly."

"Relax? Kendall, do you have any idea how important tonight is?" A loud sigh gusted over the line. "I don't know why I even bothered to ask. Of course you wouldn't, because you don't care about anyone but yourself. If you cared at all about Ethan, you would've answered the phone last night instead of worrying him half to death. But God forbid you act like a reasonable, mature adult. Instead your silence forced him to leave his own fundraiser and drive three hours to ensure his baby was all right. You haven't changed, have you? You're still as self-absorbed as ever."

"Hold it right there. You have no idea who I am. And Ethan and my personal business doesn't concern you. So keep your opinions and your—"

"You're wrong. As his campaign manager, anything that impacts his standings in the polls is my business. He needs a decisive win in the debate tonight. And instead of focusing on that, he was forced to deal with you and your jealous snit."

"You think I'm jealous of you?"

Claudia snorted. "I don't *think* you are. I *know* you are. You always have been. I'm everything your father wanted in a daughter and everything your husband needs in a wife."

"Gee, Claudia, sounds like you're the one who's jealous, not me. I obviously have everything *you* want."

"Grow up, Kendall, and for once, think of someone other than yourself. Do you have any idea how important this election is to Ethan? How badly he wants to win?"

"Yes, Claudia, despite what you think of me." *What everyone thinks of me.* "I do. And I plan to help him win."

"What do you mean?" Claudia asked, a nervous edge to her voice.

"I'll be at the debate tonight to support my husband."

"Over my dead body you're going to the debate. Let me talk to Ethan. Let me talk to him now."

"Sorry, Claudia, no can do. Ciao."

"Was that Claudia?" Ethan asked, coming out of the bathroom with a towel wrapped around his narrow hips.

"Yes," she said, muting the phone when it started to ring again. She tossed it on the bed. "I told her you'd be there soon." Since it was obvious neither Ethan or Claudia wanted her at the debate, Skye decided to keep her plans to herself. Because no matter what they thought, she knew Ethan needed her to be there tonight, and that was exactly where she'd be.

Chapter Sixteen

As Gage pulled up to the entrance of the Ritz-Carlton in downtown Denver, a wave of anxiety hit Skye. Her cell phone vibrating on the seat beside her didn't help. She ignored it like she had the last eight times. She didn't have to look to know it was Ethan's mother. Skye had hung up on her while trying on clothes at Sophia Dane's high-end ladies' clothing store, Naughty and Nice. Liz had been trying to reach her ever since.

Claudia had told Liz that Skye was planning to attend the debate, and Ethan's mother wanted to make sure that didn't happen. No surprise there. But what she'd said next had been. She'd intimated that Ethan didn't want Skye there, either, and it wasn't only because of her blood pressure. He was worried what she'd say if the reporters got ahold of her, but he was too tenderhearted to tell her so himself.

Which was probably why Skye's stomach was reacting

like she'd gone skydiving without a parachute. Maddie, who sat next to her in the back of the Suburban, picked up the phone. "It's Liz again. You should let her know you're here."

"Why? That'd just give her time to warn security to throw me out."

"Even if she did, they wouldn't recognize you. I didn't." Maddie unbuckled her seat belt and gave Skye a once-over. "I still can't believe you let Hailey and Holly give you a makeover after I warned you not to."

Skye touched her now poker-straight hair. "I thought they did a pretty good job." Twins Hailey and Holly owned the Rocky Mountain Diner. They were Christmas's self-appointed beauty experts and had arrived at Sophia's once word got out Skye wanted a makeover.

"If you were going for classy and conservative, they did. You look like a blonde version of Claudia."

"You hate it."

"No, you look gorgeous. It's just that you don't look like ... you."

Skye glanced at the cropped faux-leather camel jacket she wore over the camel dress paired with brown pleather boots. She didn't feel like herself. But that had been the whole point of the makeover. In the unlikely event that Jimmy the Knife tuned in to the Colorado news, Skye didn't want him to recognize her. Vivi hadn't been happy she planned to attend the debate, but had reluctantly agreed that it should be okay when Skye sent her a selfie.

Gage stopped in front of the entrance and turned, pointing a finger at Skye. "You behave in there."

"Why does everyone keep telling me that? I've been in Christmas for over four months, and I haven't done anything…" She probably should've stopped while she was ahead. There'd been that little incident back in June when she'd wound up in jail for breaking and entering, but the charges had been dropped. Besides, she'd been helping out Grace. "I'm here to support my husband. And whether you agree with me or not, he needs me. In the last two weeks, you can't open a paper or turn on the television without seeing Bob Bennett and his wife with their perfect little mini mes. They're promoting him as the responsible family man and Ethan as the too-gorgeous playboy. Me and Blossom are going to take care of that today," she said, patting her baby bump.

Gage frowned. "Who's Blossom?"

"My…our baby."

"Oh." He glanced at Madison. "How come you didn't name our baby?" She raised her brows. "Right," he said with a grin.

"Hey, are you making fun of me?"

"No, of course I'm not," Maddie said, but from the amused glint in her eyes, Skye knew she was. Maddie leaned forward and gave her father-in-law a gentle shake. She pulled out his earbud. "Dad, we're here."

Paul McBride scrubbed his hands over his face. "Sorry, long night." He shifted in his seat to look back at Skye. "You behave in there. I don't want your blood pressure going up."

"If one more person tells me to behave, it's going to go through the roof," Skye muttered, and went to open the door.

Gage's father narrowed his eyes at her. "I should probably check your pressure before we go in."

Okay, so maybe asking Dr. McBride to come along

hadn't been a good idea after all. Because Liz was being a royal pain in the butt, Skye had decided it was time to kick off her matchmaking plan and had encouraged Maddie to invite Paul. He'd just come off a midnight shift, but he had agreed once he found out both Skye and Maddie were going. The better to keep an eye on them, she supposed. But if her plan worked, it would be worth the aggravation.

"We're going to be late," she said, and was out the door before he pulled the cuff and stethoscope from his black bag. The three of them caught up to Skye as she entered the lobby.

"Don't be mad," Maddie said, catching her by the hand. "They're just trying to protect Ethan. And you have to admit, you haven't exactly been his biggest supporter."

"I know, but I really am trying to help him now."

"I can see that, and I'm wondering what's behind the change of heart. Anything you want to share with your best friend?"

"It's important to him."

"It is, but I think it's more than that." Maddie pulled Skye aside before they reached the ballroom's open doors and distractedly waved her husband and father-in-law on. "You're in love with him."

"What? No…" Skye trailed off as she remembered how she'd felt last night in his arms, how she'd felt waking up beside him this morning. And those warm, fuzzy feelings, the feeling of being cherished and protected, had nothing to do with how amazing he was in bed, how much he made her laugh, or how he wasn't the uptight conservative she'd once thought him to be. No, as she examined her emotions under the bright lights of the hotel's chandeliers, she had an uneasy feeling Maddie was right. She raised her panicked gaze to her best friend. "I can't be. I can't be in love with him."

"Of course you can. He's a great guy."

"I know he is. He's, well…he's pretty much perfect, and that's the problem. I'm not. It'd never work. For now, for him, I can pretend. But this"—she tugged on the cropped jacket—"this is who he should be married to. And I'm not that woman. I don't want to be. Look at my parents, Maddie. I don't want us to become them. I don't want him to end up hating me. And I don't want Blossom to grow up with parents who can't stand each other. It's horrible and scary, and I'd never do that to a child."

Maddie put her hands on Skye's shoulders. "Stop projecting. Ethan's not your father, and you're not your mother."

"But I am. My father's says I'm my mother reincarnated. And Ethan is—"

"Calm down. You look like you're having a panic attack."

"I think I am," she said, her chest so tight she could barely breathe.

"Focus on what you came here to do. This is all about Ethan and proving to these people that you support him. You can worry about everything else later."

"Right. You're right."

"You can do this. Are you ready?"

Skye put a hand on her stomach, taking a deep, calming breath. "Ready," she said with a decisive nod.

"Good." Maddie popped the ruffled collar of Skye's jacket. "There, now you look more like my best friend. It's just too bad you don't look pregnant."

"I do so," Skye said, holding the fabric of her dress tight across her stomach.

"Vivi's right—you look like you swallowed a golf ball. Come on, ten minutes until showtime." Maddie cast her a sidelong glance and started to laugh. "Are you pushing out your stomach?"

"Yeah. How many months do I look now?"

"Three."

"Ha-ha. You're so funny," Skye said as she entered the ballroom, taking in the packed room and the podiums at the front. Ethan and Bob Bennett had yet to take their places on the stage. They were shaking hands with their supporters at the front of the room. Claudia and Liz stood with Ethan. Bennett was joined by his wife and children and his campaign manager, Ted Vargas. Ted had been at Bennett's campaign office when Skye had signed on as a volunteer in August. Another reason for her makeover— she didn't want the man to recognize her.

With her shoulders back and her chin lifted, Skye walked down the red-carpeted aisle. She wasn't nervous. She'd had it drilled in her head how to behave at these events. For once she was happy for the training. Ethan, looking gorgeous in a navy suit that fit his tall, broad-shouldered frame to perfection, shook a curvy twenty-something's hand. The brunette appeared about to faint. Of course Ethan didn't realize the effect he had on the woman, but he did notice Maddie as they drew closer and flashed his movie-star smile. His gaze moved to Skye. He blinked, then simply stared at her. His mother nudged him to get his attention before following his gaze. Liz's jaw dropped and so did Claudia's.

Maddie mouthed *Good luck* to Ethan, then said "Knock 'em dead" to Skye before heading for the front row, where Gage had commandeered seats.

Skye held Ethan's gaze as she walked toward him, relief coursing through her at the warm, appreciative look in his eyes. "Surprised?" she asked when she reached his side.

A slow smile curved his lips as he leaned in to brush a light kiss across her temple. "What did you do with my wife?"

"Left her at home. You need Kendall tonight, not Skye."

Before he could respond, Bob Bennett, a short man with a florid complexion, approached. "I hope this pretty gal is your wife, O'Connor, or you're gonna be in a whole heap of trouble."

Ethan laughed and slid his arm around Skye's waist. "Bob, this is my wife…" Skye surreptitiously nudged him and mouthed *Kendall*. Ethan frowned but did as she directed. "My wife, Kendall."

"Nice to meet you, little lady," Bennett said. "We were all beginning to think you didn't exist."

And from the look on Bennett's face, he wasn't happy she did. "My husband's overly protective of me and the baby," Skye said with a thick Texas drawl. "It's a pleasure to meet you."

As she shook Bennett's hand, someone called out, "Mr. O'Connor, Mrs. O'Connor, look this way please." Word spread quickly that Skye was there and reporters shouted questions while photographers jockeyed for position. She cast an apprehensive glance at Ethan before answering a reporter's question about the baby. He didn't seem overly concerned, laughing when she shared how much the baby loved her daddy's voice. It seemed Liz had been talking about her and Claudia's fears, not Ethan's.

"All right, folks. We have to get this show on the road," Ted Vargas said a few minutes later, shooting Skye a disgruntled look as he ushered Bennett to the podium.

"I don't think your opponent is happy I'm here."

"Who cares? I'm glad you are," Ethan said, tucking her hair behind her ear.

"Really?" She got that warm, squishy feeling inside her again.

"Yeah. Really. Now go sit down and try not to get too worked up."

At least he didn't tell her to behave. "Okay. Good luck, Mr. Senator," she said, going up on her toes to kiss his cheek.

"Don't worry, honey. I'll make sure she behaves," his mother said, and patted his arm. "You can sit with me, Skye."

"Kendall," Skye quickly corrected, glancing to her right to be sure Ted Vargas wasn't within earshot. Thankfully, he was busy giving last-minute instructions to his candidate. Skye didn't relish the idea of sitting beside Ethan's mother all night, so when they reached the front row, she said, "Liz, you look a little pale. You're not having another dizzy spell, are you?"

Gage's dad, who sat two down from Maddie, stood up and gave Ethan's mother a concerned look. He took her by the arm. "Come sit with me, Liz. Don't argue. You don't want to upset Ethan, do you?"

Liz shot Skye a peeved look and plunked herself down. Feeling pleased with herself, Skye took the seat beside Maddie. "That was mean," her best friend said with a grin.

Skye laughed. "Yeah, I know."

* * *

As the debate drew to a close, Skye fanned herself with the program. "Is it just me or is it hot in here?"

"Since ninety-nine percent of the women in here are fanning themselves, and less than thirty percent of them are pregnant or going through menopause, I'd say it's the Ethan effect. Your husband is smoking hot, or hadn't you noticed?"

"Little hard not to." Skye had been attracted to Ethan from the moment she'd laid eyes on him, but tonight it was more than his extraordinary good looks that set her libido into overdrive. In her mind, there was nothing sexier than a confident, intelligent man. Ethan had it all, including that elusive *it* factor. He spoke eloquently and persuasively, a talent honed during his years in the courtroom. In comparison, Bennett came across as a bumbling fool.

Claudia looked like the cat that swallowed the canary. Ted Vargas looked like he was choking on one. There was no doubt in anyone's mind who'd won the debate. As they were about to open the floor to questions from the audience, Skye noticed Bennett's campaign manager pass a note to a man two rows behind him. Vargas lifted his chin in Skye's direction, a smug smile on his face.

"You do not want to go there with me, Vargas," she muttered under her breath as she quickly sent a text to Vivi. During the debate, Skye had been waiting for Bennett to attack Ethan's involvement with Albright Energy. When he didn't, she'd smelled a rat and texted Vivi to look into her suspicions.

"What are you muttering about?" Maddie asked.

"I think Vargas is going to use me...Hang on," she

said when her cell vibrated with an incoming text. She read the information Vivi had dug up on Bennett and smiled. She'd been right. As the moderator went to hand the mic to the curly-haired man Ted had passed the note to, Skye sent a text to Nell. Glancing to the end of the third row where Nell sat with Evelyn and Stella, Skye prayed the older woman had her cell on. She released the breath she'd been holding when Nell glanced down, then raised her gaze to Skye and gave her a thumbs-up.

"Brad Jones," the man introduced himself before saying, "I read that your wife is a Democrat. How does it feel to know she'll be voting for Mr. Bennett instead of you?"

"Dear Lord, you were right," Maddie murmured.

Skye's chest tightened in an anxious knot as she tried to ignore the furious glares from Claudia and Liz. She understood their anger. She didn't want to be the reason Ethan lost the ground he'd gained tonight.

But her husband seemed unfazed by the question when he responded, "I don't care who she votes for, as long as she does." Ethan then went on to talk about how hard people had worked and how much they had sacrificed to ensure that everyone has the right to vote. How lucky Americans are to live in a democratic society where they get to choose their representatives, and how it's their civic duty to exercise that right.

"Be that as it may, it's still gotta be tough to convince other people to vote for you when your own wife won't."

Skye stood up. There were several groans to her left, and she thought Ethan might've muttered, "Aw hell." She said, "Mr. Jones, I'm Kendall O'Connor, Ethan's wife. I don't know how the other women here feel, but when we won the right to vote, I think we also won the right to speak for ourselves." Feminine laughter erupted on both sides of the aisle, and a "Preach it, sister" came from the back of the room. "You have a couple misconceptions about me that need to be cleared up. First, I'm more an Independent than I am a Democrat. My husband occasionally calls me a bleeding-heart liberal, don't you, honey?" She smiled up at Ethan, who gave her a where-the-hell-are-you-going-with-this look.

Liz leaned across Gage to tug on Maddie's arm. "Stop her. Make her sit down," she said in a frantic whisper.

Maddie, of course, knew better than to try and shut Skye up.

"Second is your assumption that I'd vote for Mr. Bennett," Skye went on. "I understand how you'd come to that conclusion, given my political affiliations, but you're wrong. Even if I wasn't married to Ethan, after what I heard here today, I'd vote for him." Then she went on to tell them why. Vargas turned red, and Mr. Jones slowly sunk in his seat while Bennett tried to gain the moderator's attention.

"Thanks for letting me clear that up," Skye said with a smile to the audience and sat down. Applause broke out on both sides of the aisle. She wasn't sure if it was because she'd finally sat down or because they agreed with her. She was hoping for the latter.

Maddie leaned into her. "Now that, Mrs. O'Connor, sounded like a woman in love with her husband."

"A woman supporting her husband," she corrected as she sent a text to Nell, telling her to hold off on the question. Skye had handled Vargas's attempt to sabotage Ethan; no need to show all their cards just yet. And she didn't want to paint a bigger target on her back. If Vargas dug deep enough...

"Well, if the expression on your husband's face is anything to go by, he's head over heels in love with you."

Skye jerked her gaze from her phone to Ethan. He smiled, a look of pride in his eyes. No one had ever been proud of her before, and the thought that Ethan was sent a cascade of emotions through Skye: confusion, joy, desire, and... a hint of worry. Worry that maybe her best friend was right, and they were falling in love with each other. With her emotions jumbled up inside her, Skye barely registered the questions being asked or Ethan's and Bennett's responses.

"Earth to Skye," Maddie said, nudging her.

She looked up to see Bennett grudgingly shake Ethan's hand. Liz and Claudia converged on Ethan as his opponent left with his family and team. None of whom looked happy with the outcome. Ethan crooked his finger at Skye as he accepted his mother's and Claudia's congratulatory hugs. As she made her way toward him, she was stopped by a hand on her arm. Skye turned to see a stunning blonde accompanied by a silver-haired older man and a very handsome dark-haired man.

The woman smiled. "Hi, I'm Sam Reinhart, this is my father Jordan, and this is Adam Blackwell. I'm so glad you made it. I've been telling Ethan that he needed to bring you on the campaign trail with him."

Skye shook their hands and introduced them to Maddie. Ethan came up beside Skye and took her hand, warmly greeting the Reinharts and Adam Blackwell.

Sam reached up to kiss Ethan's cheek. "We've got to get going. We just wanted to congratulate you, and I wanted to rub it in that I was right. I was, wasn't I? Admit it, your wife is exactly what you needed to electrify your campaign. She was amazing."

"I admit it. You were right," he said, smiling at Skye as he brought her hand to his mouth. "She is amazing."

"We should get together next time you're in town, Skye. I'd love to get to know you better."

Given the way Ethan had just looked at her, and the feel of his thumb lightly drawing circles on her palm, it took a breathless moment for Skye to respond. "I'd like that, too."

"You've done it now, you know," Ethan said as the Reinharts and Adam left. "You're going to have come on the road with me."

Claudia, who'd just joined them said, "I don't think that's necessary, Ethan." When he raised a brow, she added, "I mean, she handled herself well tonight." Skye thought Claudia would qualify her faint praise by saying it was her own fault there was a situation in the first place. She didn't. Instead, she went for Ethan's Achilles' heel: "But it's tiring on the road, and it might not be good for either Kendall or the baby."

Liz interrupted the conversation she'd been having with Nell to give her opinion. "Claudia's right, Ethan. With Skye's blood pressure—"

"My blood pressure is fine," Skye interrupted her. She was tired of everyone acting as if she wasn't there. "I've been on the campaign trail before. It's not—"

"And we all know how well that turned out," Claudia murmured.

Skye wasn't even sure she wanted to campaign with Ethan. Of course she wanted to support him. She just didn't know if she could stand being Kendall O'Connor day in and day out. But she'd have to suck it up, because Claudia's comment just ensured that she would be by Ethan's side until election day.

"You should probably shake some hands," Skye said, gesturing at the crowd gathering in the aisle behind them.

"Skye's right, and we should get going," Gage said, clapping Ethan on the shoulder.

"Are you coming back with us?" Maddie asked Skye.

"I think I'll go home with Ethan."

"Ethan won't be able to bring you home, Kendall. I scheduled an interview for him first thing tomorrow morning. He's staying at the hotel tonight."

"Oh, I—" Skye began, barely managing a smile to hide her disappointment.

Ethan, who'd been saying good-bye to Paul, glanced at her. "Stay with me. If there's anything you need, tell Claudia, and she can pick it up for you."

Maddie hugged Skye, and whispered, "Careful—if looks could kill, you'd be dead."

Skye laughed, feeling ridiculously pleased that her husband wanted her with him. When Dr. McBride convinced Liz to go home with them, she was over the moon.

Once everyone from Christmas had left, Ethan took Skye's hand and introduced her to his supporters. Not long afterward he made their excuses, practically dragging her through the ballroom to the bank of elevators in the hall.

He impatiently stabbed at the button. "If they don't open soon, I'm going to have to kiss you right here."

She laughed. "You wouldn't."

"Yeah, I would," he said, tugging her into his arms.

"I've wanted to kiss you since you walked into that room tonight. And after your little speech, I wanted to do a whole lot more." The bell dinged, and the doors slid open. "Thank God," he said, walking her backward into the empty elevator.

Nudging her back against the wall, he framed her face with his hands and kissed her long and hard. Her knees went weak, and she wrapped her fingers around his wrists to keep from sliding to the floor.

He broke the kiss to look into her eyes. "Do you know how proud I was of you tonight? You are truly the most incredible woman I've ever met."

Touched, she kissed the underside of his jaw. "Everything I said was true. You can't turn me into a Republican, but I respect and admire you. You're a rare breed—an honest politician—and I love...I love your passion."

He held her gaze, a slow smile curving his lips. "And I love you, Kendall O'Connor," he said at the same time the elevator doors slid open.

Several people crowded in with them, saving her from responding. Her husband was in love with a woman who didn't exist. He was in love with Kendall, not Skye.

Chapter Seventeen

Ethan helped Gage carry the skeleton to the coffin lying open on the floor of his best friend's garage. "Careful you don't..." Gage began, sighing when the arm came off in Ethan's hand. Ethan managed to hold on to the arm and the head without dropping the skeleton and lowered it into the black silk-lined coffin.

"Dad's going to kill me," Gage said.

"I don't know why you had to use the real deal. What's wrong with plastic?"

"It's Annie's first Halloween party. She's never invited the kids from school over before, so we want to make it special."

"Gotcha. Get me some glue. On second thought, maybe cement will work better." He caught the doubtful look on Gage's face, and said, "Don't worry, your dad won't know the difference when I get done with this."

"Yeah, right. Remember Hippocrates?"

Ethan laughed at the memory. He and Gage had been wrestling in the McBrides' living room and had knocked the bust of Hippocrates from its pedestal, breaking his nose. "We were ten," he said. "Our orthopedic skills have improved."

Gage grinned. "We've had some good times together. I'm going to miss you, you know. You're not going to be around as much after the election."

"You're assuming I'm going to win," Ethan said, crouching beside the toolbox with Gage.

"Come on, you're way ahead in the polls. It'd take a miracle for Bennett to beat you now."

"Stranger things have been known to happen. But you're right, it's looking good."

"Never doubted it for a second. You've been working toward this since we were in sixth grade."

Ethan laughed. "Not quite that long."

"Okay, so maybe it was your dad. We didn't see you for two weeks when he was prepping you for that public speaking competition. I remember being mad at him for pushing you like he did, but I guess he knew what he was doing. You won state, and now you're going to win the state senate race." Gage handed him a tube of cement glue. "He'd be proud of you, Eth."

"Yeah, I know he would." But sometimes knowing wasn't enough. He wished his dad were here to celebrate with him. Wished the last call they had hadn't ended in anger and his dad dying.

"We're all proud of you. Sawyer's getting the Penalty Box set up for the big night. He's bringing in a couple more big screens. Has your signature drink ready for you, too. The Senator."

"What happened to the Prince Charming?"

"You won the princess." Gage grinned. "I gotta tell you, I didn't think you guys would work out. But I'm happy to be proven wrong."

"For a while there, I wasn't sure we would, either, but she's done a complete one eighty. She deserves as much credit as anyone for our surge in the polls."

"Sounds like you're in love, buddy."

"I am." He fingered the ring box in his jacket pocket. He'd been carrying it around with him for the last week. "How do you feel about being my best man?"

"I kinda was, remember?"

"I know, but that wasn't real. I want to do it right this time."

"When were you thinking?"

"I thought I'd propose to her on the night of the election. She'll probably want to have the wedding before the baby arrives. Maybe sometime around Christmas."

"Sounds good. If your baby is as reluctant to enter the world as ours, that'll give you plenty of time."

"How's she holding up?" Ethan asked. Madison was two weeks overdue. He hadn't seen her or the girls yet. Gage had roped him into helping turn the garage into a haunted house as soon as they pulled into the driveway.

"Let's just say I'm glad Skye's here to distract her. She was always good at making Madison laugh." He frowned at Ethan. "What's up?"

"Kendall. She goes by Kendall now."

"How come?"

"I'm not sure. Ever since the night of the debate, she's insisted everyone call her Kendall." He rimmed the socket with glue, pressing the ball into place. "She's different, too. More serious." And God help him, but there were times when he missed his gorgeous fruitcake. Missed her wild hair and the way she drove him crazy.

"Her hair's different and the way she dresses, but she can't have changed that much."

"Spend some time with her and you'll see."

"You don't sound happy about it."

He sat back on his heels. "Don't get me wrong, I love her. I think I have from the first day I met her. But sometimes I feel like I don't know her anymore. She's like... well, she's like Claudia."

"So what you're saying is she's turned into the perfect politician's wife."

"Yeah. And she is. I'm not kidding when I say she's the reason for the uptick in support. People love her. She can talk to anyone. Probably helps that she speaks five languages. But I think people can tell she's genuinely interested in their lives and wants to make a difference."

"None of that sounds bad to me."

"It isn't. It's just that I worry she's so consumed with being the woman she thinks I need that she's losing a part of herself." The fun part, the happy, easygoing, crazy, off-the-wall woman he'd fallen in love with.

"She's probably just tired. She's pregnant, and it can't be easy being on the road. And don't take this the wrong way, but it can't be easy for her to be around Liz and Claudia twenty-four seven. They're not exactly her biggest fans."

"She and Mom are doing better. Claudia's another story, but at least they're civil to each other. You're right, though—she's tired. We both are. I'm glad the campaign's winding down, and we can afford to take a few days off. We're going to get started on the baby's room." Maybe that was all it was. Maybe he was overreacting. No one else had commented on the changes. It was probably his imagination.

"Madison isn't herself, either, you know. Gotta be tough on them. All that hormonal crap."

Ethan laughed. It was good to be around Gage. He had a way of putting things in perspective. He'd miss his best friend if he won the election. "You know, buddy, I think it'd be safer for us not to talk about mood swings and hormones around them. They might take it the wrong way."

"Good idea. I made the mistake of asking Madison if she'd given any more thought to having a natural delivery. Dr. Evans asked her to consider it at her last appointment. I nearly got my head taken off for suggesting it."

"Hope she doesn't mention it to Kendall. She's all for a natural delivery. She picked up one of those birthing balls the other day." And now that he thought about their shopping expedition, which had included a stop at a natural health store and an eco-friendly store, he realized he'd been worrying for nothing. She was still the same woman he'd fallen in love with. He tugged on the skeleton's arm. When it didn't fall off, he said, "Maybe we should go check on our wives. I'll tell Kendall to keep her opinion on natural childbirth to herself."

"Sounds like a plan. I'm starving, anyway. Let's put this out front." Gage lifted one end of the coffin and Ethan took the other. They carried it outside. Lily and Annie were setting their pumpkins on the front steps as Ethan and Gage lowered the coffin and propped it against the front of the garage. Ethan was about to say hello when he heard Lily say, "I think the Evil Queen stole Auntie Skye's magic. She's not fun anymore."

"Nah," Annie said, "Uncle Ethan turned her into a Republican."

*   *   *

"You sure you don't want to get dressed up, sweetheart? I bet you'd still fit in your Cake Fairy costume," Ethan said as Skye buttoned Lily's hooded black cloak.

"I need my book and wand," Lily said, and took off for her room. She was going as Hermione Granger from the Harry Potter books.

Skye accepted Ethan's hand and came to her feet. "What's going on? This is the third time you asked me that. We have less than a week until election day. Do you really want a picture of your wife dressed up as a fairy princess on the front page of the paper?"

"What I want is for you to stop worrying about reporters and have fun. Do whatever makes you happy."

"What's gotten into you today?" He'd been acting weird since he'd come in with Gage earlier.

"Nothing." He drew her into his arms, resting his forehead against hers. "I just want you to enjoy yourself. You've been working hard these last few weeks."

"So have you. And I am having fun." She gave him a reassuring smile and patted his chest. "We're going to take Lily trick-or-treating, and then we'll be back to help with the party. Did you and Gage finish the haunted house?"

"Yeah, wanna come check it out?" He waggled his brows. "I can tie you up."

"Seriously, I don't know what's up with you today." She placed her palm on his forehead. "Do you have a fever?"

"Yeah, I'm hot, for you. We'll help out at the party for an hour, and then I'm taking you home."

"It'll be nice to be in our own bed for a change."

"Don't count on sleeping." He gave her a long, passionate kiss, moving away at the sound of Maddie and Lily heading their way.

"You have a guilty look on your face, Ethan O'Connor. Are you trying to seduce your wife again?" Maddie teased.

"Yeah, and I'm not having much luck."

"Ah—little ears," Skye said, nodding at Lily.

"What did you do with my best friend?" Maddie asked. "She's no fun anymore."

"Oh, please, don't tell him that." Skye looked at Ethan, who was frowning. "I'm having fun, okay? Let's go, you two," she said, ushering Lily and Maddie out the door.

"It's true, and you know it. You used to love Halloween as much as Lily. You always dressed up."

"I'm twenty-eight and pregnant and married to a man running for the state senate."

Maddie helped Lily into the Suburban. As she closed the door, her gaze searched Skye's face. "I'm your best friend. I know when something's wrong. What aren't you telling me?"

"Nothing's wrong," she said, forcing a smile.

"We are not moving from here until you tell me."

"It's the election. I'm just tired. Tired of being Kendall," she finally admitted. "It's so hard, and now that there's no doubt Ethan's going to win, I have to pretend to be someone I'm not for four years. Four years is a long time. Don't get me wrong, I'm happy he's going to win. No one deserves to become state senator more than he does. He'll be amazing. He truly wants to make a difference, and even though I don't always agree with him on the issues..."

"Take a breath and slow down. You don't have to sell me on how wonderful Ethan is. I know that. But what I don't understand is why you think you have to be Kendall. I love you just the way you are and so does Ethan. He married *you*, not Kendall."

"He married me because I was pregnant. But Kendall, she's the woman he needs by his side. And Maddie, Ethan said he loves Kendall, not me. He…he doesn't even call me cupcake anymore."

"Anyone with eyes in their head can see that you two are crazy about each other." Lily honked the horn, and Maddie went to open the driver's-side door. "Don't let this come between you. Talk to Ethan, sugar. He's worried about you, and so am I."

Maddie didn't understand, Skye thought, as she got in the Suburban. How could she? Maddie hadn't grown up with Skye's parents. She didn't think she could bear it if Ethan looked at her the way her father had looked at her mother. She loved Ethan too much to hurt his chances, to watch as his pride in her turned to disappointment and frustration. Maybe over time, she'd get used to being Kendall. It was about time she grew up. And there were parts of her new persona she liked. Not the hair or the clothes or watching every word that came out of her mouth or keeping her opinions to herself when they attended a dinner party with a bunch of muckety-mucks who were destroying the environment…Okay, so about the only thing she liked about being Kendall was that her husband loved her. Seeing the admiration and pride in his eyes made the sacrifice worthwhile.

"Let it go," Skye said to Maddie as she buckled her seat belt.

"Okay, we'll talk about something else. How's the blog doing?"

She rolled her eyes and turned to Lily. "How's school going, sweetie?"

"Good try. She's listening to her iPod. What don't you want to tell me?"

"My followers are starting to drop off, and I lost two contracts last week." She held up a hand. "Once the election is over, I'll go back to posting what I want, and the numbers will improve, and the advertisers will be back on board."

"For your sake, I hope that's the case, Skye. It doesn't matter that Ethan's wealthy. You need to be financially independent. It's important."

"I am. You know how well I'm doing. You're looking after my investment portfolio."

"True. But if your blog tanks, then what are you going to do?"

"It won't."

"I hope not," Maddie said, turning onto Nell's street. "There's Grace and little Jack." She motioned to Lily to take out her earphones. "Look, sweetie, little Jack's Superman."

"Can we go trick-or-treating with them?" Lily asked as they pulled into Nell's driveway.

"Sure, we…" Maddie sighed. Lily was already halfway to Nell's door.

They both started to laugh when Nell answered wearing a Mrs. Claus costume. "The woman is Christmas obsessed," Skye said as she got out of the SUV. "Look at her front lawn." Nell had piled three pumpkins one on top of each other to make a snowman, using sticks for arms with a Santa's hat on its head.

She frowned when Maddie didn't move. Skye rounded the SUV to help her out. "Why are..." She trailed off, looking from the wet spot on Maddie's jeans to her best friend's panic-stricken face.

*   *   *

Skye sat beside Ethan in the hospital waiting room filled to capacity with McBride family and friends. "I don't know why she kicked me out of the room," Skye grumbled to Ethan. "All I did was tell her that a natural birth is the best thing for the baby. I even offered to get my ball for her."

Ethan put an arm around her, and kissed the top of her head. "Sorry, sweetheart, I forgot to warn you. She got ticked at Gage, too, so don't feel bad."

"Maybe I should try again. Help her with her breathing."

"How about you just stay with me for a while? Do you want something to drink?"

"No, I'm good, thanks," she said, looking up when Gage entered the waiting room. "How is she?"

He rubbed the back of his neck. "I think we're in for a long night. Nell, would you mind taking the girls home?" He exhaled deeply when his aunt shook her head. Skye wasn't surprised she wouldn't leave. Nell loved Maddie like a daughter.

Liz stood up. "I'll take the girls home and stay with them, Gage. Don't worry," she quieted Annie's and Lily's protests. "Your dad will call as soon as your brother or sister gets here, and we'll come right back."

Paul came into the room, took in the situation, and said, "I'll go home with Liz and the girls."

"Perfect," Skye whispered as Paul left with Liz, Annie,

and Lily. "They'll have the whole night together." She frowned when Ethan didn't respond, then heard what he obviously had. A woman who sounded a lot like Maddie, yelling for drugs and moaning in pain. The color drained from Ethan's face. "Are you okay?" she asked him.

"No. That's going to be you in a couple months." He put his hand on her stomach and met her gaze. "I don't think I'll be able to do it, listening to you scream like that. Maybe you should reconsider the drugs."

"You're sweet to worry about me, but I'll be fine."

"You don't know that." He winced, his hand tightening on her stomach when a woman, not Maddie, started cursing at her husband for getting her pregnant. "Okay, I'll take the drugs instead," Ethan said.

"You're going to be a fainter, aren't you?" she said, unable to keep the laughter from her voice.

"I don't know how you can laugh. This isn't funny. They sound like they're dying in there."

"You'll feel better once we go to the birthing classes. We're scheduled—"

"I'm not going. Gage told about the film they showed, and—"

"You're going. It's not you who has to push a—"

He covered her mouth with his hand. "I do not need that visual in my head."

She kissed his palm, then removed his hand. "How about visualizing holding your daughter in your arms for the first time."

He leaned into her. "For now, I think I'm going to visualize her mother naked in my arms." His cell pinged. He glanced at his screen and stood up. "I've gotta take this. I'll be back in a minute."

Five minutes later, he returned to the waiting room. "I have to leave."

Skye lowered the magazine she'd been reading to search his face. A muscle ticked in his jaw, and he avoided meeting her gaze. "Ethan, what is it?"

"Nothing. I'll take care of it."

"But where are you going? What about Maddie and Gage?"

"Look, it can't be helped. I'm meeting with the team at Mom's. Claudia's on her way to pick me up." He reached in his pocket and handed her his keys.

"Ethan, tell me—"

"I've gotta go."

Without saying good-bye, without kissing her, without looking at her, he strode from the waiting room. A sense of impending doom came over Skye. Something was terribly, terribly wrong.

Chapter Eighteen

Skye lay beside Maddie on the narrow hospital bed with baby McBride swaddled between them. She angled her cell phone. "Better?" she asked Vivi, whom they'd called on FaceTime.

"He's adorable. He has his daddy's dimple," Vivi said with a watery smile. "I wish I was there." She tilted her head. "Did you break out the bubbly to celebrate? 'Cause you're looking a little loopy, mommy Maddie."

"It's the drugs," Skye said.

"You wait until it's your turn, Miss Crunchy Granola. You'll be screaming for drugs," Maddie said, slurring the words.

They talked for another few minutes, then Vivi had to take another call. "I might be a little punchy, but something seemed off with Vivi," Maddie said as soon as they'd disconnected. "And what was with the look she gave you when she said 'Call me'? Are you two holding out on me again?"

Apparently Maddie wasn't as punchy as she seemed. "No, of course we're not." Skye ignored the frisson of nerves dancing around inside her. First Ethan and now Vivi. She really hoped she'd misread the concern in Vivi's eyes. Skye had enough to worry about. Ethan had yet to respond to her text announcing the baby's arrival. He was probably on his way, she told herself. Nothing would keep him from the birth of his best friend's baby. But obviously something had.

Maybe it was a guy thing. And the unscheduled meeting of his team? That wasn't a big deal, either. Not when she considered Claudia's tendency to overreact to the most minor of hiccups. Understandably they were all on edge with the election less than a week away. All that made sense and helped Skye get her rising panic under control. "He is, without a doubt, the most beautiful baby ever," she announced, kissing the baby's head.

"He *is* pretty adorable, isn't he?" Maddie beamed, gazing down at her son. She raised her eyes to Skye and reached for her. "I'm so glad you were here to share this with me."

Skye returned Maddie's hug with a grin. "I am, too. But you weren't so happy with me a few hours ago when you told me what I could do with my birthing ball."

Maddie chuckled. "I can't believe I said that to you." They both looked up when Gage entered the room with Lily and Annie. Nell followed behind with her white hair standing on end. "You were supposed to wake me up," she grumped at Skye.

"I tried," Skye said, getting off the bed. She kissed the baby one last time before his sisters took her place. She hugged them both. "I'll let you guys get acquainted. I'll see you tomorrow. Congratulations, Daddy," she said to Gage. "Let me know if you need anything."

He put his arm around her shoulders. "Thanks for being here. You be careful driving home. It's snowing. And tell my best friend if I don't hear from him soon, I'll be ticked."

"I will." She smiled at Gage's dad when he walked in, expecting to see Ethan's mother with him. "Where's Liz?"

"She headed home a few hours ago. Something about..." He trailed off, grimaced, and patted her shoulder. "I'm sure it'll be fine, honey."

"What... what'll be fine?" she said, but he was already moving toward the bed with Gage, joining his family to coo over the new arrival. Desperate to know what he meant, Skye stood awkwardly by the door. She couldn't do it, couldn't upset this joyous occasion, because now she was nearly frantic with worry.

By the time she'd brushed the snow from the Escalade, Skye was chilled to the bone. And it wasn't only the damp night air that caused the goose bumps to break out over her skin. She'd tried to phone Ethan, and her call went straight to voice mail. She left him a message, unable to keep the fear from leaking into her voice.

She got in and cranked the heat. While she waited for the Escalade to warm up, she called Vivi. "I didn't wake you, did I?" she asked when her best friend answered, her voice more raspy than usual. Actually, it sounded as if she'd been crying. Which made sense, given that she wasn't with them tonight. Skye decided not to mention it. Vivi didn't like anyone, not even her best friends, to think she was anything other than tough as nails.

"No. I'm trying to get one person, just one fricking person, from the NYPD to take my calls. I'm going to kill him."

"Who are you going to kill?"

"Superman. He's shut me down, cut me off from all my contacts. My sources dried up overnight. And you know why he did this to me?"

Skye had a feeling she was going to find out the answer. She felt bad for Vivi, but she had to admit she was relieved the look she'd seen in her friend's eyes had nothing to do with her.

"I'll tell you why. He's a narcissistic, arrogant, self-absorbed, psychotic control freak!"

"Sweetie, calm down and tell me what happened," Skye said as she pulled out of the hospital parking lot.

"Five days ago someone broke into my apartment and tore the place apart. I'm sure it was that slimeball Jimmy. He left me a threatening note. I was so close, Skye, so close to nailing the guy, and he knew it. Gina's back in town. She agreed to talk to me. Now I can't get to her. The cops have her in protective custody, and Jimmy's gone to ground. Gina's uncle made sure he has no one to turn to. His pals have cut him off. He's desperate."

With the wind whipping up the snow and her best friend whipping up her fear, Skye pulled to the side of the road. "Vivi, Superman is right. Let the police do their job. What if you'd been at home? I'd never forgive myself if something happened to you."

"Nothing is going to happen to me, or you."

"You think he knows where I am?"

"I don't . . . yeah, it's possible. But he'll go after Gina first. She can connect him to those girls."

"So can you. You're not safe, Vivi. Come here, come to Christmas."

"Don't worry about me. Dickhead might have cut off

all my contacts, but he's got a bunch of no-necks tailing me."

Skye breathed a little easier upon hearing the news. "Don't you dare try to lose those guys. I mean it."

"I promise . . . Thank God. I've gotta go. I'll talk to you tomorrow. And for now, stay alert. I think you're safe, but it's better to be extra careful."

*   *   *

When Skye finally drove through the ranch's wrought-iron gates, every muscle in her body ached from the tension. Lights blazed in the windows of the main house, several vehicles lining the driveway. Skye turned onto the road to the guest house. Not surprisingly, it was dark. She sat for a moment, wondering what to do. Until she found out what was going on, she wouldn't sleep, no matter how exhausted she was.

Wrapping her arms around herself to ward off the cold, she trudged along the moonlit path to Liz's. The wind whistled through the bare branches while tiny whirlwinds of glistening snow danced across the lawn. Through the dining room window, she could see Ethan sitting at the table with his team.

Whatever this was about, she wanted him to tell her the news in private. She didn't want his mother and Claudia or the rest of the team there. With that in mind, Skye entered through the side door to the mudroom.

She reached the doorway into the kitchen, about to text Ethan and let him know she was there and needed to speak to him. Peeking around the corner, she caught a glimpse of Claudia. Her back was to Skye as she tossed what looked to be photos onto the table.

"We've looked at this from every angle, Ethan. You have to face facts. There's no way we can explain these to the press. I told you this was going to happen. She's ruined your chances. No one will vote for you now." Picking up a photo, she waved it at him. "Your wife worked as an escort. And I don't care if the guy says he won't go to the press if you pay him. Even if he's telling the truth, we have to assume it'll still get out."

Skye gasped, reaching for the doorjamb as her knees went weak. Jimmy. She muffled a sob with her hand when Claudia continued, "She went through millions of dollars, they've got her signature on Bennett's supporters list, they've got pictures of her smoking up, sunbathing nude, in handcuffs being hauled off to jail more times than I can count, protesting the war, and you think, you think somehow you can just explain this all away? That silly, spoiled, self-centered slut ruined your—"

"Enough, Claudia." Ethan slammed his palms on the table, half-rising from his chair. "I won't hear another word against—"

"How can you defend her? Look at what she's done." Liz shoved the photos at Ethan, several fluttering to the hardwood floor. "She's—"

Ethan sat down, spearing his fingers through his hair. "Don't, Mom. Don't say—"

Claudia cut him off. "You can't let her ruin everything. We'll put out the truth, that you married her for the baby's sake. We'll just speed up the time line. Instead of divorcing her a year from now, you can file first thing in the morning."

Skye staggered blindly to the door and let herself out. She'd ruined him. She'd destroyed his chances. Everything she'd done, all the sacrifices she'd made, were for nothing. Her past had come back to haunt her and take Ethan down. None of them cared about the changes she'd made in her life. It wouldn't matter to any of them. All they could see were those photos of her.

Stumbling along the path, she ran to the guest house. In her heart she knew Ethan wouldn't take Claudia's advice. Even if he did, because Skye was pregnant, it might backfire on him. Some of the gains he'd made in the last few weeks were due to her efforts.

The only way for Skye to save Ethan was for her to leave him. Put so much distance between them—make herself out to be the spoiled, self-centered nutcase they all thought her to be—so that he would gain the sympathy vote. And why did she leave? they'd want to know. Because she was a bleeding-heart liberal, an antigun lobbyist, a gay rights proponent, and an environmental activist who couldn't pretend to be someone she wasn't.

Her hand shook as she unlocked the guest house door. On the way to the bedroom, she tugged off her high-heeled boots and stripped off her clothes. She then pulled on a pair of jeans and a sweater. She didn't pack anything Ethan had given her. Closing the small suitcase on her meager belongings, she sat on the side of the bed and wrote Ethan a letter.

By the time she was finished, tears were streaming down her face. She loved him with all her heart, but if she told him that, he'd come after her. And if he lost the election because of her, she'd never forgive herself, and neither would he. Her swollen finger made it difficult for her to remove her wedding ring. When she'd finally gotten it off, she placed the gold band on top of the note and took one last look around the room. His gray Strum College sweatshirt hung on the doorknob. She picked it up, breathing him in one last time. Unzipping the front pouch of her suitcase, she stuffed his sweatshirt inside.

"I'm so sorry, baby. I've ruined everything," she whispered to her unborn child as she walked out the front door. Setting the suitcase down beside the Escalade, she went to open the door and realized there was one more thing she had to do. She had to say good-bye to Bandit. Skye made her way to the stables. Bandit nickered when she reached his stall. He came over and nuzzled her neck. She buried her face in his mane. "You be good, boy. Don't give them any reason to put you down." She shuddered with a sob as she patted him one last time before she left.

Lights still blazed from the main house as Ethan and his team tried to figure out how to clean up the mess that was Skylar Davis. She wondered why she was surprised that it had ended this way. The apple didn't fall far from the tree. But unlike her mother, Skye wasn't waiting for her husband to kick her to the curb. She shoved the suitcase across the front seat, climbed into the Escalade, and drove away. The main house faded from view in the rearview mirror.

When Skye reached Christmas, she parked Ethan's Escalade outside the sheriff's department and called a cab. When the cabbie pulled in beside her, she got out of the Escalade and locked the door. She'd found a piece of paper in the glove compartment, wrote Ethan's name on the front, and folded it around the keys, stuffing it in the mail slot in the door to the sheriff's department. Bowing her head, tears splashed onto the snow-covered sidewalk as she thought of Maddie, the baby, Lily and Annie, of

Grace, and Nell . . . Choking back a sob, she climbed in the back of the taxi.

"You okay, ma'am?" the driver asked, his bald head shining under the dome light.

She didn't think she'd ever be okay again. "I'm fine, thank you. I need to go to the Denver airport."

The man released a low whistle. "You sure you don't have someone, family or friends, that'd take you? Fare's going to be a couple hundred dollars."

She checked her knapsack for the prepaid Visa card that Maddie had insisted she buy. "That's okay. I don't have anyone." As the words came out of her mouth, the baby kicked her, hard. Skye startled, realizing what she'd said. She wiped her eyes and gently patted her stomach. "You're right, baby. I have you."

As they left the lights of Christmas far behind, Skye called Vivi. It took a while for her to get the story out. Despite her best efforts not to cry, she did.

"Are you sure? Are you sure you want to do this, sweetie?" Vivi asked.

"I have to. Make me out to be the bad guy, Vivi. Make me out to be so bad that people feel sorry for him. He's going to need the sympathy vote. He can't lose this election because of me. It's his dream, his and his father's. I can't be the one to ruin that for him. And release the information about Bennett's wife's ties to Albright Energy. Ethan's going to need all the help he can get after what—"

"All right, take a deep breath. You're going to get through this. I'll put the blog entry out first thing in the morning. After that, I'm going to hunt down Jimmy the Knife."

"No, don't. Please, Vivi, I can't worry about you, too. I just can't."

"Okay, don't cry. God, I hate this. I hate that you're all alone. I wish you could come here, but I don't think that's a good idea with Jimmy still on the loose."

She needed somewhere safe, somewhere . . .

"I'm going home."

*   *   *

Eight hours later, another taxi deposited Skye in front of the pink stucco mansion. She stumbled up the steps to the double mahogany doors, dragging her suitcase behind her. She barely had the strength to lift her hand to knock.

"I've got it, Willy," a loud feminine voice called before the door flew open, revealing a voluptuous blonde with mile-high hair in full makeup. The older woman, wearing a blinding yellow robe with matching mules, stared at Skye. "Well tie me to the side of a hog and roll me in the mud, it's you. Willy!" She hauled a stunned Skye into the marble entryway. "Your baby's come home," she bellowed at the same time she smothered Skye in a lemon-scented hug.

"Betty Jean darlin', what are you . . . Kendall." Her father stood at the top of the spiral staircase in a paisley smoking jacket staring down at her. His gaze moved from Skye to the older woman, and he cleared his throat. "This is a . . . surprise," he said slowly, coming down the stairs.

Betty Jean put her hands on her hips. "Now is that any way to greet your little girl?" She turned to Skye with a wide, welcoming smile. "I'm Betty Jean, hon, your daddy's fiancée."

"Fiancée?" Skye croaked. She looked at her father as he walked toward her. "You didn't tell me you were getting remarried."

"Don't get in a huff now. It's not like we had a lot of time to talk what with you breaking my ribs and your own shotgun wedding."

"You're pregnant, too?" Skye said to Betty Jean.

That set the woman off in peals of laughter. Once she got hold of herself, she said, "Just because a chicken has wings doesn't mean it can fly. I look good for my age, hon, but my eggs shriveled up a ways back."

Skye looked from Betty Jean to her father. Something wasn't right. She felt like she'd fallen into the rabbit hole. There was no way her uptight, conservative father would be in love with…And then she saw the twinkle in his eyes, the smile that spread across his face as he looked at Betty Jean. William Davis was head over heels in love with the woman. "I think I need to sit down," Skye said.

"Oh, you poor thing. Come on, I'll fix you up some breakfast. How about some French toast?"

"Thank you, that's very kind of you, but a cup of tea would be fine."

Her father followed them into the kitchen. "You'll like Betty Jean's French toast."

"But, Daddy, I—" she began, glancing at him over her shoulder.

He cleared his throat, looking a little sheepish. "Betty Jean's a vegan."

A disbelieving laugh escaped from Skye. "And next you'll be telling me she's a bleeding-heart liberal."

"Damn straight I am." Betty Jean grinned. "And we get in some good ones over that." She winked at Skye. "But we have a rip-roarin' time making up, don't we, Willy?"

Skye slowly lowered herself to the chair. "I don't—"

Her father cut her off. "All right now, I want to know what you're doing here."

"Willy!"

"I know my girl, Betty Jean. Something bad had to have happened to send her running home. She hasn't been back since she left ten years ago."

Betty Jean set the soy milk on the counter and came to Skye's side. She pulled out a chair, taking Skye's hand in hers. "You tell Betty Jean all about it, hon."

The warmth in the woman's kind eyes did Skye in, and she blubbered out her sorry tale.

"Oh my sweet girl," Betty Jean said, pressing Skye's face to her voluptuous chest and patting her back.

"You did the right thing leaving the boy. He has a bright future," her father said, pushing away from the table. "I'll make some calls. See if I can't smooth things over from my end."

Skye lifted her head. "Daddy, I don't want Ethan to know where I am. I can't...I can't talk to him right now."

For the first time she could remember, her father agreed with her.

Chapter Nineteen

Ethan rolled over and grabbed his ringing phone from the nightstand. He scrubbed his hand over his face when he noticed the time. It was past ten. The gnawing ache in his gut returned at the thought of what he had to deal with today. They hadn't reached a consensus on how to handle the publicity nightmare until four this morning.

"What the hell's going on?" Gage said, as soon as Ethan answered his phone.

"Hey. Sorry, buddy. All hell broke loose here last night. How's the baby and Madison?" He knew he should've called after receiving Kendall's text announcing the arrival of Gage and Madison's son. At the very least, he should've responded to that last message she'd left. The muscles in his stomach knotted as he remembered the tremor he'd heard in her voice. But he'd been reeling with shock and anger at the shit show she'd delivered to his door five goddamn days before the election.

He figured his lack of response was the reason she'd stayed at the hospital last night. Probably for the best that she had. He still didn't know what to say to her. If he lost the election because of this...he'd have only himself to blame. He'd ignored everyone's advice. Hell, he'd known from the start what he was getting into. He just hadn't thought it would be this bad.

"They're fine. Great. But that's not what I'm talking about. I stopped by the station and your keys had been put in the mail slot. Your Escalade's out front. It looks like whoever parked it was drunk. Someone must have taken it for a joyride—"

"How'd they get the keys? Never mind." He glanced at his watch, raking a hand through his hair. Sooner or later, he'd have to confront Kendall. He wanted to know how she got mixed up with the guy who was blackmailing him. There was no way she'd worked as an escort, but he needed answers so he'd know how to deal with the low-life. Given the timing of her signing up for Bennett's campaign, he had a fairly good idea why she'd done it. As for everything else...that was what he got for marrying an environmental activist. "I'm going to be tied up for a few hours. Any way you or your dad could drop off Kendall? She probably wants to come home and grab—"

"What are you talking about? She left the hospital around eleven last night. She was headed for home."

He shot out of bed, calling her name as he ran from room to room. "Jesus, Gage, she's not here."

"Calm down. Stay on the line with me. I'm going to check the Escalade for any signs she was taken against her will."

"She sounded scared. The last call she made, she

sounded scared." And he hadn't picked up. If anything had happened to her, to her and the baby...He slammed his fist into the bedroom wall.

"When was the last time you spoke to her?"

The sound of the wind came over the line, the opening and closing of a car door. "I haven't talked to her since I left the hospital at six." Before his best friend asked, Ethan explained why. It was when he told Gage about the blackmail attempt that panic got a stranglehold on him, tightening his chest so that he could barely get the words out. "You don't think he'd come after her, do you?"

"I've checked the Escalade. There's no sign of a struggle. I'm on my way to you now. I want to see everything you've got."

Ethan went to grab his jeans from where he'd dropped them on the floor, spotting his grandmother's wedding band on a piece of folded paper. "Hang on," he said, his voice a rough rasp. Sitting on the edge of the bed, he read her good-bye note. "She left me."

"I don't think I heard you right. Speak up."

"She's gone. She left me."

"Any sign she wrote the note against her will? Does it look like her handwriting? Is it legible?" Gage asked, the sound of a vehicle turning over in the background.

He studied the delicate sloping lines. "She wrote it, and it doesn't appear she was under duress." As he read Gage the letter, each word burned into his brain.

"It doesn't make sense. She's in love with you. Any chance at all that she heard about Bennett's smear campaign?"

"None whatsoever. And while she might be in love with me, she hated every minute of her life with me. It's obvious from what she wrote. I knew she wasn't happy, Gage. No one else saw it, but I did."

"Call Skye. We need to rule out foul play. I'll be there in ten."

Ethan disconnected and stood to get dressed. He felt like punching the wall again as his earlier fears were replaced with anger. She had to know what her letter would do to him. Had to know it would tear him apart. She'd destroyed him with the simple stroke of a pen. You don't leave someone a note when you're going to rip out their heart. You deal with your problems like adults. Talk it out. But no, she . . .

"Ethan. Oh . . ." Claudia stared at him from the doorway to his bedroom, her eyes wide, her cheeks flushed.

He grabbed the sheets from his bed to cover himself. "God damn it, Claudia. What the hell are you doing here?"

With her gaze fixated on his crotch, she moved her mouth, but no sound came out.

"Ethan, did—" his mother began as she came up behind Claudia. "We'll let you get dressed." She closed the door, then spoke from behind it. "I don't know how to tell you this, darling, but Kendall left you. I realize you think you're in love with her, but after everything you saw and heard last night, even you have to admit it's for the best."

He threw the door open as he pulled on a shirt. "How do you know she left me? If either of you had anything to do with this, I swear to God, I'll—"

His mother's eyes widened. "No, of course, we didn't."

Claudia handed him her cell phone. "She released a statement on her blog. I can see you're upset about this, Ethan, but—"

"You think I'm *upset*? My wife, a woman I adore, a

woman who is carrying my child, left me, Claudia, so 'upset' doesn't begin to cover what I'm feeling right now." He pointed a finger at his mother. "And don't patronize me by insinuating that I don't know how I feel about Kendall. I have never loved any other woman like I love her."

His mother's eyes filled, and she touched his arm. "I'm sorry, darling."

He nodded as he scanned the statement on Claudia's phone.

"You probably don't want to hear this right now, Ethan, but you can't afford to be distracted. You have an election to win. Kendall's post appeared within half an hour of Bennett's team releasing the photos. It's still too early to gauge voter reaction but, so far, none of your major supporters have pulled out."

"Keep me informed. I have to try and get ahold of someone who can tell me that Kendall and the baby are okay."

"Ethan, what *are* you going to do about the baby?"

"Right this minute, Mom, I have no idea. I have no idea what I'm going to do about anything." That may have been how he was feeling, but he also knew he owed it to everyone—his team, his supporters, and most especially his dad—to get his head back in the game.

Gage walked into the house. "Madison called Vivi. Skye's with her dad in Texas. She and the baby are fine. My wife says to tell you to fix this or else."

"Tell Madison I'm going to give it my best shot." He was torn between wanting to give his wife time to think about how good they'd been together and wanting to clear this up before it went on too long. He glanced at his watch. "I'll head for Texas now."

"No, you can't go, Ethan. I've lined up interviews for

the next few days to deal with the fallout." Claudia cast him a desperate look. "This was what I meant when I said she's spoiled and self-absorbed. She knows there's no way you can leave here with the election only days away, but she expects you to chase after her. This is a ploy to get your attention. Can't she just pick up a phone like a normal person? No, of course she can't. Instead she has to create a major drama. It's ridiculous. She's ridiculous."

"Claudia, I'm not going to warn you again. I've had it with you slamming her. You realize you're part of the reason she left, don't you?"

She threw up her hands. "That's right, Ethan, blame me. Me, who has worked twenty-four seven to get you elected. Just toss it all away on a spoiled little rich girl throwing a temper tantrum because everything doesn't go her way. If you go after her, I'm done."

"No, Claudia, wait," his mother called out as the other woman stormed through the front door. "Ethan, go after her." When he didn't immediately do as Liz said, her shoulders sagged. "You're going to throw away your dream, your father's dream, on a woman who doesn't care enough to put you first. That's what real love is, Ethan—making sacrifices."

He squeezed his mother's shoulder. It was as much her dream as it was his, and he had a promise to keep to his father. He'd win the damn race for all of them. And then he'd go to Texas and bring his wife home where she belonged.

* * *

Four days after she'd left Ethan, Skye sat beside her father in the media room with its red-and-gold damask-papered walls and red velvet drapes nervously waiting for the

election coverage to begin. Ethan had stopped calling
yesterday. As the days passed, it had become harder not
to respond to his texts and calls. She missed him desperately, but she was afraid she wasn't strong enough to say
no to him. Afraid if she heard his whiskey-smooth voice,
she'd give in. If he lost the election, he'd never be able to
forgive her. And if he won…Skye was afraid she'd end
up resenting him, end up hating herself for giving up on
everything she believed in.

She glanced at her father, who was on his iPhone
checking the exit polls while Betty Jean made popcorn
in the kitchen. She was as bighearted as her hair, and
Skye had fallen in love with her stepmother-to-be. Betty
Jean had made it her mission to repair Skye's damaged
relationship with her father. Surprisingly—or, given that
Betty Jean was as stubborn as a Texas longhorn, maybe
not so surprisingly after all—they were becoming closer.

But not so close that Skye felt comfortable asking her
father the question that had been bugging her since she
met Betty Jean. She knew she should, though. Despite
their differences, Betty Jean and her father made their
relationship work. Something Skye had been unable to
accomplish with Ethan.

She glanced over her shoulder to make sure Betty Jean
wouldn't hear her. The last thing she'd ever want to do was
hurt the woman. "I don't understand this thing with you
and Betty Jean. Don't get me wrong, I adore her. I think
she's amazing, but I remember you and Mom. I remember
your fights about her being a vegan, a liberal, and an envi-
ronmentalist. Betty Jean is Mom, only bolder and brighter
and louder. And you kicked Mom out."

He scratched his cheek, then put down his phone. "No,

I didn't. Your mother left us, Kend...Skye." Betty Jean had insisted her father call Skye by her chosen name. "I made up that story to protect you. I didn't want you to feel like she'd abandoned you."

She stared at her father, unable to believe what he was telling her. "All these years I thought...So you let me think you were the bad guy?" She shook her head, remembering what it'd been like those first months after her mother had left. "I said some pretty mean things to you that you didn't deserve. I was so angry at you for putting your political career ahead of her." She leaned back in the red velvet chair. "I wish you would've told me."

He shrugged. "You loved your mother. I understood why you were lashing out. I have broad shoulders; I could take it. You were such a little bitty thing back then." He gave her a half smile. "I thought about telling you around the time you went off to school, but by then we didn't have much of a relationship."

"I was always waiting for the other shoe to drop. For you to kick me out like you had her. You told me how much I was like her, so I didn't think you loved me, either." It was only when the words came out of her mouth that Skye realized that was how she'd felt.

"I loved you. Maybe I wasn't very good at showing you, but I did, I do."

"Admit it, Daddy, you thought I was a screw-up. And I guess I pretty much proved you right, didn't I?"

"I didn't think you were living up to your potential. You're a bright girl, but you were too busy flitting around from one cause to the other. Took you a while, but it seems like you're headed in the right direction now. I'm proud of what you've done since you frittered away all your money."

She sighed. "I didn't fritter it away, Daddy. Big Al embezzled at least half of it from me."

"Now, Skylar Davis, why in the hell didn't you tell me that? I would've put my lawyers on him."

"You can't get water from a stone. Besides, I should've been keeping a closer eye on my finances. I am now. And Maddie's looking after my investments for me." Well, she had been before Skye had left Christmas. Now she didn't think her best friend would ever speak to her again.

He rubbed his thumb over his iPhone. "You're a lot more like Betty Jean than you are your mother. The three of you had similar views, all of you vegans and environmentalists, all of you a little bit crazy, but there's a difference. You and Betty Jean are selfless and kind. You care about people as much as you care about animals and the environment. Your mother didn't. She was a radical. You did silly little things like release the horses and throw paint on Mrs. Harmon's fur coat, but you would never intentionally hurt someone. Your mother did. Two years after she left, she deliberately drove her car into a vehicle carrying several oil executives. They survived, but your mother didn't. She was a selfish and angry woman."

Skye squeezed her eyes shut. "You told me she died climbing Kilimanjaro."

"I thought it would be a nice memory for you. Kind of heroic. I didn't want you to know what she'd done."

"Geez, Daddy, I wish you would've told me the truth before I climbed Kilimanjaro in her memory. I nearly died doing that climb."

He huffed out a breath. "I don't know how I have a hair left on my head with what you got up to." He gave her an awkward hug. "I'm sorry I was so hard on you. I was worried you would turn out like her. I shouldn't have. I could see you were nothing like her where it really counted. Her parents spoiled her, gave in to her every whim. I thought if I was tough on you..."

"It's all right, Daddy." She hugged him back. "I understand why you did what you did."

"Aw, now look at what you've gone and done. My mascara's running." Betty Jean sniffed as she plunked herself down beside Skye's father with a big bowl of popcorn in her hands. The older woman never went anywhere without her face on. Ten years ago, she'd started an organic makeup line. Now Betty Jean was richer than God. Not that it was obvious.

Her father grinned and handed Betty Jean his handkerchief. He really was crazy about the woman. As they waited for the coverage to begin, Skye and Betty Jean came up with environmentally friendly products to replace the ones in the commercials. And when a paid endorsement for the Republican candidate for the Texas state senate came on, they nailed every one of his rightwing policies.

"You're not funny, either one of you," her father muttered. "Damn good thing I didn't meet you twenty years ago, Betty Jean. I don't think I would've survived the two of you."

"I wish you had, Daddy," Skye said, smiling at the older woman.

Betty Jean reached across her father. "I need some sugar from my little honey bun," she said, pulling Skye in for a hug.

Once she sat back in her seat, Skye's father put an arm

around both of their shoulders and squeezed. "You know I'm just kidding, right? I love my envirochicks."

Betty Jean leaned forward in her chair. "Did you tell your daddy?"

"Tell me what?" he asked, a nervous hitch in his voice.

"Me and Betty Jean are going into business together. We're starting a line of environmentally friendly clothing called Envirochicks."

Before her father had a chance to respond, Betty Jean whistled. "Now that boy is easy on the eyes," she said when the camera zoomed in on Ethan.

He'd just entered the Penalty Box with his mother and Claudia. He looked so handsome that Skye wanted to reach out and touch the screen. A reporter shoved a microphone at him. "Mr. O'Connor, any comments about your wife? Do you think she hurt your chances of winning the election."

A muscle ticked in his clenched jaw. "No comment," he said and turned away.

Claudia handed a white fur coat to someone off screen, revealing a winter white knit dress. She looked stunning. She gave the reporter a wide smile. "Ethan and I are confident he's going to win tonight. People understand that his marriage failed through no fault of his own. They're supporting him during this difficult time, as am I."

Skye wanted to scratch her eyes out. Claudia was making it sound like she and Ethan were together. Ethan had stepped away to talk to a table of supporters, so Skye didn't know if they were or not.

Her father and Betty Jean exchanged a look. So it'd been obvious to them, too. Claudia kept talking about the success of Ethan's campaign. The overwhelming support they'd received from the Latino community was due to Skye's efforts, but of course Claudia took all the credit.

"She's got tongue enough for ten rows of teeth," Betty Jean muttered. Texas-speak for "That girl can talk." But Claudia stopped talking pretty quick when the numbers started to come up on the big screens Sawyer had set up in the bar.

Skye reached for her father's hand. "Oh no, Daddy, Bennett's in the lead."

"It's not over till it's over," he said, giving her fingers a reassuring squeeze.

"Now there's another fine-looking man," Betty Jean said, clearly trying to distract Skye.

"That's Ethan's best friend, Gage McBride. He's the sheriff. He's married to my best friend, Maddie," she said, ignoring the pain twisting in her chest. She pointed out the people she knew, overcome by a wave of homesickness as she did. She missed the small town.

Her gaze searched for Ethan at the same time the camera found him. He stood, hands in his black pants pockets, watching as the updated numbers came in. When the station called the election in favor of Bennett, she bowed her head. She couldn't look at Ethan, couldn't see the disappointment on his face.

"I know what you're thinking, but get that out of your head," her father said. "It was a close race. The district's historically Democrat. He ran a solid campaign. He has nothing to be ashamed of."

"Other than his wife." She swiped at her eyes. "Or I guess I should say ex-wife-to-be."

"Hush. You're in love with the man. Now you have a chance to work things out. If he'd won the election, that would've been a different story. Sometimes things really do happen for a reason, you know," Betty Jean said.

A cheer went up in the bar as Ethan prepared to give his concession speech. "I don't know if I can watch this," Skye said, curling up on the chair.

Ethan flashed his movie-star smile, held up a hand to quiet the crowd, laughed when Sophia and the girls yelled that they loved him. He thanked his team, waving them over to join him. Claudia moved in beside him. He put an arm around her shoulders and thanked her for everything she'd done. She nodded, biting her lip as she fought back tears. Ethan said something to make her laugh, then turned to his mother, who swiped at her eyes. He talked about how much he appreciated having her in his corner, drawing laughs from the crowd when he told a couple of stories about her antics on the road. Toward the end of a short speech about his dad and what he'd taught him about life and politics, Ethan choked up.

Skye muffled a sob with her hand. She wanted to do something, to somehow support him, and the temptation to call him overwhelmed her.

He smiled, pulled himself together, and thanked his friends and supporters, the people of Christmas. She didn't realize until the end of his speech that she'd been holding out hope that he'd say a small something about her, or at the very least the baby, but it was like they didn't exist. It was all the proof she needed. He blamed her for the loss. She didn't know why it hurt so much. Hadn't she known from the beginning how he'd feel? Could she really blame him?

The front doorbell rang. "I'll get it," Betty Jean said, patting Skye on the shoulder before heading out of the room.

"Give it a couple of days. Let everything settle down. Then pick up the phone and call him. If you two love each other, you can get past this," her father advised gruffly.

"I ruined his chances, Daddy. Maybe that was enough to destroy any feelings he had for me."

"For you, hon," Betty Jean said, handing her a registered letter. Skye recognized Ethan's bold handwriting. She closed her eyes, hoping against hope he'd poured out his love for her in a letter. But it wasn't it a love letter. It was a notice of a petition for custody. The expensive paper fell from her nerveless fingers. "Ethan's going to take my baby from me. He wants sole custody."

Chapter Twenty

Sawyer locked the doors to the Penalty Box. Those who remained were family and friends. Ethan looked around the room; half the tables and chairs were still filled. Despite the loss, he considered himself a lucky man. Some people could count their family and friends on one hand. But there was someone missing: the one person he wanted most by his side.

Yesterday he'd come to the realization that she wasn't coming back. He was a lawyer. He dealt in facts. Her lack of response to his calls told him what he needed to know. It was time to let go and move on. He'd lost her, but he wasn't about to lose his baby, too. His mother and Claudia hadn't let up on him seeking custody. Some of their concerns about Kendall's ability to raise their child stuck in his head and led to his decision to send his wife a letter of intent. In part he hoped to get a reaction from Kendall. Any response was better than nothing.

"That was a beautiful speech, darling. Your father would have been proud of you," his mother said from where she sat beside him at the table. Disappointment radiated from her, her eyes red-rimmed, but she tried her best to put a positive spin on it for his sake.

He'd failed his father. Again. It was why he'd choked up during his speech. And why he hadn't mentioned Kendall or the baby. He'd intended to. She may have been partly responsible for his loss tonight, but she hadn't done so intentionally. She'd worked her ass off these last few weeks, and she deserved his thanks. But he couldn't do it. Not after the way his childhood memories had affected him. Mentioning her would have been worse.

He remembered how she challenged him, how she made him laugh, how she made life somehow seem bigger and brighter. How much he loved to watch her when she didn't know he was, how much he loved to hold her incredible body, kiss her beautiful face, and wake up with her in his arms. And now he'd lost her as surely as he'd lost the election.

He cleared his throat. "I don't know about that, Mom. Dad always said nothing was worth doing unless you won."

"You get thoughts like that out of your head right now, son. You should be damn proud of what you accomplished. I loved your father, but all that mattered to him was winning," Paul McBride said, clueless to Liz's furious, narrowed-eyed look. "Drove me nuts when we were growing up, and it was pure torture watching what he put you through as a kid. Nothing was ever good enough for him unless you were the best." He shook his head. "Remember the one year you missed the dean's list by two percent, Ethan? Never thought we'd hear the end of it."

"How dare you, Paul? How dare you talk about my husband like that? I thought you were his best friend."

"Okay, Mom, settle down. Paul didn't mean anything by it." Ethan appreciated what Paul was trying to do, but now wasn't the time or place.

"I was his best friend. But he was a man with faults just like the rest of us. Not the saint you've created in your mind since he died. This isn't about you and Deacon, Liz. It's about your son. Look at him. Do you want him beating himself up because he thinks he failed his father?"

Well, hell, he wasn't doing a very good job hiding his emotions if Paul could read him that easily. "What are you talking about? I'm fine," Ethan protested.

"Yes, Paul, what are you talking about? My son has nothing to be ashamed of. If it wasn't for his...Kendall, he would've won this election. The only thing he's guilty of is poor judgment and thinking with his..." She cleared her throat. "He let a pretty face distract him."

"Mom..." Ethan began.

Paul cut him off, jabbing his finger at Liz. "Skylar Davis was the best thing that happened to your son. If you would've butted out of their relationship, they would've been fine. It's about time you got on with your own life instead of living through your son, Liz O'Connor."

"How dare you!" his mother said, and tossed her drink in Paul's face.

Jesus. Ethan shook off his stunned disbelief to grab some napkins. "What the hell, Mom?" he said, handing them to Paul.

"Thanks, son." The older man wiped the red wine from his face. "Gage, you saw what she did. Arrest her."

"Arrest...arrest me?" his mother sputtered. "Are you insane?"

"Seem to remember you threatening to arrest Skye for the same thing."

"Okay, I don't know what Sawyer put in these drinks, but you two have obviously had enough. Calm down and act your ages," Gage said, "or I'll throw you both in jail."

"Now what the Sam Hill is going on over here?" Nell said when she reached their table.

"Paul said...he said Deacon..." His mother fluttered a hand at Paul and started to cry.

Ethan put his arm around her, picking up more napkins. "It's okay, Mom."

"Liz, honey, please don't cry. I didn't mean to make you cry," Paul said, reaching for her hand.

Richard, who'd flown in for the election, made his way to the table. "Lizzie, what's wrong?" He crouched beside Ethan's mother. "Now, now, darlin'. Ethan's young. He'll run again."

"It's not that," she sniffed, pointing an accusing finger at Paul. "It's him."

Richard stood up and crossed his arms. "What did you do now, McBride?"

"Stay out of it, Stevens. This has nothing to do with you."

"You're wrong, McBride. This is the woman I'm going to marry, so I—"

"What?" Ethan said at the same time Paul did.

His mother wiped her eyes, staring up at Richard. "What are you talking about? We—"

"Come on, darlin'. I'll take you home. We need to have ourselves some private time."

"Now see here, Stevens. You can't just—" Paul began.

She stood up and kissed Ethan's cheek. "Drop by the house on your way home, darling," she said, then let Richard lead her away.

"Are you just going to let her leave?" Paul asked Ethan.

"Yeah, I—"

Paul gave him a look of disgust and pushed back his chair. Gage took his father's arm. "Dad, I'm taking you home. Ethan, give me a call tomorrow."

Nell sat down in the chair his mother had vacated. She looked at Ethan and grinned. "Just a matter of time now."

"You can't actually think this is a positive development."

"Yep, I do." She sat back in the chair. "So, what are you doing to get your wife back?"

"She's not coming back, Nell. She left me. She doesn't love me."

"What the Sam Hill is wrong with you boys? Get off your heinie and go get her. You've got a baby on the way."

"I know we do. And I've done what I needed to make sure I'm a part of my child's life. But Kendall's made it clear she doesn't want to be a part of mine."

She gave a dismissive wave of her hand. "You've always gone after what you wanted in the past. Go after her or you won't be part of your baby's life."

"Yes, I will. I've informed her that I'm filing for sole custody."

"Geez Louise, God save me from foolish men," she said as if it was a prayer, then patted his hand. "It'll be tough to win her back after you've gone and done that, but don't worry, me and the girls will come up with a plan."

"Nell, I don't need your help."

"It's okay, we've got it covered." She winked, then said hello to the Reinharts and Adam Blackwell, who'd stopped at the table, before she headed off to join Evelyn and Stella. The way the three women put their heads together made him nervous. He let it go. There was nothing they could do. They were in Christmas, and Kendall was in Texas.

"How are you holding up?" Sam asked, rubbing his shoulder as she took a seat beside him.

"I'm good."

She gave him a skeptical look.

"I'll be fine, Sam. I'm going to take some time. Let it all sink in."

"Come back and work for me," Jordan said. "You were one of the best ADAs I've ever had the pleasure to work with. Never lost a case. Did I tell you that, Adam?"

"A time or ten." The dark-haired man smiled, then his expression grew serious. "I got the information you wanted on the blackmailer. Name's Jimmy Moriarty." Adam handed him a file. The second call Ethan had made the day Kendall left him was to Adam.

"And?"

"He's a dangerous guy. They've got him on two counts of murder, assault with a deadly weapon, and attempted rape. Your wife was lucky."

"She wasn't lucky, Adam," Sam said. "She was smart. She knew how to defend herself, and she did."

The thought of Kendall with a known murderer and rapist had Ethan's heart beating double-time in his chest. "What do you mean?" he asked, once he'd calmed himself down.

"Skye put him in the hospital, broke his jaw and ruptured his . . . well, you know." Sam wrinkled her nose.

Adam grinned. "What Sam is too polite to say is that your wife ruptured his balls."

"Jesus." Ethan winced.

"Yeah," Adam agreed. "I overnighted the photo and letter he sent you to the NYPD. Once they find him, they'll add blackmail to his charges." He must've read Ethan's concern for Kendall's safety, because he assured him, "Don't worry, he's holed up somewhere in New York State. They're closing in on him. The NYPD is working with a private contractor who has a personal interest in the case. They're confident he'll bring Moriarty in. This should be over in the next day or so. You might want to let your wife know there's a possibility they'll want her to testify."

"I will." Something gnawed at him. "Any idea when the incident with Kendall happened?"

"Sometime in June," Adam said.

Suddenly things started to click into place. She'd been hiding out in Christmas. And Ethan realized why she'd agreed to marry him. It had nothing to do with appeasing her father. She'd been talking to Vivi in the hospital just before she'd pushed for the marriage. Dammit, she'd been using him as a cover all along.

*   *   *

Betty Jean propped a jean-clad hip against the black granite countertop, waiting for Skye to finish making the filling for the pumpkin pies. "Let's put this in the fridge and you have a nap," the older woman said once Skye shut off the blender.

"It's just a cold, Betty Jean. I'm fine."

"We want you to feel better than fine. This is our first Thanksgiving dinner with you at home. Your daddy and I are going to pick up the tofu turkey and the rest of the fixin's for the meal."

Skye sneezed into her arm and grabbed a tissue. She blew her nose. "Maybe a nap would do me good." She hugged Betty Jean. "Don't forget the pineapple for the sweet potato casserole."

"I won't. And I'm going to stop by the apothecary to see if there's anything you can take for your cold. We shouldn't be more than an hour or two. Give us a dingle if you need anything," Betty Jean called out as Skye started up the stairs.

"I will." Skye smiled. No had ever fussed over her like Betty Jean did. And while she was happy to be with her father and her stepmama-to-be for Thanksgiving, she wasn't exactly happy about the reason she was there. But she did have a lot to be thankful for this year. She had a baby on the way, an improved relationship with her father, an older woman in her life that she loved, a blog that was doing well, and a new business that Betty Jean assured Skye was going to make her richer than God again.

The money didn't matter so much as that the clothing line was one more step in Skye's goal to prove to a judge that she was capable of being a responsible mother. Since the night she received the registered letter from Ethan, looking good on paper had been Skye's sole focus. She knew she would be a good mother despite what Ethan and Liz thought. She planned to make sure the judge did, too.

Skye wasn't going to lose custody over her child because of some stupid mistakes she'd made when she was young and . . . well, stupid. Learning about her mother had been an eye-opener. She wished her father had told her years ago. She could've avoided a lot of those mistakes if she hadn't been so angry at him, rebelling so hard against him. But that was in the past now. Old hurts that Skye hadn't even realized she'd been carrying around were now healed. She was stronger and more self-assured. Ethan had no idea what he was up against.

She ignored the hollow ache that always accompanied thoughts of him. Yesterday, she'd only experienced that hurtful throb ten times. Today, her goal was eight. She sighed, wondering if it would ever go away as she pulled the drapes across her bedroom window, blocking out the midmorning sunlight.

Crawling into bed, she propped the pillows behind her. "Okay, Meadow," she said to her baby, who started kicking as soon as Skye lay down, "time to sleep." Skye began to hum "Wild Horses." The other day she'd noticed the baby stopped kicking when she sang or hummed the song. She thought it was a coincidence, but it wasn't. Once again, the baby calmed, and Skye closed her eyes.

She'd barely fallen asleep when a sound jolted her awake. Someone was in the room with her. "Daddy," she said groggily to the large shadow at the end of her bed. She rubbed her eyes, and panic ricocheted through her. This man, and it had to be a man, was too big to be her father. She closed her eyes, praying she was imagining things, then opened them again. She wasn't. A low whimper escaped from her before she could stop it. He moved toward her, a light-colored cowboy hat hiding his face.

"Take it easy, I'm not going to hurt you," he said in a deep, gravelly voice.

Skye jolted upright. "Help!"

"For chrissakes," the man muttered and lunged for her, covering her mouth with his large hand. "Stop screaming. I told you I'm not—Jesus," he cursed when Skye slammed the heel of her palm into his nose. He let go of her to cover the blood spurting from his nostrils. "I think you broke my nose," he said, sounding more shocked than angry.

"I'll break more than that if you don't get out of here," she threatened, scrambling to the other side of the bed. Quicker than she expected, he recovered and came after her. Raising her arms in a defensive position, she bent her leg at the knee and pointed her toes.

He crossed his muscled arms and cocked his head. "What are you doing?"

"I'm trained in capoeira," she said, referring to the form of martial arts she'd studied from a master when she'd lived in Brazil. "You'd better leave. I don't want to hurt you."

She saw a flash of white under the brim of his Stetson. "Learn that while you were smoking yopo with the Yano-mami, did you?"

"How did you know that?" she asked, lowering her arms. There was no way she could take this man down. And she didn't want to risk hurting the baby. But if she distracted him, she might be able to reach the panic button on the wall behind the nightstand.

"I know everything about you, Sugar Plum." He reached in his back pocket, the movement drawing her attention to the gun tucked in the waistband of his jeans. *Gun!* He had a gun! She dove sideways across the bed, her arm outstretched in an effort to reach the button on the wall.

He grabbed her ankles. "I should've known this wouldn't be easy," he said, and swore when she got a foot loose and kicked him. Dragging her across the bed, he lifted her onto her feet and wrapped his arms around her, locking hers to her sides at the same time he trapped her legs with one of his. It was like being restrained by bands of steel.

"Now, I'm going to say this nice and slow so you understand me. I don't want to accidentally hurt you or your baby."

Her head whipped up, and she cracked him on the bottom of his jaw, his teeth clinking together with the force of the blow. "How do you know about my baby?"

She wasn't sure, but she thought he might have said "bleeping Nell"—only he used the real word; the "bleeping" was her choice. "What Nell? Are you talking about my Nell? Christmas's Nell?"

"I didn't say Nell. I have a court order to take you back to Christmas. Which I was going to show you when you tried to push the panic button."

She tried to tilt her head to look up at him, but he reared back. "Oh no, you don't. Now get dressed. This is already taking longer than I have time for."

"I'm not getting dressed, and I'm not going anywhere with you."

"Fine by me if you want me to deliver you to your husband in your pj's."

" 'Husband'? Ethan put you up to this?"

"Court order, Sugar Plum. You took your husband's baby out of state." She sneezed, and because her arms were locked at her sides . . . "For chrissakes," he cursed and let her go. He grabbed the tissue box off the nightstand and handed it to her, taking one to wipe his arm. "Be a good girl and get dressed. We have a plane to catch."

She glanced at her stretchy pink pajama top and the

matching bottoms that rode low on her hips to reveal her baby bump. "I'm not getting dressed. You'll have to take me as I am." With her plan to stay on the law's good side, she didn't want to ignore a court order. She didn't think Ethan had any rights until the baby was born, but she wasn't a hundred percent certain. Her attire alone should draw someone's attention at a crowded airport, and if a policeman happened to stop them, and the court order was invalid, he could arrest the man.

"Suits me," he said, and before she realized what he was going to do, he zip-tied her hands together.

"Hey, what do you think you're doing?" She shook her bound hands at him.

"Soon as you promise to behave, I'll take them off you."

She went to grab his gun from the waistband of his jeans, but he whipped it out of her reach.

"Jesus, you're a pain in the ass. Maybe I should do Ethan a favor and leave you here," he muttered, lifting her into his arms and heading for the spiral staircase.

"That's exactly what you should do," she said, head bowed as she focused on removing the zip ties. "Whatever he's paying you, I'll pay you more."

"Sorry, Sugar Plum. I don't think you can afford me. You're blog's doing well, but not that well."

"What? How?" She jerked upright, knocking off his champagne-colored cowboy hat. She gasped. "Superman."

*   *   *

"Why couldn't you stay asleep until we got there?" he grumbled, as they drove into Christmas.

Yes, her genius plan had backfired. How was she

supposed to know that the Man of Steel had a private plane tucked away in its own private hangar, and he knew how to fly the darn thing? If he hadn't kidnapped her, she might have thought that was kind of hot. If she wasn't still in love with her husband—yes, it was pathetic but true—she might have thought Chance McBride was one of the most gorgeous men she'd ever seen. He was all hard muscle and chiseled good looks. He'd also hurt her best friend.

"You broke Vivi's heart, you know."

"For the twentieth time, I'm not having this conversation with you."

"Well... You're in love with her." She gaped at him. "I can't believe I missed that. She's Lois Lane to your Superman."

He growled low in his throat and gave her a menacing stare. She snorted. "You don't scare me. But don't worry, your secret's safe. I'm not letting you break her heart again. And you *did* protect her."

"Pain in the ass," he muttered, patting down his pockets.

"Looking for something?" She smirked and held up his phone. He shouldn't have removed the zip ties. And while she might not have been able to get help at the airport, that didn't mean she was facing down Ethan and his family and friends without backup. She imagined that since he lost the election because of her, she was persona non grata in Christmas.

Chance took the phone from her, but his mouth quirked beneath his dark blond scruff.

As they pulled into Gage's driveway, Skye's heart started to race. There were several vehicles parked on the street, Ethan's Escalade among them. Along with the nerves, she felt a small spark of excitement and realized there was part of her that was anxious to see him. It'd been weeks since they'd talked, weeks since he held her in his arms and kissed her. She'd missed him desperately, but her pride and her anger had kept her from reaching out to him. Her fear that he didn't love her anymore or that what she thought was love had simply been lust.

Maybe this was a good idea after all. She could convince him to drop the custody suit. Tell him how sorry she was he'd lost the election because of her. And just maybe he'd realize how much he loved her. How much he'd missed her.

She pulled the visor down. Okay, so this was not the way she wanted him to see her for the first time in weeks. She looked like crap. No makeup, her nose was as red as Rudolph's, and her hair looked like she'd stuck her finger in a light socket. She pushed up the visor and whacked Chance.

He rubbed his arm. "What was that for?"

"You could've warned me everyone was going to be here."

"Feeling shy, Sugar Plum?" He grinned as he opened the driver's-side door.

"Oh, shut up and stop calling me that," she muttered. "Come get me. I'm not walking barefoot in the snow."

"Barefoot and pregnant," he said as he once again lifted her into his arms, "it suits you, Sweet Cheeks. But might have been a good idea to put on a bra."

She crossed her arms over her chest. "You are such a jerk. My best friend is better off without you."

"Yeah, she is," he said quietly as he walked up Gage's front steps.

"I'm sorry. I didn't mean that. If you hadn't kidnapped me and scared me half to death, I'd probably like you."

He gave a low, gruff laugh. "If you didn't beat the shit out of me, and you weren't such a pain in the ass, I'd probably like you, too," he said as he walked through Gage and Maddie's house.

Conversation and laughter at the dining room table abruptly ended as he set her on her feet. Everyone stared at her. Ethan sat beside Claudia at the far end of the table. They'd been smiling at one another, each of them holding the end of a wish bone, but as their eyes moved to her, their smiles faded. Skye's cheeks heated, her embarrassment magnified tenfold at the sight of them together, happy and beautiful. And then her temper flared.

"Gage, arrest them. Superman kidnapped me on *his* orders." She stabbed a finger in Ethan's direction. "And if you won't, I'm calling the...FBI. The CIA. Homeland Security!"

Chapter Twenty-One

Ethan stared at his wife. He'd imagined this moment, dreamed of it over the last several weeks, but Kendall standing barefoot in a pair of pink pajamas in Gage's dining room was not how he'd envisioned their reunion. And he sure as hell didn't expect her to demand his arrest, with her curly hair as wild as the temper sparking in her butterscotch eyes. *Wait a minute*, he thought, as he finally clued in to what she was ranting about. "Kidnapping? I didn't have you kidnapped. Why would you..."

He might as well have been talking to himself for all the good it did him. Kendall spun around. "Give me your phone," she said to the tall man who had unceremoniously deposited her in Gage's dining room. Ethan dragged his gaze from Kendall to the lethal-looking stranger. Alarm flashed through him at the realization that this guy had taken his wife, his very pregnant wife, against her will.

But since Kendall was giving the stranger hell, she

obviously wasn't afraid of him. With a cowboy hat covering half his face, all Ethan could see was the man's amused smile. "Now, Sweet Cheeks, calm down. Can't be good for your blood pressure."

Sweet Cheeks? Ethan stood up. "What's going on..." He trailed off when, in an attempt to grab the phone from the man's hand, Kendall knocked off his cowboy hat. Chance McBride. His wife's kidnapper was his best friend's brother.

Gage pushed back from the table at the same time as Paul. His stunned expression mirrored his father's. "Chance?" the two men said in unison. No one had seen Chance McBride since his wife Kate's funeral four years ago.

Paul went to greet his son, but Kendall turned on him. Somehow she'd gotten hold of Chance's phone and pointed it at Paul. "Stop right there. Did none of you hear what I said? I was kidnapped. Kidnapped at gunpoint."

"I didn't kidnap you at gunpoint, and you know it. Dad, you might want to stay back until Sweet Cheeks here gets the drama out of her system," Chance said as he picked up his hat from the floor.

"Drama?" Kendall waved the phone at Chance. "You dragged me terrified from my bed—"

"Terrified?" Chance rolled his eyes. "You don't have the good sense God gave you to be terrified."

"Hey!" She looked back at Chance and elbowed him in the gut. "I had enough good sense to defend myself against you, didn't I?"

"Yeah, your capoeira moves were real scary, Sweet Cheeks." Grinning, Chance put up his arms, raised his leg, bending it at the knee.

"Ha-ha." Kendall scowled at him. "It wasn't me who ended up with a broken nose and bruises, now was it?" she said as she pressed buttons on the phone. Chance sighed, took the phone from her, and ended the call.

No one moved, staring openmouthed at the couple as the scene played out before them. Finally Gage, as if sensing Kendall was ready to go off on another rant, intervened. "So what you're telling me, Skye, is that my brother kidnapped you at gunpoint from your father's home in Texas."

"Yes." Chance gave her a light shove. "Okay, so it wasn't exactly at gunpoint, but he did take me against my will." She shoved Chance back, then pointed at herself. "Does this look like someone who went with him willingly? If I did, don't you think I would've gotten dressed?"

Gage took in her attire and rubbed the back of his neck. "I see your point."

Chance grinned as he leaned down to whisper in her ear.

Her cheeks went as red as her nose, and she crossed her arms over her chest. Obviously, Chance had pointed out to her what had been noticeable to Ethan and every man in the room. His wife was cold and had forgotten her bra. Ethan narrowed his gaze at the man he'd grown up with and asked, "Do you want to explain to me why you kidnapped my wife?"

Kendall rolled her eyes. "Oh, that's rich. Don't put on the innocent act. This was your fault. You put him up to this."

"Skye, honey, why don't you sit down? It's not good for you and the baby to get this worked up," Paul said. At the same time he tried to get his daughter-in-law's attention, but Madison was looking at Nell, who was bent over her plate, eating her turkey as if nothing had happened.

"What did you do, Nell?" Madison said, and everyone turned to stare at the older woman.

Nell looked up, blinking her eyes. "Are you talking to me?"

Gage and Paul groaned, and Ethan pinched the bridge of his nose.

"'Fess up, Nell. You're behind this, aren't you?" Madison said.

"So she was behind it after all," Kendall said to Chance. "That's why you bleeped her."

"He bleeped me?"

"No, I bleeped her 'cause you were a pain in the ass, Sweet Cheeks. Sorry, Aunt Nell, the jig is up," Chance said.

"You can all stop looking at me like that. At least I did something. Not my fault that I'm the only one with gumption." She aimed her fork at Ethan. "What are you complaining about? All you've done is mope around since she left you."

"I wasn't moping, Nell," he protested, more emphatically than was probably necessary. "There were a lot of loose ends that needed to be tied up."

"Oh, is that why Claudia's still here, helping you tie up all those loose ends?" Kendall said, her husky voice dripping with sarcasm.

"Actually, Kendall, I'm here to support Ethan. After you destroyed his chance of winning the election and stole his child from him, he needed me," Claudia said, smiling up at him.

It wasn't true, but there was nothing he could say without embarrassing Claudia.

"Skye. My name is Skylar Davis. And this is my child." She placed her hand on her belly. "My body, my life. And all of you self-righteous, holier-than-thou right-wingers better get that through your thick skulls."

After what she'd put him through these past weeks, that was the last straw. "Are you sure that's who you are? Because I seem to remember the night we got married you were pretty clear that you wanted to be known as Kendall, Kendall O'Connor." He slapped his forehead. "That's right, now I remember. The reason you wanted to be known as Kendall O'Connor was the same reason you agreed to marry me, isn't it? You were using me to hide out from Jimmy 'the Knife' Moriarty." He jabbed a finger at her. "And that baby you're carrying is as much mine as it is yours. And I'm warning you, if you do one thing, just one thing, to put *my* child at risk, I will do whatever I have to do to protect it, including breaking the law."

Gage gave him a you've-lost-it look. Yeah, Ethan had already come to the same conclusion himself. He supposed letting out all the anger, hurt, and frustration he'd kept bottled up inside since election night wasn't the best idea. No one, not even Gage, knew how hard that had been. How hard it was to know he'd wasted a year of his life— all that time, money, and energy he could never get back. And a woman he was in love with, a woman he'd believed felt the same way about him, was indirectly responsible for that loss. But it was her betrayal, the callous, cowardly way she'd left him, the way she'd completely cut him off as if he had no right, no place in his child's life, no place in her life that was more difficult to bear.

"Ethan, darling," his mother said, touching his arm with a worried look in her eyes.

Richard got up from where he sat beside Liz and came to stand at his side. "Not the time or place for this, son," he said for Ethan's ears alone. "Why don't you sit down?"

Ethan did as Richard suggested before he embarrassed himself further.

Madison, who'd been as angry at his wife as Ethan had been, shot him an indignant look and got up from the table. She took Skye by the hand. "I'm going to get my best friend something decent to wear, and then we're all going to sit down at this table like normal people and eat the Thanksgiving dinner I slaved over for two days."

"What are you talking about? You made the carrots, and you burned them."

"Aunt Nell," Gage muttered, then kissed his wife's cheek. "I'll put everything in the oven, honey. Keep it warm until you're ready."

"I'll help you, Gage," Ethan's mother offered. Claudia's gaze flicked from Ethan to his wife. She started clearing off the table with Nell as Madison led Skye away.

"You're a big meanie, Uncle Ethan," Lily said, following after the two women.

"Geez, Uncle Eth, way to ruin Thanksgiving," Annie said as she left the table.

"Girls, wait. Come say hi to your Uncle Chance," Gage called after his daughters, but they were long gone.

"Sorry about that," Ethan apologized to Gage and scrubbed his face with his hands.

When he looked up, the four men who remained at the table glared at him. "Oh, come on, how did I end up being the bad guy in this?"

"Is that a rhetorical question?" Chance asked, taking a seat after he'd hugged his father and brother. He leaned back in the chair, picked up a bun, and fired it at Ethan's head. "She's pregnant, Einstein." It was the nickname Gage's brothers had given Ethan in grade school. One he'd hated. "And she's not feeling so hot since I dragged her out of her bed and brought her to Christmas in her pj's."

"Yeah, about that," Ethan said, lobbing the bun back at him. "What the hell were you thinking? You kidnapped her, took her across state lines, and you had a gun even if you didn't threaten her with it. You could be charged both federally and by the state with first-degree kidnapping."

"She won't charge me. She likes me. You should be worrying more about yourself. Sweet Cheeks doesn't like you very much, and she has a mean right hook." Chance grinned. "Moriarty's lucky all she did was break his jaw and rupture his balls." Jerking his thumb over his shoulder, he added, "Might be a good idea if you don't shove your new girlfriend in her face."

"Claudia is not my girlfriend," Ethan responded tightly.

"Coulda fooled me," Chance said.

"You may want to set both your mother and Claudia straight on that, Ethan," Richard said with a pointed look at the two women whispering in the kitchen.

"He can do that tomorrow," Gage said. "What he's going to do now is call a truce with his wife. Today's important to Madison. It's her first Thanksgiving with the family and the baby. And I want to salvage what's left of the day. Madison will calm Skye down, and now that she knows Nell was behind this, I hope she'll reconsider pressing charges. I'd like to visit with my brother in the comfort of my home instead of behind bars." He looked at Chance. "You are staying for a couple of days, aren't you?"

Chance shifted in his chair. "I wish I could, but—"

"Son, you haven't been home since..." Paul stopped himself, then in a pleading tone of voice said, "A day or two, that's all I'm asking for. Please."

Ethan could see that Chance was fighting an inner battle. It was as hard to watch as the hope fading from Paul's face at the resolute expression on his son's.

"Come on, Chance. It's time," Gage said quietly, holding his brother's gaze.

Chance rubbed his jaw, then slowly nodded. "Yeah, okay, Dad. I'll stick around for a day or two." He looked across the table at Ethan and grinned. "And I think in the next few minutes, Einstein here might need a bodyguard."

"I can defend myself, thanks. But I'm not going to have to, because as soon as Madison's had a couple more minutes with my wife, I'm going to go talk to her, straighten a few things out, and then we're all going to sit down for a civilized Thanksgiving dinner."

Chance started to laugh. "Best-laid plans. I figure you have"—he glanced at his watch—"about ten seconds before the cavalry arrives."

"What's he talking about?" Gage asked Ethan, as Chance began counting down the seconds with a shit-eating grin on his face.

The doorbell rang and his mother called out that she'd get it at the same time Ethan responded to Gage. "I have no idea, but he's starting to get on my—" Ethan broke off when a woman with mile-high blonde hair burst into the dining room and drew a Glock from her purse. "What have you done with my honey bun?"

*   *   *

Skye glanced at Maddie as she dragged her to her bed-room. "Considering you haven't talked to me in weeks, I'm glad to hear I'm still your best friend."

"Doesn't mean I'm not mad at you. All you've done for the last few months is lie to me. You were in danger, and you didn't tell me. What kind of friendship is that? After everything we've been through together, you shut me out. But you didn't shut Vivi out, did you?" Maddie crossed her arms, her expression more hurt than angry.

"I know, and I'm sorry. I really am. I did it for you. Gage is Ethan's best friend. I didn't want you to have to keep secrets from him."

"That excuse worked when you were keeping the baby a secret, but it doesn't cover the rest of it. You took off in the middle of the night in a snowstorm. No phone call, no nothing. You left your husband to deal with Bob Bennett's smear campaign on his own, then you publicly humili-ated him by announcing your divorce in the paper. I don't think I know you anymore." Maddie sat on the edge of the bed. "I'm not sure I want to. He loved you, Skye. Ethan loved you, and you destroyed him."

"Looks like he got over me pretty quick," she said in a flippant tone of voice, trying not to let her heartache leak into her voice. It'd been easy to hold on to her anger when he attacked her, but now the reality was setting in. She really had lost him. "I'm sure he and Claudia will be announcing their engagement any day now."

"Really, that's all you've got to say for yourself?" Mad-die looked at her, tears welling in her eyes. "I, uh, I'm sorry, but I think I'm going to have to ask you to leave."

"Why?" Skye tried to tamp down her panic at the thought she'd lost not only Ethan but her best friend, too. She sat beside Maddie. "I can't lose you, too. I can't." She gave her head a frantic shake.

"What do you mean, 'too'?"

"I love Ethan, Maddie. I probably always will."

"Then why did you leave him? Why did you—"

"Because I thought I was protecting him. I thought if I left him, he'd have a chance to win the election." She lifted her eyes to Maddie's. "I was there, that night at Liz's. I heard everything. I heard about Jimmy blackmailing him, about the pictures and what Claudia said. They were going to tell the truth—that Ethan had only married me because of the baby and was filing for divorce. There would have been backlash if he did. It was better if I did."

"Skye, why didn't you just tell him? You could have—"

"I couldn't. He would have convinced me to stay. At least without me by his side, he had a chance to win. I knew if he lost, he'd blame me as much as I blamed myself." She released a brittle laugh. "So much for my sacrifice. And, as you just heard tonight, I was right."

"I've known you for more than ten years, I should've known there was more to this." Maddie took her hand. "And what if he'd won, Skye? What were you going to do then?"

"Be glad that at least something good came out of me leaving him. Because you were right. I was pretending to be someone I wasn't. I don't think I could've kept it up for much longer. In the end, we would've ended up where we are today."

"Where are you today?"

"Here with my best friend, I hope."

"That's not what I meant. Of course we're still best friends. I was angry, and not just about Ethan. I was angry you could up and leave me after I had Connor. I needed you."

"I'm sorry. I promise, no more secrets." She tentatively drew Maddie in for a hug, not entirely sure her best friend had forgiven her. "So does this mean you're not kicking me out?"

Maddie drew back and winced. "That wasn't really in tune with the spirit of Thanksgiving, was it?"

"Nope, but neither were Ethan and me." She pointed at herself. "But I think I had a legitimate reason for my rant. Can you believe Nell sent Superman to kidnap me?"

"Uh, yeah, it's Nell we're talking about. But who's Superman? I thought Hot Bod kidnapped you."

Skye laughed. Her laughter fading when she realized this was something else she'd kept from Maddie, so she told her all about Vivi and Superman.

"I can't believe it. And you didn't tell her?"

"No, he was protecting her, and she needed protection."

"You think he's in love with her?"

"I'm not sure, but he does care about her. I don't think he's gotten over Kate."

"I'm sorry he scared you, but it's about time he came home. Paul will be over the moon. So will Gage. Maybe that was part of Nell's plan all along."

"Hey, what about me? Aren't you glad he brought me back?"

She tilted her head. "That depends. I'd like to have a happy Thanksgiving. Can you manage to be civil to Ethan and Claudia?"

Her heart fluttered beneath her rib cage. "So they are together?"

"Not as far as I know. Richard is courting Liz, though. But I have to tell you, Claudia has been there for Ethan after you..." She shrugged. "Are you planning on staying in town?"

"I think so. I've missed you guys. And Christmas would be a good place to raise the baby. Besides, Ethan and I are going to have to figure out a way to make this custody thing work. It'd be easier if we were in the same state. Easier for him to have her on weekends, that is, because I have no intention of giving him full custody." Thinking of her baby growing up with Claudia as a stepmother, she placed a protective hand on her stomach.

"You said you love him. Why don't you try and make it work?"

"He doesn't love me. And if he ever did, it was Kendall he was in love with—and I'll never go back to pretending to be her again."

Maddie was about to say something when Annie and Lily burst into the bedroom. "Auntie," Lily said, launching herself at Skye. Annie threw her arms around Skye's neck and said, "I've missed you."

Skye laughed. "How could you? We talk every day."

Maddie stood up and put her hands on her hips. "Wait a sec. You talk to my daughters every day and you don't talk to me? Okay, I know," she said when Skye gave her a pointed look.

Then Maddie started to laugh. "I should've known when I was having trouble nursing Connor and Annie suggested I try a nipple shield." She shook her head and hauled Skye to her feet. "And speaking of nipples, you need something decent to wear. Girls, I hear your brother, get him for me, please. We won't be long." Maddie opened her closet and gave Skye a once-over. "You actually look pregnant now."

"I know, it's so amazing," Skye said, rubbing her stomach. "I can't believe how big I am."

Maddie snorted. "The only thing big on you is your boobs." She handed her a pair of leggings, a long purple sweater and a bra. "Instead of looking like you swallowed a golf ball, you look like you swallowed a football, one for toddlers."

"Ha-ha, you're so funny," Skye said as she got dressed. She'd just finished tugging the sweater over the black leggings when she heard a woman yelling for her honey bun.

*   *   *

It took forty minutes to calm Betty Jean down, get Connor fed and tucked into his cradle, and the food back on the table. Skye was retrieving the last platter when Ethan cornered her in the kitchen. "We need to talk," he said, blocking her exit.

"It'll have to wait. Everyone's hungry." After what he'd said earlier, she didn't want to hear more in the same vein. Not right now. Maddie wanted a Hallmark Thanksgiving, and that was what she was going to get. Unintentionally, Skye had hurt her best friend, and she needed to make amends.

"Just give me a sec, okay? I want to apologize for earlier. I was out of line. I'm sorry."

"I'm sorry, too. I shouldn't have commented on your relationship with Claudia. It's none of my business." *Really, Skye? That's all you got?* She had so much more to apologize for, more important things. In her defense, it wasn't easy to think straight with him standing so close that she could smell his expensive cologne. The track lighting in the kitchen brought out the gold highlights in his tawny hair. He was wearing it longer now. Like the scruff on his chiseled jaw, it made him look dangerously sexy.

He shoved his hands in the pockets of his black pants. "No, it's not."

That wasn't the answer she expected or wanted to hear. She raised her gaze, trying to read the emotion in the depths of his hazel eyes. They were more green today, reflecting the color of his sweater. But he had on his lawyer face, hiding his feelings from her.

"It hasn't been your business since you left me in the middle of the night without an explanation."

"I left you a note."

He raised his brows. "The blog post was more enlightening than your note. You should've told me how much you hated it all."

"You should've known."

"I'm not a mind reader."

She shrugged. "Nothing we can do about it now. It's water under the bridge." She saw the regret in his eyes and felt the same. She wished their marriage hadn't ended the way it did. Maybe if they'd been honest from the beginning, they would have had a chance. "I'm sorry, Ethan. I'm sorry you lost the election."

"Yeah, well, it happens." His eyes drifted to her stomach. "How's the baby?" he asked, returning his gaze to hers.

"She's fine, thank you." Nerves made her response come out more clipped and formal than she had intended. The thought of him suing her for full custody was always at the back of her mind.

"You're pale. You don't look well. Have you seen a doctor?"

"Ethan"—Claudia stuck her head in the kitchen, her gaze sliding from Skye to Ethan—"everyone's waiting to start."

"We'll be right there," Ethan said, giving the woman a smile. A woman who didn't look pale and unwell, like Skye did. No, of course she didn't. Claudia looked the picture of health in a red, wraparound knit dress that hugged her willowy frame. Which might have been the reason Skye snapped, "No, I haven't seen a doctor because I don't need to see a doctor, and if I thought I needed to see a doctor, I would see a doctor. I'm pregnant, not sick."

He took her arm as she went to walk by him. "Why do you have to take a simple question and make a federal case of it?"

She jerked free of his hold. "Do not turn this on me. I know you, and I know exactly what you're thinking. The silly, spoiled, self-centered—" Her eyes widened when she realized what she'd done. She'd repeated what Claudia had said about her that night. "She doesn't know enough to take care of herself, so how could she ever take care of a baby?" she finished on a rush, praying he didn't clue in.

"No, I wasn't. But you're almost thirty-three weeks. I'll make an appointment with Dr. Evans for you. We'll go—"

"I already have an appointment with her, Ethan. I made it at my last visit. Despite what you think, I'm perfectly capable of taking care of my baby." With that, she strode out of the kitchen, slamming the casserole dish on the dining room table. "Let's eat," she said. "I'm starved."

Maddie's anxious gaze went from her to Ethan. Skye forced a bright smile. "You've outdone yourself, sweetie. Everything looks amazing. Let's give Maddie a round of applause. Yay, Maddie." She put her fingers between her lips and whistled. Then she did a fist bump across the table to her best friend. "Awesome. Best Thanksgiving ever."

Chance tugged on the back of her sweater. "Okay, Sweet Cheeks. We get it. Sit down so we can eat." She took the seat between Chance and Betty Jean, her father sitting beside his wife-to-be.

Betty Jean leaned into her. "Honey bun, we're going to have to go out and grab a bite later."

Skye eyed the platters. "Load up on carrots and green beans."

Chance grinned at her, then stuck a serving spoon into the whipped potatoes. Just as he went to put them on his plate, Lily shook her head. "We say what we're thankful for first, Uncle Chance."

"Are you shitting me?" he said in a low voice to Skye.

She surreptitiously elbowed him, even though she privately agreed with him. As Lily began, Skye tried to come up with something that wouldn't tick off the man sitting across the table from her with his mother on one side of him, Claudia on the other.

"I want to give thanks for this amazing man that I had the pleasure of working with so closely this last year. He was robbed, but I know that one day he will have his chance, and I'll be by his side to make that happen." Claudia gave Ethan a simpering smile, then patted her father's hand. "And of course I'm thankful for you, Daddy."

A big hand closed over Skye's. "Put down the knife, Sweet Cheeks," Chance said out of the side of his mouth. She didn't realize she'd been holding it, and loosened her white-knuckled grip. "You have nothing to be jealous about. He hasn't taken his eyes off you," he whispered in her ear.

"I'm not jealous," she said, but she felt a little better for him saying so.

He gently tugged on her hair. "Careful, your nose is going to grow." He cocked his head. "Actually, I think it already has, Rudolph."

"You're a pain," she said, unable to keep the smile from her voice. She liked Chance McBride. He was like an annoying older brother.

From across the table, Ethan narrowed his eyes at them. His mother nudged him. "Darling, it's your turn."

He raised his glass of wine. "To Madison and Gage, for including us today. You guys are the best. There's nowhere I'd rather be than here with all of you. Mom, I'm thankful that you've put up with me the last couple of weeks." He turned to Claudia, who smiled prettily at him. "And I'm thankful for all the help you've given me this past year. I couldn't have asked for a better friend or campaign manager." Claudia's smile fell, then she forced it back in place. Ethan held Skye's gaze. "And most of all, I'm thankful that I'm going to be a father. I plan to play a very active role in my child's life. *Very* active."

He was doing well up until that point. Skye went to say something along those lines to Chance, then remembered that he'd lost his wife and unborn child, and kept her mouth closed. When they worked their way to him, she wasn't surprised that all he said was "Thankful for all this fine food. Now, can we eat?"

Skye put her hand on his leg and gave the rock-hard muscle a light squeeze. When Chance looked at her with a raised brow, she angled her head at his father. He sighed and added, "Thankful to be here with my family. Good to see you all. Now can we eat?"

"No, it's Auntie Skye's turn," Lily said.

Skye cleared her throat. "I have a lot to be thankful for this year. I have a baby on the way."

Betty Jean reached over and rubbed Skye's stomach, "Aw, our little hon bun."

Lily giggled and Skye smiled, patting Betty Jean's hand. "And I have a stepmama-to-be who I already love to bits."

Betty Jean pulled her into a hug. "Aw, honey bun, I love you, too. Isn't she just the sweetest thing?"

Skye imagined there were some rolled eyes at Betty Jean's pronouncement, but she focused on her dad instead. "And I'm thankful for my dad. More than he probably knows. We haven't always seen eye to eye, but we're getting there."

"Aw, Willy, did you hear that? I think I'm going to cry."

Skye's father winked at her as he handed Betty Jean a handkerchief.

"And I'm thankful I have the most adorable nieces and nephew on the planet, but most of all, I'm thankful that my best friend has forgiven me because she is the sister of my heart, and I don't know what I'd do without her in my life. I love you, Maddie."

"Damn you, Skye, did you have to make me cry?" Maddie said, swiping at her eyes.

"Daddy, Mommy said a swear."

Gage grinned and put an arm around Maddie. "I'll cover her this time, sweetpea."

"'Kay, that'll be two bucks."

Chance laid a hand on his chest. "I'm wounded, Sweet Cheeks. Aren't you thankful for me?"

"Thank you for protecting Vivi, Superman," she whispered in his ear before kissing his cheek.

Once they made their way around the table, Chance said, "That was all very nice, but I'm starved. Can we eat now?"

"Hold your horses. I haven't had my turn," Nell said, her gaze lighting on everyone at the table. "I'm thankful to be here with four generations of McBrides. There's nothing more important than family, and I'm damn proud of mine. You get on my last nerve every now and then, but I love you all. And I'm thankful my great-nephew had the good sense to marry this gal right here." She waved her fork at Maddie. "Paul, you could learn something from your son. Anne wouldn't want you to be alone."

"Aunt Nell," Paul growled.

"I'm old. I can say whatever I want." She looked at Chance, and everyone held their breath. "I'd tell you the same, son, but you're not ready to hear it. I hope one day soon you will be. Don't tell the other boys, but you're my favorite. I can always count on you to do what needs to be done."

"Hey, last week you told me I was your favorite," Gage said, lightening the mood.

"And I'm thankful we're finally done with the thankful stuff. Dig in, folks," Chance said, pulling the bowl of whipped potatoes toward him. He bowed his head and closed his eyes when Nell continued, "You know what else I'm thankful for? Now that Skye's back in town, I'll be able to write the happy ending for their story. Hop to it, kids. I'm on a deadline, you know."

"Good luck with that," Ethan muttered at the same time Skye said, "Don't count on it."

Chapter Twenty-Two

"Did you hire a couple of clowns to help me entertain Annie and Lily for the day?" Ethan asked Gage as he gestured to the candy-floss-pink Smart Car parked in the driveway. And then he heard a laugh he was all too familiar with. "Tell me that's not who I think it is."

Gage nudged him back out the door and closed it behind them. "Madison thought it was a good idea, and I agree. You guys have stuff to work out, and now's the time to do it."

"I thought she was in Texas for her father's wedding." He'd heard she'd left town right after Thanksgiving. That'd been eight days ago.

"She was, but she got back last night. She's here to stay, buddy. Betty Jean's buying her a house on Sugar Plum Lane. Adoption present or something. It closes tomorrow."

"Adoption? Skye's twenty-eight." But in the end, he supposed it worked to his advantage. At least for the custody arrangement he wanted to set forth. He pushed down the disappointment that the happy marriage he'd once envisioned had turned into a broken one with visitation rights.

"Kinda crazy but sweet. I think it meant a lot to Skye. She didn't have a mother growing up, and it sounds like Betty Jean wants to make it up to her."

Ethan shoved his bare hands in the pockets of his sheepskin jacket. Snow clouds moved in over the mountain range behind Gage's place, leaving the morning air cold and damp. "Betty Jean is crazy. But you're right, it's nice for Skye. I'm just glad her stepmother lives in Texas and...what?" he asked when Gage started grinning.

"I guess Betty Jean thinks Texas is too far from her honey bun and baby bun-to-be. They've put up the ranch for sale. They're moving to Christmas."

Ethan pinched the bridge of his nose. "One crazy environmental animal rights activist is enough to deal with. What's it going to be like to have two of them in town? And Skye is sane compared to Betty Jean."

"How do you think I feel? I'm the one who's going to be dealing with the two of them, not you, remember?"

"You should probably put in a request for another jail cell," Ethan muttered. Other than their interactions about the baby, he no longer had a place in his gorgeous fruitcake's life. He didn't know how he'd handle seeing Skye day in and day out. And if she ever met someone else...

It'd driven him half crazy watching her with Chance at Thanksgiving. Though it had been nice to see the other man laughing and smiling. Ethan had just wished it'd been with someone other than his wife. Soon-to-be ex-wife, he reminded himself, as he did half a dozen times a day.

Gage laughed. "Already mentioned it to Madison. She wasn't amused."

"Are we done here?"

"Yeah—just promise me you'll try and get along. Lily and Annie are at impressionable ages."

"You know who you're talking to, right? Save the warning for the one who needs it—Skye."

"I'd agree that you're the last person I should have to warn to keep their cool, but I've seen you with her."

"You'd lose your cool, too, if Madison pulled what Skye has. Imagine how you'd feel if she tried to keep you from Connor."

Gage clapped him on the shoulder. "That's why today's so important, buddy. The baby will be here in a little more than a month. Now's the time to hammer out an agreement," he said as he opened the door.

"I thought you left without us," Madison said, a diaper bag slung over her shoulder as she tugged on her boots. They were headed to Denver to go Christmas shopping. Skye sat cross-legged on the floor cooing at Connor as she put him in his snowsuit. Annie and Lily sat on either side of her, each of them putting a mitten on his tiny hands.

"Look at you, smiling at your auntie," Skye said, giving Connor noisy kisses before handing him to Gage.

From the moment he'd met her, Ethan had thought she was the most beautiful woman he'd ever seen. But today she took his breath away. She looked all glowy and happy and so damn sexy that his chest tightened with a painful desire. Irritated at the evidence he wanted her as much as he always did, he said, "It's gas."

"What do you know? It's not gas. He loves his auntie Skye, don't you, baby boo?" She tickled Connor under the chin. This time the baby not only smiled, he laughed.

"Oh wow, that's the most beautiful sound in the world," Skye said, laying a hand on her chest. "I think I'm going to cry."

"He's only five weeks old. He's not supposed to laugh yet," Madison said, staring at the baby in amazement.

"What can I say? He takes after his auntie Skye. He's a genius."

"Make him do it again, Auntie. Make him do it again," Lily said, pushing between her sister and mother.

She did, and her warm, infectious laughter joined the baby's. "Okay, you guys," Gage said after the third time, "we've got to get going. And you've given him the hiccups."

Madison said good-bye to the girls. "We'll be home around seven. I left the number for the pizza delivery by the phone. There's a salad in the fridge for you, Skye," she said, then added something under her breath to Skye.

Skye rolled her eyes. "I already promised, didn't I? When have I ever gone back on my word?"

"Couple times that I know of," Ethan said before he could help himself. At Gage's groan, Ethan held up his hand. "Have fun. We'll be fine."

"Yes, don't worry, Gage. I'm just going to pretend he isn't here." Skye purposely bumped into him as she walked through to the kitchen. "Huh, there's nothing there yet it felt like I walked into a thick block of cement."

"Real mature," Ethan said as he hung up his coat in the front closet. He wondered if he should put it back on and head out the door when Annie said, "Do you know how many sheep died to make your coat, Uncle Eth?"

"You've been spending too much time with your aunt," he said and followed the girls to the kitchen.

"Yay, we're making gingerbread houses." Lily clapped, pulling out a stool to sit at the granite-topped island.

Skye looked up from setting out bags of candy. "Where do you think you're going?" she asked him, as he started to back out of the room.

"I'm not here, remember?"

"You're here to spend the day with Lily and Annie. So come on, roll up your sleeves, and join in the fun."

"You girls look like you have it covered for now. Call me when you need me. I've got work to do."

"Ethan, I need you," Skye called as soon he'd settled himself on the couch with his iPad.

God, he wished that were true. He bowed his head when the thought popped into his head, and he wondered how he'd get through the day without either strangling her or kissing her senseless. How was he going to move on with his life without her in it?

"Uncle Ethan, we need you," Lily and Annie called, but he heard the giggles in their voices.

He set the iPad on the coffee table and walked back to the kitchen. "What?"

"It's okay. Got it opened," Skye said, fighting a grin as she held up a bottle of red and white sprinkles.

The third time they called him, he ignored them and looked over the e-mail from the district attorney's office in New York City. He'd asked to be kept in the loop. Before Chance had left a few days ago, he'd filled Ethan in. Chance had tracked Moriarty down two days before he'd gone to get Skye in Texas. Moriarty was now in jail awaiting trial. That was one case Ethan would give his right arm to try.

"Ethan, uh, I could use some help here," Skye called. He shook his head.

Lily ran into the living room. "Uncle Ethan, Auntie Skye got her hair caught in the beaters, and it's smoking."

Jesus. He ran into the kitchen. Her hair was covered in icing, a spiral of smoke emitting from the mixer. He pulled the plug, then ejected the beater. "Ouch," she said, putting a hand to her head as he worked to free her hair.

"You're lucky all it did was pull out a few strands." He nudged her toward the sink, turned on the tap, and wet a hunk of hair. "What were you doing?"

"Nothing. My hair's long and got caught. I guess I should have—"

"She was dancing," Annie said with a smirk.

"Oh yeah, what kind of dance was she doing?" He grinned as Lily wiggled around the kitchen with her hands in the air. "Good to know you weren't doing the dance you did for me, cupcake."

Her gaze jerked to his. She searched his face before saying, in a flustered tone of voice, "Thanks. I'm good now. You can get back to work."

Gently brushing sugar from the top of her head, he said, "No, I don't think so. Probably safer for all of you if I stick around." There was something about the way she looked at him that made him think she wasn't immune to him after all. Testing his theory, he slid his hand under her hair, caressing her neck, and the soft skin there. "You have a clip or something?"

"Huh?" she said.

"A clip. So you can put up your hair." He looked into her eyes. "You okay? You're looking a little flushed." He placed his palm on her forehead, then slid it to her cheek, brushing his thumb over her full bottom lip.

She swallowed, brought her hand to the neck of her red sweater, and tugged. "It's hot in here, don't you think?"

"Getting warmer by the minute," he murmured, leaving his hands where they were. He moved closer, holding her gaze as her rounded belly brushed against him. He heard the slight catch of her breath, and saw her eyes darken from butterscotch to toasted caramel. He realized then that no matter what she'd done, no matter how much frustration and pain she'd caused him these last few weeks, he wanted another chance to make their marriage work. And not just for the baby's sake. "We have to talk," he said quietly.

She blinked, and her expression shuttered. "Later, we'll talk later." She pasted a bright smile on her face and raised her voice. "Let's get these houses decorated before the icing hardens, girls." She moved away from him to retrieve the bowl from the counter. When he didn't leave, she glanced over her shoulder. "It's okay. You can get back to whatever you were doing out there."

Now that he'd decided what he wanted, she wasn't getting rid of him that easily. He'd let her go without a fight, let the election and his mother and Claudia distract him from what he should've done the day he'd found her letter. "No, like you said, I'm here to hang out with my nieces."

"Oh, okay." She tugged at her sweater again. "I'll be right back."

As soon as she left the kitchen, Annie looked at him like he wasn't the sharpest tool in the shed. "You should've kissed her."

Lily nodded. "Yeah, that's what Daddy does when Mommy's mad at him. But it's okay. We'll help you, right, Annie?"

Thinking about how much time they spent with Nell, Lily's offer made him nervous. "Thanks, I appreciate it, but I've got this." They gave him a skeptical look. "Come on, have a little faith in me. This your uncle Ethan, remember."

Annie sighed. "That's what we're worried about."

"Hey, I've been told I'm pretty hot—charming, too."

"Auntie Skye's twenty-eight, Uncle Eth, not eighty."

He was about to tell Annie to quit listening to her father when Skye rejoined them wearing a long-sleeved T-shirt over her black leggings. She must've noticed him grinning at the evidence that he'd gotten her all hot and bothered, because she said, "Baby hormones make me hot."

"Yeah, I remember," he said. "You were hot all the time—morning, noon, and night." Her eyes widened and darted to Annie and Lily, who were listening with interest. He cleared his throat. "Ah, guess we better get decorating."

"Me and Annie are going to do this one," Lily said, pushing the other gingerbread house toward Ethan and Skye. "You and Auntie decorate this one. We'll vote who wins once we're done."

"No," Skye blurted out. "I have a better idea. Uncle Ethan and Annie will team up, and I'll team up with you."

"It'd probably be more fair if I teamed up with Uncle Ethan," Lily said. "He doesn't know how to do stuff like this, and I'm real good at it."

"Ye of little faith," Ethan said, pushing up the sleeves of his black sweater, his competitive spirit coming to the forefront.

An hour later, he popped a candy cane in his mouth and high-fived Lily. They'd won hands down.

"Get that smug smile off your face, O'Connor. You didn't win. We're not finished yet," Skye protested, her gaze moving from one gingerbread house to the other.

He saw her wry grimace before she realized he was looking at her. "Come on, cupcake. Admit defeat. You can't compete with perfection."

"Sorry, Auntie. Uncle Eth's right." Annie pointed to their house. "They've got icicles hanging from the roof, and they put strands of candy lights around the windows and doors."

"Yeah, and did you see this?" Ethan pointed to the window he'd cut out and lined with clear plastic wrap to look like a windowpane. Through it you could see the decorated tree he'd made out of Lily's green Play-Doh and placed inside the house.

"What are you talking about? You didn't even let Lily help," Skye said.

"Yes, I . . ." He trailed off as he tried to think of one thing Lily had done on the house. "She . . . she handed me the candy." He sighed. "Sorry, Lily, I guess I got carried away."

Annie laughed, Skye tried hard not to, and Lily grinned. "It's okay. You're really good at decorating gingerbread houses. I'm going to bring it to school on Monday and show my class."

"Ah, maybe you could tell them you made it, Lily. I wouldn't mind if you took the credit, you know."

"You should ask your teacher if she wants your uncle Ethan to come in and demonstrate his decorating skills for your class, Lily. You guys have Christmas craft days next week, don't you?"

"That's a great idea. I'll ask her. And Uncle Ethan doesn't have a job, so he can come anytime."

Skye grinned at him and stuck a candy cane in her mouth.

*   *   *

So far Ethan hadn't had any luck getting his wife on her own. He didn't see his chances improving as they headed outside to play in the snow after lunch, especially with the look Skye had just given his sheepskin coat.

"You're one to talk," he said, gesturing to her furry black boots.

"It's fake fur," she said, wrapping a scarf around her neck and zipping her white jacket.

"I'm on Auntie Skye's team this time," Lily said as she knelt in the snow and began rolling a snowball. They were competing to see which team could make the best snowman.

"We've got it in the bag, Annie," he said, showing her the carrot in his pocket.

Annie grinned. "You took the last one, didn't you?"

"Yep," he said. "You start rolling, and I'll hunt down some sticks for his arms." It took him a while to find what he was looking for. By the time he came back, Lily and Skye were already putting the head on their snowman. "Hey," he said to Annie, looking at the three tiny balls in the snow. "You traitor, you're supposed to be on my team."

"Losing is good for you, Uncle Eth. You need some humility."

"I think I've met my quota, don't you?" he said, referring to his loss at the polls.

The three of them looked stricken.

"I'm kidding," he said, dropping the sticks on the ground. "Don't count me out yet. It was for best snowman, not fastest snowman makers."

Once he finished, he stood back to admire his handiwork. His was twice the size of theirs and looked great in comparison. As a finishing touch, Ethan fitted mittens on the end of the sticks. His snowman looked like he was waving hello. Brushing the snow from his gloves, he laughed when they scowled at him. "Well, ladies, looks like I won again."

Skye rolled her eyes, then looked past him, an apprehensive expression crossing her face. "Ethan, I think I saw a wolf."

He followed the direction of her gaze and didn't see anything. To be on the safe side, he said, "Okay, relax. We'll get the girls inside."

"No, you have to shoo it away, my bunny lives under the tree in the back." Lily's face crumpled.

"It's okay, Lily." Annie took her sister in her arms and patted her back. "Uncle Eth will make it go away."

"Sure I will. Don't cry, sweetheart. I'll get your dad's gun…" He saw Skye's face and corrected himself, "I'll go check it out first. You guys get inside."

"Okay." The three of them nodded as he struggled through the knee-high snow toward the back of the house. Jangling the keys in his pocket, he scanned the area for tracks. When he'd visually searched the backyard and checked under the deck, he headed back. He stopped short—the three of them were laughing their heads off. They'd stolen his snowman's nose and stick arms. "Seriously? Haven't you heard about the boy who cried wolf?

Stop laughing. It's not funny. And it doesn't matter, because I still won."

"No one likes a sore loser, Ethan," Skye said, fluttering her lashes at him. "It's not a good example to set for Lily and Annie."

"Sore loser, eh?" he said and bent down to grab a handful of snow. Before he'd formed it into a ball, someone beaned him in the head. He looked up just as Skye's snowball whizzed through the air and got him in the face. Releasing an exaggerated groan, he fell to his knees and brought his hand to his eye. Skye cried out and ran to his side. "Ethan, I'm so sorry. Let me see," she said in a panicked tone of voice, cupping his face with her cold, wet gloves.

"I can't see. There must have been a stone in the snow." He groaned again, biding his time until Annie and Lily joined her at his side on their knees, then he lunged. Wrapping his arms around the three of them, he gently took them down. "Uncle Ethan," the girls yelled between their giggles as he rubbed snow in their faces.

"That wasn't..." Skye began, struggling to get out of his arms, shrieking when he shoved snow down her jacket.

"There, now you know how it feels." He grinned as he went to stand up.

"Get him, girls," Skye yelled, and they tackled him, giving him a taste of his own medicine.

Ten minutes later, the four of them lay flat on their backs in the snow. The winds picked up and the snow swirled around them. "Come on, I won't be able to find you soon," Ethan said. He glanced at Skye, who lay beside him making snow angels with the girls.

Her face was lit up with laughter as she caught snow-flakes on her tongue. An image of her playing with their own child flashed before his eyes. His chest tightened. She was going to be an incredible mother. She'd been right at Thanksgiving when she'd said she wasn't a silly, spoiled, self-centered...

Shock reverberated through him as he remembered where he'd heard those words before. Skye had repeated verbatim what Claudia had said about her that night when his team had gathered to deal with Bennett's smear campaign. Somehow she'd found...

No, there was only one plausible explanation for how she knew what Claudia had said.

Chapter Twenty-Three

You were there," Ethan said from where he lay beside her in the snow.

Skye turned with her tongue out catching snowflakes, and nearly swallowed it as his hazel eyes went soft and warm. It was a look she saw a lot when they were together. One that made her go all warm and gooey inside. She didn't appreciate him making her feel that way now.

Who was she trying to kid? No matter how much she fought against it, Ethan O'Connor would be making her feel warm and gooey until the day she died. She'd just have to get used to it. Once her heart finally stopped its excited pitter-patter, she asked him what he was talking about. *Good job*, she thought, when her voice didn't come out all breathy and needy and sad.

"You were at my mother's. You heard what Bennett was going to do, and you left because you thought I'd have a chance to win if you weren't by my side. You left to protect me." He stood up and took her hand. "Annie and Lily, it's time to go inside." He helped Skye to her feet and held her gaze. "And it's time you and I talked."

"We wanna play outside. We're going to build a fort, right, Lily?" Annie gave her sister a nudge.

"Oh, yeah, we're staying outside. You go inside with Uncle Ethan, Auntie Skye," Lily said with an exaggerated wink at Ethan.

"Okay, but stay where we can see you," he agreed as he dragged Skye toward the front steps. Ushering her into the house, he shut the door. "Start talking."

"Would you mind if I get my boots and coat off first? Thanks to you, I'm a little cold and wet," she said, taking off her hat and gloves.

"Yeah, I remember when I used to make you *hot* and wet," he muttered, shoving his jacket into the closet. "Dammit, Skye, because of your misguided attempt to protect me, we've lost a month together."

"I resent that. It wasn't misguided," she said, ignoring her sex-starved body's response to his "hot and wet" comment as she stripped off her jacket.

"And I resent you vanishing in the middle of the night, for leaving me a goddamn note"—he backed her against the wall, caging her in—"that broke my heart, for—"

"I broke your heart?"

He took her face in his hands, his eyes searching hers. "How can you even ask me that? I loved you, Skye. I loved you, and you left me."

"You didn't love me. You loved Kendall."

His brow furrowed. "What are talking about? *You* are Kendall."

She shook her head and tried to move out from under him, but he wouldn't let her escape, pressing against her with his hard, warm body. "Yes, you are," he said.

"No, I'm not. I pretended to be Kendall because you loved *her*. It was Kendall you needed, not me. I'm the one who lost the election for you, Ethan. Me, not Kendall."

"You should've told me how you felt. I loved you, *Skye*. It was always you I loved."

"Whenever you told me you loved me, you called me Kendall, not Skye."

"You're starting to piss me off, cupcake. I—"

"And that's another thing—up until today, you haven't called me cupcake in months. Today was the first time—"

He cut her off with a frustrated sound in his throat then dipped his head and devoured her mouth. Wrapping his arms around her, he lifted her off her feet, carrying her through the house with his lips fused to hers. Her dreams hadn't done him justice. Somehow she'd forgotten how he could steal her senses, turning her into a boneless mass of quivering desire with a simple kiss. Actually, it wasn't so simple. It was a long, hard kiss filled with so much passion her toes curled in her socks.

She held back a disappointed groan when he lifted his head, pushing something away with his foot. He dropped onto the couch with her sprawled over him. "You. I love *you*, Skylar Davis O'Connor. You and our baby." He moved her onto his lap. Once he got her settled, he placed his heavy hand on her stomach. "I missed my wife and our baby."

She covered his hand. "You married me because of the baby."

"You married me because of Moriarty."

"No, not just him. I—"

"Hold that thought." He raised his hip to dig his buzzing cell from his jeans pocket. "It's Gage," he told her and took the call. He didn't take his eyes off her while he spoke to his best friend. She skimmed her fingers along his jaw, amazed that only yesterday she thought they were over and now it looked like they had a second chance. If he could forgive her, then maybe they could make this work. She wouldn't have to worry about being someone she wasn't, not anymore. There would no longer be supporters and constituents to please and pacify.

The baby kicked, and Ethan blinked. Skye smiled at the surprise in his eyes. Her smile faltering as she realized it was because of her that he'd missed out on that. Missed seeing the impression of a foot or small fist move across her stomach.

He lifted his chin as if to say *What's wrong?*

She shook her head, then laid it on his chest, listening to the strong, steady beat of his heart.

"Don't worry about us," he said, stroking her hair. "I'll have the girls call you when they come inside. Yeah, we're good. No, we haven't scarred them by fighting in front of them. Might by making out in front of them." He laughed. "Yeah, right, as if they haven't caught the two of you. Okay, we'll see you in the morning." He disconnected and leaned over to put his cell on the coffee table. "Roads are bad. They're holed up in a motel in the next county for the night."

She lifted her head and looked out the window at the big, fat flakes falling heavily from the sky. "Maybe we should call the girls in."

"Two minutes. I want to know what you were going to

say, and I want to kiss you again before they come in." He slid his hand under her sweater, caressing her stomach as he held her gaze. "But before we do either of those things, tell me about the baby, how you're feeling."

"I'm good. We're both good. It's weird, though, every time I lay down, she goes crazy. The only way I can get her to settle down is to sing 'Wild Horses.'"

"Maybe she knew something was missing. Maybe she missed my hand on your belly when you went to sleep," he said, stroking her stomach with his long, strong fingers.

It was true. He'd always slept with Skye tucked against him, his big hand resting on her stomach. A heated shiver quivered up her spine as he continued to stroke and caress her. As though he sensed her reaction, he smiled. "You missed me, too, didn't you?"

"Of course I did. I didn't want to leave, Ethan. I—" She sighed when Lily and Annie called out loudly—"We're inside now"—and slammed the door.

"They're well trained." Ethan laughed, giving her a quick kiss and gently easing her off his lap. "But don't worry, cupcake, we've got all night to talk."

With the heated look he gave her, Skye wondered how much talking he intended to do. But no matter what he planned, no matter how much she wanted the same, they were finishing this conversation tonight. This time, she planned on being totally open and honest.

*   *   *

Ethan O'Connor was one very sneaky man. Somehow, without Lily and Annie noticing, he managed to touch Skye every five minutes and kiss her senseless every chance he got. Now *she* was thinking that talking was overrated.

They were all sitting around in their pajamas—well, Skye and the girls were, at least—watching *Jack Frost*.

Ethan had been trying to get them to change the channel for the last thirty minutes. "Seriously, how can this be a Christmas movie? The dad died. All right," he said when the three of them gave him a look, "I know when I'm not wanted. But you wait, in about ten minutes, you're going to be very glad I'm here." He waggled his brows, patted Skye's thigh, then got up from the couch and walked toward the kitchen.

Her gaze followed him, unable to take her eyes off his firm behind, the way those well-worn jeans encased his muscular thighs. She turned back to the TV. She had to get a grip or at least distract herself. "Wow, look at him go," she said as Charlie Frost skated down the ice.

"I didn't know you liked hockey, Auntie. Annie loves it now 'cause Trent plays. He has a game on Thursday. You should come with us."

Annie released a dramatic sigh. "Lily, I already told you, you can't come."

"You're not the boss of me, Annie. It's a free world. I can go if I want. I like hockey, too, you know."

"You can come watch me and your dad play, Lily," Ethan said as he returned to the living room. Skye eyed the marshmallows, graham crackers, chocolate bars, and metal skewer he carried with trepidation.

"That's not real hockey," Lily said. "You just play for fun."

He set his stash on the fireplace ledge. "What are you talking about? We're a real league."

Annie snorted. "Yeah, an old-timer's league."

"You play hockey?" Skye asked. Though he did have the

body of athlete, he seemed more cerebral than athletic. She just thought he'd been blessed with amazing genes.

"Don't sound so surprised," he said as he sat beside the fire, stretching out his long legs. "I was MVP last game."

"Jack said it's 'cause they felt sorry for you."

"I scored the winning goal. Jack's mad we beat his and Sawyer's team. You know, Sawyer, ex-captain of the Colorado Flurries, a *professional* hockey team. Yeah, that's who we beat." He shook his head while threading marshmallows onto the skewer. "Careful, or I won't make you a s'more."

Annie opened her mouth, and Skye caught her eye, giving her head a subtle shake. He obviously wanted to do something special for the girls, and she didn't want to disappoint him. They'd have to figure out a way to hide the fact that they would not in this lifetime eat marshmallows.

"Okay, I'm not going to let your doubts about my athletic prowess stop me from treating you to the best dessert bar none. Get over here."

Behind Ethan's back, the girl's held out their hands as if to say *What do we do now?* while Skye silently indicated she'd handle it. "Umm, smells good," she said, positioning herself a foot or so behind him, waving for the girls to do the same.

Ethan glanced over his shoulder as he knelt in front of the fireplace, holding the skewered marshmallows above the low flame. "You sure I can't change your mind about chocolate? You don't know what you're missing. All right," he conceded when she shook her head, "I'll give you extra marshmallows."

"Mm, yum," she said, trying not to gag.

He grinned, looking so adorably sweet, that she knew

she'd made the right decision. She edged the leather magazine holder closer as Ethan gingerly slid the bubbling, browned marshmallows onto the graham crackers he'd prepared beforehand with a piece of milk chocolate. "It's a little hot, so wait a minute before you eat it, Lily."

Lily rubbed her tummy. "It looks so good, Uncle Ethan. Thanks."

He smiled and tweaked her ponytail then turned to thread more marshmallows onto the skewer. "You're next, Annie."

"Can't wait," she said, putting both hands around her neck, being sure to stay out of Ethan's line of sight. Lily handed Skye her plate. She dumped the s'more in the magazine holder, covering it with papers as she gave Lily back her empty plate.

"You can't be finished already," Ethan said to Lily as he handed Annie her s'more.

"Yep, it was the best. Way better than Daddy makes," Lily said.

She's got her uncle's number, Skye thought.

Ethan grabbed a couple more marshmallows out of the bag. "Cool. I'll have to tell him you said so."

"Ethan, you have a problem," Skye said. "You might want to talk to someone about your compulsive need to compete. You're setting a bad example for the girls. Just remember, Annie and Lily, everyone's a winner."

Annie was about to give Skye her plate, when Ethan turned to them. "Don't listen to her, girls. She's living in Fairyland. Competition is a good thing. Without it, we'd be living in the Dark Ages. Nothing better than a little competition to make you aware of your strengths and weaknesses." He looked at Annie's plate. "They're better warm, eat up."

She nodded and put it to her mouth, tossing it to Skye as soon as he went back to toasting his marshmallows. "You know…" he began as he turned, then his gaze jerked from Skye to the s'more she was dumping in the magazine holder. "Really…really," he said, taking the s'mores from underneath the paper, holding them up as if they were evidence in a murder trial. "What the hel…heck? I—"

"We didn't want to hurt your feelings, but we can't eat them," Annie said.

He looked at them, lifted the s'more to his mouth, and took a big bite. "These are frigging awesome." Skye pressed her lips together to keep from laughing. He waved the half-eaten s'more at her. "What are you teaching these girls? This is perfectly—"

Lily grimaced. "Marshmallows are made from the skin and bones of animals."

He looked from the s'more to Lily. "They are not."

"Are too," said Annie.

"All you had to do was tell me you didn't want them," he said in a grumpy tone of voice, gathering up the bag of marshmallows. "I wouldn't have wasted my time."

"We won't think worse of you for eating the s'more, Ethan. It's a personal choice. Here, I'll clean up. You watch the end of the movie with the girls." Skye took the bag from him, bending down to pick up the rest. "Honestly, go ahead and eat them," she said as she straightened, pressing the s'mores into his hand.

He stood up, handed them back to her, and said low enough that only she could hear, "Chance was right. You really are a pain in the ass."

She went up on her toes and kissed his cheek. "But you love me."

"Yeah, I do," he said, lightly swatting her behind as she headed for the kitchen. The warm glow of happiness that enveloped her dissipated a little as she thought back to his earlier comments. She hadn't realized until today how competitive Ethan was. It'd been amusing earlier when they were competing over gingerbread houses and snowmen. Probably because he'd looked so irresistibly sexy, and it'd been nice to be able to have fun and laugh together again.

But now she realized, as competitive as he was, he wouldn't give up on his political career. No, he'd regroup and, with Claudia's help, run again. Skye had been fooling herself. Drying off the skewer, she placed it in the bottom drawer, wondering how she could've been so stupid getting her hopes up. There's no way Ethan would give up on his dream. And with Claudia and Liz egging him on, Skye would be right back where she started.

"Okay, movie's over. Time for you two to go to bed," she heard Ethan say.

The moment of reckoning was upon her, she thought, as she headed for the living room. It was now or never. Watching Ethan laugh with Annie and Lily as he carried them to their bedrooms, she wished she could choose never.

"You okay?" Ethan asked Skye after they'd tucked the girls into bed.

"I'm good, just a little cold." It wasn't a lie, but she doubted the goose bumps breaking out on her arms had anything to do with the blustery winds and snow battering the living room window.

"We'll sit by the fire," he said, grabbing a couple of pillows and the throw off the couch. Once he had them set up and had wrapped Skye in the red plaid blanket, he went to make her a cup of tea.

Christmas carols played on the radio, setting the scene for a perfectly romantic evening. And she was going to ruin it, just like she'd ruined his career. She stared out the window, the snow so heavy she could barely make out the mountains in the distance, wondering if she could let it go. Maybe this wasn't something they had to talk about now.

"What are you thinking about?" Ethan asked. He handed her a mug as he settled himself in behind her, and drew her into his arms.

She smiled her thanks, then said, "Us. I didn't expect this. I didn't think today would turn out this way."

He brushed his lips across the top of her head, linking his hands over her stomach. "Neither did I, but I'm happy our best friends took matters into their own hands and set us up. But if they hadn't, I'm pretty sure Nell would have." He laughed. "She has a book deadline, remember?"

"I thought it was funny when she wrote Maddie's and Grace's stories, but I don't think it's so funny now." She put down her mug, tipping her head back. "Ethan, I'm not joking. You have to stop Nell. Send her one of those cease-and-desist letters."

"Why? I bet our book will outsell Gage's and Jack's. We've got way more going on than they do."

She buried her face in her hands and groaned. She couldn't believe him. "Yeah, Grace and Maddie are normal. You're the one with the crazy wife. I'll turn into a joke on late-night television. Everyone will feel sorry for you. The man who married the woman who destroyed his dream."

"What I have is an incredibly passionate wife who gives a damn and stands up for what she believes in. And, cupcake, you didn't destroy my dream. If you would've given me a chance, we could've handled Bennett together. We didn't lose by much, and we made inroads in what was a predominantly Democrat district."

"You deserved to win, Ethan. You should've won, and if it wasn't for me, you would have. That's something I'll always regret. The last thing I wanted to do was hurt you. I'm sorry, sorrier than you'll ever know."

"If it wasn't for you busting your butt on the campaign trail, I wouldn't have had half of those votes. You did that, Skye. *You* were amazing. You worked as hard as anyone to get me elected, and even though it was unnecessary and somewhat misguided, you made the ultimate sacrifice, and that's something *I'll* never forget."

"Thank you, but in the end, I'm still responsible. Can you honestly forgive me?"

He sighed, turning her so she faced him with her legs straddling his hips. "I want you to listen to me, okay?" She nodded and he continued, "The only thing that matters to me is that you're here now. That you love me, and that we're going to raise our baby together. Having a family was as much my dream as being a senator. All that political stuff, that came from my dad. It was more his dream than mine."

"I don't understand. Your mom showed me your scrapbooks. She told me—"

"I know what she told you. She doesn't know about my last conversation with my dad. She doesn't know I told him I'd changed my mind." He stared out the window before returning his gaze to hers. The raw emotion she saw in his eyes took her aback. "I loved my job as ADA. I felt as though I'd found my calling. When I said as much to my dad, he was furious. He told me I was throwing everything he'd worked so hard for away. If I would've backed down, given in, he'd be here now. Instead, I told him if he wanted it so badly maybe he should run. He had a fatal heart attack only hours after that call."

She searched his face and didn't like what she saw. "Ethan, you're not responsible for your father's death. You know that, don't you?"

He held her gaze. "But I am. He'd never been sick a day in his life."

"You listen to me, Ethan O'Connor. He had a heart attack. You didn't cause it. I'm sure if you asked your mother there'd been signs—"

"No, I'm not talking about this with her. It would kill her if she knew. She'd never forgive me."

"But, Ethan—"

"Skye, I've never told anyone about this, not even Gage. I'm trusting you to keep this to yourself. Promise me you won't say anything to anyone."

Seeing the pain his guilt caused him, she wasn't sure it was a promise she could make. "This isn't healthy. You need to talk to someone. Talk to Paul. Please, he'll keep your confidence, and he out of anyone will know if your dad had health issues that you were unaware of. Because, Ethan, I'll guarantee you that he did."

"No. This goes no further than us."

"Okay." She reluctantly gave in, realizing that for now, there was no way she would change his mind. But somehow she had to banish the sorrow from his eyes. She angled her head. "So, what you're telling me is that I saved you. I saved you from making the biggest mistake of your life." She gave him a long, passionate—and she hoped—healing kiss, then lifted her head and smiled. "I'm your hero, Ethan O'Connor."

He shook his head with a laugh. "What you are is a gorgeous fruitcake."

"Hey." She lightly swatted his chest. "I'm not a fruitcake."

"I love fruitcake, and I love you," he said, swallowing her "I love you, too" with one of his off-the-charts, toe-curling kisses.

Minutes into their hot and steamy kiss, there was a loud bang. The lights flickered, then went out. "Wow," Skye said, lifting her head to look around the room. "I'm impressed. I knew your kiss packed a wallop, but I didn't think it was strong enough to knock out the electricity."

Once he stopped laughing, he said, "I'm going to make a couple of calls, check to be sure it was the storm that caused the outage. And then, cupcake, I'll take you to bed and show you just how powerful I am."

"If we were alone, I'd race you to the bedroom, but we're not. Annie and Lily—"

"—are asleep, and I'm pretty sure Gage and Madison—"

"Uncle Ethan, Auntie Skye, I can't see anything. What happened?" they heard Lily call from her bedroom at the same time as a bright flashlight shone in their faces.

"It's okay, Lily," Annie said. "I'll come get you. We'll camp out by the fire with Auntie Skye and Uncle Eth. They've got it all set up."

Lily yelled "Yay!" at the same time Ethan groaned.

Chapter Twenty-Four

Ethan held Skye's arm as they made their way down the icy driveway to where he'd parked the Escalade. They were headed to Grace and Jack's for a tree-trimming party. "Thanks," Skye said when Ethan took the container of food from her hand. She glanced at the pile of snow where her car should have been. "Hey, you guys forgot to shovel me out."

As soon as Gage and Maddie had arrived home this morning, the two men left to help out the snowed-in residents of Christmas. Skye and Maddie spent the day wrapping presents and cooking for the party.

"We thought it was safer if the egg didn't hatch until spring."

"Ha-ha, you're hilarious."

He grinned and opened the passenger's-side door of the Escalade. Once she was settled inside, he handed her the plastic container and kissed her. "You don't need a car. I'll take you wherever you want to go."

"That's going to be a little difficult once you're work-ing," she said, then cast him a nervous glance. "You are accepting your old job as ADA, aren't you?" She'd been over the moon when Ethan told her about Jordan's offer this morning. And not just because it meant he wasn't going to run for political office again, though, admittedly, the thought had happily crossed her mind. No, she was thrilled that he'd be doing something he loved, something he was passionate about.

"I am. I'm meeting with him tomorrow morning to firm up the details. He said Sam's e-mailing you a couple of places to look at. They're downtown."

After he'd informed Skye of his decision, they'd dis-cussed living arrangements. They'd stay in Denver during the week and Christmas on the weekend. Which suited Skye just fine, until she realized Ethan meant for her to sell her new house on Sugar Plum Lane. He wanted to spend weekends at the ranch. She knew he loved his mother, but what she also knew, even if he wouldn't admit it, was that the decision probably had more to do with Ethan's guilt than love.

And that was something Skye didn't like. For Ethan's sake, she had to make him see how detrimental to his well-being it was to hold on to his mistaken belief that he'd killed his father.

Given his reaction last night, it wasn't something to bring up now. So she took up the conversation where they'd left off. "I like my independence, Ethan, and despite what you think of my car, it's safe."

"Wait for us," Lily yelled, as she and Annie ran down the front steps.

"I love those two, but I was hoping we'd have at least

ten minutes on our own. Careful!" he called out as they started down the driveway. Then he said to Skye, "We'll stay for an hour at the Flahertys'. Make an excuse to leave. Tell them you're not feeling well."

Skye had to admit that she felt the same as Ethan. They had a lot of lost time to make up for, and she was looking forward to being alone together. "If I say I'm sick, and Dr. McBride's there, he'll probably make me go to the hospital. Why don't we just tell them the truth?"

"What . . . that I want to ravish my wife? That I want to get her in my bed and not let her out of it for the next week?"

"Geez, Uncle Eth, TMI," Annie said, opening the back door.

Ethan's face reddened, and he gave Skye a you-could've-warned-me look.

She'd been too busy staring into her husband's beautiful eyes to notice anything but the way her body reacted to his heated promise. "I didn't realize she was there," Skye said, unable to keep the laughter from her voice. She couldn't remember seeing the unflappable Ethan O'Connor blush before.

"It's not funny," he muttered, closing her door and helping Lily inside before rounding the SUV.

"Put the radio on, and we can sing carols," Lily said, bouncing in the backseat.

"Someone wanna tell me how we got stuck with you two and not your parents?" he said, doing as Lily asked.

"Mommy has to feed Connor. And you better not be grumpy or Santa won't give you your present tonight. It's a really good one."

"Lily." Annie elbowed her sister.

"What? I'm not going to tell him."

"Tell me what?" Ethan asked as he pulled onto the road.

He didn't get his answer. The girls were too busy singing "Grandma Got Run Over by a Reindeer" along with the radio.

"I'm glad you think it's so funny," he said to Skye. "You know what they're doing, don't you? I'll guarantee it's not feeding the baby."

"You're just jealous," she said, then joined in with the girls.

"Yeah, I am," he agreed, then started singing, too.

As they turned onto Sugar Plum Lane, Lily leaned forward, pointing out the window. "Wow, look at the lights." The residents on the street had gone all out. Every Victorian, except for Skye's, was lit up with colorful Christmas lights.

"Did you call the Realtor?" Ethan asked, as they passed the yellow Victorian that only a few days ago Skye thought she'd be making her home.

"No, I've decided not to sell. I don't want to hurt Betty Jean's feelings."

Ethan didn't look happy with her answer. "I thought we'd settled this. I'm sure she'd understand."

"We did, but it doesn't mean I have to sell the house. I've been thinking we'd run Envirochicks out of it. If the street's commercially zoned, we could have a storefront."

"You're going to be in Denver most of the time. Wouldn't it be better to set up shop there?"

"No, Betty Jean and I already agreed on Christmas."

"As long as you don't think it's going to be too much for you. I don't want you running yourself ragged. You're going to be busy once the baby comes, you know."

"I know. But I have you to help out. It's not like I'm raising the baby on my own, right?"

"Okay, you made your point, cupcake. We'll work it out." He pulled behind Nell's truck in front of Jack and Grace's purple Victorian. They'd decorated the house, trees, and shrubs all in white lights. Paper luminaries lit up the path to the front porch. "Girls, be careful. It's slippery out there," he warned Lily and Annie, as they got out of the SUV.

They ignored him, racing each other to the house. Ethan came around to Skye's side and helped her out of the SUV. He took the container from her and set it on the seat.

"What are—" At the feel of his hot, greedy mouth on hers, she forgot what she was going to ask. She curled her fingers in his jacket, holding on when her knees went weak.

"Get a room," a deep male voice said. Skye opened her eyes to see Sawyer Anderson laughing as he walked by with a stunning brunette on his arm.

Ethan rested his forehead against hers, his breath a rough rasp. "He's right. We should just skip the party and go home."

"We can't. Grace has been planning the party for weeks." Skye grabbed the container of sugar cookies. "Besides, we have all night to make up for lost time."

"It's going to take a lot more than one night," he said, pressing the Lock button on his keys and taking her hand.

She looked up at him. The Christmas lights cast his face in an ethereal glow. There were times, like now, when she looked at him and couldn't believe this amazing man was her husband. And how close she'd come to losing him. "Good thing we have forever then."

*   *   *

An hour later, the party was in full swing. The Flahertys' house was overflowing with friends and neighbors. In the living room, Skye looked up from where she sat, by the fire with Grace and Maddie, to see Ethan laughing with Gage, Sawyer, and Jack.

"Now that is some serious eye candy," Maddie said, following her gaze. "I wonder if we could get them to pose for a Christmas calendar. It would sell like hotcakes."

"Your brain never stops, does it?" Skye laughed, feeling happier than she had in weeks. It was good to be back in Christmas with her friends. Admittedly, her happiness probably had more to do with the man looking at her from across the room. She smiled at her husband who winked and mouthed *Fifteen minutes*.

"No way," Maddie said, catching their exchange. "You can't leave, not until Santa comes. And the kids are expecting you to read the Sugar Plum Cake Fairy story."

"Sorry, I think I'm a little too big to fit in the costume."

"Nell altered it," Grace said with a smile. "But you can just wear the crown if you don't feel like getting changed. I like your sweater, by the way."

Skye wore cream corduroy leggings with a lilac sweater. "Thanks, Betty Jean had it made for me. It's a new type of acrylic that we're going to use in our sweaters. It looks like cashmere, doesn't it?"

Maddie rubbed her arm. "Feels like it, too. I'm proud of you, you know. And I'm very glad you're setting up shop in Christmas. Ethan will be, too. It'll be great for the local economy."

"I'm not sure how happy he is, since we're going to be living in Denver."

With a mischievous glint in her eyes, Maddie patted Skye's knee and stood up. "I think he might have a change of heart before the night is out."

"What are you up to?" Skye asked.

"You'll just have to wait and see." She tugged Skye to her feet. "Come on, ladies. Let's help the kids decorate the tree."

"Are you sure you want to do this, Grace? We might make a mess of your tree," Skye said.

"Don't worry about it. With little Jack around, I have a feeling we'll be redecorating it every other day or so." Grace gestured to the adorable, dark-haired little boy who was the spitting image of his gorgeous father. Little Jack ran around the Christmas tree with two toddlers chasing after him.

Maddie and Skye organized the kids with Annie's help, and Grace handed out ornaments with Lily. Once they began decorating the tree, Nell and her friends called out instructions. Skye was reaching up to put a gold ball on one of the upper branches when warm hands settled on either side of her waist. "Need some help, cupcake?"

"Keep doing that," she said when he nuzzled her neck, "and I'm going to drop this ball."

"Can't have that," he said, putting his hand over hers to hook the ball on the branch. He lowered his voice. "I figure ten more minutes, and we're good to go."

"More like half an hour. After we finish the tree, I have to read the Cake Fairy story to the kids. But don't worry—I'll read fast."

Liz, who'd been showing baby Connor the Christmas tree lights, turned to her son. "You can't leave." Ethan's mother had been doing her best to avoid Skye. She'd barely said ten words to her all night. Obviously, while Ethan had forgiven her, it was going to take Liz O'Connor some time to do the same.

"Ho ho ho, Merry Christmas," Santa said as he arrived in the living room with a large red velvet sack slung over his shoulder. The kids jumped up and down, converging on the realistic-looking Santa. With his full belly and white beard, there was no way this was Gage.

"It's Calder Dane," Maddie whispered as if reading Skye's thoughts. Rumor had it the older man and Nell McBride had a romantic history. Considering how Nell's cheeks pinked when she glanced at Santa, Skye thought the rumors might well be true.

Jack pulled up a chair beside the tree, and Santa took a seat. The children gathered on the floor at his feet.

"Aw, they're so cute," Skye said, looking at the bright anticipation on their faces.

"You're pretty cute, too. Wanna sit on my knee?" Ethan asked, drawing her onto the couch beneath the front bay window.

"Behave," she said, nudging him with her elbow.

By the time Santa had given the last of the children a present, Skye was more than ready to leave. Ethan had been doing his best to drive her crazy with his subtle touches and caresses. "Cut it out," she whispered. "We have an audience." And they did. Everyone had turned to them with smiles on their faces.

"Ho ho ho," Santa said, digging in the bottom of his sack. He pulled out a brightly wrapped present. "Ethan

O'Connor, I hear you've been a very good boy this year. Get up here, son."

Friends and neighbors clapped when Ethan got up from the couch and walked over to Santa. "I'm not sitting on your knee," he said, looking somewhat bewildered. He opened the present and held up a key at the same time Nell and her friends unraveled a sign that said, "Mayor Ethan O'Connor for State Senate, 2018."

Skye's pulse quickened as her mind raced through the implications. Surely he'd put a stop to this. But one look at his expression as he took in the cheering crowd told her she was wrong.

"Ethan," Maddie said, "the town council voted, and we want you take over as mayor."

"You can't say no, and we're all backing you for another run at the state senate," Nell McBride told him.

"Here." His mother handed him a cell phone. "It's Claudia. She and Richard are already working on your campaign, and Nell has started a fund-raising committee in town. This time, darling, nothing will get in the way of you winning."

Nothing meaning me, Skye thought, a heavy weight bearing down on her chest. She wanted to tell them that he didn't want this, that it wasn't his dream but his father's. To leave him alone and let him get on with his life.

Instead she got up from the couch. No one noticed as she retrieved her jacket from the overstuffed hall closet, shoved her feet into her boots, and left the house. They were too busy listening to Ethan on the phone, making plans for the next election.

Hands shoved in her pockets, head bowed, Skye didn't know how long she'd been walking when a vehicle crunched in the snow beside her. She heard a window go down, then a familiar male voice said, "Where do you think you're going?"

She stopped, turning to look at him. "Did you tell them that you didn't want to be mayor, Ethan? That running for the state senate wasn't your dream but your father's? Because if you didn't, I don't think we have anything to talk about." She started walking.

He cursed and a door slammed. Seconds later, he caught her by the arm and turned her to face him. "What did you want me to do?"

"Tell them the truth."

"Are you sure this is about me and not about you?"

"Of course it's about you. It's always been about you, don't you get that? You loved your job as ADA, and now you're going to give up that opportunity to make everyone else happy. Again. You can't keep doing this, Ethan. You have to tell them the truth."

"You were there. You saw how excited they were, how much they wanted this."

"They want it because they love you and they think it's what you want. All you have to do is be honest with them. If you can't…"

"If I can't, what? Are you going to leave me again?"

"No, but if anyone asks me how I feel about it, I'm not going to lie. I'm going to tell them the truth."

"It's not your truth to tell, Skye. It's mine."

"You're right, it is. And I hope you do tell them, Ethan, because take it from me, it's not easy pretending to be someone you're not. Just so you know, I won't make that mistake again. If you take another run at the senate, I'll support you, but it'll be me, environmental animal rights activist Skylar Davis—not Kendall, and not another Claudia clone. So if you're going to do this, you better be sure it's me you want by your side." She shook off his hand and headed for the SUV. "You'd probably have a better chance of winning if you have Claudia by your side."

"She's already offered her services—but you were there, you know that," he said as he got in the Escalade.

"I meant as your wife, Ethan. And I'm pretty sure you wouldn't have to twist her arm." She looked out the window at the Christmas lights. He didn't respond, didn't start the engine, and she glanced at him.

"How can you say that? You know much I love you, so how the hell can you even say something like that?"

Chapter Twenty-Five

Skye woke up cold and alone in Ethan's bed the next morning. Which wasn't a surprise, given how their night had ended. The drive to the ranch had been a silent one. As soon as they got there, she'd gone to bed, leaving Ethan sitting by the fire on his phone fielding calls.

Thinking over how she reacted last night, Skye realized she'd handled the situation badly. Her intentions were good—she'd wanted to protect him—but it wasn't what he'd needed from her. He'd needed her support. This was a difficult time for him, and his issues with his father's death only made it worse. It was really a no-win situation unless Skye could free him from his guilt. Now more than ever, she needed answers, and she needed them quick.

Skye rolled over and picked up her phone from the nightstand. It was almost ten. She couldn't believe she'd slept that late. There were a couple of missed texts: two from Maddie, and one from Ethan. In her first text,

Maddie wanted to know what was wrong with Skye. In her second, she seemed to have figured out the problem and apologized. As Skye had realized months ago, Maddie's loyalties were torn. But it was Ethan's text that caused a swell of hopeful emotion in Skye's chest. He hadn't canceled his meeting after all. Surely, if anyone could convince him to take his old job back, it would be Jordan Reinhart. And if Skye found out what she needed to know before he came home, they could put this all behind them and get on with their lives.

With a plan beginning to coalesce in her brain, she showered and got dressed, then went in search of Liz. She found her mother-in-law in the barn. "Good morning," Skye said in a cheery tone of voice.

Liz, dressed in jeans and a sheepskin coat, leaned on a broom and arched a brow at her. So maybe this wasn't the day for subtle digging after all.

Suck it up, buttercup, Skye told herself. She had more important things to worry about than the fact her mother-in-law didn't like her. But they did bond over horses, sort of. "How's Bandit doing?" Skye asked as she walked further into the barn, her gaze moving to his stall. It was empty. "Where is he?"

Liz briefly closed her eyes and shook her head. "He's gone."

"What do you mean, he's gone? What did you do to him?"

"We didn't do anything, Skye. It was Bandit's owner. If we'd known he was fighting the seizure, maybe we could've stopped it. But we didn't. And when the agent didn't show up in court to face the owner's complaint that the search was improper, the judge threw the case out."

"So what if the search was improper? Bandit was abused. You should have done something."

"Like what? His owner arrived with a court order last week and took Bandit. Ethan's making sure the Department of Animal Cruelty closely monitors the situation."

Skye felt sick at the thought of Bandit in the hands of his abusive owner. If she hadn't left Ethan, she would've been here. She could've done something to protect Bandit. "Where's the ranch? I need an address."

"Why? What are you going to do?"

"I'm going to make sure Bandit's all right. And if he isn't...I don't know, I'll take pictures or something. Surely after a second complaint against the man, they'll remove Bandit right away." Tears prickling behind her eyes, she looked at her mother-in-law. "We can't let him hurt Bandit again."

Liz worried her bottom lip between her teeth. "You're right, but..." She leaned the broom against the wall. "Okay. Come on. We'll take my truck," she said. "But you have to promise you won't do anything crazy or I'm going on my own."

Skye sighed as they headed out of the barn. "Despite what you and Claudia think of me, I'm not crazy. Maybe I did some stupid things when I was younger, but I believed in what I was doing. I thought I could make a difference. I just went about it the wrong way. I'm sorry, you know, about the election. When I found out what Bennett was up to, I tried to protect Ethan."

As they reached the black pickup, Liz stopped and stared at her. "That's why you left him...to protect him?"

"I love Ethan, Liz. I would never do anything to

purposely hurt him," she said, opening the passenger's-side door.

"Then I don't understand what last night was about. I thought you'd be happy for him. Happy to live in Christmas."

"I would be if it was what he wants, but it's not." This was the opportunity she'd been waiting for, but in telling his mother the truth, she'd be breaking her promise to Ethan. She weighed the consequences, putting herself in Liz's shoes and then Ethan's. If he found out she'd told his mother, he wouldn't forgive her, but for his sake, Skye had to take the risk. "If I tell you something, do you promise to keep it between us? Ethan can never know what I'm about to share with you."

Liz cast her a sidelong glance, then nodded as she drove through the wrought-iron gates. Skye hesitated at the thought of breaking his confidence, and then she remembered the tortured look in his eyes. "Ethan blames himself for his father's death," she said, and repeated their conversation to Liz. By the time she'd finished, tears were streaming down his mother's face.

"I'm sorry," Liz said and pulled to the side of the road. "I need a minute."

Skye opened the glove compartment, found some tissues, and handed them to Liz. The older woman blew her nose, leaning against the headrest. "I can't believe he's kept that to himself for all these years. How could I be so blind?"

"You'd lost your husband. You were grieving."

"It's no excuse." She covered her face and shook her head. "And as much as I'm angry at myself, I'm angry at Deacon. Damn him for putting all that pressure on Ethan."

Skye rubbed Liz's arm. "I'm sorry. I didn't mean to upset you. But now that you know, you can fix this. Did your husband have health issues before his heart attack?"

"Yes, but he didn't want the kids to know. He had high blood pressure and high cholesterol. Paul warned him it was only a matter of time if he didn't change his lifestyle. I tried, you know, but he was stubborn. He thought he was invincible. I guess I did, too, or I would've pushed him harder."

"Don't blame yourself, Liz. It won't help Ethan. But I think I've come up with a way that will."

"How?"

Skye filled her in on the plan as Liz pulled onto the road. All they had to do was get Dr. McBride on board. Knowing how Paul felt about the O'Connors, Skye didn't foresee a problem. All she had to do was insist Ethan have a physical. And given that high cholesterol and blood pressure ran in his family, it was something he needed to do anyway. Then Dr. McBride could reveal his father's medical history.

"Paul was right," Liz said, casting Skye a sidelong glance. "You are the best thing that happened to my son. I owe you an apology. I hope we can start over."

"I'd like that." Skye smiled, feeling more hopeful that Liz would keep her promise. But just in case... "Liz, you understand the risk I took telling you, don't you? Ethan would never forgive me if he found out."

"You did it for his own good. Honestly, I can't believe he didn't confide in me. He tells me everything."

Okay, so now Skye was getting nervous. "But you're not going to tell him, right?"

"No, of course not. I hope once Paul makes him understand he wasn't to blame, that he'll tell me himself."

Good, that was good to hear. And while she was at it, Skye thought she might as well do a little matchmaking. It was a selfish move on her part, really. Skye didn't want Liz to end up with Richard, because that meant Claudia would be her stepsister-in-law. She shuddered at the thought of years of holiday dinners with Claudia sitting across the dining room table from her. "It's probably best if you explain the situation to Dr. McBride. I don't know him very well, and the two of you are so close."

Liz turned onto the highway, keeping her eyes on the road. "It might be better if you talk to him. Paul and I aren't exactly on speaking terms these days."

"Really? How come?"

"We had words the night of the election. I, um, threw a drink at him. I probably should apologize. He said I needed to get a life and stop living through my son." She glanced at Skye. "Do you think I'm living through Ethan?"

Um, yes. "No, I mean you were very involved in his campaign, but that's natural, right? What do you normally do? Are you involved with any committees, local charities?"

"No, I just pitch in whenever anyone needs me."

"I guess you keep busy with the ranch."

"Raul likes to run things his way. I help out where I can." She grimaced. "Damn the man, he was right again."

Skye held back a laugh. "I've heard you're a fantastic seamstress. If you're interested, Betty Jean and I will be hiring in the New Year." Her amusement faded as Liz pulled to the side of the country road down from a run-down house and barn. "I have a better idea. Open a sanctuary for abused horses and become an advocate." She turned to her mother-in-law. "This isn't right, Liz. Look at this place. How could they give Bandit back to him?"

"I don't know. And Bandit wasn't the only horse they took from him. They placed the others with ranches throughout the county." Liz leaned forward, peering through the window. "Someone's home. There's smoke coming out of the chimney. We're going to have to be careful. I don't want to get caught trespassing."

Neither did Skye. "We'll be in and out in two minutes. Just long enough to take a couple of pictures." They both got out of the pickup, quietly closing the doors behind them.

The barn was past the house. It was also out in the open, which didn't help their cause. Liz motioned for Skye to crouch down and follow her up the snow-covered driveway. As they got closer to the barn, the smell was enough to make them gag. Liz covered her mouth with her gloved hand. Skye zipped up her jacket and buried her mouth and nose inside.

By the time they reached the barn, their eyes were watering.

"I'm afraid to go inside," Liz whispered. "I'm afraid what we'll find."

Skye nodded. She shared her fears. Taking Liz by the hand, Skye pulled open the door. It was worse than she imagined. There were six stalls, and none of the horses moved when they entered. There didn't appear to be any water or hay. The cement floor was covered in filth, and a cold wind was whistling through the broken timbers.

"We can't leave them here. Not in these conditions."

The old Skye would've damned the consequences and released the horses. But as hard as it was, she knew they had to go through the proper channels. "We don't have a choice," Skye said, taking pictures with her cell phone as she moved toward Bandit's stall. He lifted his head. Skye nearly started to cry at the dull, resigned look in his eyes. "I'm so sorry, boy." She reached for him. It took several heartbreaking seconds before he nudged her hand.

Liz came to stand beside her, stroking the brandy-colored horse in the stall next to Bandit. "I wish we thought to bring them something to eat. They've only been back a week and you can already see signs of mal-nourishment. Look at their coats."

Skye took pictures of Bandit and the other horses. As she was about to take one more, they heard a door slam. Liz's gaze jerked to hers. Skye rushed to the other side of the barn, and peered through a hole. A man, a very large man, was coming their way with a double-barreled shot-gun in his hand.

Running to Liz, Skye grabbed her hand. "We've gotta go. Now."

*   *   *

Gage met Ethan at the front of the Logan County Sher-iff's office. "Don't go in there half-cocked," Gage said. "He only fired a warning shot. They're all right. He's charging them with trespassing, but I've talked to Sheriff Walker, and he thinks with a little persuasion Russo will drop the charges."

"This is why I didn't tell her. I knew she'd do some-thing stupid. I just didn't know she'd drag my mother along with her," Ethan said.

"I saw the pictures, Eth," Gage said, opening the glass doors. "Russo must have friends in high places, because there's no way those animals should've been returned to him. Walker's looking into it now."

And that bothered Ethan the most. All Skye had to do was call him. He would've told her that an agent from the Department of Animal Cruelty had been scheduled to visit Russo at the beginning of next week. But no, his pregnant wife and mother had to take matters into their own hands.

"Maybe I should let Walker leave them in the cell overnight. Let them think about it for a while," Ethan said as he followed Gage into the station.

Gage glanced at him over his shoulder. "They're not in the cell. They're in his office with my dad."

Of course they were. And that was another thing that irritated him. They'd called Gage instead of him.

A tall, auburn-haired man in a sheriff's uniform, with a beleaguered expression on his face, tried to calm down a muscle-bound guy in leather, who said, "They should be locked up, and you know it. They were trespassing, and the crazy one attacked me."

Ethan pinched the bridge of his nose. Great, just great. His pregnant wife went after a gun-toting, tattooed Neanderthal.

"If it wasn't for the little blonde pulling her off me, she would've done some serious damage."

Gage, who obviously knew what Ethan had been thinking, held back a grin.

Ethan ignored him, and introduced himself to Walker and Russo. By the time Ethan got through with the man, he'd agreed to drop the charges. After thanking Ethan,

the sheriff followed Russo from the station. He'd decided
to check out the stables himself.

"Always did enjoy listening to you speak legalese.
You're scary good at it. You sure you don't want your old
job back?" Gage asked.

"Between you and me, yeah, I do. Jordan gave me a
couple days to think it over."

"I know you, buddy. Don't let your mom, Nell, or Claudia influence your decision."

"What about Skye? Should I let her influence it?"

"What do they say...a happy wife is a happy life? So
yeah, it wouldn't hurt to have her on board. From what I
saw last night, you two are on the same page. She doesn't
want you to take the job as mayor, does she?"

"No. But don't mention anything to anyone. I'm
going to keep my options open. Think about it over the
weekend."

"Sure thing," Gage said as he opened the office door.

Ethan stepped into the office and froze when he heard
his mother say, "All this time he's been blaming himself
for Deacon's death, Paul. What kind of mother am I that I
didn't see what was going on? I was so wrapped up in my
own grief..." Liz broke off on a sob and Paul drew her
into his arms.

"Now don't start blaming yourself, honey. We'll..."
Paul trailed off as he caught sight of Ethan standing in the
doorway.

"Mom?"

Skye half-rose from her chair, and turned with a
stricken expression on her face. His mother frantically
wiped at her face. Stepping away from Paul, she faced
Ethan with a forced smile. "Hi, honey."

He stared at Skye, his gut twisting at her betrayal, at the anguish he saw in his mother's eyes. "You told her, didn't you? You promised me you wouldn't, but you did. God damn it, Skye, that was not your call to make. You couldn't leave things alone, could you?"

Gage put a hand on his shoulder. "Eth, take it easy."

"You haven't got a clue what she's done, Gage. I'm so sick of—"

Skye stood up. His mother reached for her hand. "I'm sorry. I didn't mean for him to find out this way."

"It's okay, Liz. In the end, it's probably for the best." Skye came to stand in front of him. "Whether you believe me or not, I did it for you, Ethan. I knew there was a risk you wouldn't forgive me, but I was willing to take it."

"Good to know, because I can't. I can't forgive you for this. It never ends with you, Skye. There's always—"

"Ethan, son, I know you're upset, but don't say anything you'll regret. Skye had your best interests at heart."

"I wouldn't want to see what my life looked like if she didn't. Because she's done a pretty good job trying to destroy it up until now," he said, and as he did in the courtroom, he paced, stating the evidence to support his claim.

He didn't realize she had left until Gage said, "I don't know what the hell is going on here, but you went too far. She didn't deserve that. I'm taking her home to Madison. And you better get your head out of your ass or you're going to lose her."

As Gage strode from the room, Paul called after him, "Son, tell Walker we need his office for a few minutes. And you"—he pointed at Ethan—"sit. You're going to listen to me, and once I've said my piece, you're going

IT HAPPENED AT CHRISTMAS

to listen to your mother. And then you're going to find your wife and apologize to her. Because as far as I'm concerned, Skye saved you from sharing the same fate as your father."

* * *

Ethan stood in his old office at the town hall, looking down at himself. He couldn't believe he let his mother and Nell talk him into this. Gage sat with his boots propped on the desk, his arms crossed behind his head. "Did princes really wear purple tights, or are you just special?"

"Put a sock in it. If you would've told my wife to answer her phone like I asked, I wouldn't be standing here looking like an idiot." And since Skye refused to see or talk to him, this was what it had come down to. The "grand gesture," as Nell referred to it. He was making an appearance as Prince Charming in the Santa Claus parade tonight.

"Honey, you don't look like an idiot," his mother said, coming into the office with something gold and sparkly hanging over her arm, "You look very handsome. And it's not Gage's fault. It's your own. You were a jerk."

"Thanks, Mom." It was true, he had been. But in his defense, Skye had shared with Ethan's mother his deepest, darkest secret. Yes, in the end, it turned out she'd done him a favor. The ensuing conversation with Paul and his mother had changed his life. He'd walked out of the sheriff's office a free man. Free from the guilt and pain that had dogged him for the last five years. But if his wife didn't forgive him, if this grand gesture didn't work, none of that would matter.

"Found it," Nell said as she walked into the office

holding up the crown Ethan had won at the hamburger-eating contest. She shoved it on his head. "There." She gave him a once-over, then tugged the purple sparkly tunic down. "Don't want to scar the children, now do we?"

Once he stopped laughing, Gage said, "Come on, Prince Charming. The parade is about to begin."

His mother took Ethan's face in her hands. "Skye loves you. She'll forgive you." She kissed his cheek, then attached the gold sparkly cape around his shoulders. "Good luck, darling."

He had a feeling he'd need it. And so, it seemed, did Nell, because as he and Gage were leaving the office, he heard her say, "If she pushes him off the float, the crown should protect his head."

"Nell, she wouldn't do that," his mother said.

"She killed him off when she read the Cake Fairy story. Just sayin'."

As though he sensed Ethan might be getting cold feet—and he was—Gage added, "Lily says it'll be just like in the movies, and Skye will love it. She gave the plan two thumbs up."

"All right, let's get this over with." Ethan opened the front doors to a blast of frigid air. As they walked outside, a float rolled by across the street. Sawyer, wearing his hockey uniform, sat in a penalty box decorated with white lights, and two blondes dressed as referees in short skirts snuggled up on his lap.

"Well, hell, the parade's already started. You better get going, buddy."

Ethan cursed under his breath and took off down the street. "Sawyer, where's the bakery's float?" he yelled as he jogged alongside them. He hit a patch of ice and grabbed the garland hanging on the side of the float to regain his balance. The crowd standing along Main Street cheered. He gave them a royal wave.

"If it isn't Prince Charming." Sawyer grinned. "You looking for your princess?"

"Yeah, you know where she is?" he asked, as the float picked up speed. He held on and scrabbled for purchase in his treadless, knee-high black boots.

"About four down. In front of the band. Careful," he said when Ethan's feet slid out from under him and he nearly disappeared under the float. "Might be safer if you hitch a ride with Fred." Sawyer called out to the older man.

Riding a red four-wheeler, Fred, dressed as an elf, motored over. "Sheesh, and I thought my costume was bad. Hop on."

"Fred, slow down," Ethan said, holding on to his crown as they zoomed past the Mountain Co-op's float. Kids sat around a fake mountain tossing candy canes. "Hi, princess." A little girl in a pink snowsuit waved.

Fred laughed.

"I do not look like a girl," Ethan muttered, waving as they putted alongside the Naughty and Nice float. Sophia Dane, the owner of the clothing store, dressed as a centerfold elf, stood in front of a gingerbread house.

"Ethan, you look so pretty," she said in her heavily accented voice.

"Can't get past the band," Fred yelled over the high schoolers' rendition of "Santa Claus Is Coming to Town." "Better get off here."

Ethan grabbed hold of a majorette as he slipped and slid his way through the band members. He was ready to call it quits when he saw Skye, wearing a white fake-fur cape, standing in front of a cardboard castle waving to the kids.

Relieved that he'd finally reached his destination, Ethan quickened his pace and hit another patch of ice. He crashed into the bakery's float. Clinging to the side, he looked up to see his wife staring at him with a stunned expression on her face.

"Cupcake, I kinda need a hand here." Her lips flattened, and she turned her back on him. "Jack," he called out, "slow down."

The dark-haired man stuck his head out the truck's window and started to laugh, but he eased on the gas. Once Ethan regained his footing, he went to pull himself onto the float and got tangled up in the Christmas lights. "You have every right to be mad, sweetheart," Ethan said, "but I'm going to burn some important parts if you don't give me a hand here."

Seeing his predicament, the crowd started to laugh. Skye sighed, then kneeled down and unhooked the strand of lights. She stood up and helped him to his feet, curtsying to the now-cheering crowd. Out of the side of her mouth, she said, "You look like an idiot."

He looked into her eyes. "But you love me."

She shrugged, throwing candy canes to a group of kids. "I'll get over it."

"I don't want you to. I love you." He took her by the shoulders and turned her to face him. "I'm sorry. I shouldn't have said what I did. You were right. It helped—talking to Mom and Paul helped."

"Good. Now I have to get back to work." She looked past him, waving.

"Tell me what I need to do to make it up to you. Tell me what I need to say."

"You said I've pretty much destroyed your life, so I don't know why we're even having this conversation."

"Come on, you know why I said that. I was angry and—"

"You put me on trial."

He bowed his head, then lifted his gaze to hers. "I know. And you didn't deserve that. The truth is, you saved me. My life would be boring and predictable without you in it. You're my sunshine. I can't lose you. I won't lose you."

The look in Ethan's eyes as much as his words soothed some of the hurt his anger had caused earlier. She'd known the risk she'd taken, known he'd feel betrayed no matter how good her intentions. And yet here he was in all his purple, sparkly glory asking for her forgiveness.

He went down on one knee and retrieved a small box from his cloak. He opened it. "Marry me."

She touched the wooden wedding band. She'd met the designer a few years ago at a Wellness Expo. The ring was made from black walnut and crushed Tibetan stone. It was exquisite. The perfect choice for her. "You had this made for me?"

"Yes." He took her hand, sliding off his grandmother's ring, his intent gaze searching her face. "I know who you are. I love who you are. Please say you'll marry me."

And with those words, he swept the last of her doubts and hurt away. But as the float jolted to a stop in the middle of Main Street, she realized there was one more thing she needed to know. She looked over the crowd, then back at him. "Are you going to be mayor of Christmas?"

"No, I'm getting my old job back. But, cupcake, I have to be honest, one day I might want to run for the state senate again, or maybe I'll run for DA. And if I do, I want Skylar O'Connor by my side, not Kendall O'Connor."

Skye thought about that, thought about how her dad and Betty Jean dealt with their differences. It wasn't really that difficult, as long as you respected and loved each other. And there was no doubt in her mind that she loved and respected him. For Ethan, she could do about anything. Including support him if he decided to run for political office. Only this time, she'd be as true to herself as she was true to him.

She smiled. "Yes, I'll marry you."

Chapter Twenty-Six

It was two o'clock in the afternoon on Christmas Eve, and the McBride household was in a frenzied state as everyone got ready for the big event. "Can someone help me, please?" Skye called from her old bedroom as she tried to zip up her wedding dress.

"Sorry, that was Liz..." Maddie trailed off from where she stood in the doorway.

Lily, Annie, and Betty Jean, who had also answered Skye's summons, plowed into her.

"Oh, honey bun," Betty Jean cried, peeking over Maddie's shoulder, "you look like a fairy princess."

"You really do," Maddie said, coming into the room. "That's the most beautiful wedding dress I've ever seen."

Skye thought so, too. The strapless bodice had mother-of-pearl beading, and the skirt consisted of layers of tulle with muted shades of pink at the bottom. She'd found it in a secondhand store.

"Can I wear it when I get married?" Lily asked.

"Sure, you can. But look at all of you," Skye said as they followed Maddie into the bedroom. "You guys look amazing." They all wore vintage pink dresses.

Betty Jean zipped Skye up, then placed the delicate tiara on her head. She leaned back, arranging Skye's long, curly hair over her shoulders. "Perfect," she pronounced.

"Thanks." Skye smiled, then asked Maddie, "You said Liz called. Is something wrong?"

"No, she just wanted you to know that everything's ready for the reception." They were having it at the ranch. "But she still hasn't heard from Chloe and Cat. And with the snowstorm, Richard and Claudia can't make it."

She didn't mind that the Stevenses were unable to attend, but she'd hoped that Ethan's sisters would be able to. They were part of the bridal party. "Any word from Vivi?"

"I'm sorry, sugar. I don't see how she can get here if they can't."

"Now don't you count that gal out yet. If anyone can make it, she will," Betty Jean said at the same time the doorbell rang.

Lily and Annie raced to answer it. At the sound of a familiar, raspy voice, Skye lifted her skirts and ran from the room with Maddie on her heels. "You made it," Skye said, throwing her arms around a bedraggled-looking Vivi.

"I don't want to interrupt your reunion, honey bun. But we better get a move on."

Skye swiped at her eyes and took a step back. "Betty Jean's right. You have to get dressed, Vivi."

"How did you manage to get here?" Maddie asked.

"Think the mother in *Home Alone*—that was me. So if I have time, I wouldn't mind a shower." She smiled at

Betty Jean and extended her hand. "Nice to finally... oomph." Betty Jean pulled her in for one of her bone-crushing hugs.

When she finally released Vivi, Betty Jean gave her a thorough once-over and grimaced. "You look like you've been rode hard and put up wet, hon."

"I wish." Vivi sighed.

Skye laughed. "She means you look exhausted, not"—she glanced at Lily and Annie—"you know."

"By the time I get through with you, I guarantee one of these gorgeous Christmas boys will make your wish come true," Betty Jean said as she led Vivi down the hall.

The phone rang again. It hadn't stopped all day. "Okay, I'll get them ready," Maddie said to whomever was on the other end. "Girls, your grandfather's coming to get you. Check your rooms and make sure you have everything you need." Once they were out of earshot, Maddie said, "I want to make sure we're on the same page. As far as Vivi knows, it was Chance that kidnapped you. We're not mentioning that he's Superman, right?"

"Right. The girls and Gage won't say anything, will they?"

"No, I don't think they even noticed that you called him Superman. Will Ethan?"

"No, so we should be good."

"Okay, go fix your face. Your mascara ran."

Thirty minutes later, her mascara was running again. Ethan had called to tell her he had a Christmas present for her and to go outside. "It's bad luck for you to see me," she said.

"Cupcake, we're already married. But I'm not there, just your present is. Go on, open the door."

Betty Jean, Vivi, and Maddie gathered around her as she did as he asked. At the end of the driveway sat a beautiful, old-fashioned sleigh. Raul, wearing a Santa hat, held the two horses' reins. Skye had to lean halfway out the door, squinting through the falling snow, to get a better look at the animals. It was Bandit and the brandy-colored horse from Russo's ranch. The two horses had bells around their necks and bright red bows. "Oh, Ethan, you saved them. That's the best present anyone has ever given me."

"Bandit's yours, and so is his friend. Hey, are you okay?" he asked when Skye started to sob.

Maddie took the phone from her. "We're going to be late. You just ruined her makeup... I'll tell her. See you in a few." She disconnected. "Your husband said to tell you he loves you and to hurry the hell up."

"Told you it was a good idea for you to stay at Maddie's till the wedding," Betty Jean said, taking some tissues from her purse and dabbing under Skye's eyes.

It had been kind of fun to pretend they were dating for the last two weeks. But now she was ready for their life together to begin. She wanted to be with him every waking moment and fall asleep wrapped in his arms.

By the time they finally made it to the church, they were fifteen minutes late. Raul jumped down and helped them out of the sleigh. Skye pushed back the hood of her fake white fur cape and kissed his cheek. "Feliz Navidad, Raul."

"Merry Christmas, Mrs. O'Connor." He gave her a half smile. "Ethan always was a smart boy. He picked the right woman. Now go make him a happy man."

"I plan to," she said, pleased to have won over the

taciturn older man. As her friends headed for the church, Skye rounded the sleigh and pulled two apples from her muff, feeding them to Bandit and... "You need a name, don't you, pretty girl? How about Blossom?"

"Skye," Maddie yelled at her from the stairs, "get a move on."

With one last pat to the horses, she joined her friends. Her father opened the church doors. "About time," he said. "Your husband's pacing." His eyes got bright when Maddie took Skye's cape and Vivi took her muff. "You look beautiful, sweetheart."

"Thanks, Daddy." She kissed his cheek and snuck a peek inside the packed church. Her throat tightened at the sight of Ethan in his black tux, talking to Paul, Gage, and Jack.

She caught Vivi anxiously scanning the pews. "Chance is out of the country," she told her.

"I wasn't..." Vivi rolled her eyes at Skye's raised brow. "Come on, let's get this show on the road."

Betty Jean kissed Skye and her father, then took Sawyer's arm. He was one of the ushers. She glanced back at them and mouthed, *Oh my*.

They all laughed, then turned as the door to the church opened. Grace carried little Jack inside. "Sorry we're late," she said, setting the toddler on the ground. Little Jack was their ring bearer. Lily, who was their flower girl, ran over and took his hand. Grace hung up her coat, then took her place in front of Vivi.

"Are we ready now?" her father asked as he straightened his bow tie.

"All..." The door to the church opened again. Two beautiful dark-haired women stepped inside. Identical twins, they had Deacon O'Connor's coloring, but they looked a lot like their brother. The woman with the short hair was Catalina, the former police officer—or Cat, as she preferred to be called. Only a woman with Cat's fabulous bone structure could carry off the Halle Berry haircut. Chloe, the actress, had model-perfect long hair.

"You really do look like a fairy princess. A very pregnant fairy princess." Chloe laughed and grabbed Skye's hands, air-kissing her on both cheeks. Shrugging out of her floor-length, sable fur coat, she glanced at her sister. "Cat, be a doll and take this."

"Good thing there's no paint around," Skye's father murmured.

Cat's lips pursed, and she took the coat. As she removed her own serviceable dark wool jacket, she said, "Sorry, we're late, Skye." She kissed Skye's cheek, then introduced herself to everyone. While she did, Chloe stood at the entrance into the church, calling out to people she knew, blowing kisses to the guests waiting patiently in the pews. Cat looked at her sister and pinched the bridge of her nose.

Chloe turned to them, fluffing her hair. "I should probably freshen up first. Can't have a picture of me ending up in the tabloids looking less than my—"

"Chloe, take your place."

Maddie and Vivi caught Skye's eye as if to say *Have fun with that one*. Ethan had already warned her that Chloe was a drama queen.

With a huffed breath and a flick of her hair, Chloe did as she was told.

Maddie motioned to someone in the church and turned

to Skye. "Your husband made a last-minute substitution." Instead of Wagner's Wedding March, Annie's incredible voice drifted from the front of the church. She was singing Billy Joel's "Just The Way You Are."

Vivi groaned when Skye sniffed. Her father reached in his pocket for a hankie as they started up the aisle. "Figured you'd be needing this."

Ethan turned to watch her walk down the aisle. He got a look in his eyes that she would cherish forever. Love and tenderness radiated from him. It was if everyone faded away in that moment and they were the only ones there.

Her father leaned in and kissed her, then took her hand and placed it in Ethan's. "You take good care of her, son. She's precious to me."

"I will, sir," Ethan said, looking into her eyes. "She's precious to me, too."

"Tissues, Cat. I need some tissues before my mascara runs," Chloe said from behind Skye.

"Too bad she didn't get snowed in somewhere," Ethan muttered under his breath.

"She's not that bad," Skye whispered back.

"Just wait," he warned, then smiled down at her. "You look amazing, cupcake."

"You look pretty amazing yourself."

"Hello again," said the preacher who'd married them the first time. "Are you two ready to do this?"

"More than ready," Ethan said, his expression softening as he took Skye's hands in his. "Skylar Davis O'Connor, you are everything I want and need in a wife. You complete me. I promise to cherish you and protect you, to care for you and respect you. To encourage your dreams and to do my best to make them come true. To be the husband and father you and our baby deserve." He brought her hands to his lips. "I love you now. I'll love you for always."

He gave her a tender smile as she struggled to keep from crying. "You going to be okay?" he asked.

She looked into the eyes of the man she adored and nodded. "Ethan O'Connor, you are my Prince Charming. You are my love and my life. I promise to cherish you and respect you, to care for you and encourage you. To make our family's happiness my priority. To walk beside you, hand in hand, through the good times and the bad." She brought his hands to her lips. "I love you. Now and forever."

When Ethan lowered his head, about to kiss her, the preacher chuckled. "I know you're anxious, but the ceremony's not quite over." Ten minutes later, he announced, "Ladies and gentlemen, Mr. and Mrs. Ethan O'Connor."

Everyone stood and clapped. Several people, Maddie and Vivi included, whistled loudly.

To their guests' delight, Ethan framed Skye's face with his hands and gave her one of his long, toe-curling kisses. When he finally let her up for air, he said, "What do you say we skip the reception, Mrs. O'Connor?"

"Your mom went to a lot of work. We can sneak…" She trailed off when she felt a gush of water run down her leg.

Ethan stepped back and looked at his now-soaked shoes.

Skye grimaced. "Sorry, my water broke."

"Your water?" His eyes widened, and the color leached from his face. "The baby…you're having the baby now?"

She squinched up her nose. "Merry Christmas, honey."

"It'll be okay, cupcake." He lifted his frantic gaze from her, calling out, "Someone call 911. We—"

"Buddy, I *am* 911, remember? Now calm down. Skye has lots of time," Gage assured him.

"Calm, you expect me to be calm? My wife is having a baby. She's not supposed to be having a baby. Not now. It's two weeks early." Ethan tried to pick up Skye, but with her voluminous skirt, he was having a hard time figuring out how to do so.

"Ethan, I'm fine. Put me down," she said, as he awkwardly lifted her.

Betty Jean, her dad, Liz, and all their friends crowded around as he set her on her feet. Everyone was talking over one another, offering everything from advice to transportation. "Her water broke. It's not false labor, Chloe," Ethan snapped at his sister.

"Ethan, I know more about this sort of thing than you do," Chloe said with exaggerated patience. "I was a doctor on *Days of Our Lives*, remember?"

"I warned you this could happen, Liz," Dr. McBride said to Ethan's mother. "You should've listened to me. Skye didn't need the added stress of planning a wedding."

"You can't be serious. You're actually blaming me for Skye going into early labor?"

"If the shoe fits..."

When Betty Jean began arguing with Skye's father about God knew what, she'd had enough. She lifted her skirts and headed down the aisle.

"Skye," her husband called after her, "where are you going?"

"The hospital."

* * *

"Look at her. She's glowing," Maddie said to Vivi, who sat on the other side of Skye's hospital bed. "I looked like death warmed over, and she looks like she's ready to go out and party."

Vivi nudged Skye and said with a straight face, "Must've been all those drugs you took, Maddie."

"Joke all you want. Wait until it's your turn. Not everyone has twenty-minute labor," Maddie said.

"Forty-five, and it was pretty painful, you know."

"Right, that's why I heard you laughing."

"I was laughing at Ethan. Don't tell him I told you, but the poor guy practically fainted."

"Yeah, Mr. Calm, Cool, and in Control was definitely not in control today," Vivi said.

Ethan came into the room with their pink bundle of joy in his arms. "I heard that," he said as he walked to Skye's side, tucking their daughter in beside her.

"What did Nurse Ratched say?" Skye asked her beaming husband. He'd caught sight of the older woman a few minutes ago and had gone to show off the baby.

"The only thing she could say—that our daughter is perfect. And that her mother is, too."

"Sure she did," Skye laughed, putting a hand on her stomach when it growled.

"You hungry?" he asked.

"Starved," she admitted.

He kissed her forehead and the baby's. "I'll go get you something to eat."

As he left the room, Vivi said, "He's going to be one of those obnoxious fathers. You know that, don't you?"

Skye stroked her baby's soft cheek. "I know. He's going to spoil her rotten." And Skye had a feeling that if she let him, he'd spoil her rotten, too.

"She really is gorgeous," Maddie said. "And I'm not just saying that because she's my niece." She lifted her smiling eyes to Skye. "Remember in July when I told you that one day you'd look back and realize all the crappy stuff going on in your life then would turn out to be the best thing that could've happened to you? I was right, wasn't I?"

It seemed so long ago that Skye could barely remember how desperately scared and lost she'd been. "You were. Everything really does happen for a reason. And Ethan and this little one were my reasons." She glanced at Vivi, catching the wistful expression on her face and covered her hand with hers. "One day you'll get your happily-ever-after. I know you will."

Vivi pulled a face. "That only happens in fairy tales."

"Hey, what about us?" Maddie said, gesturing to herself and Skye.

"You two are an anomaly."

Before either of them could respond, Betty Jean helped Skye's dad carry a decorated Christmas tree into the room. "Told you I'd find one. Set it up in that corner, Willy."

"Where did you get it?" Ethan asked, following them in carrying a tray of food.

"Out there." Betty Jean absently waved her hand.

As Ethan put the tray on the table in front of Skye, he said, "You stole it from one of the waiting rooms, didn't you?"

"I borrowed it. I'll put it back tomorrow." Betty Jean

nudged him aside. "Can't have my little baby bun without a tree on her first Christmas, can we, snookums?" she said to the baby, nuzzling her cheek. "You are the most precious thing I've ever seen. Just like your mama. Willy, come kiss your girls. We're going to head over to Liz's and give her a hand."

Ethan's mother and Cat and Chloe had left half an hour ago. Liz had decided they'd have the reception without Skye and Ethan.

"We'd better go, too," Vivi said after Betty Jean and Skye's father had left. She kissed Skye and the baby. "I'll see you guys tomorrow."

"We'll be home in the morning."

"Tomorrow. You're going home tomorrow?" Maddie said.

"Sweetheart, maybe you should stay another couple of days."

"I'm not spending our first Christmas in the hospital." At Ethan's anxious expression, she said, "I already checked with Dr. Evans. It's fine."

"That reminds me, here's…" Vivi took a book from her black messenger bag. Her gaze moved from the baby to Skye. "Is her name Clover or Meadow?"

Ethan got a nervous look in his eyes as he waited for her to answer.

"I was thinking Snowflake or Snow. What do you think, honey?" Skye asked Ethan while struggling to keep a straight face.

He shot a pleading look at her friends. When he didn't get any help there, he said, "I think I like Peanut better."

"I'm teasing. It's Christmas Eve, so I thought Eve might be nice. I like Ava, too." Skye tucked the pink blanket around her sleeping daughter's angelic face. "Evie, she looks like an Evie, don't you think?"

Her best friends and husband agreed that she did, and Vivi signed the book, handing it to Skye. It was the new Sugar Plum Cake Fairy Christmas story.

Ethan closed the door after they left, shut off the lights, and turned on the Christmas tree. He came back to the bed, nudging her over so he could crawl in beside her. He picked up their peacefully sleeping daughter and placed her between them. "So"—he lifted his chin as Skye flipped through the book—"do I get to live in this one?"

"Yes, we live happily ever after with our little cupcake."

He gave her an amused smile and wrapped his arm around her shoulders. "What about the Evil Queen—how does she make out?"

"She's not evil, after all. And I have a feeling she'll find her own Prince Charming very soon, and we'll all get our happily-ever-afters."

As he lowered his head to kiss her, he said, "I like that ending."

Charlotte Bailey needs a miracle. She came to this sleepy little Colorado town to keep the local hospital afloat, but now her scrooge of a boss is demanding she close it down. Charlotte is going to need all the help she can get, even from Dr. McSexy—er, Dr. Matt Trainer—if she's to save Christmas before, well, Christmas!

Please turn the page for more holiday romance in Christmas, Colorado, with this bonus short story, "Miracle at Christmas."

Chapter One

Dr. Charlotte Bailey's first thought as she slid across the cracked vinyl backseat of the yellow New York cab was that she'd made it. Her year in purgatory was finally over. As she powered down the passenger side window to take in the mad swirl of humanity, the sights and sounds of the city, a smile stretched the underused muscles of her face.

Underused was an understatement.

In the year since she'd been banished from her beloved New York to the backwoods of Colorado, Charlotte could count on two hands the number of times she'd smiled. The majority of which had happened today. The first instance had been earlier that morning when she'd locked the door of the tiny rental in the small town of Christmas, Colorado. Knowing she wouldn't be back, her lips had twitched and then curved as she tested the lock one last time.

Her next smile hadn't been so much happy as bittersweet.

She'd forgotten to leave Jane Randall, her replacement at Christmas General, a note of welcome and had run the half block to the hospital, bumping into the gorgeous ER doctor who'd been making her pulse race since she'd first arrived in town. No easy feat, no matter how gorgeous or sexy he was, and Matt Trainer was both.

Charlotte had arrived in Christmas last December with a huge chip on her shoulder and an even bigger case of manhating-itis courtesy of her cheating ex-husband, who hadn't been her ex when he cheated. So racing pulses? No, they shouldn't have been a problem at all.

They probably wouldn't have been if Matt hadn't proven to be as incredible to watch with his patients as he was to look at. The man was a brilliant doctor with skills she greatly admired. He was also caring and kind. A lethal combination to any woman, but especially to one whose heart had recently been broken. Luckily for Charlotte, she'd had her priorities straight and kept her eye on the prize. She had a job to do and didn't have time for a lover or a friend.

Something she constantly had to remind herself eight months later, when her heart had healed and being in close proximity to Matt's all-around awesomeness day in and day out proved almost as hard to resist as a one-way ticket home. She managed to, though. Barely, but she did.

Her saving grace had been her position at Christmas General. As CEO, she was Dr. McSexy's boss, and she couldn't afford the complication or a lawsuit if things went south. And there were several nurses and doctors who would've taken great pleasure ensuring that they did. Not everyone at CGH had approved of Charlotte's cost-saving measures.

Still, she couldn't deny feeling a touch of longing and regret as she wished the gorgeous Matt Trainer a merry Christmas and a happy life that morning outside the hospital's revolving door. Or that her third smile of the day wasn't tinged with those very same emotions when he gave her a friendly hug goodbye. The man was tall with an athletic physique, and he smelled amazing.

Still, no matter how delectable Matt was, he couldn't compete with the draw of her hometown. And half an hour later, excitement curved her lips as she left the small town of Christmas, Colorado, in her rearview mirror.

She rested her head against the back of the cab's seat, annoyed at the evidence of just how pathetic she'd become. Seriously, who knew the exact number of times they smiled in a day and the reason why? It definitely wouldn't have been her a few years before. She'd been that woman who was always smiling, a glass-half-full kind of girl. She didn't need to look far for the reason she'd changed. Her best friends, Abbie and Kate, took immense pleasure in pointing it out. They'd warned her not to marry Jeremy. It had been love at first sight for her, hate at first glance for them.

They didn't have to worry about her ignoring their advice any longer. Now that she was home for good, she'd gladly put them in charge of her love life. She was ready to get back in the dating game. *Back in?* More like getting into it for the first time. And wasn't that a scary thought for a thirty-seven-year-old who'd wasted ten years and eight months of her life on a man who'd never loved her as much as she loved him. Which he'd proven at last year's Christmas party with Bailey Healthcare's most influential board member, Samantha Delray.

As much as Charlotte would like to think she'd eventually extirpate from her brain the image of her husband with his pants around his ankles having sex with Samantha on the boardroom table with "Santa Baby" playing in the background, she hadn't had much luck getting rid of it so far.

Banishing the couple from her brain wasn't as easy as their success in banishing her to the boonies. It still grated that her father had caved to Jeremy and Samantha's demands and forced her to work in Christmas. Though she supposed she understood why. Money talked, and so did lawsuits.

Which they'd threatened within five minutes of Charlotte stumbling upon the pair. Because as much as Jeremy and Samantha had done the dirty and unforgiveable deed, Charlotte may have gone a tad crazy on the couple. Who was she trying to kid? She'd gone bat-crap crazy. Nothing that three stitches on Jeremy's backside hadn't taken care of though, and what was the loss of a few strands of hair? Samantha wore extensions anyway. But according to the couple, Charlotte had created a scandal of epic proportions by opening the doors wide for all the guests to get a full-frontal view of the adulterous pair, including Samantha's much older husband.

So maybe time did heal after all, she thought, when laughter bubbled up inside her instead of anger and tears as she recalled the looks on everyone's faces. Time and the knowledge that her father would name Charlotte chief medical officer of Bailey Healthcare at tonight's board meeting.

Benjamin Bailey wasn't a man to hand out praise or promotions willy-nilly, but he did both during last week's

phone call. She'd turned Christmas General's underper-
forming trauma center around, exceeding both the terms
of her one-year contract and her father's expectations.
She'd not only overcome last year's scandal, she'd won his
respect. *Take that, Jeremy and Samantha*, she thought,
her cheeks stretching in a true ear-to-ear grin.

In the rearview mirror, she caught the driver raising a
bushy white eyebrow. Okay, so it was possible that, in his
eyes, Charlotte's over-the-moon smile looked like she'd
soon be howling at the moon. If she wasn't careful, he'd
drive her straight to Bellevue Hospital's psychiatric wing
instead of Park Avenue.

She'd been about to stick her head out the open passenger side window and into the cold December night air
to celebrate being home with a rendition of Alicia Keys's
"New York" but thought better of it. Instead, she hummed
the song while taking in the city's bright lights and revel-
ing in the familiar cry of sirens and blasts of horns and
the smell of car exhaust and fried food.

"First time in New York?" the cabbie asked.

She pressed a hand to her chest. The idea he thought
she was a tourist was like a knife to her heart. If she was
one of those women who poured out their life's stories
to perfect strangers, she'd try to explain how it felt being
back in her beloved city after a year away. "Born and
bred, actually. You?"

He lifted his white-bearded chin, his lips bunched as
he looked at her in the rearview mirror. "Huh. I can usually make a New Yorker straight away. You don't have the
vibe."

She looked down at herself and fake-sobbed in her
head. He was right. Beneath her unbuttoned camel coat,

she wore the goodbye Christmas present from her assistant, Sheila, a holiday sweater that was guaranteed to take top prize should Charlotte ever enter an ugly Christmas sweater contest—and her dark skinny jeans were tucked into practical snow boots that screamed *country bumpkin*.

It didn't help that her caramel highlights had at least six inches of dark brown regrowth or that her usually sleek corporate-styled hair had devolved into loose bedhead waves that fell to her shoulders. Nor did she have a speck of makeup on her face. She opened her purse and dug inside for a tube of lipstick.

"My suitcases were left on the tarmac in Denver. I was stuck...posted in Colorado for a year." She'd need more than the coat of crimson she swiped over her lips to project the image of chief medical officer at tonight's board meeting.

The cabbie opened his mouth to respond, but the sound of "Jingle Bells" coming from his cell phone stopped him. She looked at her own phone when he answered his with a playful "Ho, ho, ho! Nick here."

She smiled as she punched in her password, thinking *Nick* probably made a killing this time of year impersonating the jolly old elf. Too bad he wasn't the real deal. Right about now she could use some Christmas magic. Abbie and Kate had yet to respond to the panicked text she'd sent upon discovering her suitcases hadn't joined her on the flight. She'd asked them to bring her a change of clothes to the office.

They worked for Bailey Healthcare, too. Kate, bookworm and wine snob, as a paralegal, and Abbie, fashionista and red lipstick aficionado, as executive assistant to Charlotte's father.

There wasn't a message from either of them, which surprised Charlotte as much as them not showing at the airport. They were as excited about her moving back to New York as she was... or so she'd thought. Then again, her flight had been delayed due to a freak snowstorm, so maybe they couldn't get away from the office. Still, it was odd they hadn't let her know.

She checked to be sure her phone wasn't on airplane mode—it wasn't—then re-sent the text, along with an apology for bothering them, but she was desperate. Thanks to her plane being delayed, she was already cutting it close for the meeting. If worse came to worst, she'd switch clothes with Kate. They were both five eight and close to the same weight. Used to be, Charlotte reminded herself. The break-up of her marriage had taken a toll. She'd dropped almost twenty pounds her first two months in Christmas.

The cabbie glanced at her over his shoulder as he turned onto Park Avenue. "I would've called it. Denver," he said when she gave him a questioning look. "You've got that laid-back vibe."

Well, that was a first. No one had ever accused her of being laid back before. Type A with a tendency to OCD, definitely. Though he may have a point. The last week in Christmas she'd found herself slowing down some. Most likely because she no longer had anything to prove and was going home.

"You seem pretty laid-back yourself."

His smile reminded her a bit of her earlier one. "I'm retiring at the end of the month. My wife and I bought ourselves one of those tiny houses and a piece of land in Florida. Quiet little place with a post office and country store. Our own slice of Mayberry."

His rapturous smile deepened the lines at the corners of his twinkling blue eyes. No way would she rob him of his innocence or steal his joy by uttering the warning that had immediately come to mind. He'd find out soon enough that small-town living wasn't all it was cracked up to be. "Sounds amazing. Congratulations. I hope your new life is everything you and your wife want it to be."

She wanted to add *New York will always be here if it isn't.* Just like it was for her, she thought, as he pulled the cab in front of a modern glass and steel building. Home to Bailey Healthcare for the past thirty-five years.

"I have no doubt it will be, thanks," the cabbie said as he turned in the seat and tapped a finger to his temple. "All you gotta do is believe." His chuckle was somewhere between a snort and a *ho.* "I see by your expression you're the untrusting kind. Gotta see it to believe it, don't you? Take it from me. All you need is a little faith."

Oh yeah, thanks to Jeremy, Charlotte didn't trust much of anything these days. She played along anyway. "And hope?"

"Yep, and charity," he said, holding out his hand with a wink. "For the retirement fund, you know."

She laughed and added a generous tip to his fare. She liked his chutzpah. "Too bad you're leaving town. I could've used a driver like you."

He took out a card, wrote something on the back of it, and then handed it to her. "I'm still around for a couple of weeks. My pal Henry will look after you when I'm gone. He's almost as charming as me." He leaned over to look up at the building. "You want me to wait?"

"I'm good, thanks. I'm staying at a friend's tonight. But I'll give you a call next week. I prefer taking a cab when

I work late." And she planned to put in a lot of long hours over the next few months. The last thing she wanted was her father regretting his decision to promote her or to give someone the opportunity to say nepotism was the only the reason she got the job.

At least there were two Bailey employees who would never question her ability to do the job, she thought as her best friends raced from the building wearing killer heels and killer dresses. The wind whipped Kate's long black hair around her gorgeous face while Abbie's perfectly styled red hair stayed firmly in place.

Her father's executive assistant knew more about beauty products than the buyers at Sephora. Actually, Abbie knew more about anything than anyone, especially when it came to the goings-on at Bailey Healthcare. Which raised the question, what exactly was going on? Because the smiles on her best friends' faces didn't say *Welcome home!* They screamed *Start the car!*

Chapter Two

Y ou're here!" Abbie and Katie cried, helping Charlotte from the car and into a group hug. It was obvious they were thrilled that she was home, but just as obvious something wasn't quite right.

"Charlotte, don't forget. Keep your eyes and heart open to miracles. They happen when you least expect them. All you have to do is believe," Nick called out to her.

Later, she'd wonder how Nick knew her name, but right then, she was caught up in the moment. She was home and with the two women she loved best in the world.

They looped their arms through hers and hustled her to the glass doors.

"Come on, let's go to Kate's office, and you can fill us in on everything about Christmas," Abbie said, holding the door open before once again putting Charlotte's arm in a stranglehold. "Kate picked up the wine, and I went to the deli and bought you those mini paninis with roasted eggplant, zucchini, and fontina that you love. And, wait for it... a double order of grilled polenta topped with truffled mushroom ragout. Sounds delish, doesn't it?"

It sounded so amazing that Charlotte's mouth actually began to water. She was to food what Kate was to wine and Abbie was to beauty products. The last time Charlotte had a decent meal was two days before the infamous board meeting at Per Se with her lying, cheating husband. Still, as much as she was tempted to make a mad dash to Kate's office, a warning alarm went off in her head. Even though she'd promised her father not to talk about the promotion with Kate and Abbie, they knew there was a board meeting tonight.

Which is why when her best friends tried to bodily drag her to the bank of elevators, Charlotte dragged her booted feet and yanked them to a stop. "What's going on? And don't say 'nothing.' You know everything that goes on at Bailey, Abbie, which means you know that, in less than fifteen minutes, my dad is going to introduce me to the board as the new chief medical officer." She crossed her arms when her best friends fake-gasped and shared a look that was more *Now what?* than *OMG, that's amazing!* "Don't try and pretend that you both didn't know. As soon as Abbie found out, she told you, Kate."

They deflated right before her eyes, and her heart deflated along with them. "He already told the board, and they shot him down, didn't they? That's why you didn't respond to my texts or pick me up at the airport." She squeezed her eyes shut and squinched up her face in an attempt to keep her emotions at bay. Her father was all about the stiff upper lip. He probably wouldn't care that she looked like an idiot keeping her emotions in check, as long as she did so.

She'd been looking forward to seeing the faces of the board members the moment her dad announced her promotion. It was the public vindication she'd been craving this past year. For years, her father had treated Jeremy like the son he'd never had, and she'd started to feel like the daughter he'd never wanted. And as much as she may have understood why he kowtowed to Jeremy and Samantha's demands and sent her away, standing in front of the board as he rendered his decision in their favor that night had hurt almost more than Jeremy cheating on her.

"No, that's not it at all. It's—" Abbie broke off as the doors to the elevator opened, and she gently nudged Charlotte inside.

"Don't keep me hanging. What is it?"

"Just a minute," Kate said as she and Abbie stared at the doors. They waited until they closed and Kate had pressed the button to the twenty-fourth floor before turning to face Charlotte, who by then had sagged against the gold-veined glass wall, suddenly more tired and disappointed than the week she'd been banished to Christmas.

"Maybe you should sit on the floor," Kate suggested, obviously concerned Charlotte might end up there anyway.

"The elevator hasn't been mopped yet. She'll get her coat dirty," Abbie said, though she looked like that might not be such a great loss. "Just...lean against the wall, take a couple of deep breaths, and..."

"Jeremy's hedge fund bought up shares in Bailey, and he now holds a seat on the board. Between him and Samantha, they control thirty-five percent of the company. Twenty minutes ago, he called for a vote to remove your dad as chairman of the board." Kate blurted it all out so quickly that she was breathless by the end.

So was Charlotte. She covered her mouth with her hands to slow her breathing before she hyperventilated and passed out. "Please tell me the board didn't do that to my father," she said, her voice muffled by her hands.

Abbie closed her eyes and nodded.

"We were trying to come up with a way to stop them. That's why we didn't return your calls or pick you up at the airport. We were... There was nothing we could do. I'm so sorry." Kate rubbed Charlotte's arm, glancing at Abbie.

Charlotte lowered her hands from her mouth. "There's more, isn't there? What aren't you telling me?"

"You know how Samantha's husband, Harold, died last month?" Kate asked.

From the look on her best friend's face, Charlotte had a good idea where the conversation was headed and didn't know how she felt about it. She didn't love Jeremy anymore, of course. How could she after what he'd done to her and now to her father? She just wished he'd go away and leave them alone. "He married Samantha, didn't he?"

Kate made a pained face and cast a glance at Abbie, who nodded and then added quietly, "They're having a baby, honey."

"Oh." This time neither a stiff upper lip nor eyes squeezed shut could cover Charlotte's reaction to the emotional hit. For years she'd tried to convince Jeremy it was time to start a family. He always managed to come up with an excuse that sounded reasonable and shut her down. And now he was going to be a father with someone else. Samantha had gotten everything Charlotte wanted, the baby, her family's company, and her husband. "Merry Christmas to me," she murmured.

Her response made her think of what Nick the cab driver had said to her only moments before. It was almost like the older man was psychic and knew what she was about to walk into. She didn't believe in miracles, but boy, could she use one now. There had to be some way to stop them. "What about me? I have a voting share. They held the meeting before the posted time. We'll demand another vote. I'll talk to the other board members." The doors slid open, and she took off, running toward the boardroom before Kate and Abbie could stop her. She wouldn't let Jeremy and Samantha win.

"No, wait. Don't go in there, Charlotte! You're supposed to be in Christmas," Abbie yelled after her.

The warning didn't really register, but it wouldn't have made a difference if it had. Charlotte had already pushed open the doors and everyone had turned to stare. Including her impeccably groomed ex, who'd claimed her father's seat at the head of the long boardroom table. The table where he'd first boinked his new wife. Who knew, though? Maybe it hadn't been their first time. Charlotte stepped further into the boardroom then froze when her gaze moved from Jeremy to his perfectly coifed blond wife, who sported a healthy pregnancy glow.

Jeremy frowned, looking decidedly unhappy to see her. What he didn't look was ashamed or apologetic. "Well, this is a surprise. What are you doing here, Charlotte? As I understood from your father, your contract at CGH isn't over until next month. Part of the agreement was that you weren't to return to New York until your—"

"Really, after what you've just done to my father, what you did to me, you have the nerve to sit there and—"

From behind her came a groan, and then Kate was

there, grabbing her by one arm while Abbie's fingers wrapped around her other arm. Charlotte's father leaped from his chair, moving to stand in front of her, blocking her view of Jeremy's smug face.

Benjamin Bailey put his hands on her shoulders and whispered frantically, "We changed the term on your contract to protect you. It's ironclad. He can't break it without opening the door for you to sue. I told Jane we decided it was best to transition in the new year and gave her the month off with pay."

"I have to go back to CGH? What about the job you promised me? I thought—"

Her father's hazel eyes reflected the same desperation she'd seen in her own gaze in the months and weeks leading up to the night she caught Jeremy with Samantha. Charlotte blinked, startled by the thought. It didn't make it less true, though. She just hadn't been ready to face it until now. Her marriage had begun unraveling long before that infamous night.

"Please, do this for me. I'm not going to let them push me out, but until I can come up with a plan to fight back, I need to know a member of this family is still part of Bailey Healthcare," her father pleaded, looking older than his sixty-eight years.

"Sorry to break up the reunion, but I'm sure, like me, the rest of the board would like to know what Charlotte is doing here. It must be something urgent for her to show up looking like..." He trailed off with a shudder, as if personally affronted by what she chose to wear to the meeting.

Abbie's and Kate's fingers tightened around her arms. "He's just trying to goad you into giving him an excuse to fire you," Kate whispered.

"It's okay. I won't let him get to me," Charlotte promised as she shook off their hands and stepped around her father. "I'm here to present my interim report to the board."

"Do you really think an interim report on the revenue of a small-town hospital in the middle of nowhere warranted a trip to New York? You've probably expensed the company more than CGH earned in the entire time you were there. Hmm, Danielle," he lifted his chin at the woman sitting to his right, "make a note that Ms. Bailey's expense account for the past year is to be verified down to the last cent. Now, if there's nothing further…"

Charlotte curled her fingers into fists, fighting the urge to launch herself across the table and wrap her hands around Jeremy's scrawny neck. There was nothing she wanted more than to wipe the self-satisfied smirk from his cocky face. She wouldn't let him get to her. She wouldn't let him win. "No, nothing at all," she said in a measured tone.

"Good, then we'll expect you at your desk at CGH at nine a.m. tomorrow morning." He shared a self-congratulatory smile with his wife.

When Charlotte thought about it later, she'd realize that wasn't the moment that made her head explode and lose control of her temper. It was when her husband's new wife held Charlotte's gaze and rubbed her noticeable baby bump with a smile that said, *I won.*

Her fingernails digging painfully into her palms, Charlotte managed to force her face into an apologetic expression. "Samantha, how rude of me. I forgot to offer my condolences on the loss of your husband. You have my deepest sympathies, truly. Harold was such a kind and generous man. It must bring you some measure of solace to know that he'll live on through his child. Did he know you were pregnant before he dropped dead?"

Several members of the board gasped.

"What? Did I say something wrong?"

*   *   *

"Hold it! Hold the elevator, please!"

Now that was a voice Matt Trainer hadn't expected to hear again—unless he did something stupid like call her. As far as he knew, Dr. Charlotte Bailey, former CEO of Christmas General, had left yesterday morning with no intention of ever coming back. The woman couldn't wait to shake off the snow of his beloved town, which was how he'd known it would be a complete waste of time to even think about contacting her, no matter how attracted he was. And he was very attracted to Dr. Charlotte Bailey. He had been from her first day at CGH.

But while Charlotte had practically been salivating at the idea of returning home, Matt would never leave the small mountain town. The citizens of Christmas had welcomed him with open arms when he'd most needed it. No one here knew his story or why he'd turned down a lucrative position in California after his last tour of duty.

"Stop! Stop the elevator!"

Charlotte. Right. Matt stuck his arm between the doors and pushed back the left one to see the woman he'd hugged goodbye less than twenty-four hours before staggering toward the elevator with a large red purse hooked around her neck—swinging from side to side—while she attempted to drag three suitcases behind her. Continuing to hold the door open with his shoulder, he lifted his booted foot and hit the Stop button on the panel while stuffing the elaborately foil-wrapped box of chocolates from the local candy store, Sugar and Spice, inside his leather jacket to free up his hands. Dr. Paul McBride, the chief of staff, was away and had asked Matt to deliver the chocolates to Charlotte's replacement

"What happened? Did they end up canceling your flight on account of the snow?"

"If only," she muttered and gave the handles of her bags a hard tug when their wheels apparently stuck to something on the floor. Which caused the third and smaller suitcase to wing across the white tiles and bounce off the suitcase in her right hand, throwing her off balance. She tilted to her right and then overcorrected and lurched forward. His hands now free of the chocolates, Matt grabbed her before she took a header into the elevator. The purse swung around and whacked him hard.

"What have you got in that thing? Bricks?" he asked, unable to let her go to rub his shoulder.

Charlotte looked up at him, her eyes bloodshot and glassy. She was one of the most self-possessed and unflappable women he knew, but if he hadn't already guessed that she was about to cry, the quiver in her bottom lip would've given her away.

"Hey, I was just teasing. It didn't hurt that bad. Honest." He smiled. But instead of reassuring her, she hiccupped a sob and did a face-plant into his chest.

Chapter Three

Matt held Charlotte as close as her purse allowed. He liked the feel of her slender body in his arms, her spicy floral scent. Her perfume smelled like lemons and lilies. It smelled like her—elegant and seductive.

Her hair got caught on the stubble on his chin, and he lifted his hand to remove the silky strands. Instead he found himself stroking her tousled mane. She usually wore it sleek and straight. The casual look suited her better—at least he thought so.

She turned her face as though to get more comfortable on his chest, and he noted the pallor of her typically glowing skin. The light dusting of cinnamon-colored sprinkles on her high cheekbones and across the bridge of her narrow, upturned nose that were barely visible most days, today stood out in sharp relief. Exhausted or not, there was something about the woman that appealed to him.

And it wasn't just her fresh-faced looks, willowy frame,

or seductive scent he was attracted to. He admired her. She was bright, ambitious, and committed to ensuring the patients at CGH received the best of care. As much as she demanded of the staff, she demanded more of herself. In the year she'd been here, she'd rarely left her office on the eighth floor. Which hadn't exactly endeared her to the rest of the staff or the citizens of Christmas.

She hadn't gotten involved in the community or made friends. As far as he knew, he was the only one she spent time with. And the only time they spent together had been here. It was an odd sort of friendship they had, he and Dr. Charlotte Bailey.

"Ow," she cried as she'd tried to snuggle closer. She let go of the handles of her suitcases and lifted her head to touch her mouth. "What have you got inside your jacket?" she grumbled at the same time her luggage crashed to the floor. She let go of the other handle and that suitcase fell, too.

"Chocolates for your replacement," he said as he lifted the straps of her purse over her head, inadvertently pulling her hair as he did so.

She moved her hand from her mouth to her head. "That hurt."

"Sorry for trying to save you from strangling yourself." He shook his head, exasperated, wondering what was up with her. This wasn't the woman he knew and cared for.

He handed her the purse and then picked up her suitcases. Once he'd placed them in the corner of the elevator, he took her gently by the shoulders, turning to position her back against the wall. She obviously needed something to lean on. "Your office?"

She nodded, sniffed, and then blinked. "Oh gosh. The

time. What time is it?" She unzipped her purse and began digging inside. Her head jerked up. "Matt, the time?"

His hand automatically lifted in a what-the-hell gesture, but her head was now half-buried in her purse, so it wasn't like she noticed. Reaching into the pocket of his jacket, he withdrew his smartphone and checked the screen. "Six fifty-five. Now are you going to tell me what's going on? Because something is clearly going on with you, Charlotte."

"I will. I'll tell you as soon as I get to my office. Can't this thing go any faster?" She moved past him and repeatedly stabbed the button for the eighth floor. "You know what, never mind." The elevator shuddered to a stop on the second floor, and she wedged herself through the barely open doors.

He stuck his head out of the elevator to call her back but she'd already disappeared around the corner. She'd figure it out soon enough. The run might do her good. She'd burn off some of her anger and frustration, because the woman was clearly experiencing both.

He leaned in to press the Stop button. Seconds later, he heard her frustrated cry from down the hall followed by the sound of her snow boots slapping against the tiles. "Stop! Don't leave!"

Holding the elevator doors open with his shoulder, he cocked his head as she pushed past him. "You're welcome."

"You could've told me they'd blocked off the stairs for repairs."

"I would have if you'd given me half a chance. But I thought you'd figure it out since I only ever take the stairs. Plus you're the one who ordered the repairs."

"The job was supposed to be completed by now."

"No, it was supposed to be completed by nine this morning. It's only six fifty-eight. Now, are you going to—"

She cut him off with a panicked yelp. "Hurry. Call me. Call my office," she ordered, her voice muffled. Her head was stuck in her purse again. She pulled it out, staring at him through a curtain of honey-brown hair. "Matt!"

"If you don't tell me what's going on, I'm stopping the elevator."

"No! I'll lose my job if I'm not sitting at my desk in two minutes." She looked at her phone and half-sobbed. "In one minute and twenty-six seconds. Please, I'm begging you. There's two lines. If we both keep calling them and leaving messages, they'll get a busy signal and think I'm there."

"You've lost me. When you left yesterday, you were headed home to accept a promotion, and now you're telling me they're going to fire you if you're not at your desk by seven in the morning?"

"Nine in the morning their time, I think. I should've asked if it was nine a.m. Eastern or Mountain, but at that moment I was thinking of ways to murder my ex-husband without getting caught."

"What does Jeremy have to do with this?" Matt knew all about Charlotte's ex. She'd opened up about her failed marriage at Thanksgiving. After she refused the McBrides' invitation to join them for dinner on account of work, Matt had brought it to her. They'd eaten in her office and talked the night away. It'd been one of the best *dates* he'd been on in a long time.

"He has everything to do with it." She brought her

phone to her ear and gestured for him to do the same. While they alternated between leaving messages on her office voice mail and tying up the phone lines, she filled him in on what happened in New York.

As the elevator shuddered to a stop on the eighth floor, Matt tucked his phone between his shoulder and ear and handed her the smaller suitcase. He grabbed the other two. "Look, I know it's not easy for you to leave this for your dad to handle, but if he says he'll take care of it, I'm sure he will. You'll eventually get the promotion he promised you. And hey, you've gotta admit, being stuck in Christmas over the holidays isn't so bad."

She shot him a Grinchy look as she strode from the elevator. "You can't be serious. Christmas in New York is magical, Matt."

"Compared to here? No way. This town looks like it belongs on a Christmas card or in a snow globe. It's so Christmassy, even Santa set up a second workshop here."

His remark earned him an eye roll.

"Right, as if that can compete with skating in Central Park, the tree in Rockefeller Center, the Rockettes, and tea at the Russian Tea Room."

"The only reason you say that is because you haven't given this town a chance. Wanna bet I can change your mind?" Underneath the teasing challenge in his voice, he was serious. He wanted to show her what she was missing. Maybe it was just wishful thinking on his part, but he didn't think she'd be so anxious to leave if she gave the town half a chance. Then again, maybe he just wanted her to give him one.

"Even if I wanted to take you up on your bet, which I don't, but if I did, I wouldn't have the time. Jeremy's looking for any excuse to get rid of me. I made a promise to my dad, and I can't go back on my word. I won't. This is *Bailey* Healthcare, and I'll be damned if Jeremy pushes me out, too."

Her lips moved silently as she swiped her key card at her office door. Her shoulders relaxing when the knob turned under her hand. "Thank God, I thought they might've deactivated my card. Maybe my luck is finally turning around."

It was a good thing the phone on her desk rang just then. He didn't have to point out that Jeremy would most likely fire her when her contract was up in a month's time—if the guy didn't find a way out of her contract before then. Matt scrolled through his contact list and sent Ethan O'Connor a quick text. Ethan was a district attorney and an all-around good guy. Now and again, he took on pro bono work for the hospital. It wouldn't hurt to have him check out Charlotte's contract.

As Charlotte registered the ringing phone, she released a panicked gasp, letting her suitcase and purse drop to the floor as she raced across the office to the massive cherry wood desk that sat in front of a wall of bookshelves. Her desk was on the left, a small seating area made up of a charcoal-gray couch, a glass coffee table, and two modern-looking chairs to the right.

It was an impressive office for an impressive woman, but what made it spectacular in Matt's opinion was the view. Straight across from where he stood in the doorway, the bank of windows framed the snow-covered Rockies and below, nestled in the tree-lined valley, Main Street with its cobblestone streets and pastel-painted storefronts decorated for the holidays.

He didn't know how Charlotte, who'd looked at that

view for the past year, couldn't see what he did. Like her, he'd been a city boy, and his love life hadn't ended much better than hers. He'd go so far as to say it had been worse. But he'd healed with the help of the people in Christmas. Charlotte hadn't.

Oh, she talked a good game, and she was definitely in a better place than when she first arrived, but until she found a way to let go of her anger and hurt, she'd have trouble moving on to the life she deserved. And the woman deserved a wonderful life.

"Christmas General, Charlotte Bailey speaking." Her mouth turned down, and she pulled the phone away from her ear to strangle it.

Okay, so definitely someone from New York, and if Matt was a betting man, he'd say it was Jeremy. And... he'd be right.

"It's five minutes after seven, Jeremy. I've already been on the phone for the past ten minutes dealing with hospital business." She looked at Matt and lifted a shoulder. Probably because she was lying through her clenched teeth, and, as Matt knew from experience, Charlotte Bailey was a stickler for the truth. Other than someone not taking responsibility for their mistakes, nothing irked her more than someone lying to her face. Like her husband had, repeatedly, for years.

Matt decided it might be better if he came back later. Before he gave in to the urge to take the phone and tell Charlotte's ex what he'd do to him if he upset or threatened her again—and as a former special ops medic with the Rangers, Matt was well trained in not only healing a man but making him suffer—he left the two suitcases by the door. Once he'd gathered up her smaller suitcase and purse, placing them with the rest of her luggage, he removed the now-squashed foil-wrapped box from inside his jacket and walked over to put the chocolates on her desk.

Through all of it, she sat quietly listening to whatever her ex had to say. What he hadn't noticed before then was that she wasn't only quiet, whatever color she'd had left on her face was gone, and her bloodshot eyes were no longer only glassy, they were wide with panic.

"No, no way. You'll never get the board to agree to this." She brought a hand to her mouth and slowly shook her head. "I can't. There's no way I can close CGH within a matter of weeks."

He felt like he'd been sucker-punched and uttered a strangled sound of disbelief.

As though she'd forgotten he was there, her gaze shot to him. She covered the receiver and whispered, "I'll talk to you later, Matt."

"Charlotte, you can't do this. You can't—"

"Just go, okay. I can't deal with both of you right now."

He turned on his heel, anger dogging his every step as he strode to the door.

"Yes, I'm here, Jeremy. And what you're asking me to do makes no sense. CGH is operating in the black, which is more than...Of course I want to come back to New York, but...I don't understand. What's going on? Why would my promotion and my father's reinstatement as chairman of the board hinge on me closing Christmas General by the beginning of the new year?"

Matt swung around to stare at her. She wouldn't meet his eyes, just shook her head and waved him out.

*   *   *

The next morning, Charlotte arrived at her office at the more reasonable hour of nine. She preferred to start her day at eight, but this morning she'd had trouble getting out of her bed at the lodge. Probably because she'd spent half the night trying to figure out how she was going to face Matt. She hadn't seen him since he'd stormed from her office yesterday. He was angry, and he had every right to be. He wouldn't be any happier with her today or tomorrow. None of the staff would.

Yesterday, she'd spent the entire day and early evening on the phone with her father, Bailey's lawyers, Abbie, Kate, and then every single board member trying to understand what was behind the decision. Well, every board member except Samantha. None of their answers made sense to Charlotte, but she soon learned there was nothing she could do to change their minds. Jeremy had the board members wrapped around his crooked little finger.

Either Charlotte closed CGH, or they'd send in someone who would. And if she couldn't do her job, she was out of one. The unspoken inference was as clear as if they'd said it aloud: *Good luck finding another executive position in healthcare if you don't do as directed.* There was no doubt in her mind that Jeremy and Samantha would make sure no one hired Charlotte or her father if they didn't toe the line.

Today was going to be a long one. People's livelihoods were on the line, and she was all too aware of the impending holidays. It was a difficult time of year for a tenth of any community's population to receive pink slips, but more so she imagined for the citizens of a town named after the holiday. Her stomach tossed and turned like she'd taken a ride on Santa's sleigh. She could use a little Christmas magic right about now.

Only Charlotte didn't believe in Santa or magic, and never had. The only way out of this mess was to come up with a solution that would work for Jeremy and the board, and the citizens of Christmas. She'd been mulling over an idea since late last night. Neither side would get exactly what they wanted, but if she could get them both on board, she might have a chance of pulling it off. First, she had to talk to Matt.

"Sheila, would you do me a favor and schedule a meeting with Dr.—" Charlotte began as the door to her office opened. She stopped and stared at the man who walked in with two takeout cups in his hand. "You're not Sheila." Though the handsome man with the red-framed glasses and model-perfect dark hair looked vaguely familiar.

"What gave me away?" He grinned and set a purple to-go cup that read SUGARPLUM BAKERY on her desk and then took a seat across from her, crossing his legs. He wore black pants with knife-edge creases and a black wool vest over a silk shirt that matched the frames of his glasses.

The divine smell wafting past her nose distracted her, and she picked up the cup and took a careful sip. Cocoa and candy canes. It tasted as divine as it smelled. "Oh my gosh, this is amazing."

"Yes, I am."

"I was actually talking about the hot chocolate. Thank you, though. Uh, is there something I can do for you?" she asked, choosing to go for the politer version of *What are you doing in my office?* She knew for a fact she didn't have any appointments scheduled for today, because she wasn't supposed to be here. She was supposed to be in her beautiful corner office on Park Avenue looking out at the gorgeous view of her beloved city. Not at a crystal blue sky and snow-covered mountaintops.

"*Pour moi?* No, no, it's what *I* can do for *you*. And darling, let me tell you, I can do a lot for you. Starting with your hair." He put down his cup and rose from his chair to come around to hers.

She stared at him as he fluffed the hair she'd spent twenty minutes straightening this morning.

"First, I think we'll—"

Shaking off her shock, she raised a protective hand to her head. "Who are you?"

"Ty. The owner of Diva's Hair Salon and Diva's Catering. I'm also right-hand man to the mayor, Chloe McBride, and now, part-time assistant to *tu*."

"Who's *tu*?"

He laughed and lightly swatted her shoulder. "You, silly."

She may have had next to no involvement in the community, but that didn't mean she hadn't heard about Mayor Chloe McBride and her right-hand man. "No, I'm good, thanks. I already have a full-time assistant. Sheila. Sheila, can you come here, please?" Charlotte called out with a nervous hitch in her voice, hoping her assistant had finally shown up for work. She'd never been late before.

Chapter Four

Abbie and Kate leaned forward, their faces filling the computer screen. "Why are you whispering?" Abbie asked.

Charlotte was at her desk, talking to her best friends via Skype. "Because I swear I heard him outside the door. He's probably got his ear pressed to it now."

"You better hope not. You more or less accused him of kidnapping Sheila to take her place," Abbie said before she took a bite of what looked like the grilled polenta slice Charlotte would've eaten two nights before if she hadn't been forced to take a red-eye back to Colorado.

"I know you think I'm overreacting, but you guys haven't heard the stories I've heard." She frowned. "Why are you looking at each other like that?"

"Well, the thing is, I've not only heard the stories, I've read them." Kate held up a paperback: *The Trouble with Christmas.* "It says the author is Debbie Mason, but I think the town's matriarch, Nell McBride, actually wrote it."

"I've met her. The town matriarch, I mean. She's the chief of staff's aunt."

Kate gave her a knowing nod. "And the town's match-maker. You're lucky she's retired, or she'd be trying to marry you off to one of the single men in town. That's what she did to Madison Lane in *The Trouble with Christmas*. And Madison hated the holiday and small towns even more than you do. You probably know her; she's Dr. McBride's daughter-in-law."

"Dr. McBride's mentioned Madison, but I haven't actually met her. And I don't hate the holiday or small towns. I just love New York, and want to spend the holidays with you guys." The thought of spending another Christmas here was depressing. She'd never felt so alone or lonely as she had last year.

"You know I'd come if I could, but my mom's not doing well," Kate said, taking a bite of her polenta slice. Charlotte's stomach growled. All she'd had was the hot chocolate Ty had brought her that morning. She'd passed on lunch, and it was close to four in the afternoon. Her best friends had stuck around after work to talk to her.

"And Mark won't let me take Emma out of state," Abbie said, referring to her five-year-old and her ex, who was almost as bad as Jeremy.

"I'm sorry for being so whiny. You guys have enough on your plates without me going on about my problems. I'm sorry Mark's being a jerk, Abbie, and that your mom's not improving with the new meds, Kate."

"Stop. If anyone deserves to whine, it's you, and you never do. We're going to do everything we can to help you from here, but we'd both feel better if you had someone in Christmas to support you."

"Abbie's right. I know the situation isn't ideal, but you and Matt seemed to be getting along really well before you left. For a while there, Abbie and I thought you guys were dating. Didn't we, Abs?"

"Okay, don't even go there."

"Why not?" Abbie said. "It's been a year since you and Jeremy split up. It's past time you got out there."

"Says the woman whose been divorced for two years and hasn't gone on a single date."

"It's not the same. I have Emma to think about. But trust me, if I met someone like your Dr. McSexy, I wouldn't be single for long. That man is—"

"He's not mine." And she didn't need to be reminded how amazing he was. Matt probably hated her now, and she wasn't about to let her friends know how much that bothered her. It was one of the reasons Charlotte hadn't asked Ty to schedule a meeting with Matt yet. The other reason was she had to find Sheila and convince her to come back to work before she did anything else. Ty obviously had an agenda, and it didn't coincide with Charlotte's.

"The only reason Matt isn't yours is because you put up roadblocks every chance you get," Kate said with a raised eyebrow, challenging Charlotte to deny her accusation

Which she couldn't, because after spending an incredible night with Matt at Thanksgiving and having one glass of wine too many, she'd confessed as much to Kate and Abbie via Skype.

"And before you try to deny it, remember who you're talking to. No one knows you better than we do. We've had the feeling something was going on between you and Matt long before Thanksgiving. He's perfect, and he's perfect for you."

"No one is perfect," Charlotte grumbled.

"So, you're telling us that if Matt lived in New York, you wouldn't be practically engaged by now?"

She may have had that fantasy every now and again. Not the engaged part; the part where Matt lived in New York. "First, you're forgetting that I'm stuck in Colorado. And second, that I'll never be engaged to anyone since I'm never getting married again." From behind the door, someone laughed. "Did you hear that? I told you Ty's spying on me. Somehow, they've found out that I've been ordered to close CGH."

"Do you think Matt told someone? It's a small town. Once one person knows—" Abbie began before Charlotte cut her off.

"No, Matt wouldn't do that. He's not like that." He was loyal and dependable with a deep sense of moral integrity. Quite simply, he was the most incredible man she'd ever met, and she was going to have to fire him if she couldn't convince Jeremy and CGH to get on board with her plan.

"It wasn't Matt," she reiterated, thinking back to yesterday. "It was Sheila. She came in while I was on the phone with one of the board members. I stopped talking as soon as I saw her, but she could've been there a while before I noticed." If Charlotte was honest, someone could've been standing in front of her and she might not have noticed. By then, she'd been up almost thirty-six hours straight.

"So that means everyone in Christmas knows," Kate said, making a face that Charlotte could take only one way. Her goose was cooked, as her maternal grandmother used to say. Then again, Kate had been power eating. Maybe she had heartburn. Charlotte was able to hold on to that hope for about half a second before her best friend added, "You know the old adage about knowing your enemy? Maybe you should pick up a copy of *The Trouble with Christmas*."

                    *   *   *

Christmas General Hospital needed a miracle, and it looked like the folks in town had decided Matt was it. It felt like half of Christmas had paid him a visit today, and another one was on her way. He leaned his elbow on the table in the hospital cafeteria and raised his hand to the side of his face in hopes the mayor wouldn't notice him, inwardly groaning when the chair across from him scraped across the tile floor.

"Matt, what are we going to do? I can't have the babies at home. I have an incredibly high pain tolerance, but I'm not ashamed to say I want drugs. Whatever kind of drugs you can give me, I want them."

He reached across the table and patted Chloe's hand. A former soap opera star, the beautiful brunette was affectionately known in town as Diva #1, and her sidekick, Ty, was known as Diva #2. "Relax. The last thing we want is your blood pressure to go up. You're months away from your due date. If necessary—and I highly doubt it will be—there's lots of time to come up with a new birth plan."

She relaxed in her chair. "Of course, you're right. The babies will be fine, and so will I. What I'm really worried about is the town. The hospital is our biggest employer. Not to mention the best healthcare provider in the state. How will we survive without it?"

"I think it's premature to go to the worst-case scenario. Charlotte's smart. I'm sure she'll figure out a way to save the hospital." He hoped his voice sounded more confident than he felt. From what he heard of her conversation with Jeremy, both Charlotte and her father would be pushed out if she didn't close CGH as directed. And if she tried to fight her ex-husband, what then? No doubt they'd send someone else to do the job.

"What if she can't? Sheila told me Charlotte spent most of yesterday trying, and it didn't get her anywhere."

"I heard Sheila quit. She should've at least given Charlotte two weeks' notice." He'd meant to go up and check on her a couple times today, but between patients, concerned citizens, and shoring up the staff's morale, he hadn't had a chance. And maybe, if he was honest with himself, he'd admit he didn't want her to validate his fear that this was happening and there wasn't a damn thing any of them could do to stop it.

"Oh, don't worry about Charlotte being left high and dry. She has a new assistant."

Her grin made him nervous. "Chloe, what did you do?"

"You sound like Easton," she said, referring to her husband. "It's not like I was up to anything nefarious. All I did was suggest Sheila come work for me, and Ty would work for Charlotte. We need someone like him on the inside if we want to keep ahead of this. Oh, look, there he is. Ty!" She waved him over.

Matt sat back in the chair and crossed his arms. "Whatever you two are planning, the answer is no."

Chloe pouted and batted her long eyelashes.

"Yeah, and that's not going to work on me. Save it for your husband."

"Diva, you're looking divine as always." The two air-kissed, and then Ty leaned in to do the same to Matt, sniffing him as he did. "Yum, you smell edible, McSexy."

"I think it's whatever you've got in the bag, Ty."

The other man looked down and chuckled. "You see, that's what happens when I'm around you. I forget myself." He handed Matt the bag.

"What's this?"

Ty frowned down at Chloe. "You didn't fill him in on the plan?"

"He said no before I got a chance."

"Is that right?" Ty wrapped one arm around his waist and used his other hand to cup his clean-shaven chin. Slowly moving his head from side to side, he tapped his forefinger on his lips.

He made Matt more nervous than Chloe did. "Look, Ty, I don't know what you two are up to, but I don't want any part of it."

"Is that so? Well, if you don't go along with our plan, I'll have to bring in the big guns."

Chloe sighed. "Nell's retired, Ty. You know that."

"I have my ways. So, what's it going to be, McSexy, us or Nell?"

Nell McBride's matchmaking schemes had a one hundred percent success rate. Any couple she set her sights on ended up married within the year. As much as Matt liked Charlotte, he didn't want to marry the woman. He'd been down that road before, and it didn't work out so well.

He stood up and looked into the bag. "Christmas cupcakes and cookies? What about real food?"

Ty shrugged. "That's what Chloe told me to get. And chocolate's an aphrodisiac."

Matt reminded himself that Ty and Chloe were the lesser of two evils and kept his mouth shut. He'd pretend to go along with the plan. No harm, no foul. "I'm taking it Charlotte never left her office today. I'll pick her up a couple of chicken wraps."

She turned up her nose at pretty much everything else on the cafeteria menu. A few months ago, he'd challenged her to come up with a better one, but at the time, she'd been busy requisitioning new equipment for the cardiac unit. His own heart squeezed at the thought it would all be for naught if Jeremy had his way.

Matt didn't know what he'd do if they closed the hospital. He'd been working here for more than five years. It was his home away from home. They were like one big, happy family. Not all the time, of course, but what family was? Certainly not his. He'd disowned his brother after his betrayal.

Ty waggled his eyebrows. "Chicken wraps? It sounds like the man knows his woman."

"She's not my woman."

"Well—" At the sound of a low moan, Ty turned to Chloe. "Diva!" He took away the bag she'd slipped from Matt's hand and held it protectively to his chest as he returned his attention to Matt. "Charlotte's friends didn't believe her any more than I believe you when she said you weren't her man. Now come here and let Uncle Ty fix you up a bit."

Before he realized what Ty was up to, the other man had his fingers in Matt's hair. "So thick, and just, oh, what I wouldn't do to get you in my chair. To think all of this male goodness is real. And you're smart too, and nice." He tousled Matt's hair and then patted his chest. "Good God, your muscles have muscles."

"Okay, I think I'm good now. I'll just go up and . . . What exactly is it I'm supposed to do?"

He should've kept his mouth shut. After he picked up

the chicken wraps, Chloe and Ty spent the elevator ride up to the eighth floor instructing him on the art of seduction. He sent them back down to the third before they decided to join him on his *date*.

There was no reason for Matt to be nervous. Okay, so there was when it came to the future of Christmas General, but not his future with Charlotte. He had to remind himself he was just playing along with Chloe and Ty to get them to back off. He'd shared coffees, lunches, even dinners with Charlotte on many occasions, and this was no different. Even if it sort of felt like it was because of Chloe and Ty's romancing-the-CEO pep talk.

He knocked on her office door, cracking it open when she didn't answer. "Charlotte, you got a minute?"

She was on the phone and waved him in. "Jeremy, I'm going to put you on speaker. Dr. Trainer is here representing Dr. McBride, our chief of staff." She raised her eyebrows at Matt as though asking if that was okay. He nodded, and she put her ex on speaker. "I have a proposal I want you both to review. I've e-mailed you a copy. Dr. Trainer, here's one for you. I realize it's not ideal, but Jeremy, I think by closing the long-term beds and focusing on outpatient and emergency services, we can generate the profit you're looking for while retaining at least fifty percent of the jobs and services the town has come to rely on."

"You're kidding, right?" Matt asked as he tossed the file on her desk. "This isn't close to acceptable."

"I agree, and I don't appreciate you wasting my time or the board's, Charlotte. I want notices to go out this week. Assets sold off and Christmas General closed by January first."

"I'll see you both in court. By the end of the day, I'll

have at least two hundred employees signed on to a class-action suit."

"Matt," Charlotte said, sounding shocked and hurt by his threat.

"On what grounds?" Her ex's voice came through the speaker, his tone condescending and smug.

"The WARN Act. You're required to notify local and state governments sixty days in advance when more than one hundred people will be put out of work."

"Fine. Consider them notified. And Charlotte, as of now, I'm verbally extending your contract until February tenth. Paperwork to follow."

Charlotte sat there without saying a word. Matt shook his head, disappointed that she didn't try to intervene. He dropped the bag of cupcakes, cookies, and chicken wraps on her desk and strode to the door. He opened it, and Ty fell into him.

"Not a word," he told the other man when he opened his mouth.

Ty sent both Matt and Charlotte a tight-lipped look before hurrying back to his desk and picking up the phone.

As Matt strode across the reception area, he heard him say, "Nell, it's Ty. This is a direct order from your mayor. The town needs you. Get your butt over to Christmas General, ASAP."

Chapter Five

Five long and agonizing days after Matt confirmed he officially hated her by threatening to sue Bailey Healthcare, Charlotte walked into her office and immediately walked back out. She glanced at the empty desk to her right. She wasn't in the wrong office; it was definitely Ty's desk. He wasn't in yet—because God forbid he actually got to work on time—but there was no mistaking the dancing Santa and the bowl of neon candy canes.

She took a deep breath and once more opened her office door to slowly walk inside. Someone liked pink, a lot. Christmas, too. Feathery pink garland was looped from one end of the wall of windows to the other. At least fifty glass snowflakes dangled in a symmetrical line from the window frame. The heat pouring from the vents caused them to spin in the bright morning sunlight, turning her office into a glittering rainbow. She'd need to wear sunglasses if she hoped to make it through the day without developing a migraine.

As she made her way to her desk, she noted the ornaments strategically placed on the bookshelves. A pink tree in the corner was tastefully decorated with miniature white lights and glass icicles, which no doubt would glitter and shine once the sunlight made its way to that side of her office.

"All I Want for Christmas Is You" blasted through the speakers, and she jumped. Even though she should be used to it by now. The onslaught of Christmas music signaled Ty's arrival.

It had been the same routine every morning since Matt confirmed Charlotte's worst fear that he hated her. She gave herself a mental slap. It was like she couldn't stop thinking about how Matt felt about her. And it seemed to be getting worse. She supposed that shouldn't be a surprise. Her days were getting worse, too.

But Ty was at least twenty minutes earlier than usual. She knew why when he ushered a woman into her office. He made a Vanna White gesture with his hands to the attractive woman with blond hair. "Christmas's favorite New York girl, Madison McBride."

Charlotte managed a smile and put down her briefcase to shake Madison's hand or, as Kate referred to her, the butt-kicking heroine of book 1 in the series. Her best friend was officially addicted to both the books and the town of Christmas. Which was annoying when the citizens of said town hated Charlotte as much as Matt did.

She gave her head an exasperated shake. She'd done it again. It was like she was obsessed with the man. *She wasn't, was she?*

She ignored the silent question. Losing her mind was apparently a consequence of living in a town where

99.9 percent of the population hated her. An image of He Who Shall No Longer Be Named popped into her head, and she pushed him out. Maybe it was a good thing Ty had once again ignored her no-more-appointments directive.

Over the course of four days, Chloe McBride had stopped by three times. And now that Charlotte thought about it, she had a fairly good idea who was behind her office re-do. The woman liked pink and was Ty's best friend.

Charlotte also had the grave misfortune of dealing with Sheriff Jill Anderson on a daily basis. Several times a day, actually. Because that's how often a member of the charming little mountain town (Kate's words, not hers) leveled a fictitious charge against Charlotte. Yesterday, she had supposedly been seen in the grocery store fighting with someone over a head of lettuce, which resulted in an older woman falling and breaking her wrist. She also had reportedly been seen leaving the local bar under the influence and driving away in her car. Neither incident had taken place, of course.

Oddly enough, the one person who hadn't demanded an appointment with Charlotte was Nell McBride. As Charlotte had been led to believe, nothing happened in Christmas without Nell getting involved. Kate had been even more surprised than Charlotte that the seventy-something woman hadn't demanded an audience. Albeit for an entirely different reason.

As her best friend had learned, and shared, Charlotte's new assistant had begged Nell to come out of retirement...She'd refused. According to Nell, via Ty, then Kate, the town's matriarch's gift couldn't be forced.

Unless the couple in question hit the top of her chemistry meter, she wouldn't waste her time. Apparently, that was the case with Charlotte and Matt. They had no chemistry. He wasn't her one and only, and she wasn't his.

"Charlotte." Ty nudged her. "You fell asleep with your eyes open again."

"I wasn't... Sorry, I just have a lot—"

Ty talked right over her. "She hasn't been sleeping. All you have to do is look at her to know that, right? The bags under her eyes have turned into suitcases since yesterday. Look—" he said to Madison while pinching Charlotte's cheeks—"the color disappears in seconds. She glows in the dark."

Charlotte nudged him away, forcing an isn't-he-cute smile on her face as she took a seat behind her desk. "Thanks, Ty. I think Madison gets it."

"At least her hair looks fan-tab-u-lous, doesn't it? I gave her the full treatment yesterday. We turned her office into a salon. Poor thing, it's safer for her here than out on the streets."

"I'm right here," Charlotte reminded him.

Obviously Madison decided a distraction was in order. "Ty, I'd kill for a Sugarplum Bakery gingerbread latte. Charlotte, what about you?"

"Definitely. I'll have a salted caramel latte, and—" Charlotte began.

Ty rolled his eyes. "I know, three of the bakery's Christmas cupcakes. Might as well make it a half a dozen," he said when Madison raised two fingers.

"I hope you don't mind me stopping by, Charlotte," Madison said once Ty closed the door behind him, taking a seat across from the desk. "My father-in-law asked me to check on you. He knows how hard you worked this past year for CGH, and he feels horrible that everyone has turned against you. They're just scared, you know."

Charlotte didn't know what it was about Madison, maybe it was Dr. McBride's words of support, or knowing the other woman was originally from New York, but she suddenly found herself spilling her guts about how awful the past week had been. Nothing like this had ever happened to her before. Well, of course the scandal with Jeremy and Samantha had been horrible, too, but this situation was so much worse. Madison was right. People were terrified about losing their jobs and not being able to find another one. And Charlotte had no idea how to fix it.

As she shared just how bad it had been, Madison nodded like she understood her plight completely. Once Charlotte fell silent, the other woman said, "You know when you're talking to someone and sharing how crappy your life is and they can't just listen and make sympathetic noises and tell you it's going to be all right?"

Charlotte nodded.

"Well, I'm not that woman, Charlotte. I'm honestly not. But let me tell you, when I first came to Christmas, I couldn't wait to leave it in my rearview mirror. People here were horrible to me. They basically ruined my reputation. I lost my job because of them. And as much as I hated small towns before, nothing compared to how I felt about this one. But everything changed once I got to know the people in town and they got to know me. You've been here a year, and none of us really know you. I'd like to, and my friends would, too. If you gave have us half a chance, I think you might be pleasantly surprised."

"I'm sorry. It honestly wasn't my intention to bury myself in work. I wasn't in a good place when I first arrived, and it had nothing to do with the town. My marriage had just ended, and not happily."

"I know. Ty told us. I'm sorry. Your ex sounds awful, and so does his new wife. Believe me, we've all dealt with jerks, and in the end, they get what they deserve. My friend Skye would say it's karma."

"You and your friends are all from New York, aren't you?" At Madison's nod, she said, "Don't you miss New York? I'm not trying to be rude; I'm just trying to understand how you can go from living in New York to living *here*."

"If it wasn't for my husband, Gage, I might still be in New York. But I'm happy here. Happier than I ever thought possible. Of course that's because of Gage and our children, and his family, who've become mine. We've all made great lives here. We have wonderful friends. If you gave Christmas a chance, I think the town would grow on you, too. And the people. They're good, decent, hardworking folks. It's like I said before, you just have to let them get to know you."

"They might've been more open to getting to know me last year, but I'm pretty sure they'd be just as happy if I left town. Honestly, I don't blame them. I understand why they're angry. I am, too. I didn't sign up for this. I've tried everything I can think of to stop them from closing CGH. Obviously, neither side was happy with my idea to keep the emergency and outpatient services running, but I haven't been able to come up with anything else." She lifted the piles of notes she'd made over the past couple of days. "I've heard you're a financial genius and consult with local businesses. If you have any ideas, I'm open to them. I'll take whatever help I can get."

"I'm happy to hear you say that, because I've already had a look."

Charlotte sighed. "Ty."

"Ty, and my father-in-law. And just so you know, they weren't questioning your ability or willingness to do the job. They just thought a second set of eyes would help."

"Did they?" Charlotte asked hopefully.

"No, I would've suggested exactly what you did. Like you, I'm at a loss. And as much as people complained about your cost-saving measures, you did an incredible job turning CGH around. If I was a shareholder in Bailey Healthcare, I'd be recommending you for promotion."

"Thank you. I appreciate the vote of confidence. And you probably should know, I will be promoted, and my dad will be reinstated as chairman of the board if I wind down CGH by the deadline and at a profit. If I don't, we're both out."

By the look of surprise on Madison's face, that was news to her. And not happy news. Only Matt had overheard that part of Charlotte's conversation with Jeremy the other day. She'd known all along she could trust him to keep her confidence, and this proved her right.

"I'm not going to lie: I'll do whatever it takes to ensure my father and I don't get ousted from my family's company. The way I see it, I have a couple weeks to convince the other board members to vote Jeremy out and reinstate my father. If I can't, I have no choice but to begin winding down operations at Christmas General." She'd already begun closing long-term beds. It's why people were picketing outside the hospital.

"If I were you, I'd probably do the same," Madison said, although she didn't look happy about the admission. "That's more or less what I was doing when I first came to Christmas. Hartwell Enterprises, the company I worked for, wasn't my own, but in some ways I felt like it was." Madison frowned. "You know, maybe we're looking at this all wrong. The deal Harrison, my boss's nephew, was trying to push through for Christmas was a smoke screen for a get-quick rich scheme of his own. So maybe you have to figure out what's in it for Jeremy. Why is he focused on Christmas General? Is he closing down any other hospitals?"

"Not that I'm aware of, but I can't think of any way closing Christmas General would benefit Jeremy personally."

"You keep thinking, and I'll have my friend Vivi look into Jeremy, too. She's an investigative reporter and owns the *Christmas Chronicle*."

"Thank you. I'd appreciate it." Charlotte smiled, looking up when Ty walked in carrying a bag and balancing a tray of coffees in one hand, his phone in the other.

"My New York BFFs wanted to check on their girl. See," he said to the blurry faces on the screen, "she doesn't look depressed anymore. I told you I'd find her some friends."

Madison waved and said hi to Kate and Abbie.

"We'll all get to hang out next summer. Kate, Abbie, and little Emma have promised to visit Charlotte then. We'll have so much fun."

"But I won't be here next summer," Charlotte said.

Ty laughed like he knew something she didn't.

*   *   *

Charlotte had spent the rest of the day before thinking about what Madison said. It made sense. There had to be some financial reward in it for Jeremy. The man was motivated by money. Every decision he ever made revolved around the almighty dollar. Charlotte had planned to practice family medicine, but the ink had barely dried on her degree when Jeremy called a family meeting, insisting that she take her rightful place at Bailey Healthcare.

Her mother, a pediatrician, had still been alive then. She'd wanted Charlotte to follow in her footsteps, but Charlotte's father and Jeremy had overridden both their objections. Granted, Charlotte's had been half-hearted. Head over heels in love with Jeremy, she would've done just about anything to make him happy, even if it meant giving up on her own dreams.

She supposed that's something she should think about when all this was over. Whose life was she living, her own or the one Jeremy had mapped out for her? Right now, he was definitely still pulling the strings. She planned to put a stop to that. She'd spent, or she should say Ty spent, the entire morning trying to reach the CEO of Valley Ridge Medical Center. In the end, they'd given up and driven the forty minutes to track down the woman themselves.

Valley Ridge Medical Center was the hospital most likely to benefit from Christmas General's demise. They were also owned by a for-profit corporation who had expressed an interest in buying out Bailey Healthcare a few years back. It wasn't beyond the realm of possibility that Jeremy was in bed with that company now, weakening Bailey Healthcare's position and leaving them vulnerable to a hostile takeover. For which Jeremy would no doubt be handsomely rewarded.

Only Charlotte didn't have any evidence, and it didn't look like she was going to get any today. "She must have left early. We'll try again on Monday," Charlotte said to Ty, who'd insisted on accompanying her to Valley Ridge Medical Center.

He shook his head and rattled the knob on Maureen Cheever's office door. "I don't think so. Everyone we talked to said she's here. She's hiding from us, which means that we can try to set up a meeting with her all we want, and it's not going to happen. She'll wait us out."

Up until fifteen minutes ago, Charlotte had begun to think she was reaching, seeing conspiracies where none existed. But Ty was right. Valley Ridge's CEO was definitely avoiding them. "I don't know what else to do. We can't break into her office."

"Why not?" He crouched in front of the knob. "It can't be that hard to—"

She grabbed his arm and pulled him to his feet. "Because that would be breaking the law, and there are cameras. Trust me, I know how important it is that we get to the bottom of this and put a stop to Jeremy. But we have to go about it legally." She looped her arm through Ty's and guided him toward the elevators.

"Ma'am, I think you dropped something."

She turned to see a man standing outside Maureen Cheever's door. He was dressed in white coveralls and leaning on a mop, holding up a business card between his fingers.

"Thanks, but I don't think—" Charlotte began, only to be cut off by Ty, who half dragged her back down the hall saying out of the side of his mouth, "He's a janitor, and janitors know everything."

Charlotte smiled at the thirty-something man with the attractive, angular face, a heavy lock of dark hair flopping over his forehead and left eye. "Thank you," she said, accepting the card. It read NICK CLAUSE, NEW YORK CAB CO. She turned it over, and there, written in ink, were the words *Believe* and *Miracles happen every day. Open your eyes and your heart to see them.* She checked the zipper on her purse, trying to figure out how the card had fallen out. It didn't make sense. She'd put the card in her wallet.

"Charlotte, Henry's going to open the door and let us wait in Ms. Cheever's office for her. Isn't that nice of him?"

"Yes, that's wonder...Henry? Your name's Henry?" she asked, thinking back to what Nick had said that night about his partner. She could've sworn his name was Henry, too. Henry was a common name, but still...

The man grinned. "That's me. There you go." He held the door open. "Good luck finding what you need, Ty. Ms. Bailey."

"Thank you," Charlotte said as she looked around the room. They might have gotten in legally, but she didn't want to be here any longer than was..."Wait, how do you know my—" She turned to face Henry, but he wasn't there. She leaned out the door. The hall was empty. "Ty, did you tell him our names?"

"Of course. He's hot. I gave him my number, too," he said, as he rifled through some files on Maureen Cheever's desk. "Not sure if I told him your name though. Why?"

"Nothing," she said as she joined him. "I just..." She trailed off as her eyes landed on the photograph on the far corner of the desk. She picked it up and smiled, Henry all but forgotten. She knew exactly what Jeremy was up to and why.

Chapter Six

Smile," Ty said just before he took a picture of Charlotte on the drive back to Christmas. The flash nearly blinded her.

She blinked the stars from her eyes to focus on the taillights ahead of her. Wrapped tight around the steering wheel, her hands began to cramp. After a year in Colorado, her defensive driving skills had improved, but today's road conditions would be trying for the best of drivers. "No more pictures. If you haven't noticed, it's snowing and the roads are a mess."

"It's not your best side, but it'll do. I can see the headlines now: *Charlotte Bailey saves Christmas.* I'm going to suggest it to Vivi. Catchier if she leaves off General," Ty said as he worked his phone. "Wait, this is even better." He lifted his hand and punctuated each word. *"Miracle at Christmas."*

"Don't start celebrating just yet. I don't mean to be a

downer. I'm excited about this too. But you heard my dad. We don't have any evidence that Jeremy is colluding with Maureen."

"Yeah, but he's calling an emergency board meeting. So he must think he has a good chance of getting them to oust Jeremy."

"You don't know my ex like I do, Ty. If anyone can spin this, it'll be Jeremy. I'm just hoping the board members will see through him. It all depends on whether my dad can lay out the case against him."

"Maybe you should do it. You laid out a pretty good case when you were talking to your father."

"Thanks, but I just stated the facts." Ty was right, though. Despite not having solid evidence of collusion, they had a pretty good circumstantial case. It would be up to the board members to connect the dots. Maureen Cheever was Harold Delray's daughter and could legitimately contest her father's will. Charlotte imagined there was no love lost between Harold's daughter and his second, much younger wife. Samantha was the reason Harold had left Colorado for New York. And until today, no one at Bailey Healthcare had even known Harold had a daughter. As far as anyone knew, Samantha was Harold's sole beneficiary.

If Harold had indeed cut his daughter out of the will, Samantha's pregnancy would provide Maureen with the ammunition she needed to prove her stepmother had been unfaithful. Even if a judge didn't overturn the will based on the evidence, Maureen could tie up the money for years. And that wouldn't suit Jeremy's purposes at all. Especially with a baby on the way. Every time Charlotte had suggested they start a family, money had been the number one excuse he'd used to put her off.

Given how things had turned out, it was for the best. She returned her attention to Ty. "And I didn't have Jeremy arguing against each fact as I presented it. Or Samantha, for that matter. Which is what my dad will be up against," she added. "And, like he said, if they offered to close CGH as a bribe, Maureen won't come forward."

"Why not? She stands to gain a lot more money if she goes after her father's fortune."

"No, the odds of her overturning Harold's will are negligible. Even if she did, it would take years, and Samantha would still receive the majority of Harold's fortune. If Maureen was lucky, she might get a couple hundred thousand dollars. But after paying her legal bills, she'd walk away with next to nothing. This way, the closure of CGH ensures a huge increase in Valley Ridge's revenues and solidifies Maureen's position as CEO, as well as ensuring she'll surpass her targets. Her bonuses alone will more than likely be in the hundred-thousand-dollar range. She'll also look good to the higher-ups, which puts her on track for a promotion."

"Okay, your father has as much on the line as you, but trust me, you're the best one to present this to the board. You're one of Samantha and Jeremy's victims. You're proof he lies and cheats and doesn't care who he hurts. I'm not dissing your father. But I'd feel better knowing the fate of Christmas was in your hands and not his."

Ty had hit a sore point. Charlotte hated to be seen as a victim. Which made the idea of being the one to bring Jeremy and Samantha down hard to resist. However, it was the thought of telling Matt that Christmas General and his job were safe that made the decision for her. "I'll go."

"Yay! I knew you would. Did you hear that, ladies? She

said yes. Call every scalper you know and scrounge up four tickets to the Rockettes. We'll have lots to celebrate. Later." He made kissy noises into the phone.

"Who was that?"

"My girls?"

"Your girls?"

"Yeah, my girls. Abbie and Kate. I can't wait to see them."

"You're coming with me?"

"Of course, I am. You need me. Besides, my job has become hazardous to my health. I need a holiday. All day long I take calls from angry people threatening you and people sharing what's going to happen to them if CGH closes. One minute I'm shaking like a leaf and in the next crying like a baby."

She knew exactly how he felt. He took thorough notes and made sure she—and the sheriff—got each and every one.

"That girl is good," he said, holding up his phone. "Abbie's got us covered. Emergency board meeting is scheduled for tomorrow night. We leave first thing in the morning."

"Ty, you might want to look outside." She nodded at the near white-out conditions through the windshield.

"Good God, when did that happen? Charlotte, watch out!"

She reacted without thinking and slammed on the brakes. The car fishtailed, skidding sideways into the truck ahead of her. There's was a crunch and screech of metal scraping metal and then the loud *whoomph* of the airbag on Ty's side bursting open, pushing his body into hers. They bumped heads.

"Ouch," they both cried at the same time.

Charlotte raised a hand to her temple, Ty to his forehead. Someone rapped on her window. "Charlotte."

It was Matt, looking big and strong, his handsome face concerned. She opened the door, so glad to see him she wanted to jump into his arms and share the news that they might've found the answer to saving CGH. And then she realized how and why he'd arrived so quickly at the scene. She winced. "That's your truck, isn't it?"

He nodded and leaned in, looking from her to Ty. "You guys okay?"

"No, I'm sure I've broken several bones. I'll need a thorough examination," Ty said, casting a hopeful glance at Matt.

"He's fine," Charlotte said, attempting to undo her seat belt. "What about you? Are you okay?"

"He looks more than fine to me."

Matt ignored Ty and reached in to help with her seat belt. "There's a fifteen-car pileup. We'll be here for a while. You'll be safer waiting it out in my truck."

She nodded while trying not to react to the feel of his strong hands or to how close his face was to hers. Until then, she hadn't noticed how long his eyelashes were. Like his hair, they were golden-brown and had a slight curl. Dark stubble shadowed his square jaw, and she got a whiff of his aftershave. He smelled like snow falling on cedars and warm leather.

"Bailey, you look like you're going to lick the man," Ty groused, then sighed. "I guess I can't blame you. Just do it and get it over with."

Matt turned his head, his whisky-colored eyes holding hers. "You want to *lick* me?"

No, she wanted to kiss his corded neck and his strong jaw and that sensuous mouth with the full bottom lip and... The corner of his mouth kicked up. She shot Ty a killing glare, and said, "Of course not. Ty's just being Ty. I'm not a dog." *No, I'm an idiot. Why did I say something like that?* Her seat belt popped free. Her "Thank you" came out a little breathy and squeaky. She sounded like she'd sucked in a lungful of helium.

"Are you sure you're okay?"

"She's fine, but I'm being smothered by a giant marshmallow. Not that either of you seem to care."

Matt extended his hand. "It'll be easier to get him out the driver side."

"Right. Of course." She put her hand in his and stepped from the car into ankle-deep snow. Only underneath it was ice, and her heel went out from under her. Matt's arm shot around her waist, saving her from falling backward. It didn't save her from embarrassment, though. From the waist down, she was pressed against him, resulting in another breathy "Thank you."

He stared into her eyes as she lay over his arm like a heroine on a romance cover. There was something about the way he looked at her that made her think he wanted to kiss her as much as she wanted to kiss him. Even if he didn't, at least he wasn't looking at her like she'd disappointed him when she pretended to go along with the plans to close CGH and that made it feel like everything was finally right with the world. Through the snowflakes pelting her face, she smiled up at him. "We might've found a way to save the hospital."

The smile he gave her softened his ruggedly handsome face, telling her more than any words could. Dr. Matt

Trainer liked her, a lot. Maybe as much as she liked him. Slowly, he drew her upright until they were thigh to thigh, chest to chest, the frosted clouds of their breath intermingling. "I always believed you would, Dr. Bailey."

This time something more than admiration lit up his eyes. He didn't just want to kiss her; he was going to. It would be the perfect ending for what was turning into a perfect day. Other than being involved in a fifteen-car pileup and smashing into his truck, she supposed. She went up on her tiptoes, and he began to lower his head when from within the car Ty said, "Seriously?" And from down the road, "Doc Trainer, is that you?"

Matt straightened, easing Charlotte from his arms. "Ted, what's going on?" he asked the older man hurrying toward them.

"A young woman. Think she was the one who caused the pileup. Car went off the road. Someone just spotted it. She's hurt bad. Unconscious. Two young 'uns in the back. Shaken, but I think they're all right."

"I'll get my medical bag out of the truck and be right with you." He handed Charlotte his keys. "Get Ty out of the car and into my truck. Be care—" His head shot up, and he grabbed Charlotte. "Ty, brace. Ted, run. Not between the vehicles," he ordered as he slammed the car door shut and took off at a run, half dragging her with him. She turned her head and saw what he had, headlights coming through the wall of snow, and they were coming on fast.

"Oh God," she cried out, just before the SUV crashed into her car, followed by two more. The ground shuddered as if there'd been a mini earthquake. A drawn-out, ear-piercing screech and the sound of metal crunching like accordions vibrated in the early evening air. And then it was over. Low moans, an anguished cry, and the hiss of steam replaced the sounds of moments before.

Matt snapped into action. Once he'd confirmed she and Ted were okay, he moved to her car and checked on Ty, and then the on the passengers in the vehicles behind. She hurried after him, wishing not for the first time today that she'd worn practical boots.

"Charlotte, call the sheriff's office and ask where the hell they are. I called them ten minutes ago. And unless they have emergencies, get on with the fire department and Search and Rescue. We need all the help we can get."

Less than fifteen minutes later, Matt had proven, at least to her, why he was called Dr. McSexy. His gorgeous face, chiseled six-pack, and rock-hard pecs that his scrubs couldn't hide were probably why he'd been given the nickname. And of course those attributes put him at the top of anyone's sexy meter.

But in Charlotte's eyes, he'd never been sexier than he was when he took control of the situation. He was confident and commanding, and no one doubted they'd be safe with Matt Trainer on the job. He wasn't only a doctor; the man had been a special ops medic and volunteered with Search and Rescue. It's how he was able to outfit Ted and his friends in some form of reflective wear. They were stationed a few hundred yards down from them with flashlights in hopes of preventing the pileup and the number of injuries from getting any larger.

At last count, there were twenty vehicles involved and at least fifteen people injured. Matt had gone to look after the unconscious woman and her children while Charlotte took care of the rest. Most of them had sustained minor injuries, including Ty, who'd broken his nose. He currently wasn't speaking to her. Aware of his dramatic tendencies, she'd thought it best not to warn him before she reset his nose.

From where he sat cross-faced and cross-legged in a snowbank, he grumbled at the distant wail of sirens, "About time. Now a real doctor can fix my nose."

The woman whose arm Charlotte was putting in a splint glanced from Ty to her. "Don't worry, I'm a real doctor," she assured her patient while shooting a zip it look at Ty. He lifted his nose and sniffed, and then his face contorted in a pained grimace.

Moments later emergency vehicles filled the other lane of the highway. Two tall men got out of the sheriff's white Suburban. They were extremely good-looking, so Charlotte wasn't surprised when Ty flagged them down. "Gage, can you check my nose?" he asked, lifting his chin at the dark-haired man.

"Ty, I was a paramedic, not a doctor. Looks fine to me, though."

Apparently not happy with his answer, Ty looked to the fair-haired man for advice. "Chance, tell me the truth. Has she ruined my face forever?"

"Put some ice on your nose, take two ibuprofens, and you'll be as good as new." Chance winked at Charlotte, and she blinked. No wonder Madison and Vivi didn't mind leaving New York.

"Can I call you in the morning?" Ty asked, but the two men had already walked off to make themselves useful.

Charlotte continued to treat the injured until the paramedics took over. She helped them load an elderly man complaining of chest pain onto a stretcher.

The younger woman thanked Charlotte and then said to her partner, "Matt said we're to take everyone to CGH."

"Will do," her partner responded with a nod.

"No, I'm sorry. You'll have to take them to Valley Ridge," Charlotte said.

"Sorry, ma'am, but we take our orders from Dr. Trainer."

"Yes, and Dr. Trainer takes his orders from me. I'm CEO of Christmas General, Dr. Charlotte Bailey, and you will do as I—"

"Charlotte, what do you think you're doing?" asked a deep and unhappy voice from behind her.

She turned around. "Matt, we're not equipped to—"

"I don't have time to argue with you about this, Charlotte. Everyone is going to Christmas General." He lifted his chin at the paramedic, who nodded and wheeled the patient away.

Charlotte stared after the woman and then looked up at Matt. "I can't believe you countermanded my order like that. We're down to a skeletal staff. We can't handle—"

"We can, and we will. Now I have a patient to get back to." He turned and walked to one of the other ambulances. Tucking supplies under his arm, he waved over the McBrides. "Hey guys, I could use a hand."

Ty was gone, and most of Charlotte's patients had been loaded in the ambulances or taken away in other emergency vehicles. She started to walk in the direction Matt had taken but then turned back. If he wanted her help, he would've asked. Obviously, he wasn't happy that she'd wanted to send the patients to Valley Ridge. She wasn't happy with him, either. Which proved she'd been right all along. She couldn't afford to get involved with an employee, no matter how much she wanted to.

She walked over to where the dark-haired sheriff stood beside the white Suburban with a picture of Santa on the door. Jill was on the radio. The call sounded serious. She didn't mean to listen in but couldn't help herself. It sounded like the call was about Matt's patient.

The woman's children were being transported to Christmas General now. The jaws of life had finally cut through the vehicle, and the woman was being removed. From what Jill said, it was only because of Matt's heroic efforts that she was even alive.

Charlotte turned and ran down the road. Matt had to listen to her. The woman was in a life-and-death situation. CGH was already overextended. Charlotte had closed most of the long-term beds. The rest were filled. She had to make him see reason.

The *beep, beep, beep* of an ambulance backing toward the side of the road was barely audible above the engines and howl of the wind. Lights from the emergency vehicles lit up the path the McBride brothers and two paramedics walked along as they carried the woman on the stretcher toward the waiting ambulance. Matt stood beside the mangled car with two firemen. It was dark now, and the snow was still heavy so it was difficult to see what he was doing, but he appeared to be treating one of the firefighters.

Someone shouted. From where she was, it was hard to make out the words. In seconds, she didn't need to hear what they yelled to know Matt and the firefighters were in trouble. Carried on the wind was the smell of gas. The McBride brothers pointed something out to Matt. A spark. A flame. He was already moving away from the car. And then it was like someone had turned a camera on slow motion. Matt's face was lit up in an orange glow as he looked over his shoulder. One of the firefighters had tripped and was struggling to get up. Matt started back, heedless of the danger.

"Matt!" she screamed.

Boom! A ball of fire lit up the night sky.

Chapter Seven

There was standing room only in the emergency room at Christmas General, where Matt waited for someone to stitch his head. At least he had company to keep him entertained. The McBride brothers, their great-aunt's best friends Ted and Fred, and a few guys from the old-timers' hockey league Matt played on, including the sheriff's husband and owner of the Penalty Box, Sawyer Anderson. Jill was there, too. So was Ethan O'Connor, three guys from Search and Rescue, and two of Matt's firefighter friends.

And that right there was why he loved the town of Christmas, Colorado. He counted himself blessed. And lucky. Other than a mild concussion, some scrapes and bruises, and a minor head wound, he'd survived tonight's explosion in one piece. Both firefighters had escaped with minor injuries, too. The person Matt was most worried about was the young mother they'd extracted from the car just before it blew.

He raised his voice to make himself heard. His visitors were getting loud. "Jill, how are Jane Doe's kids?" Whatever could've helped them identify the woman was now destroyed by the explosion, and, as far as Matt knew, the kids weren't talking. Matt suspected the older boy—who was maybe four—was in shock.

"They were having a hard time. Dr. Bailey thought it might help if they saw their mom. She has them in the room with her now. Before you ask, yes, she's still unconscious, but she's stable. Thanks to you and your field work."

It was more thanks to his time in the military. He'd learned to think on his feet and improvise. "Cold weather helped some."

"So, you and Dr. Bailey, anything to share?" Gage asked Matt.

"Ah, no, and I'm not sure why you're asking."

"He can't help himself. He has three daughters," his older brother Chance said.

"What do you mean you don't know why Gage is asking? The only reason a woman runs toward danger instead of away from it is—"

Matt cut Ted off before he said what he thought he was going to. Insinuating that Charlotte was in love with him wouldn't do either of them any good, especially in a small town. Especially given their last exchange. He had little doubt his *boss* had a few things to say to him about overruling her at the scene tonight. "I wasn't actually thinking or seeing clearly for a few minutes. But the only reason Charlotte would run to my aid is because she's a doctor."

"No, siree, the woman had tears streaming down her face. She thought you were dead. Ain't that the truth, Ted?" Fred asked his best friend of seventy years.

They reminded Matt of Jack Lemmon and Walter Matthau in *Grumpy Old Men*. Fred was Walter, and Ted was Jack. Only it wasn't Ted and Fred who worried him. It was their best friend, Nell McBride.

Maybe Matt's hearing had been affected by the blast or his concussion was worse than he thought. Because he was pretty sure Fred had just said Charlotte was crying. He glanced at Jill, figuring it was safer to ask her than Fred or Ted.

"So, how about the big game last night?" he said, knowing that would get the conversation started and distract them from the one he planned to have with Jill. Christmas was a big hockey town, thanks to Sawyer Anderson. He used to be captain of the Colorado Flurries.

Sure enough, they were all eager to share their opinion of the game. It helped that a couple of guys were cheering for the opposing team. As soon as the conversation got heated, Matt turned to Jill, who sat on the edge of the bed.

He'd made a slight miscalculation: He'd forgotten that Jill was as big a fan of the game as the rest of the guys. "You're joking, right? He's a baby. See how many goals he scores without his team protecting him."

Before he lost his chance, Matt nudged Jill. "Fred said Charlotte was crying. Did she hurt herself?"

"No, you idiot. She thought you were dead."

"Keep it down, would you?" He should've known better than to ask Jill.

"Why? It's a good thing, isn't it? If she gets that upset at the thought of you dying, she's probably in love with you. And if she's in love with you, she'll fight to ensure that you keep your job and that Christmas General stays open. Way to go, Matt." She raised her hand to high-five him.

The guys stopped arguing and turned to look at him.

Sawyer laughed. "If you expected Jill to keep it on the DL, you must've hit your head harder than we thought."

"Okay, just so you all know, that wasn't what it sounded like. Charlotte and I are friends. That's it. That's all."

"Won't be for long. Nellie's coming out of retirement," Fred said.

"No, she's not," Matt said, his voice rising an octave. Everyone laughed at him.

"Yes, she is," Ted said, turning his phone around. "She just announced it on Facebook."

*   *   *

Charlotte cast a nervous glance at the older woman sitting with the two little boys on the couch in her office. Nell McBride had been waiting for them when they returned from visiting with the boys' mother. Charlotte supposed she should be grateful for the older woman's presence. Nell had come straight from Santa's Village, where she'd been performing in her role as Mrs. Claus, and was providing a welcome distraction from the little boys' grief and fear as she read them a Christmas story.

Charlotte's gratitude was tempered with worry only because Nell's reputation preceded her. Perhaps she was worrying for nothing. At the moment, the older woman looked sweet and grandmotherly with her rosy cheeks and smiling blue eyes. As though she sensed Charlotte's perusal, Nell raised her gaze from the page. "Why in the Sam Hill are you staring at me? Go see to Matt."

Nell had no idea how much Charlotte wanted to do that, but she had to ensure the children were taken care of first. She knew Matt would feel the same. "I will as soon as I've met with social services."

They were looking for someone to take in Jane Doe's sons while they searched for their extended family. Both boys had curly light brown hair and hazel eyes. Charlotte guessed the youngest to be somewhere between two and three, and the oldest to be between four and five. So far, neither of them had said a single word. Although she'd seen signs they were communicating with each other. The oldest was sweetly protective of his baby brother.

His wary gaze narrowed on her over the top of the book, and she had a feeling he understood more than she'd thought. Charlotte smiled at him. "It's just a temporary arrangement until your mother gets better. We're going to make sure you and your brother stay together and that's there's lots of toys for you to play with. You'll see your mom every day, I promise. I'll bring you to the hospital myself. Okay?"

The boys shared a glance, and then the oldest looked at her and shook his head. Charlotte moved to the chair closest to them and sat on the edge. "If you told us your names and where you live, it would help us find your family. Can you do that? Can you tell us your names?"

An emotion sparked in his eyes just before he lowered his gaze to the book. Fear or panic, she couldn't be sure which. He'd reacted the same way when she'd questioned him earlier. At the time, she'd put it down to worry about their mother and being among strangers. Now, though, she had a feeling it was something more.

"We don't need social services involved, do we, boys? How would you like to stay with Dr. Bailey? She lives a couple blocks from the hospital."

"Well, um, I'm living at the lodge right now, and that's not really a suitable…" Trapped by two pairs of hazel eyes set in adorable, scared little faces, she trailed off helplessly when the oldest gave her a tiny nod.

"You're right, the lodge is no place for two little boys during the Christmas season. You need a big yard to play in and a house to decorate, don't you?"

Thank God, Charlotte thought, *Nell's taking them home with her.* Charlotte stood up, her relief turning to delight at what looked to be a gleam of excitement in the oldest boy's eyes. And she might be mistaken, but she thought she caught a hint of a smile on the toddler's face just before he stuck his thumb in his mouth.

"All right, you get on the horn and tell social services we've got the boys set, and I'll put out a request for toys and clothes on Facebook. When you go down to check on Matt, ask him how he's set up in the way of Christmas decorations. I can put out a call for them, too, if need be."

Charlotte froze with the phone in her hand and slowly turned to look at Nell. "Why do you want to know if Matt has decorations?"

"You're a smart girl, why do you think? Kids like to decorate with colorful lights for the holidays, don't you?" she asked the boys, who nodded. "And Matt lives in a nice, big, family-sized house just around the corner. I'll feel better knowing you're with him on account of the head injuries he sustained playing hero tonight, Dr. Bailey. Seems to me we've found the ideal solution for everyone."

This time there was no mistaking the expression on the boys' faces, and no matter her near panic at being caught in the crosshairs of Christmas's resident matchmaker,

Charlotte would not be the one to make their smiles disappear. Which, as evidenced by her satisfied grin, Nell McBride knew full well.

Ten minutes later, after clearing the arrangement with social services and leaving the boys in the capable hands of the manipulative Mrs. Claus, Charlotte went in search of Matt in emergency to break the news. It wasn't difficult to figure out where he was; all she had to do was follow the sound of male laughter. Opening the door was more difficult. She heard a grunt as she shoved it open. Crossing her arms and raising an eyebrow, she leaned against the doorjamb. The laughter in the room trailed off then died.

"Uh, oh, looks like you're in trouble, Trainer," the firefighter in the corner said.

"Take good care of our boy, Doc. It's a busy time for Search and Rescue. We can't afford to have him out of commission for long," a hulking man said as he and his friend gave Matt a fist bump.

Matt was watching her as warily as the little boy had fifteen minutes before. Ha. He should save his wary looks for a woman who warranted them. But Nell was the least of her worries at the moment. Charlotte had received the radiologist's report on Jane Doe on her way to see Matt. And now that she saw him, she didn't like his coloring or the blood seeping through the gauze on his forehead.

"Your boy should've been taken care of an hour ago." Charlotte leaned back to look for a nurse.

"Charlotte, they're overrun, and I'm fine."

"You're not fine. And they're overrun because someone vetoed my directive to send the accident victims to Valley Ridge," she snapped, and then winced at the expression that came over the other men's faces. In their eyes, she'd officially become the witchy Dr. Bailey. Given the way Matt's mouth flattened, he thought so, too. Wait until he found out the witchy doctor and two children were having a sleepover at his house tonight.

Two grizzled older men stood up. She recognized them from the pileup this afternoon. They said their goodbyes to Matt and gave her polite nods as they walked past.

When they were a few feet down the hall, she heard the taller one say, "Ted, I'm thinking Nell's been retired too long and doesn't have it anymore. Those two are no Maddie and Gage."

Charlotte had no idea why, but she felt slightly offended by the older man's remark.

"Good thing you got here when you did, Charlotte. He's been threatening to stitch himself up. I offered, but he didn't take me up on it," Gage said as he and his brother filed out with the rest of the men. They'd officially introduced themselves to her after Matt was loaded in an ambulance. By that time, she'd recovered from her meltdown. She'd been so certain Matt was dead that she'd lost it. Like completely lost it. She hadn't been as upset about losing Jeremy as she'd been at nearly losing Matt.

Her cheeks heated with embarrassment at the thought. His friends had probably told him she'd made a fool of herself. She went to the small sink in the room and washed her hands, wishing she could splash cool water on her face. She felt the weight of Matt's gaze on her back.

"Have you had a CT scan?" she asked, keeping her voice professional and detached.

"No, and I don't need one."

She turned, her mouth open to argue only to realize he

was no longer sitting on the bed but moving to the door. "Get back on the bed. I need to examine you and stitch your head."

"You're not stitching my head or examining me. What you can do is sign me out."

"Yes, I am, and no, I will not. And if you don't allow me to do so, I won't clear you for work."

"Fine. I'll wait until one of the other docs is available."

"I'm afraid that's impossible. You'll have at least a two-hour wait, and the boys need to be put to bed before then. They've had a trying day, and so have I. Of course, you have, too. So would you please just do as you're told and not make such a fuss about it so we can go home?"

He rubbed his temple as he returned to the bed. "You know, I might have hit my head harder than I thought. Because for a minute there, it sounded like you and I were married with children..." He groaned. "Ted and Fred weren't joking, were they? Nell's come out of retirement, hasn't she?"

"On the one hand, I'm pleased to report that, given how quickly you figured that out, you're probably only mildly concussed. While on the other hand, I'm sorry to report you're right. Thanks to Nell, I'm moving in with you, and so are Jane Doe's sons. And before you give yourself a headache trying to come up with excuses, the boys smiled when Nell told them, so we're staying." At his stunned expression, she explained how it had transpired. As she did, she also began removing the gauze from the wound on his forehead.

"You shouldn't have let her in your office." He pulled his head away. "And don't think I didn't notice what you're doing."

"You need stitches. So why don't you lie back and let me do my job? And while I do, you can tell me if anyone has ever been able to stop Nell McBride from doing exactly what she sets her mind to."

"To be honest, I'd prefer a doctor who's practiced in the past couple years and who doesn't have an ax to grind."

"I'll be wielding a needle and thread, not an ax. And while I may be out of practice, I do know what I'm doing. But if you'd prefer a plastic surgeon..."

"No, I don't scar easily," he said, and she knew he'd given up fighting the inevitable. Once she'd found a nurse to bring her supplies, she got down to business. He lay back on the bed.

Feeling his eyes on her as she numbed the site, she glanced at him. "Second thoughts?"

"No, I know you'll do a good job. You wouldn't be doing it if you didn't think you could."

"Thank you for the vote of confidence, Dr. Trainer." She smiled while beginning to stitch the interior of the wound. It was deep and would need two layers. She'd glue the external layer. She found her eyes straying back to Matt's. *Focus*, she told herself. It might be a simple procedure, but she couldn't afford to be distracted, and being this close to Matt was distracting. Maybe she should've had someone else take care of him after all.

"How's Jane Doe doing?"

Just the distraction she needed as long as she didn't look him in the eyes or pay attention to the way her hip brushed his muscled arm. She cleared her throat. "The general consensus is she wouldn't be here if you hadn't done a tracheotomy in the field. Under the conditions you were in, I don't know how you did it, Matt. She's lucky you were there today. Lucky to be alive."

"I hear a *but* in your voice."

"No, it's just that the radiologist's report came in."

"And?"

"There are signs of old injuries, breaks that haven't healed properly. They're consistent with someone whose been abused. I think our Jane Doe is in an abusive relationship." She told him about the oldest child's reaction to questions about his extended family. "He's scared, and not just because of the accident. There's a shelter outside of town. What if that's where she was going?"

"I volunteer at Interval House a few hours a week. I'll contact Gail and see if she knows anything. What? You okay?"

"Yes, of course," she said, and refocused on stitching his wound instead of thinking about Matt volunteering at a home for abused women. Just when she thought the man couldn't be more perfect, she found proof that he was.

"You seem angry."

"I am," she said without thinking.

"And why's that?"

"Because you nearly went and got yourself killed today, you stupid, stupid man. What would those women do without you? What would we do without you?" *What would I do without you*, she thought, squeezing her eyes shut and squinching up her face.

"Look at me."

"No, I'm busy."

He wrapped his fingers around her wrist and drew her hand from his forehead. She let her hand fall to her side and bowed her head. "Matt, don't," she said as he sat up and drew her between his legs.

"I'm sorry I scared you." He reached up and tucked her hair behind her ear. "Will you look at me, please?"

She did as he asked. His face swam before her eyes. Then his lips touched hers, and his strong hand curved behind her neck, bringing her closer. She didn't realize until that moment how long she'd been waiting, wanting, this man to kiss her. Today, she'd nearly lost her chance.

There was a loud knock. "Everyone decent in there?" Nell's voice came through the door. "The boys are tired and need to get to bed. Folks have already started dropping off toys and clothes at your house, Matt. Hop to it, now."

Chapter Eight

As Matt and Charlotte tiptoed from the spare bedroom where they'd set up the boys, he glanced at her, taking in the determined line of her delicate jaw and the set of her narrow shoulders. All evidence of the soft and willing woman he'd held in his arms an hour before was gone. What he wouldn't give to get those moments back.

"Do you think they're warm enough?" she whispered.

"They're wearing flannel pjs, you added an extra blanket to the two already on the bed, and you used practically every pillow in the house to barricade them in there, not to mention the ten stuffed animals you tucked around them."

"I know but—"

"You know what? I think you're projecting. You're the one who's cold, not the boys. And you know why you're cold?"

She looked down at her red pjs and nodded. "I should've packed warmer pajamas. Can I borrow a sweatshirt?"

The silky fabric outlined the sweetly feminine curves of the body he'd held in his arms and more than anything wanted there again. He raised his gaze to her face, watching her mouth move but not registering the words. All he could think about was that moment when he'd had his lips on hers.

He took her hand.

She took it back and said quickly, nervously, "It's okay. I don't need a sweatshirt. I'll just take an extra blanket if you have one."

"You don't need an extra blanket or a sweatshirt. You've got me to keep you warm." He closed the distance between them, backing her against the wall. "We crossed the line tonight. We can't go back. I don't want to. I want you, Charlotte. I have for a long time. And I think you want me, too. Am I wrong?"

"No, of course you're not wrong. But we're adults. We both know just because you want something doesn't mean it's good for you."

He tried to keep from smiling. "You think I'm bad for you?"

"Yes, you're like Di Fara pizza, polenta with mushroom ragout, Sugarplum's cupcakes, and chocolates from Sugar and Spice. They taste amazing, but they're addictive and you can't stop at just one bite."

"Ah, so you're afraid you'll become addicted to me and not be able to give me up."

She nodded, raising her hand to play with the button on his shirt.

"That's easy to fix."

"How?"

"Don't give me up." His brow furrowed as the words

came out of his mouth. It wasn't something he expected to say. Until that moment, he didn't think it was something he even wanted again. It spoke of long-term commitment. But maybe like Charlotte, his near-death experience had affected him more than he'd been willing to admit.

She rested her forehead against his chest and shook her head. "I didn't want this to happen, Matt. I don't want to want you. I don't want to want this."

"But you do?"

"Yes." Her hands fisted in his shirt, and she went up on her toes and touched her mouth to his. "Please tell me we won't regret this in the morning."

He deepened the kiss and walked her backward to his bedroom without answering. Her mouth was soft and warm. She tasted like sugar and spice and everything good and nice and right. And he knew then that the only reason he'd regret being with her tonight is if she regretted it. Because Charlotte Bailey had done what no one had done in a very long time: She made him believe there was such a thing as a second chance at love.

*   *   *

The only regret Charlotte had about last night was that she and Matt had wasted so much time. Though, in fairness to him, her friends were right. Charlotte had, metaphorically, held up a massive stop sign every time he got too close, every time she'd felt like melting in his arms and kissing his delectable mouth.

She released a happy sigh and then smiled. She was happy, deliriously so. And it was an incredible feeling. She couldn't remember the last time she felt that way. She searched her mind to a time long ago when she'd experienced the same incredible sense of...joy. That's the only word she could think to describe this deep sense of contentment, of being exactly where she was meant to be. With someone who cherished her, believed in her, and loved her for who she was and not who they thought she should be.

Other than with Kate and Abbie, the time she'd most felt that way was with her mother. Something had been missing since her mom died. Even between Charlotte and her father. Nothing had been the same, and Jeremy hadn't filled the void. In some ways, he'd deepened the chasm between Charlotte and her father.

But as much as it was tempting to put the blame squarely on Jeremy's shoulders, she couldn't. She was the one who allowed him to take over her life and control her every move and her every waking thought. In some ways, he was still doing that now. And she was letting him.

She picked up the fresh basil leaves from the wooden cutting board, inhaled deeply of the aromatic scent of pepper and mint, and then snipped the leaves into tiny slivers over the big pot of soup bubbling on the back burner. The sweet smell of fall filled the air. Matt's gorgeous gourmet kitchen was all warm woods and dark quartz. If she hadn't already fallen in love with the man, his kitchen would've put her over the edge.

The thought should've had her falling face first in the pot of soup. She wasn't in like or lust with Matt; she was in *love* with him. She smiled, held up the scissors, and cut the air with a dramatic flair. It was time to cut Jeremy out of her life for good.

At the sound of Matt's deep voice coming from the front of the pretty white Victorian on Candy Cane Lane,

Charlotte's heart gave an excited leap. "Oh, Bailey, you've got it bad," she said to herself, then put down the scissors and went to greet him and the boys.

He'd taken them to see their mom, and then they'd gone off on a secret mission. At the smell of pine drifting in the house on a blast of cold, arctic air, she had a feeling she knew what they'd been up to. If she had any doubt, the excited light in the boys' eyes gave the secret away.

They spotted Charlotte and waved her over, pointing at the eight-foot spruce tree Matt was wrestling through the door.

He looked up and grinned. "It might not be as big as the tree in Rockefeller Center, but this one was picked especially with you in mind, wasn't it, boys? It took them a whole hour and a half to decide on which one they wanted for Dr. Bailey."

She took in their rosy cheeks and red noses, and struggled not to laugh at the image of the good doctor in a tree lot with two uncommunicative little boys, trying to find her the perfect tree. And along with the tears of laughter in her eyes there were tears of another kind. The gesture touched her right to the heart of her soul.

Clearing the tight ball of emotion from her throat, she crouched in front of the boys. "Really? You picked that gorgeous tree out just for me?" They answered her question with solemn nods, and she pressed her palm to her chest. "That is the best present anyone has ever gotten me. Would it be okay if I give you a thank-you hug?"

They shared a glance and then the oldest lifted a shoulder and the youngest nodded before sticking his thumb in his mouth. Charlotte drew them into her arms and held them tight. They smelled like fresh air and candy canes.

"I hope you guys didn't ruin your appetites. I made a special lunch," she said as she let them go and came to her feet.

They looked at Matt, who was propping the tree against the bookshelf in the living room. She caught his wince before he'd fully turned to face them. "Guys, take your stuff off and put it in the front hall closet, okay?"

"You brought back lunch, didn't you?" she said, trying not to let the disappointment creep into her voice. "It's okay. We can have what I made for dinner."

He smiled and drew her into his arms as the boys trotted off to do as he'd asked.

She shivered. "You're cold."

"Tell me about it." He kissed the tip of her nose. "But it was worth it to see your face and theirs. Do I get a thank-you hug, too?"

"I thought that's what we're doing. How about a thank-you kiss?" She touched her lips to his stubbled jaw. "You know what? After all the trouble you went to, you deserve a you're-an amazing-man kiss too." And she gave him what she hoped was a kiss worthy of his amazingness, drawing away when she heard the pitter patter of stocking feet. "So, lunch," she said in a breathy voice as she moved out of his arms.

"After that kiss, my mind skipped to bedtime snacks. Them eating theirs and going to bed, and then me getting mine." He waggled his eyebrows suggestively.

"Did you have anything special in mind?"

"I think you know exactly what I had in mind, Dr. Bailey."

"I do, and I think that can be arranged, Dr. Trainer. Now lunch?"

"We went to the grocery store, and the boys picked out mac and cheese and hot dogs. But what do you say we eat what Charlotte made us for lunch and have yours for dinner, guys?"

They looked at her.

"Come on, I'll show you, and you can decide." They followed her into the kitchen, and she lifted the pot off the stove to give them a look inside. "I've got some delicious butternut squash soup, toasted sage garlic bread, and a wonderful spinach, escarole, and radicchio salad with sugared pecans. And for dessert..." She looked at their faces. "Okay, so mac and cheese and hot dogs for lunch it is."

They high-fived each other and then ran off to the family room, where Matt had put the majority of toys people had dropped off last night.

"It's not that funny," she said as she returned the pot to the stove.

Matt came up behind her and moved her hair to press a kiss to the sensitive place just below her ear. He smiled against her skin. "It kind of is," he said, taking her by the shoulders. He turned her to face him. "But I'm definitely having that for lunch. It looks and smells incredible. Just like you. And I want you for breakfast, lunch, and dinner." He pulled back, his brow furrowed. "Three-year-olds and five-year-olds still have afternoon naps, don't they?

*   *   *

Matt walked into the family room. It was dark except for the colored lights on the decorated Christmas tree, quiet except for the soft sounds of Kenny G's Christmas CD playing in the background.

Lowering himself beside Charlotte, he handed her a glass of red wine and put his feet up on the coffee table. He let his head fall back against the brown leather couch and turned to look at her. "How do people do this day in and day out?"

"I have no idea. I'm exhausted, and it's only eight o'clock." She put her feet up on the coffee table beside his and rested her head on his shoulder. He slid his arm around her, careful not to spill her wine.

"Yeah, and they don't talk. Can you imagine what it'd be like if they did?" He winced. "I shouldn't have said that."

"I know what you meant. I was thinking the same thing. Did you have any luck with your friend at the shelter?"

"Nothing stood out. They get e-mails and calls from women all the time. Typically, they don't leave any identifying information, just ask questions."

"Now that you've looked at the scans, what do you think?"

"Same as you, same as the radiologist. But it's not just the scans, it's the boys. It's obvious they can talk. I'm pretty sure I heard them whispering to each other after we tucked them into bed. And they're comfortable with us now. They're laughing and smiling, playing, eating and sleeping well. So there's only one reason for them not to talk. They're afraid, if they do, we'll force them to tell us who they are, and that once we know, we'll get in touch with whoever's been hurting their mom."

"Sadly, they're right. We'd have no choice but to inform social services, and they'd have to make the call. There's no way we can protect them unless they tell us what's been happening at home."

"We might not be able to protect them even then. It depends on who's been hurting them and how well he's been hiding the abuse. Mom's a wildcard, too. It all depends on what kind of hold he has on her. How long the abuse has been going on."

"If we're right about the situation, and I have no doubt that we are, she's made up her mind. She left with her two kids and very little else from what you told me. She's ready to take her life back, and we're going to help her do that when she wakes up." She looked up at him, her eyes glassy. "Even if I have to hide those kids, and her, I'm not letting them go with anyone until we're sure they'll be safe."

Noting the determination in her eyes, the stubborn set of her jaw, he fell a little more in love with Charlotte Bailey. "You know I'll have your back and theirs, but if you have to take a stand while she's still in the care of CGH, without evidence to support our claim of abuse, you're opening us up to a lawsuit, as well as giving Jeremy cause to fire you."

With everything that had gone on yesterday, Charlotte had postponed today's emergency board meeting in New York. They were going to hold off until they found more evidence that Jeremy was using the closing of CGH to bribe Maureen Cheever.

"I know. And I don't care anymore. Maybe I'm wrong about Maureen. What if this is about me? Maybe what Jeremy wanted all along is me to quit."

"You're thinking about quitting?"

She swirled the wine in her glass and nodded. "I am. If it wasn't for my dad, I would've tendered my resignation today."

"Don't you think it's time you thought about yourself for a change?" He worked to keep any emotion from his voice. He didn't want to influence her decision one way or another. Even though whatever she decided would obviously impact their relationship. Somehow, in the past twenty-four hours, he'd forgotten that the woman he was falling in love with had her heart set on living in New York.

"You know, since yesterday, I really have been thinking about myself and doing what I wanted."

He smiled down at her. "In the last twenty-fours, you say? Do you think it's an odd coincidence you've been here with me about that long?"

"Really? How strange. And wonderful," she said, wrapping her arm around him. "It has been wonderful, Matt. I can't remember when I've been this happy."

And he would do everything he could to keep her that way.

Chapter Nine

The next day, they were standing in Santa's tiny house in the village, holding hands. Charlotte's fingers were breaking his. She might be delicate-looking, but the woman had a bone-crushing grip. He forgave her, though. She was too sweet not to. Her eyes were squeezed shut, and her face squinched up. It's what she did when she was emotional and trying not to cry.

He couldn't say he blamed her. Watching the brothers sitting on Santa's knee brought back memories Matt had spent years erasing. They'd been tainted by a memory from five years before, the day he'd come home unexpectedly from his last tour of duty. It was two months before their wedding. Lara had been complaining about how difficult it was planning everything without him, so he'd thought to surprise her. Only he ended up being the one who was surprised.

He'd been smiling as he walked up to the house they'd

bought together in Denver, imagining the look on her face
when she saw him. He'd been so caught up in the fantasy
that he hadn't registered his baby brother's truck parked
up the street. He didn't register the sounds coming from
their bedroom, either. He assumed she had the TV on.
Until he opened the door and his fantasy came crashing
down around him.

At first there'd been tears and pleas for forgiveness,
but they'd soon changed to recriminations. *What did
he expect when he was gone so much?* Oh, just loyalty
from a woman who said she loved him and a brother he'd
grown up protecting. The wedding went on as planned;
she simply traded one Trainer brother for the other. He
hadn't attended the wedding or spoken to either of them
since.

"Matt, are you okay?" Charlotte whispered, pulling
him out of his head.

He looked up to see the boys handing Santa pictures
of what they wanted for Christmas. He and Charlotte
thought this might be the day they'd talk, but the kids
were smarter than they were. When Matt had told them
where they were going this morning, they'd disappeared
into the family room, found a couple of catalogues, and
started ripping out pages. If it wasn't exactly what they
wanted, they used markers to make the changes.

"I'm fine," he said, but he'd lost her attention. She was
making funny faces at the boys to make them smile for
the camera. Matt laughed, leaned in, and took one of her
with his phone.

"You didn't." She grabbed his hand to see the picture.
"Oh my God. Delete it."

He held it over her head, the camera shaking as she

jumped in an effort to take it from him. "Mrs. Claus is giving you the evil eye. You better stop or she'll kick you out."

She stopped but whispered up at him. "Look again. That's not the evil eye. That's an I'm-the-matchmaker-extraordinaire look," she said, rubbing the tips of her fingers on her winter jacket.

"We probably should give her some credit. Without Nell setting us up, we might not be where we are today," Matt said.

"You could say the same about the accident and the boys."

"If you want to look at it that way, you could say the same about what happened with Jeremy and Samantha and my brother and Lara." He wondered what his chances were of her not picking up...

"What about your brother and Lara? I didn't even know you had a brother. And who's Lara?"

"What are my chances of you letting this go?" She gave him a dream-on look. "Yeah, that's what I thought."

He gestured to Nell that he and Charlotte would wait outside. The boys were opening an early present from Santa. Given their circumstances, everyone in town was making an extra effort to make their Christmas special.

Matt joined Charlotte, leaning against the white picket fence decorated with cedar garland and bright red bows. Then he told her the same story he'd relived only moments before. No doubt it's why he'd blurted out his brother's and Lara's names.

"I'm so sorry, Matt. I can't imagine how it must've felt to have your brother betray you that way. I bet you were an amazing big brother. You must miss him, just a little."

He smiled as the boys barreled out of the house. "To be honest, I haven't thought about him much until the past couple of days. Having the boys around reminded me how close we once were."

"You should call him."

"We'll see. Now we're taking you to high tea at Dame Alexander's tea shop. It probably won't be what you're used to at the Russian Tea Room. But Dame Alexander says she's related to the royal family, so it should be pretty good."

She wrapped her arms around him and kissed his cheek. "If you do talk to your brother, tell him thanks for me."

"I'd tell you to thank Jeremy for me, but he's still messing with you, so I'd rather beat him up."

She laughed and waved the boys over. "That I'd like to see. And it was sweet of you to want to take me to high tea, but I think the Sugarplum Bakery might be more the boys' speed. Don't you?"

"Yeah, you're—" Charlotte's phone rang, and she glanced at the screen. "Sorry, I have to take this. Dr. Bailey here." She frowned, and then her eyes went wide. She looked up at him, her expression stricken. "Don't tell him what room she's in. Don't tell him anything. Say whatever you have to stall him, and I'll back you up. I'll be right there. Get security on her floor."

Matt swore under his breath. "Give me two minutes. I'm coming with you." He was just about to ask Nell to look after the kids when she appeared at the door.

"You go. Take care of this. We've got the boys." Nell clapped her hands and the boys looked up from the snowballs they were rolling. She waved them over. "Our elves never showed up for work. We need replacements, and you two are the perfect size. Come on, you'll be Elvis, and you'll be Elfie."

Matt took Charlotte's hand and gave it light squeeze before saying to the boys, "We'll go get some Christmas shopping done and pick you guys up at four. How does that sound?"

*   *   *

Charlotte knew as soon as they arrived at the hospital that word had spread throughout the town. Gage and Chance McBride, who'd both been former sheriffs of Christmas, and the current sheriff met them in front of the elevators. "Jill, tell them what they're dealing with," Gage said as he held open the elevator door.

"Okay. Jane Doe is Heather Brickman. Husband is Alan Brickman, a wealthy developer. Oldest son is Alexander and baby brother is Oliver. Brickman called the station and lodged a formal complaint. He's not a stupid man. He knows he's being stalled, and he knows why."

"Is she in the system? Has she been admitted for suspicious injuries in the past, or has her family physician registered any concerns?" Charlotte asked.

"Nothing came up."

"Brickman has enough money and influence to ensure that it doesn't. Easton's on it now. Chance is working his connections, too." Gage nodded at his brother, who was currently on his phone.

"Jill, do you think he's good for this?" Matt asked.

She nodded. "He didn't ask about the boys or the extent of his wife's injuries. His biggest concern was how quickly he can move her out of CGH. He also didn't like dealing with me. Which is often the case with abusers. They don't like women in a position of authority."

"So, if I can get Brickman to threaten me, you can hold him for forty-eight hours without charging him, right?" Charlotte asked Jill.

"What are you talking about? You're not—" Matt began.

Jill talked over him. "That'd be tough. The guy knows people. Now, if you could get him to physically attack—"

"Dammit, Jill. Don't give her any ideas."

"Matt, I'm CEO. My job is to protect my patients and my staff, and that's what I'm going to do." She leaned around Chance McBride and pressed the button for the fifth floor.

"Well, I'm making it my job to protect you."

"I don't need protection. Heather Brickman does, and so do Alexander and Oliver. They know you, Matt. They trust you. I do, too. Please, go back to Santa's Village and watch over them. I'll be fine. Jill will be with me. And Gage, if you and your brother could provide extra security for Heather, I'd be in your debt."

"That's what we're here for."

"Thank you. Matt, can you show them to Heather's room and check her vitals before you leave?"

"Yeah, but I'm not happy about it, Charlotte. Jill, you take care of her. Don't let her do anything stupid."

"Matt, I'm perfectly capable of—"

He cut her off with a hard, fast kiss. "I know you are. It doesn't mean I have to like it though."

"So it looks like Dr. McSexy has met his match," Jill said as the elevator door closed behind the three men.

"Looks good on him. Guess Nell will be coming out of retirement permanently if you two head to the altar."

"No, there's not going to be an altar. I mean, wedding. Matt and I aren't the marrying kind."

Jill laughed. "That's what they all say."

Before Charlotte could respond, the elevator dinged. "Showtime," she murmured, wishing she'd been able to change into more professional attire. She wore a powder blue ski jacket over jeans and a cream sweater. At least she'd worn boots with heels instead of snow boots.

Ty sat behind his desk, stiff and pale. She wasn't surprised he'd come in on his day off. Alan Brickman had no idea what he was up against.

"Mr. Brickman, I'm Dr. Bailey, CEO of Christmas General. I'm sorry to keep you waiting," she said to the man sitting across from Ty wearing a three-piece gray suit beneath his navy cashmere coat. His black hair was slicked back from an attractive face. His dark eyes flicked over her dismissively as he came to his feet. He was a tall, well-built man.

"Just tell me where my wife is, Dr. Bailey. I've been kept waiting long enough."

"I understand, and I'm sorry to keep you from Mrs. Brickman any longer, but your wife was seriously injured in a car accident two days ago and remains in a coma. It would be helpful to know her complete medical history." Charlotte held his gaze. "I'd like to speak to your family physician about Heather's previous injuries. They're extensive, Mr. Brickman. Extensive and concerning."

He took a menacing step toward her, and then she could see him visibly rein himself in. "What are you implying?" He smoothed over the anger in his voice. Jill was right. He was a smart man. He wasn't going to threaten Charlotte verbally or physically in front of witnesses. She needed another plan to buy them time.

She ignored his questions and opened the door to her office instead. She gestured him inside.

"Obviously, I'm going to have to go over your head, Dr. Bailey." Brickman brought his phone to his ear.

"You're wasting my time and yours, Mr. Brickman. If you had your wife's best interest at heart, you'd want to help us get a clearer picture of her medical history."

He walked by her as he spoke to someone on the phone, close enough that his body pushed her back against the door. "Sorry, I didn't realize it was such a tight fit. That's the problem with being big."

"That's the problem with being an asshole," Jill said under her breath. "You okay?"

"Perfectly fine. Have you met our sheriff, Jill Anderson, Mr. Brickman?" she asked when he ended his call.

"For all the good it did me, yes, I've spoken to her. Why is she here?"

"To ensure the safety of my patient. Now, I'll ask you one more time for your wife's complete medical history."

He sat on the couch and examined his nails. Seconds later, her cell phone rang. Brickman looked up and gave her a contemptuous smile.

"What the hell do you think you're doing?" Jeremy yelled as soon as she answered.

Charlotte took the seat across from Brickman. "My job."

"You won't have a job much longer if you don't let that man see his wife and have her transferred to a private clinic in Denver. His lawyers are threatening to sue me personally, and you, and Bailey Healthcare, and CGH. So if you don't comply within two minutes, you're fired."

He had no idea how much she wanted to quit and never have to deal with him again. But that wouldn't help Heather and the boys.

She held Brickman's gaze. "Really? And what clinic was Mr. Brickman planning to have Mrs. Brickman transferred to? You may not be aware of this, but she's in a coma, Jeremy. I can't sign off on a transfer that could possibly endanger her."

"How the hell should I know what clinic he's transferring her to?"

"Mr. Brickman, could you please give Sheriff Anderson the contact information for the private clinic? It would be helpful if it's the same one you've brought Mrs. Brickman to for her previous injuries."

He didn't respond. He was back on the phone with his lawyers.

Charlotte got up and moved to the window that overlooked Main Street. Lowering her voice, she made Jeremy aware of her concerns. He was a lying, cheating slimeball, but even he wouldn't protect a man who was physically abusing his wife. She hoped. She prayed.

"Now what am I supposed to do with that? Dammit, there's his lawyers again. You need proof, Charlotte. Unless you have proof, my hands are tied. And you better make sure it sticks, or we all go down." He disconnected.

Charlotte rested her forehead against the cold window pane. She didn't have proof. She had a feeling, deep down inside, that if she released Heather and the boys to Alan Brickman's care she was signing the woman's death warrant.

Her eyes were drawn to the snow-covered rooftops and the giant candy canes outside Santa's Village. Matt was there keeping the boys' safe, and she was about to release them into a monster's care. They needed a miracle. The thought had barely passed through her mind when Whitney Houston singing "When You Believe" blasted through the office's speakers.

"What the hell?"

She turned to see Brickman and Jill looking around the room. Ty peeked in her office, frowned, and then hurried back to his desk. The music went off.

Charlotte closed her eyes and said a silent prayer. Then she moved back to the chair across from Brickman.

He stood up. "Either you release my wife into my care, or I'll have you charged with kidnapping."

"Mr. Brickman, is there a reason you haven't enquired into the well-being of Alexander and Oliver? I would think you would be as concerned for them as you are in removing your wife from our care. As much as your wife's previous injuries tell a story, your sons do, too. They're lovely little boys. Very, very smart. Observant, too."

"What did they say? They're two and five. You can't believe what they say. It won't stand up in court."

"Perhaps not. Although I believe them, and I imagine a judge and jury would, too. Regardless, phone records don't lie. Did you know your wife was seeking shelter in a home for abused women, Mr. Brickman?" She clenched her trembling hands tighter, praying that the beads of nervous perspiration at her hairline didn't begin trickling down her face. She turned to Jill. "I'd liked to bring a charge of spousal abuse against Mr. Brickman, Sheriff Anderson."

*   *   *

In less than an hour, Alan Brickman would be free to remove his wife from CGH and take his children. Charlotte tried not to cry as she closed the freezer door. "Looks like we're out of ice cream, boys. Would you like to go to the store with me?" She didn't know where she'd take them, but she wouldn't let Alan Brickman have them. She'd put them in grave danger by lying.

She felt the weight of someone's gaze and looked over her shoulder to see Matt watching her. He smiled, softly. "Honey, I know you're scared, but you're not going into hiding with the boys. Trust me, someone will find something we can use against Brickman."

There was a blast of cold air, and then a voice called out from the front hall. "Mrs. Claus here. I've come to pick up Elfie and Elvis. Only one week until the big day, and me and Santa are doing a trial run."

"Great, someone else trying to kidnap the boys," Matt muttered, and walked to the front door where Nell waited, dressed as Mrs. Claus. Her husband, Calder Dane, dressed as Santa, waved and *ho-ho-ho*ed from where he stood on Candy Cane Lane behind a sleigh pulled by a team of eight huskies.

"Nell, you and Calder can't take the boys," Matt said.

"Why the Sam Hill not?"

"Because who's going to keep the spirit of Christmas alive if you and your husband end up behind bars?" a voice from the dark said, and then a man stepped out from behind Matt's truck. It was the janitor from Valley Ridge.

"Henry?"

"Fancy meeting you again, Ms. Bailey." He sauntered

up the walkway with a wiggling package in his hands and winked at Nell before addressing Charlotte. "You mind if I talk to Alex and Oliver? I have a special delivery."

"I guess. Matt?"

"Sure. Just don't call them by their names. They don't know we know who they are. We didn't want to scare them."

Henry patted Matt's shoulder as he strolled by. "You'd be surprised what kids can handle. They know when you're keeping something from them. More often than not, what they're imagining is way scarier than the truth."

Matt watched Henry head for the stairs. "He's right, you know. We have to tell them. We can't let them be blindsided."

"About time. I've said right from the start you should tell the kids what's what," Nell said.

"We were hoping for a miracle," Charlotte murmured, wondering if Henry was it.

Matt's cell rang. "It's Gage." He answered the call. "Please tell me you have news...That's great, right?...Oh, okay. Yeah. I will. Thanks." He disconnected. "They found Heather's sister. Brickman cut her family out of Heather's life years ago so they couldn't testify to the abuse. But they'll be arriving in Christmas sometime tomorrow. Gage says they won't roll over for Brickman."

"It won't matter. What we need is information about the clinic and the doctor who treated Heather previously."

"Easton's getting close. He needs another hour."

"Brickman's out in less than forty-five minutes."

Alexander and Oliver came flying down the stairs. Alexander held up a doe-eyed puppy, who yipped and yapped and wriggled and squirmed. "Look what Santa gave us. We have to go to the hospital and wake up Mommy. Henry says all she needs is to hear us talk. It's important. Really, really important."

Oliver nodded, his thumb in his mouth. He took it out. "Weally portant."

"Okay, let's go. Hurry, Matt. We have to go."

Matt was staring up the stairs. "But that guy . . . Where did he go?"

"Back to the North Pole. He's Santa's head elf," Alexander said.

Chapter Ten

The citizens of Christmas were praying for another miracle to save CGH. In their minds, Heather Brickman coming out of her coma five minutes before her husband walked into her hospital room was a miracle. As a doctor, Matt could give them several medically sound reasons why that wasn't the case.

It had only been a matter of time before Heather regained consciousness. Hearing her sons' voices had no doubt played a part, and having a roomful of determined and supportive strangers, along with her boys, had no doubt helped Heather find the strength and courage to bring charges against her husband moments after he arrived with the sheriff.

Henry was harder to explain. And Matt was fine with that, because, like the citizens of Christmas, he was hoping for a miracle, too. He only had a matter of weeks to convince Charlotte to stay, and a lot of folks in town were making her feel less than welcome. He'd go so far as to say they were making her feel like she'd be lucky to survive the next month while she sold off the hospital's assets.

No one understood their fears and frustrations better than he did. After all, he'd soon be looking for work like everyone else. But Charlotte didn't deserve to be treated like a cold, heartless woman. They had no idea how much she empathized with them or how hard she'd worked to try to save the hospital. To no avail.

Jeremy had outmaneuvered them. Somehow, he'd gotten wind that they were looking for evidence of collusion with Maureen Cheever to present to the board. Yesterday, he'd called an emergency meeting to address the charges. Maureen had appeared before the board via Skype. Nothing short of a miracle could save Christmas General now.

As Matt drove his truck up to the entrance, he leaned on the horn to move the protesters out of the way. They were marching in front of the hospital carrying signs sporting the Grinch. They looked similar to the ones folks in town had used to protest against Madison McBride a few years before. Charlotte had the misfortune of the closure being announced at Christmas. It would've been bad regardless of the time of year, but the holidays made it seem worse.

Matt left the truck running and hopped out. "Back off, and back off now. Sherriff Anderson is on her way." He bodily pushed people aside to reach Charlotte, who was making her way through the angry crowd, holding her purse over her head. She never fought back or defended herself. Maybe she was right. Nothing he said had gotten through to the protestors, and he tried every day. Some of them had even taken to calling him...

"Trainer the traitor!"

Charlotte stopped in her tracks and removed the purse from her head to stare down his detractor. One word against Matt and the woman who wouldn't defend herself was ready to take on thirty sign-wielding protestors. Which made him groan in aggravation and smile, just a tiny bit, at the same time.

"You can say whatever you want about me, but you don't get to say one negative word about Matt. He's the heart and soul of Christmas General. He's everything good about this hospital and town, so if you—"

He made it to her side and drew her against him, shielding her from the waving signs. "Save your breath."

"Trainer the traitor! Trainer the traitor!" It sounded like the guy from maintenance had gotten a few of his friends on board.

"Look, he's had a problem with me since I reported him for drinking on the job," Matt told Charlotte, tightening his hold on her as she tried to wriggle free and shout over his shoulder. "I don't care what they say about me. What I do care about is you, and I won't be able to show you just how much if you're sitting in jail or in the emergency room. So let's leave peacefully and enjoy the night."

She nodded as he guided her to his truck with a protective hand at her back. Jill arrived, and almost immediately the crowd dispersed. Pulling out of the lot, Matt waved his thanks.

"There's a bag for you in the back. Grab it and see if they fit. We still have time to stop by Hardy's Mountain Co-op if they don't."

She leaned around the seat and reached into the bag. "Skates?"

"Yeah, our rink in the park is twice the size of the one in Central Park, and the trees are all lit up for the holidays."

"Um, Matt."

He glanced at her. "Yeah?"

"Well, the thing is, while watching people skate at the rink in Central Park is something I love to do during the holidays, I don't actually do it."

"You just like the idea of watching them?"

"I watch them, but I don't actually skate. I don't know how."

"No problem. It's easy. I'm a pro. I'll teach you."

*   *   *

Forty-five minutes later, Matt worked to keep the frustration from showing on his face when he fit his hands under Charlotte's arms and hauled her to her feet.

She tipped her head back to smile up at him, her cheeks and nose pink. "I nearly had it that time."

Shockingly, she actually seemed to believe that. Matt was afraid she was going to break something, but didn't have the heart to tell her he had met toddlers who learned to skate faster than she did. Or at the very least stand up on their skates, on their own, for longer than sixty seconds.

"All right, you can let me go now."

"I thought maybe we could skate like this for a few minutes. You just lean back and relax against me."

"But I'm not doing anything."

Which is why you're still upright and not taking out the other skaters, he thought but didn't say. "Indulge me. I like holding you in my arms." And even though he was pushing her around like she was a corpse, it was kind of nice.

It was the perfect night for a skate. The stars were out, and it wasn't too cold. The rink wasn't packed. Well, it had been until Charlotte got out there and took out half the skaters. He smiled at the thought and kissed the top of her head.

"Why are you laughing?" she asked, turning to look back at him.

"No, don't..."

Her feet began to scrabble, and her right leg went one way, her left between his. She cried out, fisted her hands in his jacket, and brought him down with her. He got his hands behind her head just before it hit the ice.

*   *   *

"It was a good idea to take a little break," she said, smiling up at him from the bench.

He handed her a hot chocolate and sat down beside her. "Yeah, we should probably call it a night. You don't want to overdo it your first time."

"No, I'm fine," she said, and he worked to hold back a groan.

He was about to suggest that they do something else when her cell phone rang. "Facetime. It's Kate and Abbie. Wait until they see me skate," she said as she held up her phone.

The smiling faces of Charlotte's dad and her best friends Abbie and Kate filled the screen. The three of them wore Santa hats and held Champagne flutes. They looked like they were in a partying mood. Charlotte put down her hot chocolate and waved. "You guys! You look so cute. I miss you!"

The three of them looked down at the phone in the

redhead's hand as if waiting for a text. There was an audible *ping*, and then their heads popped up. They beamed. "Look over your shoulder. Do you see the sleigh?" Abbie asked.

Matt followed Charlotte's gaze. At the edge of the park, Calder Dane dressed as Santa stood behind his sleigh, the dogs yapping as they tried to catch the lightly falling snow.

"Yes, why?"

"Santa's making your wish come true. You're coming home for Christmas! There's a private airport fifteen minutes away. Your plane's waiting for you." The three of them squealed liked three-year-olds who'd been given their Christmas wish.

Charlotte frowned. "I don't understand. Jeremy—"

"You never did like to be surprised," her father grumbled, and then sighed. "I don't know why we expected you to change. All right, we might as well tell her now. Are you ready?" Her friends nodded, and the three of them held up their Champagne flutes. "Cheers to our new chief medical officer at Bailey Healthcare, Dr. Charlotte Bailey!"

"What? How?"

The three of them groaned. "Charlotte!"

"I know, it's amazing. The best news ever. It's just that I don't understand how it happened."

Matt was confused, too, as much by Charlotte's reaction as the news. She looked at him. He forced a smile, nodding as if it were the best news ever when, for him, it couldn't get much worse. But it was everything she wanted.

"I was reinstated as chairman of the board fifteen minutes ago. Jeremy's out, and so is Samantha," her father said.

"And it's all thanks to your friend Nick," Kate said.

"Nick who?"

"Nick from the New York Cab—" Abbie began before Charlotte's dad cut her off with a laugh.

"Nick Clause, can you believe it?" her dad said. "He even looks like Santa. Anyway, your friend Nick found Jeremy's briefcase in the back of his cab and was returning it to his office. Only the briefcase popped open on the elevator, and Jeremy's papers went all over. Which wouldn't have been a big deal if the head of the hedge fund hadn't been the one to help Nick pick up the papers and discovered what Jeremy had been up to at Bailey Healthcare. Like colluding with the CEO of one of their major competitors for personal gain. You were right all along, Charlotte. Jeremy worked out a deal with Maureen Cheever, just like you suspected. But that wasn't what brought him down. He'd lost heavily on several trades last year and needed authorization before acquiring shares, which he didn't do when he bought out a majority of Bailey Healthcare on behalf of the hedge fund. The good news is they think we're a solid-performing company, and they're holding their shares as well as buying up Samantha's."

"Wait!" Charlotte raised her voice to be heard over their cheering. "This means Christmas General stays open? No cuts to staff or beds?"

"Yes. Now get on Santa's sleigh and come home where you belong!" her father said.

"Go, go!" her friends cried, waving ticket stubs. "We have front row seats for the Rockettes tomorrow night!"

"Can you believe it? Christmas General isn't closing. No one's losing their jobs. You're not losing your job." She threw herself in his arms. "It's a miracle, Matt. A Christmas miracle."

It was. And he was happy for her, for the town, for his

friends and colleagues. It just wasn't the miracle he'd been hoping for. "You better get going. Santa's waiting."

She pinched herself. "This feels like a dream. It's all happened so fast."

"It's what you want, though, isn't it?"

"Yes, of course. I just didn't expect it to happen." She glanced over her shoulder. "I guess I better go. I'll call you. We'll talk, okay? We'll—"

"Go. You'll miss your flight."

"I'll miss you. I...." She cupped his face between her mittened hands. "Merry Christmas, Matt." She kissed him and his arms went around her, holding her tight, praying that she'd change her mind.

She didn't.

*   *   *

Two days after Matt had watched until the sleigh was out of sight, he was packed and ready to head to the airport. If his flight wasn't delayed, he'd land in New York on Christmas Eve. He planned to surprise Charlotte. He hoped it would be a happy surprise. She'd only been gone a couple of days, but he missed her like crazy. He loved her, so much so that he was willing to relocate to the Big Apple. He hadn't told anyone of his plans. Who knew? Charlotte may not feel the same. But Matt was willing to take the risk. So he'd taken the week's holiday owed him, and here he was, doing one last check of the house to make sure everything was turned off.

A wave of nostalgia washed over him as he walked through the bedrooms. He'd put a lot of love into the old place. It wouldn't be easy to say goodbye to either the house or the people who'd become a family to him. Then again, there was no comparison to the thought of being without Charlotte in his life.

He glanced at his phone, checking to see if she'd responded to his last couple of texts. She hadn't. He reminded himself that it didn't necessarily mean anything. She was busy. It was like she was packing all her holiday traditions into a single day. She'd sent pictures of herself at the Russian Tea Room, at Rockefeller Center, at the Radio City Christmas Spectacular, and decorating a tree with her dad. She'd been up on a ladder, putting the angel on top. She looked beautiful and happy, excited to be home with her father and friends.

His front doorbell rang, interrupting his thoughts. Which might've been a good thing because he was questioning his decision to fly to New York. He left his bags on the upstairs landing and went to answer the door. Later, he'd wonder if he'd made his decision to stay home then. He opened the door. It was only the memory of Charlotte's voice that kept him from slamming it shut. *If you ever talk to him, tell him thank you for me.*

His baby brother hadn't changed much since the last time Matt saw him. Only this time he was fully clothed. They had the same light brown hair and light brown eyes and, once, the same taste in women.

Ryan took a step back, and his hands went up. "Your girlfriend must have read you wrong. Sorry." His brother turned to walk away.

"What are you talking about?"

"Charlotte. She called me yesterday. She wouldn't happen to be a cop, would she?"

"No, why?"

"Because she asked about a hundred and ten questions

before telling me to haul ass up here to spend Christmas with you. She thought it was time we talked. She thought you were ready to. I guess you're not."

And there it was, the reason he wasn't already halfway to the airport. She obviously didn't want him to be alone for Christmas, but she didn't want him with her. If she did, she would've invited him herself or responded to his texts.

"You made the drive. You might as well come in." He stepped back, gesturing him inside.

"Yeah?"

He saw the hopeful gleam in his brother's eyes and had a sudden memory of him tagging after him. He remembered all the Christmas Eves and all the Christmas mornings. Their mother's funeral, and two years later, their dad's. For years it'd just been the two of them, and then the three of them, and then for the past five years Ryan with Lara, and Matt on his own.

There was no longer any anger that accompanied the thought. Maybe just sorrow at all he'd missed out on with his brother. Matt nodded and then smiled. "Yeah."

He saw the tears swim in his brother's eyes before he grabbed Matt and hugged him hard. "I'm sorry. You have no idea how sorry I am."

"I know," he said, returning the hug.

His brother let him go and stepped back, rubbing the sleeve of his jacket across his eyes and nose. Then he turned to wave at the black SUV parked just up the road. Matt briefly closed his eyes. While Charlotte was having the Christmas of her dreams, Matt was being visited by the ghost of Christmas past.

As Ryan went to help his wife out of the vehicle, Matt texted Christmas General to let them know they could put him back on call tonight. He heard a woman's voice and prepared himself before raising his gaze.

"Jen?" He frowned at the dark-haired woman waddling up his driveway beside his brother. Growing up, Jen had been their next-door neighbor and Ryan's high school sweetheart. Matt had loved her like a sister.

She elbowed Ryan. "Did you let him think you'd brought Lara for Christmas?"

"I told his girlfriend. I thought she would've filled him in," his brother said and rubbed the side Jen had jabbed with her elbow. Then he grinned. "You must've really missed me if you were going to let me and Lara stay for Christmas."

"I'm sure he's beginning to wonder why he missed you," Jen said before smiling at Matt and moving in for a hug. Then she reached up as much as her generous baby bump allowed to whisper in his ear, "He was an idiot, but he regretted it the moment he married her. He loves you, Matt. He's missed you like crazy. We both have."

He met his brother's gaze over Jen's head. "He's not the only one who's been an idiot."

*   *   *

It wasn't the Christmas Eve Matt had dreamed of, but it was better than he'd hoped for, much better. And he owed that to his *girlfriend*, who he'd been trying to reach for the past several hours. He stood outside the bank of elevators at Christmas General to check his smartphone for about the hundredth time. Still nothing.

"Matt. Merry Christmas, son. Thanks for coming in," Dr. McBride said and patted Matt's shoulder.

"No problem. How was the cruise?" He held the elevator

door open for the older man. Paul had called Matt in for a second opinion on a new admission.

"Great, even better that we came home to such wonderful news." Paul pressed the button to the fifth floor. "I was all set to get off at the next port of call and come home, but both my aunt and Charlotte assured me things were under control."

Matt waited for Paul to pump him for information about his relationship with Charlotte, but the older man was busy looking at the chart in his hands. His aunt had no doubt filled Paul in on their status—somewhere between limbo and over. *Way to depress yourself*, he thought.

"Do you have any specific concerns about your patient, Paul?" Matt asked as they walked down the fifth floor's almost empty hall. Anyone that could go home was gone long ago.

"Heart, I think," he said as he opened the door to the room and then frowned. The room was in complete darkness. "Where's the switch?"

"On the wall," an older woman's voice came out of the dark.

"Nell!" several people yelled, sounding peeved at the town's matriarch.

Paul sighed, and the room lit up. It had been decorated for the holidays, though packed as it was, it was hard to tell.

"Surprise! Surprise! Surprise!" pretty much everyone Matt knew in Christmas cried. Even Alexander and Oliver, who were there with their mom and her sister.

They were all looking his way so obviously the surprise was meant for him. "Thanks. But you know it's not my birthday, right?"

Nell peered at the person lying prone on the hospital bed. "Is she dead or asleep?"

"Nell!" several people yelled, once again in those peeved voices that seemed to be reserved for the seventy-something woman.

Ty leaned over and shook the person under the covers.

It wasn't the patient's heart they had to worry about, it was Matt's. It felt like it was beating outside his chest as he walked to the bed. And then it fell at her feet when Charlotte sat up, her hair all over the place, her face pale, her eyes bloodshot. "Surprise," she said, and held up her hands.

He laughed and took her in his arms. "I've had a couple of surprises today. I have to say you're the best one."

"I better be," she said. "Oh God, I'm so tired. Lie down with me. Just for a minute."

"We can stay here all night if that's what you want. I'll be happy as long as I have you in my arms."

"Aww, that's so sweet. Isn't that sweet?" said the man staring at them from the foot of the bed with his hands pressed to his chest.

"Ty!" Jill grabbed him by the collar and half dragged him from the room.

"Merry Christmas!" at least thirty different voices whispered, and then the lights went out and the door closed.

"They grow on you, don't they?" Charlotte murmured, snuggling close.

"That they do. Just like you. I didn't know how much until you were gone. Did I tell you how glad I am that you're here?"

She opened an eye, winked, and said, "I can tell." She kissed his chin. "It's good to be home."

He pushed up on his elbow and looked down at her. It was too dark to see her expression, and he took his penlight from his pocket and shone it in her face.

"Matt!"

"Sorry." He moved the light out of her eyes. "But this is important. You said *home*. I want to know what you mean."

"Home is where the heart is, and you stole mine. You're my heart, Matt. I love you." She gave him a weak smile. "It's okay if you don't feel the same. I—"

He placed a finger on her lips. "You just gave me my Christmas miracle, Charlotte. You're all I want. All I'll ever need. I love you. Letting you go, watching you leave were two of the hardest things I've ever done."

"I needed to do it for me, and for you too really. I needed to know this is what I wanted."

"How long did it take you to figure it out?"

"When I was on the sleigh and looked back and couldn't see you anymore." She smiled and stroked his face with the tips of her fingers. "But my dad and Abbie and Kate were so excited, I couldn't disappoint them. So I fit in as much Christmas as I could with them without missing out on my Christmas with you." She yawned. "How do you feel about spending the holidays in bed?"

"How do you think?" He laughed and got off the bed, leaning over to scoop her into his arms. He picked her up and headed for the door. "But I don't want anyone saying I'm getting special favors from the boss, so I think we better go home."

She frowned and waved her hand at the room they'd just left. "That's what all this was about. I'm not your boss anymore."

"I must've missed something because all I heard was

surprise, and then *is she asleep or dead*. After that, all I saw and heard was you. So if you're not my boss, who is, and what are you going to do?"

"Paul is the new CEO of Christmas General, and I'm your new colleague. Well, I will be once I receive my license to practice here."

"And I didn't think my Christmas could get much better. It's going to be fun working with you, Dr. Bailey."

"Likewise, Dr. Trainer."

His phone pinged, and he set her on her feet outside the elevator, pressing the Down button before checking his message. "I was wrong. My Christmas just got better. Paul asked me to take over as chief of staff. Say hi to your new boss," he said as they got on the elevator.

She sighed and wrapped her arms around him. "I guess that means we'll have to be discreet."

"I'm good with whatever you want. But I kinda like the idea of sneaking around. At least for a while." He lifted her in his arms and pressed her back against the wall. Then he hit the stop button with the toe of his boot. "Merry Christmas, Dr. Bailey."

"Merry Christmas, Dr. McSexy."

USA Today bestselling author
Debbie Mason presents another
heartwarming holiday tale in
The Corner of Holly and Ivy.
When hotshot lawyer Connor
Gallagher returns to town, high
school sweetheart Arianna Bell
finds herself falling for him
all over again.

Please turn the page for a preview.

Chapter One

Arianna Bell awoke with a start at the sound of a drawer slamming outside her closed bedroom door. She blinked, trying to get her bearings. Was it morning or night? The blackout curtains in her bedroom made it difficult to tell. Down the hall, someone continued their frenetic opening and closing of drawers, and she sat up in bed.

Burglar or her grandmother? she wondered. Not in the least alarmed either way. After barely surviving the fire that destroyed her business and three others, nothing much fazed her these days. Besides, it wasn't like they had anything of real value in the small Cape Cod home where she now lived with her grandmother, Helen Fairchild.

Another drawer slammed. "Where did you put the damn car keys? I have to hit the campaign trail."

Arianna's stomach muscles tightened in response to her grandmother's angry question, making a lie of her claim that nothing fazed her anymore. At that moment, she'd moved beyond slightly fazed to really worried.

And not because her grandmother was hitting the campaign trail. At eighty, Helen was the oldest woman to run for mayor of Harmony Harbor, a small town less than an hour from Boston. Her grandmother's habit of misplacing something was nothing new either. But over the past few weeks, Helen's forgetfulness hadn't been so easily explained away.

As much as Arianna would like to blame moments such as this on the stress of the mayoral race or the typical forgetfulness of old age, she couldn't. Her grandmother had given up driving a decade before and had sold her BMW around the same time. Unless she was referring to Arianna's car, which had been lost in the fire two months before.

Cradling her injured arm to her chest, Arianna scooted off the bed. She could count on one hand the number of times she'd gotten out of bed of her own volition in the past seven weeks. Which the piles of books, water glasses, and tea cups on the floor by her bed attested to. One benefit of spending so much time in the dark was that she seemed to have developed bat-like sonar and safely made it through the obstacle course and to the other side of her bedroom without knocking something over or falling on her face. She reached for the doorknob with her good hand.

"Arianna, where—" The door flew open, shoving Arianna and her elbow into the wall at her back—"the hell are the keys to my Beemer?"

So much for Arianna's bat-like sonar, she thought, trying to breathe through the pain. It felt like someone had whacked the elbow of her damaged arm with a tuning fork, the ache vibrating up and down her forearm and hand. Which might have been a good thing, not the pain in her arm obviously, but her inability to speak. She had no idea how to deal with this. She didn't know whether she should tell her grandmother the truth or protect her with a lie.

"Where is that child?" her grandmother muttered, her voice raspy from years of smoking.

"Standing behind the door, Glamma," Arianna said through clenched teeth.

Her grandmother had coined the moniker *Glamma* long before it became popular. Not a surprise since Helen had been forty for as long as Arianna could remember. She was all about fashion and glamor. Once a highly sought-after runway model in Paris, she'd returned to Harmony Harbor to raise her daughter (Arianna's mother Beverly) and open Tie the Knot, a bridal shop on Main Street. The shop she'd passed down to Arianna a decade before. The same shop the mad man had burned to the ground in July.

"Don't go there," Arianna told herself firmly. She relived that night over and over again in her dreams and refused to relive it when she was wide awake.

"Don't go where?" her grandmother asked, clapping her hands

Arianna came out from behind the door. "Nowhere. You can stop clapping, Glamma. The lightbulbs are burned out. I have to replace them."

Arianna had a thing for Clap On! Clap Off! lights. Her baby sister Jenna knew about her secret addiction and replaced the lights in Arianna's bedroom with Clappers the day she came to live with her grandmother. Jenna was the sweet, thoughtful sister. Much sweeter than Arianna deserved after the way she'd treated her growing up.

Her grandmother's lips thinned. Helen's silver blond

hair was pulled back from her face, the severe hairstyle giving her an instant facelift and showcasing her pale blue eyes and exquisite bone structure. "You mean, I will. You haven't been out of the house since the day you got home from the hospital," she said as she walked to the window on the other side of the bedroom.

Arianna was so relieved her grandmother remembered exactly when she'd last ventured outside that the sarcastic tone in her voice didn't get under her skin. Besides, half of what came out of her grandmother's mouth had bite. She'd always had a dry sense of humor, something she'd passed on to Arianna. Although Arianna's sense of humor had been missing for quite some time.

The blackout curtains rattled along the rod as her grandmother whipped them open with strength and purpose. Just like her walk, Arianna thought with a smile. She must have been imagining things. There was nothing wrong with her grandmother, nothing wrong at all. Arianna felt like sinking to the area rug in relief. She might have if the bright autumn sunshine pouring through the window wasn't half blinding her.

Squinting, she turned away from the sun's rays. Big mistake. The position put her in direct view of the mirror on her dresser. There was a time not so long ago when catching a glimpse of her shoulder-length blond hair, blue eyes, and thin frame in the mirror wouldn't have bothered her. It did now.

"All right, I'm off to . . ." Helen frowned and then rubbed her forehead as though she'd forgotten what she'd been about to say, or maybe where she'd been about to go.

That wasn't unusual though. People complained about forgetting why they walked into a room all the time. You couldn't go a day on social media without a meme about it popping up. Women in their menopausal and post-menopausal years posted them all the time. No doubt if Glamma was on social media, she would too.

Helen lowered her fingers from her forehead and bent to pick up a copy of the town's local newspaper, the *Harmony Harbor Gazette*, from the floor.

Arianna was impressed. She wasn't nearly as flexible as her grandmother and checked off another box in the "Glamma's fine" column.

Helen's face cleared. "Campaigning, that's it. I have to get out there and pound the pavement. I'll see you later, darling. I won't be back until late. Don't forget to eat."

Arianna took in her grandmother's attire as she passed her on the way out the door. Just like she suspected, they were pajamas. Pink satin pajamas. "Wait. You don't mean you're leaving right this very minute, do you?"

"That's exactly what I mean. I have to get a leg up on the Gallagher boy."

This wasn't good. Not good at all. Arianna's heart began to gallop. She could barely look after herself. How was she supposed to look after her grandmother? "Why don't we both get dressed and go together? It's about time I got out there on the campaign trial with you, don't you think?" Arianna said, working to keep the panic from her voice.

Her grandmother blinked at Arianna's suggestion and then blinked again like a sleepy owl. Arianna wasn't sure whether it was because Helen didn't recognize her or she was stunned by her offer to accompany her.

"You want to come on the stump with me?"

Thank goodness, it was the latter. Wait a minute.

What had she been thinking? She'd just agreed to leave the house! "Yes, unless you think it's going to rain and we both should stay home." She looked out the window, hoping to see water-logged black clouds darkening the cerulean sky.

Her grandmother's lips flattened. "I knew you'd back out."

"I'm not backing out. I'll bring an umbrella just in case."

"We don't need an umbrella. We'll take my car."

Arianna bowed her head and then lifted it to look at her grandmother. "Glamma, you—"

Helen interrupted her with a snap of her fingers. "I don't know what came over me. I haven't had that car in years."

She didn't know whether her grandmother truly remembered or had picked up on

Arianna's distress. Memory issues aside, Helen Fairchild was one sharp cookie.

Arianna gave her grandmother a reassuring smile. "We all forget things now and again. No big deal, right?"

"Right. Right," she said in a voice that didn't sound nearly as confident as Arianna's.

*   *   *

An hour later, her heart pounding like she'd run a one-minute mile, Arianna stepped out of the house on the corner of Holly and Ivy. Positive she was about to faint, she turned back to the door, fumbling for the knob with her good hand.

Obviously, she hadn't learned from her past mistakes. She knew better than to allow strong emotions to influence her decisions. That was the one benefit that had come out of the fire on Main Street, Arianna no longer had feelings or acted upon them. She'd been an apathetic shell holed up in her room for the past seven weeks. Now look at her, venturing outside when she'd be perfectly content never to set foot out of the house again. A fact she couldn't share with her closest friends and family because they had no problem sharing with her that they thought she needed professional help.

In the middle of the night when she woke up beneath sweat-soaked sheets and gasping for air, she agreed with them. But then morning would arrive and push back the shadows that haunted her, and she'd come to her senses. Nothing a therapist could say or do would help her recover from the Nightmare on Main Street.

Her grandmother called out to her from where she stood smoking, leaning against a white picket fence draped in ruby-red vines. "Come on now, the primary is next week, and the *Gazette* says the Gallagher boy is in the lead. We don't have a moment to lose."

If her grandmother had been running a strong second, it would have been okay. Next Tuesday's primary election narrowed the field to two candidates from the seven currently in the race. However, according to the *Gazette's* latest poll, that was not the case. Helen Fairchild was running dead last in the mayoral race.

Arianna reluctantly released the door knob. Her eighty-year-old grandmother had a dream. She wanted to be mayor to protect her beloved home town from the vision Daniel Gallagher had for Harmony Harbor's future.

Arianna knew a little something about dreams herself. Before the Nightmare on Main Street, she'd lived and breathed her dream of becoming the next Vera Wang and of Tie the Knot becoming the next Kleinfeld Bridal. A thirty-six-year-old (admittedly bitter) divorcee, it seemed her entire grown-up life had revolved around ensuring every bride had the wedding dress of their dreams.

She'd spent twelve hours a day, seven days a week, working with customers who could turn into a bridezella or a weepy mess in the blink of an eye. But the most difficult for her to deal with had been the sweet, wide-eyed innocents who thought their lives would be perfect the moment they said *I do*.

She'd survived the daily drama and stress without sarcastic rejoinders and eyes rolls because of what awaited her at the end of her day. The moment she retired to the windowless room above her shop on Main Street, everything else faded away. It was the place where the magic happened.

Sometimes she'd be holed up there from dusk to dawn hand sewing lace, crystals, and pearls onto the tulle and organza gowns, turning them into one-of-a-kind works of art. And while the hours were long and the work sometimes tedious and back-breaking, she'd never once complained. After all, she'd been following her passion, living her dream.

Her dreams were over now. Everything had gone up in smoke. But it was more than guilt at the loss of her grandmother's legacy and worry about her that forced Arianna out of the house today, it was her deep and abiding love for the woman who was at that moment regarding her through narrowed eyes and a cloud of cigarette smoke.

"What on earth are you wearing?" asked the woman who only an hour earlier planned to knock on doors in pink satin pajamas.

Arianna looked down at the mocha-colored lounge pants and top she wore beneath a calf-length blush velour cardigan. In deference to her damaged arm, the right sleeve was empty and the top two buttons fastened to conceal the sling she still wore. In deference to Helen, Arianna had changed out the pink sneakers her sister Jenna had paired with the outfit for brown suede ankle boots.

"It's the new trend. Loungewear chic," Arianna informed Helen, who'd obviously recovered from her momentary fashion lapse and looked effortlessly elegant in wide-legged cream pants and a blouse with a bronze-colored sweater draped casually around her shoulders and bronze ballerina slippers on her feet.

Arianna, who'd once been as style conscious as her grandmother, didn't care about that sort of thing anymore. Comfortable and cozy pajamas were her wardrobe of choice these days, which her sister knew. Not that Arianna would mention Jenna to Helen. She didn't blame the Nightmare on Main Street on her sister, but her grandmother did.

Helen's brow furrowed, the expression on her face turning from distaste to concern. She approached the step where Arianna stood poised to take flight. She could handle the distaste, the concern...not so much. But she didn't have time to run back inside. Helen was surprisingly fast for an eighty-year-old. She lifted her walking stick—most people would refer to it as a cane but not her grandmother—and moved Arianna's cardigan aside. "You're too thin."

The statement took her aback. In Helen Fairchild's book, you could never be too rich or too thin.

Arianna was saved from responding by their neighbor

from across the road. Mrs. Ranger looked up from raking the autumn leaves into a pile and smiled. "Arianna, it's so good see you, dear. How are you doing?"

She didn't expect the truth, did she? What if Arianna said *fine* like she always did and Mrs. Ranger wanted specifics—like how was her arm? It would open up a conversation about the Nightmare on Main Street, wouldn't it? Of course it would.

Obviously, Glamma had caught her at a weak moment. Arianna had been out of her flipping mind agreeing to accompany her today. Because no matter how much she loved her grandmother and didn't want to see her hurt or embarrassed or her dreams dashed, Arianna wasn't up to interreacting with people who weren't family or her closest friends. She had a difficult enough time interacting with them. And it'd be a cold day in hell before she'd talk to anyone about what happened on that warm summer night. Her sister Serena had been smart. She'd left town two days after Arianna was released from hospital.

"I'm fine, Mrs. Ranger. Thanks for ask—"

Her grandmother interrupted her with a horrified gasp, which was immediately followed by choking from inhaling a stream of cigarette smoke.

"How could you, Irene?" Helen said once she got her coughing under control. "We've known each other for more than sixty years." Before Mrs. Ranger had a chance to respond, Helen strode down the leaf-littered flagstone walkway and flung open the front gate.

Arianna frowned, confused by her grandmother's angry outburst until she spotted Daniel Gallagher's campaign sign on the far side of Mrs. Ranger's front yard. And there it was, the main reason Arianna should have convinced her grandmother not to put her name in the race. Helen wouldn't take defeat well, and she had a temper. A temper that sometimes made her act without thinking.

Arianna protectively cradled her right arm to her chest to keep it from bouncing against her body as she hurried after her grandmother, who was already halfway across the road by then. "Glamma, you get back here right now."

Now in a face-off with Irene on her front lawn, Helen ignored Arianna. She wished Mrs. Ranger would do the same to her grandmother. Instead, she'd apparently decided to add fuel to the fire. "Yes, we have, and you're the same age as me, Helen. Far too old for this sort of thing. It's time to give the younger generation a chance."

"Speak for yourself. I don't look a day over sixty, and I don't feel it either. And why should I give a man like him a chance?" She slapped the lawn sign with her cane. "He's going to ruin this town with his modern ideas. He hasn't lived in Harmony Harbor for decades. He's an outsider now."

Stuck on the other side of the street thanks to slow-moving traffic, Arianna waved the rubberneckers on. "Nothing to see, folks. Move it along before you cause a pile-up."

"Helen, he's a Gallagher. Without his family, Harmony Harbor wouldn't exist."

Arianna groaned. Her grandmother blamed Daniel Gallagher's nephew Connor for ruining Arianna's life. Connor had represented her ex in their divorce, and Arianna had walked away without anything to show for the years she'd given to her marriage.

But she and Connor had a history long before Gary and

their divorce. Connor Gallagher had been her first love. And, at one time, she thought he'd be her only love. She considered herself lucky that her grandmother had no idea the price Arianna had paid for her teenage love affair with Connor. It was a price she'd continue paying until the day she died.

"Don't talk about them as if they're something special. William Gallagher was a pirate who made his money on the high seas, burning and pillaging. The rest of them are no better. Especially him." She whacked the sign again, taking out one of Daniel Gallagher's blue eyes.

At Mrs. Ranger's outraged gasp, Arianna held up a hand and darted between the two idling cars on the street. She reached her grandmother just as she put her cane through Daniel's toothy grin.

"It's time we were on our way, Glamma. Sorry about that, Mrs. Ranger. The heat of the campaign and all that. I'll, ah, I guess I could call and ask for a replacement sign. I'm sure the Gallaghers have plenty on hand."

Tugging on her cane, her grandmother glared at her. Arianna glared back. It's not like she wanted to call the Gallagher campaign headquarters, but what did Helen expect her to do? She'd defaced the sign. It was a punishable offense. One of them had to be the responsible adult.

"I don't know, dear. There's been a run on the signs since Daniel's nephew Connor was put in charge of delivery and set-up. He's a high-powered attorney, you know? Such a handsome boy. Charming too, just like his uncle."

Okay, so she wasn't going to be calling for a replacement sign after all. The last person she wanted to talk to was Connor.

She glanced at the cars idling on the street. Their audience had grown. Instead of four cars, there were now six. Seven, she amended when a black Porsche slowed to a crawl. She sagged with relief when the Porsche pulled around the idling vehicles. Maybe now the others would get the idea they were blocking traffic and move on. Except the Porsche didn't keep driving, it pulled alongside the curb and the others followed suit.

"You think Connor Gallagher is charming, do you, Irene? Well, have I got news for you," her grandmother said with another vicious tug of her cane, which remained firmly attached to Daniel Gallagher's mouth.

"Don't even," Arianna muttered close to her grandmother's ear and closed the fingers of her good hand around the cane. "Let me do it."

While Arianna tried to wrestle the walking stick from the sign, her grandmother trash- talked the Gallagher men and Irene Ranger defended the handsome, blue-eyed devils. Frustrated with both women and her inability to unstick the cane, Arianna lifted her booted foot and kicked Daniel Gallagher in the head.

It felt so good to release some of her pent-up anger and emotion that she did it again, and then again. A loud grunt escaped from her mouth each time she hit the sign with a solid *thwack*. It took a moment for her to realize that the only sound she heard was *thwack*, *grunt*, *thwack*, *grunt*. Helen and Irene were no longer arguing. Except for the god-awful noises Arianna was making, it was uncomfortably quiet.

She glanced over her shoulder to see her grandmother and Mrs. Ranger staring at her open-mouthed, and just beyond them, a handsome blue-eyed devil watched her from where he leaned against the black Porsche.

About the Author

Debbie Mason is the *USA Today* bestselling author of the Christmas, Colorado, and the Harmony Harbor series. Her books have been praised for their "likable characters, clever dialogue, and juicy plots" (RTBookReviews.com). When she isn't writing or reading, Debbie enjoys spending time with her very own real-life hero, their three wonderful children and son-in-law, and their two adorable grandbabies in Ottawa, Canada.

Learn more at:
AuthorDebbieMason.com
@AuthorDebMason
Facebook.com

Fall in Love with Forever Romance

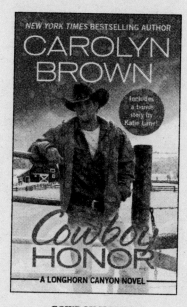

COWBOY HONOR
By Carolyn Brown

New York Times bestselling author Carolyn Brown delivers a sweet cowboy romance with a heart bigger than Texas itself! After her SUV runs off the road in the middle of a Texas blizzard and her cell phone stops working, Claire Mason is about to snap. Getting back home to Oklahoma with her four-year-old niece is top priority. And, lucky for her, help comes in the form of a true Texas cowboy... Also features the bonus story *O Little Town of Bramble* by Katie Lane!

Fall in Love with Forever Romance

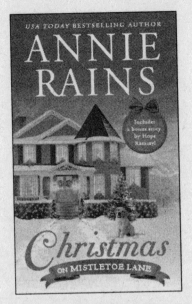

CHRISTMAS ON MISTLETOE LANE
By Annie Rains

Mitch Hargrove wants nothing more than to put his hometown in the rearview mirror, but his plans get derailed when he learns he's now half owner of the Sweetwater B&B. The fact that he's given only two months to make the inn a success is a huge problem, but it's his pretty—and incredibly headstrong—partner Kaitlyn Russo who's the real challenge. She's inherited the other half of her grandparents' charming (if a little rundown) bed and breakfast. With the grand reopening fast approaching, will Mitch keep running from the ghosts of Christmas past...or will he realize the true gift he's been given? This special 2-in-1 edition features *A Midnight Clear* by Hope Ramsay!

Fall in Love with Forever Romance

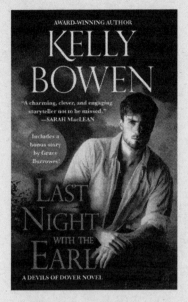

LAST NIGHT WITH THE EARL
By Kelly Bowen

War hero Eli Dawes was presumed dead—and would have happily stayed that way. All he wants is to hide away in his country home, where no one can see his scars. But when he tries to sneak into his old bedroom in the middle of the night, he's shocked to find the beautiful Rose Hayward. Eli might be back from the dead, but it's Rose who makes him feel *very* much alive. This special 2-in-1 edition features *Respect for Christmas*, a bonus novella by Grace Burrowes!

Fall in Love with Forever Romance

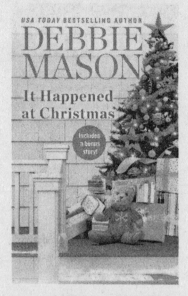

IT HAPPENED AT CHRISTMAS
By Debbie Mason

Out of money and out of options, Skylar Davis returns to Christmas, Colorado, seeking the comfort of the small mountain town all decked out for the holidays. There's no place Skylar would rather be...until she comes face-to-face with one of her biggest mistakes: the town's gorgeous mayor. Skye's never been able to forget her time with Ethan O'Connor. With snow in the air and the magic of the season all around them, will a Christmas miracle bring them back together at last? This special 2-in-1 edition features Debbie Mason's **never-before-in-print** novella *Miracle at Christmas*!